Praise for Jillian Hart and her novels

"Jillian Hart's *Every Kind of Heaven* is a warm, tender story in the McKaslin Clan miniseries."
—*RT Book Reviews*

"Jillian Hart's compassionate story will most certainly please readers."
—*RT Book Reviews* on *Everyday Blessings*

"It's a pleasure to read this achingly tender story."
—*RT Book Reviews* on *Her Wedding Wish*

"A heartwarming story with likable characters."
—*RT Book Reviews* on *His Country Girl*

"Jillian Hart conveys heart-tugging emotional struggles."
—*RT Book Reviews* on *Sweet Blessings*

Jillian Hart

EVERY KIND OF HEAVEN

and

EVERYDAY BLESSINGS

HARLEQUIN® LOVE INSPIRED® CLASSICS

Recycling programs
for this product may
not exist in your area.

ISBN-13: 978-0-373-60116-5

Every Kind of Heaven and Everyday Blessings

Copyright © 2015 by Harlequin Books S.A.

The publisher acknowledges the copyright holder
of the individual works as follows:

Every Kind of Heaven
Copyright © 2007 by Jill Strickler

Everyday Blessings
Copyright © 2007 by Jill Strickler

(H) HARLEQUIN®

Printed in U.S.A.

™ www.Harlequin.com

CONTENTS

Jillian Hart grew up on her family's homestead, where she helped raise cattle, rode horses and scribbled stories in her spare time. After earning her English degree from Whitman College, she worked in travel and advertising before selling her first novel. When Jillian isn't working on her next story, she can be found puttering in her rose garden, curled up with a good book or spending quiet evenings at home with her family.

Visit the Author Profile page
at Harlequin.com for more titles.

EVERY KIND OF HEAVEN

I consider that our present sufferings
are not worth comparing with the glory
that will be revealed in us.
—*Romans* 8:18

Chapter One

Baker Ava McKaslin stopped humming as she stepped back from the worktable to inspect the wedding cake. Her footsteps echoed in the industrial kitchen, nearly empty except for a few basics—the sink, countertops and the few pieces of equipment she'd managed to buy off the previous tenant. They'd considered it too cumbersome and expensive to move the industrial oven and fridge, which was just her luck.

She might not have the bakery of her dreams *yet,* God willing, but it was a start. Besides, her cake was spectacular, if she did say so herself.

But what was with all the silence? She cut a look to the long stretch of metal counter behind her. The CD had come to an end. She'd probably forgotten to hit Repeat again. Okay, she forgot most things most of the time. Since her hands were all frosting coated, she hit the play button with her elbow. The first beats of percussion got her right back into the creative mode. Although some people found it hard to think with bass blasting from her portable boom box, she thought it helped her brain cells to fire…or synapse…or do whatever brain cells did.

As the Christian music pulsed with an upbeat rhythm, she went back to work on the top tier. The delicate scrollwork took patience, not to mention stamina. Her wrist and arms were killing her, since she'd been at this for six hours straight. Ah, the price of being a baker. She ignored the burn in her exhausted muscles. Pain, that didn't matter. What mattered was *not* failing.

Before she'd bought this place, she'd been unofficially in business by using her oldest sister Katherine's snazzy kitchen off and on for a few months. This was her very first wedding cake in her own bakery. How great was that? And it was actually going well—a total shocker. So far there were no disasters. No kitchen fires. No last-minute cancellation of the wedding. It was almost as if this business venture of hers was meant to be.

Maybe she hadn't made a disastrous mistake by jumping into this entrepreneurial thing with both feet. And, best of all, the remodeling contractor would start work soon transforming this drab commercial space into a cheerful bakery shop in less than a couple of weeks. That was another reason why she was in such a great mood.

"Hello?" a man's voice—a stranger's voice—yelled over the booming music.

She screamed. The spatula slipped from her grip. What was a man doing in her kitchen? A man she'd never seen before. Her brain scrambled and her body refused to move. She could only gape at him in wide-eyed horror.

Oh, no. What if he was the backdoor burglar? The thief that had been breaking into the back doors of restaurants and assaulting and stealing? What if this dude was him?

It would be smart to call 9-1-1, but she had no idea where her cell was. There was no business phone installed yet. Even if she did have her cell or a working landline, it wouldn't matter since she was paralyzed in place.

"Uh…uh…" That was the best speech she could manage? *Get it together, Ava. You're about to be robbed.* "I've seen your face, so I can identify you in a lineup."

The burglar stared at her. Wow, he was really handsome. And he looked startled. His strong, chiseled jaw was clenched tight in, perhaps, fury and his striking dark eyes glittered with viciousness…or maybe that was humor. The left corner of his mouth quirked up as if he were holding back a grin.

Great, she had to get an easily amused thief.

"I've got two bucks in my purse. That's it, buddy. There's not another cent on the premises. You've picked the wrong place to rob. So t-t-turn around r-right now and go away. Go on. Shoo."

There, that ought to scare him off *or* confuse him. She really didn't care which. Adrenaline—or maybe it was terror—started to spill like ice into her veins.

"Go ahead, call the cops." He called her bluff, crossing his arms over his wide chest. He had the audacity to lean one big shoulder against the door frame, as if he had all the time in the world. He looked more like a movie star than a criminal. "Explain to the police how you left the front door unlocked."

"No, I—" Wait, she *did* forget to lock stuff. And if he'd come in the *front* door, then he wasn't the back-door thief. Maybe. Unless he'd changed his M.O. and was that very likely? She didn't think so. "I did leave the door unlocked, didn't I?"

"Anyone could walk right in. Even the backdoor burglar. That's who you thought I was, right?"

Okay, her mind was starting to unscramble. He didn't look like any criminal she'd seen on TV. To make matters worse, he looked *better* than any man she'd seen on TV. He was handsome to a fault. His thick black hair fell with disregard for convention over his collar. He wore a short-sleeve polo shirt—black—with the little expensive insignia. His clothes—including his baggy khaki shorts and exclusive manly leather sandals—were top-of-the-line. Expensive.

It was likely that the backdoor thief didn't dress like that or have such a perfect smile. She hit Pause on the boom box. "Okay, I feel dumb now. What were you doing surprising me like that? You just can't go walking into any place you want."

"I'm looking for you, Ava McKaslin." His grin broadened enough to show off a double set of dimples.

Oops. This must be about business, and mistaking a potential customer for a burglar was so not professional. "You've come with a cake order, haven't you, and after meeting me, you've changed your mind."

"No, but it's tempting." The sets of dimples dug deeper as his grin widened. "I've been sent to check on the cake."

"Chloe's cake?" Oh, no. That can't be good. Suddenly her great mood tumbled. "Has she called off her wedding?"

"Nope."

"Changed her mind and eloped?"

"Not to my knowledge."

"Has she gone with another baker and forgot to tell me? Has she postponed the wedding?"

"Let me guess. You're more of a glass-is-half-empty kind of girl, aren't you?"

"Hey, disasters happen. I'm a realist."

Ava knelt to retrieve the spatula. She tossed it into the sink and washed her hands, turning her back to the guy. He wasn't a burglar. She'd leaped to a wrong conclusion, but his being a thief might be better because he'd come with bad news. She knew, although he had yet to admit it, that he'd come to cancel the first cake she'd made in her bakery.

Total doom.

She grabbed a paper towel to dry her hands. "Tell Chloe I appreciate that she went with me, even if it didn't work out. Is she all right?"

"I hope so, since she's getting married tomorrow."

"The wedding's still on?"

"Sure it is."

She was as cute as he remembered. Brice Donovan took a step closer, trying to act like he wasn't stunned. He'd never met any woman who looked so funny and gorgeous all in the same moment. It was the eyes. Those big violet-blue eyes filled with one hundred percent vibrant emotion. They radiated such heart and spirit that he was sucked right in, like being caught in the vortex of a black hole.

It ought to be terrifying, but he didn't mind it so much. He was glad to see her again. She didn't seem to remember seeing him at Chloe's wedding shower, considering she'd mistaken him for a burglar. But he sure remembered her. How could he not? She was unforgettable.

And absolutely adorable. Not that he could see much of her; she was standing behind the most unusual cake he'd ever seen. One large heart-shaped layer was stacked off-center on another, and another over that. Satin-textured, smooth ivory frosting adorned with amazing gold lace and ribbons of some kind of frosting, and colorful sugar flowers everywhere.

Unlike her cake, the designer wasn't as perfectly arranged. She had globs of icing all over her. A streak on her cheek, a dried crown of it in her light blond hair, which was neatly tied back, and a blob just above the tip of her cute little nose.

When he'd agreed to check on the cake's progress for his sister, he'd thought the address was familiar. He knew why the instant he'd pulled into the lot. His construction company had won the bid for renovation—starting next week. The moment he'd spotted the shop's proprietor hard at work, he'd known why Chloe had sent him. She was meddlesome, but then a guy had to tolerate that from his baby sister. Not that he wasn't grateful.

Over the past year, he'd noticed Ava McKaslin around town a couple of times. They didn't belong to the same social circle or church, and didn't live in the same parts of town, so he'd never had an opportunity to talk to her before. There was something about her that always made him smile. Just like he was doing now.

"I've been sent to make sure the cake is on schedule." He stalked forward, wanting to get closer to that smile of hers. "It looks on schedule to me."

"I'll need thirty minutes tops, and then it's done. Chloe doesn't have to worry about a thing. I'll deliver it bright and early at the country club, just as I promised, no sweat."

"She'll be thrilled." He splayed both hands on the table and leaned toward her, drawn by those eyes, by everything.

Up close, there was nothing artificial about her. She was radiant. She had a fresh-faced complexion and dazzling beauty, sure, but she was unique. She was like the light refracting off a flawless diamond. Hers was a brilliance that was impossible to touch or to capture.

He'd really like to get to know her. "You said you've got thirty minutes until you're done?"

"I promise. You and Chloe have nothing to worry about. Your wedding cake will be perfect." Ava crossed her heart like a girl scout, as cute as a button.

Captivated, Brice felt blinded in a way he'd never been before. He definitely would like to see what this violet-eyed, flawless Ava was really like. He took in the little gold cross at her throat and the sweet way she looked. What was such a good, amazing woman doing single?

She scooped a short spatula into a stainless steel bowl, fluffy with snow-white frosting. "Did you want to come back when I'm done?"

"I'd rather stay, if you don't mind."

"Stay? You don't want to do that. You'd be bored."

"I doubt that. I could watch you work. I've never seen anything like this. It's beautiful, the work you do." He took a breath. Gathered his courage. "If you don't mind, when you're done, we could talk, just you and me."

Ava stared over the top frills of the cake. She blinked hard, as if she were trying to bring him into focus. Or make sense of what he was saying. "Talk?"

"Sure. We've met before, don't you remember? Maybe we can go down the street for a cup of coffee. Get to know each other better."

"What?" The spatula dropped from her supple artist's fingers and clattered on the metal tabletop. "You want to get to know me *better?*"

Uh-oh. She didn't look happy about that. He'd never had that reaction from a woman before. Okay, maybe he'd jumped the gun. "Do you have a boyfriend? I should have asked first. I noticed you weren't wearing a wedding ring and I assumed—"

She cut him off, circling around the table like a five-star army general. "You *assumed?* What's wrong with you?"

He couldn't believe how mad she looked. "Hey, what did I do? I just wanted to talk."

"Talk? Oh, is that what men like you call it? You need to get some morals."

Well, at least she was a lady with serious principles. He liked that. He respected Ava's inner fiber. It was a little passionate, but he liked that, too. He held up both hands, a show of surrender. "Hey, I didn't know you were attached. Why wouldn't you be? Look at you. Of course you have a boyfriend. He probably worships at your feet."

"No, I don't have a boyfriend, but what about you and Chloe? You're getting married! You should leave. Go."

Normally, he might take offense at her dismissal, but he didn't seem to mind.

No boyfriend, huh? Okay, call him interested. No, call him dazzled, that's what he was. She fascinated him, all pure inner fire and feeling. But this wasn't going well. Usually he got a better response than this.

"What am I going to have to tell your bride?" Her sweetheart-shaped face turned pink with fury. "The poor woman thinks she's getting married to Mr. Right. Little does she know you're Mr. Yuck, wanting to get to know me the evening before your wedding. I don't think you want to chat either!"

So, that was it. Whew. For a minute there, he was afraid she really didn't like him. "You misunderstood."

"Misunderstood? Oh, I don't think so."

Men, Ava fumed. What was wrong with the species? *This* was why she wasn't married. Too many of the gender were just like this guy, and nothing made her madder. Spitting mad. "I'm a good Christian girl. Get a clue, buddy. Are you misunderstanding me now?"

"Uh, no. I noticed the gold cross. You look like a very nice Christian girl to me."

He was being agreeable now, but it didn't matter. "Poor Chloe. Now what do I do? Do I tell her? Or do I make you do it? A man like you doesn't deserve a nice wife like her. What kind of man would do that to the woman he was about to marry?"

He chuckled. Actually chuckled, the sound rich as cream. His dimples deepened. Tiny, attractive laugh lines crinkled around his kind, warm brown eyes.

That was the problem. He didn't look like a cheater. He looked like a nice guy. What did a girl do in a world where icky men could look as good as the nice ones?

She'd had this problem before. This was why she had a newly instated policy of staying away from every last one of them, unless they needed to buy a cake from her, of course. She intended to stick to her current no-man policy one hundred percent. "This is the last time I'm telling you to leave."

"Okay, stand down, soldier." He held up both hands as if he were surrendering. "I'll go. But please accept my apology. I'm sorry. I don't know what I was thinking."

"Obviously you weren't thinking at all. Or you thought that I looked easy, and let me tell you, you couldn't be more wrong."

"Ava McKaslin, you look like class to me. I can't help noticing that you aren't happy with my interest."

"You got that right. Hey! You're not heading toward the door."

"We're not done discussing the cake." He had the audacity to grin again.

That grin became more charming each time he used it, Ava thought, making him look like the absolute perfect guy.

She'd been fooled by dimples and charm too many times before. "The cake will be ready and delivered at the country club's service entrance by nine tomorrow morning, as agreed. There. Discussion done."

"Chloe will be relieved. You aren't going to mention this little misunderstanding to her, right?"

Didn't that take the prize? "I don't know. I may have to consult my sisters and my minister on this one. She should know the kind of man she's marrying."

"I'm not the groom."

"Oh, *sure* you're not." Ava rolled her eyes. Some men would resort to anything. Men like him had made her give up dating. Perhaps forever. Good thing she'd vowed to turn all her energy to making a success of her business, because it would be impossible to make marriage work considering the men running around these days.

She reloaded her spatula with frosting. "You're not gone yet."

He sighed, resigned as he backed through the kitchen doorway. "I guess I'll see you at the wedding, huh?"

"Not if I can help it." Really, what gave this guy the idea that she was interested? "I'd better follow you to the door to make sure you really leave. Then I'm going to lock it, so no more riffraff can get in."

"At least I'm not the backdoor burglar, or you would have really been in trouble. That spatula loaded with frosting wouldn't be much of a weapon against a revolver." He paused in the front door, framed by the brilliant June sunshine. His grin went cosmic. "By the way, you have frosting on your nose. It's cute. Real cute."

"You're not so attractive, Mr. Yuck."

"Ava, listen. I'm *not* the groom. When you deliver

the cake, stick around for the wedding. You'll see I'm the best man. So, how about it?"

She grabbed his arm and gave him a shove. It was impossible not to notice he felt like solid steel. Once he'd rocked backward a step, she was able to slam the door. Not that he was harmful, she thought as she threw the dead bolt, but she'd had enough of not-so-stellar men.

So why did she gravitate to the front windows that gave her a perfect view of the parking lot?

Because she wanted to make sure he left, the horrible man, trying to pick up a woman on the night before his wedding. Despicable.

It was hard to believe a human being was capable of behaving so badly, but she'd been propositioned like that before. Three wedding cakes ago. Darrin Fullerton had thought that when she delivered the two-tier caramel coconut cake that she was ready to serve up something else, too. It still shocked her. Too many men needed to spend more time reading their Bibles. Filling their minds with uplifting and spiritual subjects. Learning to recite the Psalms. List the seven deadly sins. That kind of thing.

The groom climbed into a bright red luxury sports car—not surprising—and zipped away. As he passed by the shop's glassed front, his driver's side window whipped down and he lifted his designer aviator sunglasses to give her a wink.

Horrible. Anger turned her vision to pure crimson. Seconds passed until she could see normally again. The parking lot was empty, the red sports car long gone.

Her cell phone chimed. The cheerful jingle came

from very near. She looked down and found it in her apron pocket. The display said it was her twin sister, Aubrey. "Howdy."

"I'm just pulling up into the lot. I can see your frowny face from here."

"I have more than a frowny face on. It's my down-on-men face."

"Wow. What happened?"

"Oh, another groom trying to get one last party in before he commits." Ava spotted her bright yellow SUV cautiously creeping across the empty lot. Her sister had borrowed it and was coming closer. "What is it with men and commitment? I don't get why it's so terrifying. It's not any more frightening than a lot of things. Like premature baldness."

"Crow's feet."

"New car payments. Now *that's* scary. Which is why I'm glad I've given up on dating. Who cares if I ever get married?"

"*You* do."

"Too true." Ava sighed. "I've got a few more minutes to finish up, and then I'm good to go."

Aubrey brought the vehicle to a slow stop at the curb outside the window. She leaned forward, squinting through the windshield. "You brought a change of clothes, right? Or are you going to the movies like that?"

"I knew I forgot something." Ava snapped the phone shut. Who needed a man when she had enough disaster in her life?

Too bad the kind of man she needed—perfect in

every way, no selfishness, no flaws or questionable morals—didn't exist.

So what was a nice girl to do? Settle for Mr. So-So or Marginally Moral? As if!

Ava unlocked the door for Aubrey and went back to work. There was the wedding cake in all its loveliness, fresh and beautiful like the new promise a wedding should be. But would she ever know what that new promising love felt like? No.

Disappointed, she grabbed a clean spatula from the drawer by the sink and went back to work, making sugar roses. Trying not to dwell on the sadness that was buried so deep inside she could *almost* pretend it didn't exist. She didn't want to live her life without knowing true love.

But with the men she kept running into, she had no other choice.

Chapter Two

The next morning, Brice pulled into the country club's parking lot and killed the engine. It was 8:53 a.m. Hadn't Ava promised the cake would be delivered by nine?

He climbed out into the hot sunshine, made hotter by the monkey suit he had to wear. He hooked a finger beneath his tie and tugged until he had a little more breathing room. After remoting the door locks, he hadn't gone five steps before his cell rang. He thumbed it from his pocket. Seeing his sister's number on the call screen made his step lighter. "Having cold feet yet?"

"No way. I can't wait to get married. I don't have a single doubt. Where are you?"

"Where do you think?"

"Ha! You're up to something. You're not answering me." She sounded happy, her voice light and easy.

Brice was glad for his little sister. He wouldn't mind having that kind of happiness in his life. He checked his Rolex. Another minute had ticked by. He shouldered through the club's main door. "Where I am is none of your business. Is Mom giving you problems?"

"When isn't she giving me problems? She means well. At least, that's what I keep telling myself so I don't flip out. She's made two of my bridesmaids cry. She's decided the wedding planner isn't capable and is trying to take over."

"Do you need me to come run interference?"

"Do you know what I need you to do?" Chloe sounded as if she was very glad he'd asked. "I'd love it if you could swing by the club and check on the cake."

I know what you're up to little sister, he thought. But he didn't mind. He hadn't been able to stop thinking of Ava since he'd left her shop yesterday.

It ate at him that she thought he was the groom. She was right—from her mistaken perspective he did look like a Mr. Yuck. Now, that was a misperception he had to change, even if he had to show her two forms of ID to do it.

Because he didn't want to encourage his sister, he tried to sound indifferent. Not at all interested. "Tell me what you know about this baker you went with."

"Ha! You like her. I know you do."

"I don't know her." *Yet.* But he intended to change that.

As he began looking around the room, he spotted her through the closed French doors into the ballroom and he froze in place. Ava. Seeing her was like the first light of dawn rising, and that was something he'd never felt before. *Ever.*

"I met Ava when we were volunteering at the community church's shelter kitchen." Chloe sounded very far away, although the cell connection was crystal clear. "She's sweet and kind and hysterical. We had a great time, until they asked her to leave."

What had she said? Brice's mind was spinning. He couldn't seem to focus. All he could think of was Ava. Her thick, shiny hair was tied up into a haphazard ponytail, bouncing in time with her movements. She was busily going over the cake, checking each colorful flower and sparkling golden accent.

She hadn't noticed him yet and seemed lost in her own world. She had a set of earbuds in, probably listening to a pocket-sized digital music player. She wore jeans and a yellow T-shirt that said on the back "Every Kind of Heaven" in white script.

Was the saying true? It had to be. She *did* look like everything sweet and good in the world.

"Brice? Are you listening to me?"

He felt dazed, as if he'd been run over by a bus. He couldn't orient himself in place and time. Any minute Ava would look up, and when she saw him, she'd leap to the same conclusion as before—that he was Mr. Yuck. If he didn't act quickly, would she start lobbing frosting at him?

He'd never quite had that effect on a woman before.

"Look, Chloe. I gotta go. Call if you need anything, okay?"

"Sure. You'll make sure Ava doesn't need any help, right? She's just starting her business and she hasn't hired anyone yet. She'll need some assistance with all the favors we ordered. Remember, if you change your mind and decide to bring a date to my wedding, feel free."

"Sure. Right," he said vaguely.

Ava. He was having the toughest time concentrating on anything else. His thoughts kept drifting to the woman on the other side of the door.

When he opened it, he heard a lightly muttered, "Oops!"

Ava's voice made his senses spin.

Think, Brice. He clicked off his phone and stepped into the ballroom.

Morning light spilled through the long row of closed French doors and onto her. She looked tinier than he remembered. Maybe it was that she had such a big personality that she gave the impression of stature. She was surprisingly petite with slender lines and almost skinny arms and legs. There was no one else helping. How she'd delivered that big cake by herself was a mystery. It had to be heavy.

He knew the moment she sensed his presence. The line of her slender shoulders stiffened. Every muscle went completely rigid. She pulled the earbuds out of her ears, turning toward him in one swift movement.

"You." If looks could kill, he'd at least be bleeding. "What are you doing here? You're just like Darrin Fullerton. He showed up when I was delivering the cake to beg me not to say anything to his bride. He'd been drunk, he'd said, and didn't know what he was doing when he propositioned me. As if that's any excuse!"

Quick, Brice, look innocent. He held up both hands in surrender. "Wait. I'm nothing like that Fullerton guy. I'm a completely innocent best man. Really."

"Innocent? I don't think so."

Ava gave him her best squinty-eyed look. He was

bigger than she remembered, a good six feet tall. When she'd shoved him out the door of her bakery, it had been like trying to move a bulldozer.

She went up on tiptoe so she could glare at him directly, not exactly eye to eye, but it was the best she could manage, being so short. "Are you ashamed of yourself? At all?"

He didn't look unashamed. "Chloe's going to love that cake. You did an amazing job."

"Now if only I can control the urge to lob the top tier at you."

"Do you think you can restrain that urge for a few seconds? I've got something to show you." He reached into his back pocket.

Men were much more trouble than they were worth, she concluded. But why did he have to have such an amazing grin? That's probably what Chloe saw in him; it obviously blinded her to all his multitude of faults. Poor Chloe. "You should be getting ready for your wedding, but what are you doing? Trying to get me not to tell—"

He flashed a card at her. "This ought to clear up the confusion."

"I'm not the one who's confused. You owe me an apology and your bride an enormous apology and—"

He waved the card in front of her. "Look closer."

She squinted to bring the card into focus. Not a card. It was a driver's license. Some of her fury sagged as she realized the picture, which was, of course, perfect, matched the man standing before her. The name to the left of the photo was Brice Donovan.

What? Her mind screeched to a sudden halt. She

sank back onto her heels, staring, feeling her jaw drop. Brice Donovan. Chloe Donovan's *brother*. Not the groom.

"I'm the best man," he said, wagging the card. "Do you finally believe me?"

His eyes darkened with amusement, but they weren't unkind. No, not at all. A strong warmth radiated from him as he leaned close, and then closer.

That thought spun around in her brain for a moment, like a car's engine stuck in Neutral. Then it hit her. She'd insulted, yelled at and accused a perfectly innocent man.

It was hard to know just what to say. Talk about being embarrassed. Had she really said all those things to him? She felt faint. Wasn't he on the city's most eligible bachelor's list? It was just in last weekend's paper. She couldn't believe she hadn't recognized him.

Why did these things always happen to her? She clipped her case closed. He was probably waiting for an apology. An apology for the accusations. The fact that she'd been beyond rude to him, one of the wealthiest men from one of the most prominent families in Montana.

Lovely. Her face heated from the humiliation starting to seep into her soul. "Oops. My bad."

"You think?" He crooked one brow, amusement softening the impressive impact of all iron-solid six feet of him.

The effect was scrambling her brain cells, and that wasn't helping her to think.

"Chloe's going to really love what you've done with this cake." He jammed his hands into his pockets, looking like a cover model come to life. "It's going to make her so happy. Thank you."

Now what did she say? She'd been awful to him and he was complimenting the cake she'd worked so hard on. It made her feel even worse. "I'm trying to figure out how to apologize, but *sorry* seems like too small a word."

"Don't even worry about it."

"Thanks," she said shyly.

Brice Donovan's smile made her even more muddled. Before he'd walked into the ballroom she'd been so happy, thinking how pleased Chloe was going to be. But now? Her heart twisted with agony. Her face was so hot and red from embarrassment, she could feel her skin glow. What she could see of her nose was as bright as a strawberry.

This was no way for a professional baker to behave. Feeling two inches tall, she looked up to Brice's kind eyes. He wasn't laughing at her. No. That was one saving grace, right?

"I am sorry. Really. Tell Chloe best wishes. This cake is my gift to her."

"But she hired you to bake it."

"So she thinks. I've got to go, I have another project to work on, but this, the groom's cake and the favors, it's all from me to her. She was a good friend to me when I really needed one." Her chest felt so tight, she felt ready to burst. Embarrassment had turned into a horrible, sharp pain right behind her sternum.

Doom. She'd just made a mess of this. Would there ever be one time—just *once*—when she didn't make a mess of something? There was no way to fix this, and the cake was finished. There was nothing else to do but grab her case and her baseball cap.

Somehow she managed to speak without strangling on her embarrassment. "Goodbye, Mr. Donovan. And I am s-sorry again."

"Wait, don't go yet, I—"

"I have to." She was already walking away. She had work waiting and she couldn't face him a second longer. She'd humiliated herself enough for one day and it was only 9:15 a.m. She hadn't even had breakfast yet. *Way to go, Ava.*

She wasn't aware of crossing the room, only that she was suddenly at the kitchen. But she was aware of him. Of his presence behind her in the spill of light through the expansive windows. She didn't have to look at him as she pushed through the kitchen door to know that he was watching her. She could feel the tangible weight of his touch between her shoulder blades. What was he thinking?

Lord, I don't want to know. She kept going. She hit the back service doors and didn't slow until she felt the soothing morning sun on her face.

She skidded to a stop in the gravel and breathed in the fresh morning air. The scents of warm earth and freshly mowed grass calmed her a little. She breathed hard, getting out all the negative feelings. There were a lot of them. And trying not to hear her mother's voice saying, *You wreck everything you touch. Can't you stop making a mess for two seconds?*

She'd been seven, and she could still hear the shrill impatience. She still felt like that little girl who just didn't know how things went wrong no matter how hard she tried.

You're just a big dope, Ava, she told herself. What kind of grown adult had the problems she had? Wasn't she going to turn over a new leaf? Start out right this time? Stop making so many dumb mistakes?

Well, no more. She wasn't going to think about the way she'd embarrassed herself back there. She'd been hoping that by doing a good job with Chloe's cake, she'd get some word-of-mouth interest and her business would naturally pick up.

But after this, what were the chances that anyone was going to remember what the cake looked like?

None. All Brice Donovan was going to do was to talk about the dingbat cake lady who mistook him—the city of Bozeman's golden boy—for a philandering groom.

Her SUV blurred into one bright yellow blob. She blinked hard until her eyes cleared and reached into her pocket for her keys.

The only thing she could do was go on from here. Simply write off this morning as a lesson learned. What else could she do? She reached into her other pocket, but it was empty. No, it couldn't be. Her heart jackhammered. Where were her keys?

She did another search of her pockets. Jeans front pockets. No key. Back pockets. No key. Those were the only pockets she had. Panic began to stutter in her chest. *Where were her keys?*

There. Sitting right in plain view on the rear passenger seat. *Inside* the locked vehicle. Right next to her cell phone and her sunglasses.

Super-duper. What did she do now?

"Looks like you need help," said a rumbling baritone from behind her. A baritone she recognized. Brice Donovan.

Could the morning get any worse? How was she going to save her dignity now—or what was left of it? "H-help? Oh, no, I'm fine."

"Fine, huh? Aren't those your car keys inside the car?"

"I believe so."

"I don't know too many people who can actually lock their keys in the car with a remote. Don't you need the remote to lock the door?"

"Yes." She plopped her baseball cap on her head and pulled the bill low, trying to hide what she could of her face. Her nose was bright red again.

Brice studied her for a moment before realization dawned. Oh, he knew why she was acting this way, shuffling away from him, head down, avoiding his gaze. She was embarrassed. Well, she didn't need to be. "Hey, it's no big deal. This kind of thing happens, right?"

The tension eased from her tight jaw and rigid shoulders. She shrugged helplessly. "I've only had this car for a few months and I haven't figured out all the settings yet. It's too technologically advanced for me."

"I doubt that." Tender feelings came to life and he couldn't seem to stop them. Maybe her keys getting locked inside the car was providential. Just like the fact that he was here to help at just the right moment. "I have a knack for this kind of thing."

"Thanks, but please don't bother."

She still wouldn't look at him. Instead, she stared hard at the toes of her sunshine-yellow sneakers. Yellow, just like her SUV. There was nothing mundane about Ava McKaslin.

He liked that. Very much.

She surprised him by sidestepping away, heading back to the service doors.

"Hey, where are you going?"

"To find a phone."

"To call...?"

"My sister to come with the extra set of keys."

Wow. She really didn't want his help. Getting a woman to like him used to be easier than this, although he *had* been out of the dating circuit for a long time. After all, he'd dated Whitney two years before he'd proposed to her, which had turned out to be a much longer engagement period than either of them had expected. That put him nearly four, no, almost five years out of practice.

But still, he just didn't remember it being so difficult. "Your sister doesn't need to go to the trouble of driving out here. I'll break in for you."

She paused midstride.

He could sense her indecision, so he tried again. "Let me help. It'll take a minute and then you can be on your way."

"But I was so rude to you."

"So? If you're worried about retaliation, forget it. I'm a turn-the-other-cheek kind of guy. And I won't leave a scratch on your new car. Promise."

"And just why does a man like you know how to break into a car without leaving any evidence?"

"Chloe used to lock herself out of her car, too. I need a coat hanger. I'll be right back." He shouldered past her, pausing at the base of the concrete steps.

Why was her every sense attuned to this man? She felt Brice's presence like the bright radiant sun on her back, almost as if she was interested in him, but, of course, she couldn't be. She was done with thinking about any guy, and done with dreams of falling in love.

She was done with dreams like Brice Donovan.

Chapter Three

"Mission accomplished. No trouble at all."

His voice moved through Ava like a warm breeze. She turned toward him as her car's alarm went off. While the vehicle honked and the headlights flashed, he calmly opened the back door, grabbed the key ring with the remote and pressed the button. The horn silenced, the headlights died.

For him, it had been simple. But for her? She'd had to stand here and watch him, knowing he was helping her out of sympathy. Because he'd felt pity for his little sister's friend.

She would rather fall through a big black hole in the ground than have to look Brice Donovan in the eye one more time. Sure, he was being gallant and incredibly nice, but it wasn't as if she could erase the things she'd said to him. She heard all the adjectives she'd called him roll around in her head. *Mr. Yuck. Riffraff.* She'd told him to *get some morals.* How could she have not recognized him? How could she have made such a mistake?

"All done. And without any damage, thanks to the caterer." He finished bending a wire hanger back into place, but his gaze seared her from six feet away. "Lucky for us she had this in her van."

"Yep, lucky for us." But she didn't feel fortunate. Her nose was still strawberry red, but now it felt hot, too, as if it were glowing under its own energy source.

He opened her driver's side door, looking every inch the handsome millionaire in the designer tux he wore, which fit him like a vision. Of course. He appeared every inch the proverbial prince. And suddenly she knew how Cinderella felt in her ragged dress, wishing she could put on a fancy dress and change her circumstances.

"Here are your keys." They rested on his wide, capable palm.

She couldn't help but notice how strong his hand was. Calluses roughened his skin, as if he worked hard for a living. But that couldn't be. Wasn't he a trust fund kind of guy?

"Thanks, again."

It took all her willpower to meet his gaze. His eyes were so kind and tender. Clearly, he wasn't holding the mistaken identity thing against her. What a relief.

"Goodbye, Brice." She scooped the keys from his hand as quickly as she could, but her fingertips brushed his hand.

It was like touching a piece of heaven. A corner of serenity. The shame within her faded until there was only a hush in her soul. She didn't know why this happened, but it couldn't be a good sign. She hopped into her car, grabbed her belt as Brice closed her door. Their gazes met, held through the tempered glass, and her world stilled. Her heart forgot to beat.

Probably from the aftereffects of a lethal dose of embarrassment and nothing else—surely not interest, she told herself as she started the engine. But she knew, down deep, that wasn't the truth. The truth wasn't something she could examine too closely.

She drove away, into the sun, purposefully keeping her gaze on the road ahead. She resisted the urge to peek at her rearview mirror and see if he was standing there, watching her go.

Chloe had cried in happiness at her first glimpse of the wedding cake. The cake had been cut, pictures taken, and everyone in the ballroom had been served, and still he could hear the conversation buzzing about the unbelievable cake. It had looked like a porcelain creation of art and beauty, impossible that it was edible. But every piece, from the intricate lace ruffles to the golden beads to the delicate curls of rose petals, had tasted as sweet as heaven.

Each of the two hundred carefully stacked serving boxes, printed to match the lacework of the cake, held an individual cake for the guests to take home. A heart-shaped version with sugary miniature rosebuds and golden ribbons. He thought of the woman who had done so much work as a gift to his sister. Chloe didn't know it yet since he hadn't found the moment to tell her. She looked as happy as a princess in her frosty-white gown at her husband's side.

Brice thanked God for his sister's happiness. He wouldn't mind having some of that kind of joy of his own. He took a gulp of sparkling cider, draining the glass. This was the spot where Ava had stood earlier this morning, with the pale morning sunshine sprinkling over her like a blessing.

Then she'd driven away. What had she been thinking? Did she like him at all? She hadn't acted like it, and yet he'd thought he'd glimpsed something in her eyes. Something that made him think she might be feeling this, too.

Then again, she'd driven off pretty fast. That couldn't be the best sign.

"*There* you are, big brother. You've been hiding." Chloe swept close in her cloud of a dress.

"You know me. All this fancy stuff makes me itch."

She slipped her arm through his. "You look dashing. Five of my former sorority sisters asked me if you were seeing someone."

"And you said…?"

"That you seem to be interested in someone. But if I'm wrong, I have a long list of available women I can set you up with, Mr. Most Eligible Bachelor."

"You know I had nothing to do with that. It's not me." That only made him feel more out of place. Like he was a rich playboy looking for a fast lifestyle or a great catch for a debutante—both equally wrong.

All he wanted was to trade in this getup for his favorite T-shirt, jeans and his broken-in work boots. That's who he really was, and all this glam and glitter made his palms sweat. He swept his hand toward the cake. "You don't need to set me up with a date. I can do it myself."

"Would you rather Mom did it? She's working on it, you know. I was just trying to help out."

"I know." If anyone knew how rough of a time he'd had after the breakup with Whitney, it was Chloe. She meant well. "I can handle it from here."

"I never doubted it." She rose up on tiptoe to brush a sisterly kiss to his cheek. "I want you to be happy. I saw how you looked at Ava at my shower."

"Exactly how was that?"

"Like you were glimpsing heaven. Don't worry, I haven't said anything to her, but you should ask her out. I bet she says yes."

"I've tried that, but I don't think she likes me." Like he needed his baby sister's dating advice. He could handle his own love life just fine. "She said no."

"And since when does Brice Donovan take no for an answer?" She flounced away, grinning over her shoulder at him. "Try again, silly. Look out, here comes Mom."

The problem was, his mother had been dropping some pretty strong hints lately. Now that she had Chloe successfully matched, she must be refocusing her energy on him. She seemed determined as she barreled through the crowd. Flawless, dressed in diamonds and flowing silk, she looked deceptively like a genteel upper-class lady instead of the five-star general she really was.

"Brice. You have been hiding again." She tugged at his tie, unknotted and hanging loose. "This isn't a barnyard. And what are you doing all the way over here? What are people going to think?"

He accepted the china dessert plate a server handed him. "Maybe people will think that I'm having a second piece of cake."

"Yes. The cake. Horrible, that's what it is. I don't know what Chloe was thinking going with that McKaslin girl."

"That she wanted her friend to make her wedding cake."

"Ridiculous. That cake is unsophisticated and completely unacceptable. And the taste of it, why, it's much too sweet. What is wrong with that girl? I told Chloe. I said, you're going to regret going with her."

"Mom, stop. You're doing it again."

"But did she listen to me? No, she had to have her own way. We ought to have gone with a professional, not some iffy girl who thinks because our family is richer than hers, she has the right to charge us an arm and a leg."

He laid a hand on his mom's arm to stop her. Sometimes she got such a wind going—sort of like gravity's effect on a snowball rolling downhill—that she simply couldn't realize what she was saying. "Chloe's happy, and that's all that matters. Besides, how much did Ava charge?"

"Ava, is it?" Mom's face pinched, something only she could do and still look dignified. "I wouldn't be so familiar with her if I were you. Her family has money, goodness, but that mother of hers."

"People have been known to say the same thing

about Chloe." He said it gently, because he knew his mother didn't mean to be harsh. She simply wasn't aware of it. "I think Ava did an amazing job. So does everyone else in the room. Maybe you should learn to like sweet. You're awfully fond of the bitter."

"That had better not be a veiled reference to me, young man." His mom smiled and tried to hide it, but her eyes were twinkling. "I work hard for this reputation. If people aren't afraid of you, they take advantage. Now, come with me and say hello to a few of my dear friends."

"To the *daughters* of your friends, you mean."

"Crystal Frost is back from her disastrous divorce to that big real estate broker in Seattle. She's perfect for you."

"Perfect? I don't think so." He took a bite of cake, and sweetness flooded his mouth. The frosting was as rich as cream cheese, and the cake was delicious and buttery. *Perfect.*

"Hello, Brice. Excuse me." One of his mother's friends had sauntered over and gestured toward the cake. "Lynn, this is all so lovely. I came to plead for the name of the designer. My Carly must have a cake like this for her wedding."

Brice knew it would probably drain his mother of her life energy to say something kind about anyone. She was his mom, so he tried to save her from herself. And he wanted to help the cute baker, even if she didn't want to have coffee with him. "Ava McKaslin is the designer and I highly recommend her. Chloe loved working with her."

"Oh, let me think which McKaslin girl. Oh, of course. The friend of your sister's. One of the twins?"

"Yep. She has a shop off Cherry Lane. My company starts renovation on it this week."

"I know which shop you mean. Why, thank you, Brice. You do know that my Crystal is back from Seattle. She's here somewhere." Maxime scanned the room. "Where did she go?"

Uh-oh. Time to escape while he could. "I have to go. Mrs. Frost, it was good seeing you again. Bye, Mom."

He left quickly and didn't look back. It wasn't until he hit the foyer that he realized he still had hold of his dessert plate. Ava's cake. As if he couldn't quite let her go.

The only reason Ava heard her cell ring was because of the break between songs. The electronic chime echoed in the silence of her shop's kitchen. She set down her pastry cone, hit the Pause button on her CD player and went in search of her phone.

Not in her apron pocket. Not on the kitchen counter. She followed the electronic ringing to her gym bag. She unzipped the outside compartment and *ta da,* there it was.

As she grabbed her phone, she realized it was after four. Mrs. Carnahan was supposed to drop by for the birthday cake in ten minutes! Good thing it was almost done. Well, it *would* be done if she'd stop fussing. But after this morning's disaster, she wanted this cake to be perfect.

She flipped open the phone. "I'm late, I know. I was supposed to call an hour ago. My bad."

Instead of her sister's sensible response, a man's resonant chuckle vibrated in her ear. "Keeping your boyfriend waiting?"

It took her a moment to place that voice. Brice Donovan. If he was calling, that could only mean one thing. "Chloe wasn't happy with the cake?"

Disappointment drained her and she sank onto the floor next to her gym bag. Not only had she failed at something she'd tried her hardest at, something that she was good at, but she'd let down a friend. "I'm so sorry."

"Now, wait one minute. That's not why I'm calling."

"It's not?"

"No." His voice warmed like melting chocolate, kind and friendly. "I'm calling to thank you. You made her very happy. She didn't want to cut into the cake because it was too pretty."

"Really? Chloe was happy? Whew!" That was a relief. Now, if she could just forget flinging insults, she'd be doing well. *Don't even think about what happened,* she told herself. Look forward, not back. *Don't dwell on what went wrong.*

Problem was, that was easier said and not so easy to do. She took a quivering breath. "Good. Then my work is done."

"And your work is?"

"To make this world a sweeter place one cake at a time. I know it's not solving world strife, but it's the only talent I seem to have, so I'm going with it."

"Surely that's not your only gift."

"Uh, you don't want to hear the long list of disasters I've left in my wake. Speaking of which, I have a cake to get ready and box for a client."

"You can't do that and talk to me?"

"If I want to drop the cake. I need two hands."

Don't think of him in that tux, she thought. Or how amazing he looked. Or how kind he'd been when he'd helped her recover her keys. What had he been thinking when she'd driven away? That unreadable expression in his eyes came back to her now and unsettled her. Why?

Just forget it, Ava. Just forget him. "I appreciate the call. Thank you."

"Well, now, I'm not done with you yet."

"Why am I not surprised?" She couldn't keep the curiosity out of her voice. Or the smile. Both the humiliation she'd felt and the failure seemed far away. Maybe it was because she knew this was a pity call. He felt sorry for the dopey cake lady. Face it, he was Mr. Wow, and she was lucky to keep the date and time straight.

That meant this was a business call. How great was that? She hadn't totally embarrassed herself beyond redemption after all. Cool. "Hopefully you're interested in placing an order?"

"You've got a renovation coming up. How are you going to fill your orders?"

He probably knew about the upcoming renovation because Chloe had been the one to recommend a construction company. "I'm planning on using my sister's kitchen. She's spending most of her evenings with her fiancé and his daughter, so I've commandeered her condo."

"Then maybe you and I can talk later. Say, Monday morning, bright and early?"

"Oops. Can't. I have construction dudes coming by bright and early."

"That's a coincidence because I—"

"I'm totally sorry, but my customer is here. Can I call you back and we can make an appointment? I can show you my catalogue and have some samples ready."

"Why don't I come by on Monday sometime?" Brice leaned back in his car seat and could see the bakery's front door over the curve of the side mirror. There was a grandmotherly woman at the front door, waving at Ava through the glass.

"Thanks, Mr. Donovan. I really appreciate this. Bye!" There was a click in his ear.

He slid his sunglasses down his nose to get a better view as the front door swung open and there was Ava, dressed in her jeans and that yellow T-shirt, her hair tied back and her genuine smile bright as she waved her hands, talking away to her customer.

Okay, this wasn't how he figured things would go. Again. Ava wasn't going to make this easy for him.

She caught his gaze again, moving back into sight with a cake made like a giant dump truck. The red chassis and the bright blue bed made it look like the real toy. Even from a distance, he could see the details. The driver behind the steering wheel, the big black tires, and real-looking dirt.

When she opened the other box, he watched the grandmother's face brighten a notch. There were what had to be small cake rocks about the size of his thumb in chubby yellow buckets. One for each little guest, he figured.

The grandmother looked delighted. But it was the sight of Ava that drew him, multifaceted and flawless, shining like one perfect jewel. She probably didn't realize how she shone from the inside out when she was happy. How caring she was as she refolded the side panels and tucked the lids of the boxes into place. How she waved away what was probably a compliment with ease. She was like no one he'd ever seen before.

Something happened inside him when he looked at Ava. Something that made his spirit come more alive.

He was going to try again. She was a sparkle he could not resist.

He put the car into gear and started driving. Her cheerful words replayed in his mind. *Hopefully you're interested in placing an order?* She'd sounded so full of joy. How was he going to tell her he hadn't meant he wanted to order a cake, but to talk to her about that cup of coffee he'd mentioned earlier?

And what about the renovation? She'd sounded as if the construction guys who were coming had nothing to do with him and his company. She did know he was a part owner, right?

Then again, Ava might not have noticed. His business partner, Rafe, had handled the contracts and the scheduling, and was supervising this project.

Brice hit the speed dial on his cell and waited for it to connect. He'd see if Rafe wouldn't mind switching jobs. Being around Ava every working day for the next two weeks sounded like a good idea. No, a brilliant idea, considering how much he wanted to get to know her.

How would she take it? He was definitely anxious to see the look on her face when he walked into her shop bright and early Monday morning. What would happen then? Only God knew.

One thing was for sure, it was going to be a whole lot of fun to find out.

"Good news!" Ava announced as she sailed through the front door of their apartment. "Mrs. Carnahan loved the cake. She said her little grandson was going to be so happy. And your idea about adding bonus party favors at no charge—it was brilliant. She loved the little rocks I made."

Her twin, Aubrey, poked her head out of the kitchen. "What did I tell you?"

"I know, you're *always* right. I don't deny it." Ava rolled her eyes, shut the door with her foot and dropped her purse, gym bag and keys on the floor. "Instead of take-out burgers, I splurged and got Thai. Cashew chicken, stir-fried rice and that noodle dish you love."

"Well done." Aubrey's smile turned full-fledged as she reached for the big take-out sack. "Hurry up, get changed. I'll get us all set up."

"I'm late, I know. But it was an excellent day despite it all. Who knew?" Ava took off for her bedroom, a total disaster. One day when she got enough time, it would be the epitome of orderliness. But since she wasn't sure when that would be, she had to go with the flow.

Knowing Aubrey was waiting, she tossed her clothes on the floor, kicked her sandals toward the closet and dug around in the laundry basket of clean clothes for her favorite sweatpants and T-shirt. After she found her fuzziest socks, she flew down the little hall.

Aubrey was in the living room setting two heaping plates of food onto two TV trays facing the wide-screen TV they couldn't afford but got anyway. Not smart, and her poor credit card was bent from the weight of debt, but it was nice to watch Clark Gable in forty-two-inch glory.

"If you would have remembered to call before I hit the video store, you would have had some say in tonight's movie," Aubrey said as she settled down on the couch.

"Hey, the cell waves work both ways. You could have called me."

"I'm always calling you." Aubrey reached for her napkin and shook it open over her lap. "So, I take it the Donovan cake delivery went well this morning. You haven't mentioned the groom. What happened with that?"

"Oh, that's a disaster. Total doom. You know me." While she'd told her sister about insulting Brice Donovan, she hadn't given her the day's full update.

"Men." Aubrey shook her head, disapproving. "And to think Chloe's groom, Mark Upton, is supposed to be like last year's most eligible bachelor. Philanthropic. An upstanding Christian. I guess it just shows, you never know about some men. They show one face when they really have another."

"Well, now, that's not exactly the case." Ava slipped behind the TV tray and plopped onto the couch. "Whew, I'm starved. Your turn to say the blessing."

"What happened? Are you telling me that he showed

up this morning at the country club and apologized? Or no, there was a mix up. He didn't proposition you, did he? You jumped to conclusions like you always do and accused him of it. Right? When it wasn't true?"

"You're partly right. I was asked out to coffee, sure, but it wasn't by Mr. Upland. I thought it was, but you know me, like I can remember everyone I've ever met."

"We went to school with Mark *Upton*. Don't you remember?"

"I was busy in high school. How was I supposed to know everyone? Besides, I don't recognize a lot of people. I'm not good with faces."

"Or names."

"Or names." How could she argue with that? She wanted to keep things light and funny, that's the way she felt comfortable with everything. Anything serious or painful, well, that made her feel way too much. And once you started really feeling, then you had to face all the other emotions you were trying to avoid.

Avoidance was a very good policy. At least, she was doing fine avoiding the things that hurt the most. Take today. She didn't have to think about the fact that Brice Donovan might think she was a disaster, too, but he wanted to order a cake. She'd concentrate on the cake part, and try hard not to think about anything else.

Not that she was having the greatest luck with that.

"So what really happened?" Aubrey asked, taking possession of the remote before Ava could grab it and divert her with the movie. "It's okay. You can tell me. It isn't as bad as you think. Really."

Easy for Aubrey, who thought things through before she opened her mouth. Aubrey who never made a mistake of any kind, who never embarrassed herself, who never locked her keys in the car.

Remembering how Brice Donovan's voice had sounded, kind and not belittling, made the yuck of her morning fade a few shades.

"I'll tell you after the movie." Ava shrugged. Some things she didn't even want to talk about, even with her twin. That wasn't the way it was supposed to be, and she knew it made Aubrey sad to be shut out like that, but she didn't want to share every detail.

She wanted to do things right for a change—not just try really hard and then fail, but to really stay focused and careful and committed. One day, maybe she could be the girl who didn't make a mess, who didn't insult Bozeman's most eligible bachelor or who frustrated people so much they simply left her for good.

As Aubrey bowed her head, beginning the blessing, Ava bowed her head, too. But she added a silent prayer to Aubrey's. *Show me the way, Lord. Please, I don't want to mess up anymore. Show me how to be different. Better.*

There was no answer, just the click of the remote as Aubrey hit a button. The TV flared to life, showing a classic movie with a silver-screen hero. Maybe if she met a man like that, she might make an exception to her no-man policy.

She grabbed her fork and dug into the cashew chicken, but did she pay attention to the movie? No. Who was she thinking about?

Brice Donovan and how he'd looked like a real gentleman in his tux. How he'd looked like one of her forgotten dreams when he'd been standing in the full brightness of the morning sun, looking as vibrant and as substantial as a legend come true. But it was just a trick of the light. Legends didn't exist in real life, and real love didn't happen to her.

Chapter Four

It was a beautiful Monday morning, and Ava was on her way to meet the construction dudes. Okay, in truth, she was going to ply them with her special batch of homemade doughnuts and signature coffee. She might not be the brightest bulb in the pack, but she wasn't the dimmest. It was only common sense that people worked better when they were well fueled.

This renovation was a step toward her dream. Tangible and real, and all the hammering and sawing and dust to come would transform the dingy little place into a baker's delight. This was fabulous, something to celebrate, right?

Right. At least, she *should* be feeling so buoyant with happiness that she ought to be floating. But sadly her happiness felt subdued and superficial like icing on the cake, and nothing deeper. Why?

She'd been down a little ever since Brice Donovan's call. Did that make any sense?

No. So what was all this being sad stuff about?

Concentrate on the positive, Ava.

She screeched into the closest parking space since her favorite spot—right beneath the shade of a broad-leafed maple—was already taken by a big forest green pickup truck. It was the ostentatious kind that looked as if it cost more than a house. There was a lot of chrome glinting in the low-rising sun and big lights on top of a custom cab. It probably belonged to one of the construction guys.

Yep, there was one standing on the sidewalk with his back to her. He seemed to be looking over the front of the shop with a contractor's discerning eye.

She cut the engine and grabbed her cell from the console and her bag from the front passenger seat. It was still early, only ten minutes to seven. She'd have time to get the coffee canisters set up and the doughnuts laid out before the rest of the workers arrived. She elbowed the door open, stepped down from the seat and the second her shoe touched the ground she felt it. Something was wrong, but she couldn't put her finger on what.

The construction worker hadn't moved. He was still staring at the front windows—and she could see his reflection as clearly as she could see her own. He looked remarkably like Brice Donovan. That handsome face, sculpted cheekbones and chin, straight nose and strong jaw were all the same. Except for one thing— how could that be Brice? It made no sense. She gave the door a shove to close it.

She had Brice Donovan on the brain. *That's* why her emotions were all off-kilter. *That's* why she wasn't fully enjoying the beautiful morning or this first momentous day of construction.

Brice Donovan. It wasn't as if she even liked him a tiny bit. Really. So what was going on? Maybe it was stress, she decided as she circled around to the back of the vehicle and realized she hadn't hit the door release.

No problem. She looked down at her cell phone. Where were her keys?

The automatic locks clicked shut all on their own.

Great. Wonderful. Terrific. She'd done it again! Why wasn't she paying better attention?

Well, if she hadn't been thinking of Brice Donovan, then she wouldn't have been distracted. See? *This* was why she had to stick to her no-man policy—all the way. No exceptions. Even thinking of him just a little caused problems.

She leaned her forehead against the rear window and took a deep breath. All she needed was to call Aubrey. Plus, there was a silver lining in all this. At least this time she hadn't locked her cell phone in, too. Hey, it could be worse.

She flipped open her phone when a startling familiar baritone rumbled right behind her. "Let me guess. You're in need of rescuing again."

Brice Donovan? She turned around and there he was, looking totally macho in workmen's clothes. The lettering on the light gray T-shirt he wore said it all: D&M Construction, the name of the company she'd hired for the renovation. How on earth did he have a shirt with that company name? Did he work for them?

Then it hit her. Maybe the *D* stood for Donovan. *Wow.*

He jammed his hands into his pockets, emphasizing the muscled set of his shoulders. "You don't look happy to see me."

"Surprised." So surprised she had to lean against the fender for support. "What are you doing here?"

"Rafe Montgomery was going to do the job, but I sweet-talked him into trading."

"Lucky me." Ava's mind swirled. Montgomery must be the *M* in the company. Rafe had been a nice man who'd been her contact. "But why are you here in workman's clothes. Aren't you like an investment broker or something?"

"That would be my dad. Rafe Montgomery and I got to talking one night while we were studying for our graduate school exams. What we were really dreading wasn't taking the test, it was being cooped up in an office all day. Just like our dads. Don't get me wrong, I don't mind putting in a good hard day's work, but I felt put in a box. It wasn't for either of us. So we pooled our resources and went into business."

That was the most unlikely story she'd ever heard. MBA dudes who built stuff? "I'd like to think you had woodworking training. A certificate of carpentry competence."

"I'm good at what I do, believe me."

Oh, she did believe him. And how was it possible that he looked even better dressed for work than he had the other day in a tux? Today he looked genuine, capable and very manly.

"Let me get a coat hanger." He strode to the green pickup and opened the crew-cab door. A big golden retriever tumbled out and ping-ponged in place in front of Brice, tongue lolling. "Whoa there, boy."

Okay, she melted. She couldn't help it—she was a softy when it came to dogs. "What's his name?"

Goofy brown eyes fastened on her. That big doggy mouth swung wide, showing dozens of sharp teeth. The huge canine launched toward her, tongue out and grinning, moving so fast he was a golden-brown blur.

"Rex, no! Come back here." Brice reached for his collar to catch him.

Too late.

Ava didn't have time to brace herself, because the dog was already leaping on her, plopping one front paw on either side of her neck, almost hugging her. His tongue swiped across her chin. Happy chocolate eyes studied hers with sheer joy.

"Brice, I'm in love with your dog." She couldn't help it. The big cuddly retriever hugged her harder before dropping down on all four paws. As if he knew how much he'd charmed her, he posed handsomely, staring up adoringly with those sweet eyes.

"Excuse him. He's very friendly. Too friendly." Brice grabbed his collar. "This may come as a shock to you but he failed every obedience class he's been in. From puppy school all the way up to the academy."

"Academy?"

"I hired professionals, but in the end, he won." Brice turned his attention to the retriever, his face softening, his big hand stroking over the crown of the canine's downy head. He received a few swipes of that lolling tongue and laughed. "Life's hard enough, isn't it? Without being told what to do every second of the day."

Ava couldn't believe it. The big, macho, most eligible bachelor was tough looking with all his masculine strength and charm, but she knew his secret. He was a big marshmallow underneath.

Not that she was interested. Really.

"This'll only take a second, now that I have the routine down." He took a wire hanger—she hadn't even noticed when he'd fetched it from his truck—and unbent it enough to slide it between the frame of the door and the roof.

True to his word, a few seconds later he'd hit the lock and was pulling her key from the ignition and silencing the alarm. He hit the back door release for her.

Okay, he was really a decent guy. On the surface anyway, and that's the only level on which she intended to know him. He was the *D* in D&M Construction, so that meant for better or worse, she was stuck with him. Not that she thought for a moment he actually did the hard work. No, he was probably more of a figurehead. He probably just oversaw projects. He was Roger Donovan's son, right?

She lifted the back and slid out the bakery box, and Rex bounded up to sniff at it.

"Hey, buddy, these are not for you." Ava might be charmed by the big cuddly dog, but she wasn't that big of a pushover. "Sit."

The retriever grinned up at her with every bit of charisma he possessed.

"Look at him drool. That can only mean one thing. There must be doughnuts in that box." There was Brice, as large as life, wrapping one big, powerful hand around the canine's blue nylon collar. "Need any help carrying those?"

"I suppose you like doughnuts, too."

"Guilty." His warm eyes and dazzling grin, those dimples and personality and his hard appearance made him look good down to the soul.

She had been fooled by this type of guy before, but not this time. "These are not for you. They are for your crew. For the men who actually work for a living instead of walking around owning companies."

"Hey, I work hard."

"I don't see a hammer." She reached for a second box, but he beat her to it. It was heavy with big thermos-type coffee canisters. "I see you eyeing the thermoses and no, you may not have any of that either. Not unless you're a construction dude, and I don't see a tool belt strapped to your waist."

"That's not fair. My tools are in my truck."

She rolled her eyes. "Oh, *sure* they are."

Brice shut the door and hit the remote. Rex bounced at his hip, the dog's gaze glued to the pink bakery box. "You know I'm the on-site manager of this project, right?"

"I'll have to see it to believe it." She snapped ahead of him with that quick-paced walk of hers, her yellow sneakers squeaking with each step. "I still don't get why you're here. Why I'm plagued with you and that dog of yours."

She eyed him like a judge awaiting a guilty verdict, but she didn't fool him. Not one bit. He saw in her eyes and in the hint of her smile what she was trying to hide. He wasn't the only one wondering.

Maybe he wasn't the only one wishing.

"Where do you want these?" he asked of the stuff he was carrying.

She gestured to the worn wooden counter in front of them, where she'd set the bakery box and was lifting the lid.

He did as she asked and nearly went weak in the knees at the aroma wafting out from the open box. Sweet cake doughnuts, the comforting bite of chocolate, the richness of custard and the mouthwatering sweet huckleberries that glistened like fat blue jelly beans.

"Where did you get these?" The question wasn't past his lips before he knew the answer. "You made these. You."

"Okay, that's so surprising? I'm a baker. Hel-*lo*." She rolled her eyes at him, but it was cute, the way she shook her head as if she simply didn't know about him. Yep, he knew what she was trying to do. Because whatever was happening between them felt a little scary, like standing on the edge of a crumbling precipice and knowing while the fall was certain, the how and what of the landing was not.

She pulled a bag of paper plates from her big shoulder bag, ripped it open and pulled out a plate. She slid the berries-and-cream-topped doughnut onto the plate and handed it to him. "I saw you eyeing it."

Had she noticed how he'd been looking at her? He thought she was two hundred times sweeter than that doughnut. "How about some cups?"

"Here." She pulled a bag of them from her mammoth bag. "Which doughnut should I give your dog?"

Rex gave a small bark of delight and sat on his haunches like the best dog in the world. His doggy gaze was glued on the bottom corner of the bakery box.

"He'd take every last one. Don't trust him if you leave that box uncovered."

"Oh, he's a good guy. It's you I don't trust," she said with a hint of a grin. "You said you traded with Mr. Montgomery. I want to know why."

Just his luck. He filled two cups with sweetened, aromatic coffee and handed her one. "How about grace, first?"

"I've already had my breakfast." She took the coffee.

Their fingertips brushed and it was a little like being hit by a lightning strike from a blue sky. His heartbeat lurched to a stop. What was it about Ava that seemed to make his world stand still?

She gave him another judgmental look like a prim schoolmarm as she put a glazed doughnut on a second plate. Rex's tail thumped like a jackhammer against the scarred tile floor. She knelt to set the plate on the floor.

"What a nice polite gentleman," she praised, and gave him a pat.

Rex sat a moment to further fool Ava into thinking he was a perfect dog before he wolfed down the doughnut in two bites.

"You're welcome," she said as she patted him again and removed the plate. "Oh, some of the men are driving up now. Good."

Brice tried not to let it bother him that she disregarded him completely as she disappeared through the kitchen door. This was *not* how most single ladies reacted to him. He considered the steaming cup of coffee he held and the plate with the delectable doughnut.

Lord, I'm gonna need help with this one. If it's Your will, please show me the way.

The doors swung closed as if in answer, swinging open again to show a glimpse of Ava, washed in sunlight from the large window. Inexplicably, the sun shone brighter.

Could the morning be going any more perfectly? The homemade doughnuts were a hit. With promises of more sweet surprises for tomorrow morning, Ava made sure the fridge was stocked with plenty of liquids—it was important to keep the workers hydrated—and gathered up her stuff.

Time to get out of their way. Dust was already flying. Walls were already missing. As curious as she was to see absolutely everything, she knew she'd only be in the way. Besides, she had to work at her family's bookstore because she had her share of the rent and utilities to pay at month's end. Not to mention her car payment. Oh, and credit card payments. And her school loans. She grabbed her bag and was in the middle of hunting down her keys when she suddenly realized she wasn't alone.

"Ava, I'm glad I caught you." There was Brice, shouldering through the door. "Before you go, I want to go over your final plans."

"I already did that with Mr. Montgomery. When we talked the other day on the phone, you know, after Chloe's wedding, you said you wanted to stop by on Monday morning. I assumed that meant you were interested in ordering a cake. But this is why, isn't it?"

"I can order a cake if you want."

"It isn't what I want that's the question." Really, that grin of his was infectious. Dashing and charming and utterly disarming. What was a girl to do? How was she supposed to *not* smile back? She was helpless here. *Lord, give me strength, please.* "I haven't forgotten that you tried to ask me out. I mean, I know you changed your mind once I started insulting you."

"The post-traumatic stress is better, by the way. Although standing in this kitchen might give me a flashback or two." His grin deepened right along with his dimples. "You're questioning why I'm here, right? Remember I said that you made my sister happy with her wedding cake?"

"I do." Leery, that's what she had to be. On guard. The kindness of his smile was like a tractor beam pulling her in. If she wasn't careful, she was going to start liking this man.

Liking men at all—even platonically—wasn't a part of her no-man policy. Because that's how it had happened with Ken, the chef she dated about five months back, and that had ended in disaster. If she didn't learn lessons from her ten billion mistakes, how was she ever going to feel better about herself?

Brice came closer, his dog trailing after him. "You made Chloe happy, and now I want to return the favor."

Okay, she could buy that reason. It was actually a nice reason. Which only made him a nicer man in her eyes.

He set a coffee cup down on the metal table between them and gave it a shove in her direction, obviously meant for her. She hadn't noticed what he'd been carrying.

How could she have not noticed that he was hauling with him a rolled up blueprint, too?

Keep your mind on business, Ava, she ordered herself. Really, it was that smile of Brice's. It ought to come with a surgeon general's warning. Beware: Might Have the Gravitational Pull of a Black Hole And Suck You Right In.

"I know you've gone over the plans with my partner." Brice plopped the blueprints on the metal worktable and spread out them out with quick efficiency. He anchored each corner with a battered tape measure and hammer he plucked from his tool belt. "But what I want to know is the dream of what you want. The heart of it. Beyond the computer-generated drawings of this place."

Okay, that wasn't what she expected and it disarmed her even more. Emotions tangled in her throat and made her voice thick and strange sounding. "I showed Mr. Montgomery a few pictures of what I had in mind."

"I'd like to see them."

Their gazes met, and a connection zinged between them. A sad ache rolled through her and she didn't know why. She refused to let herself ask. Instead, she fumbled through the top drawer in the battered cabinets. She'd left the magazine pictures here to show the woodworker, just in case.

But turning her back to him gave her no sense of privacy or relief from the aching she felt. Somehow she managed to face him again, but her hands were shaking. She didn't want to think too hard on the reason for that either. "Here. I'm not looking for exactly this. But something warm and whimsical and unique. In my price range."

She spread the three full-color pictures on the metal

table, turning them so they were right side up for his inspection. Long ago, she'd torn them from magazines she'd come across, tucking them away for the when and if of this dream. The white frame of the pages had dulled to yellow over time, and the ragged edges where she'd torn them from the magazine looked tattered. But the bright glass displays and the intricate woodwork remained as bright and as promising as ever.

"It's probably beyond my budget, I know, that's what Mr. Montgomery said. But he thought he could scale it down and still get some of the feeling of the crafts-manship."

Brice said nothing as he studied the photos, sipping his coffee, taking his time. "Why baking? Why not open a bistro? Or stay working at your family's bookstore?"

Surprise shot across her face. "You know about the bookstore? Wait, Chloe knows. She probably told you."

That wasn't exactly true. Everyone knew about the bookstore. Ava's grandmother's family, a wealthy and respected family and one of the area's original settlers, had owned the store forever. "I need to know what this means to you before I start on the woodwork. Isn't that what you do before you design a cake for someone?"

"Exactly." She took a sip of the sweetened coffee and studied him through narrowed eyes, as if she were truly seeing him for the first time.

He could see her heart, shining in her eyes, whole and dazzling. He leaned closer. Couldn't stop himself.

She turned one of the pictures around to study. "You wouldn't understand what I want, being Bozeman's most eligible bachelor and all."

"You know, I have relatives who work on the local paper. That's where the list came from. I had nothing to do with it. I'm just a working man, so I bet I can understand. Try me."

A cute little furrow dug in between her eyes, over the bridge of her nose. Adorable, she shrugged one slim shoulder, and for a moment she looked lost. *Sad.* "My mom really wasn't happy being a wife and mother. I know that. But when I was little it felt like I was the one who made her unhappy. I was always spilling stuff and knocking into furniture and forgetting things. Not that I've changed that much." She shrugged again. "This isn't what you want to hear."

"This is exactly right. Exactly what I want to know."

He laid his hand over hers, feeling the warm silk of her skin and the cool smoothness of the magazine page. One picture was of bistro tables washed in sunlight, framed by golden, scrolled wood and crisp white clouds of curtains. It looked like something out of a children's storybook, where evil was easily defeated, where every child was loved and where love always won.

That's what he knew she saw on the page, he knew because he could see her heart so clearly.

She drew in a ragged breath, her voice thin with emotion, her eyes turning an arresting shade of indigo. "One thing that always went right was when I was with Mom in the kitchen. She wasn't much of a baker, but I had spent a lot of time with Gran in the kitchen, she taught me to bake, and I liked the quiet time. Measuring sugar and sifting flour. Getting everything just right."

She paused as if noticing for the first time that his

hand still covered hers. She didn't try to move away. Did she know how vulnerable she looked? How good and true? He didn't think so. He feared his heart, hurting so much for her, would never be the same.

"This reminds you of baking with your Mom," he said.

"Sort of. I remember the kitchen smelled wonderful when the cookies or the cakes were cooling. And afterward there was the frosting to whip up and the decorating to do. It's the one thing I could always do right. It made everyone happy, for how ever little time that happiness lasted, it was there."

"And then your mother left?"

Ava gently tugged her hand out from beneath his. She lowered her gaze, veiled her heart. That was a scandal of huge proportion. Everybody had known at the time, and in a small city that was really just one big small town, everybody still remembered although twenty years had passed. "I want this to be like a place where customers feel like they've stepped into a storybook. Not childish, just—" She couldn't think of the word.

"You want a place where it feels as if wishes can come true."

How did he know that? Ava took a shaky breath and tucked away the honesty she shouldn't have hauled out like dirty laundry in a basket. She was *so* not a wishing kind of girl. Not anymore.

She grabbed her bag again, not remembering when exactly it had slipped from her shoulder to the floor. "I'd better get going. I'm late for my shift at the bookstore."

"Do I make you uncomfortable?"

"Yes." The word popped out before she could stop it.

He winced. "Well, that's not my intention. We got off on the wrong foot. Is that what's bothering you?"

"No. Yes."

"Which is it?"

"I don't know." All she knew was that he felt *way* too close, although she'd crossed half of the kitchen on the way to the door and it still didn't make any difference. She took a shaky breath. "I should have recognized you. I mean, I'm usually so busy in my own little world, I don't notice everything I should."

"Well, I didn't introduce myself, so when you think about it, it could be all my fault."

"You're being too nice."

"That's better than being Mr. Yuck, right?"

"Maybe."

That made his dimples flash. "What do you do with your time, besides baking incredible cakes?"

"Hang out with my sisters, mostly. Doing my part to contribute to consumer debt. That kind of thing." And that was all she was going to share with him because anything else would be way too personal. "Okay, what did I do with my keys?"

"I might have 'em." He reached into his back pocket and then there they were in the palm of his hand.

Oops. It looked as if she would have to move closer to him to get them. Her chest tightened and her emotions felt like one big aching mess. Was it because of the story she'd told him, about baking with her mother? Or was he the reason?

She knew the answer simply by looking at him.

His appearance—the worn T-shirt, battered Levi's and beat-up black work boots—all shouted tough guy, but in a really good, hardworking way. Add that to his kindness and class—and he was totally wishable.

Not that she was wishing.

As he strode toward her with the slow measured gait of a hunter, she didn't feel stalked. No, she felt *drawn*. As if he'd gathered up her tangled heartstrings and gave them a gentle shake. There were no more knots, just one simple, honest feeling running up those strings and straight into her heart.

She didn't want to be drawn to any man. Especially not him.

She grabbed the keys, careful to scoop them from his hand without any physical contact. But something had changed between them and she couldn't deny it.

"Thanks," she said in a practically normal-sounding voice. "You have my cell number if there's a problem, right?"

"Right."

She could feel him watching her as she yanked open the door. Rex bounded toward her and she almost forgot about Brice. She knelt down to give his head a good rubbing. "It was very nice meeting you, boy. I'll bring some muffins tomorrow. Is that all right by you?"

Rex lapped her cheek and panted in perfect agreement.

She had one foot over the threshold when Brice's voice called her back. "See you tomorrow, Ava. And thanks for sharing a cup of coffee with me."

Coffee. That made her screech to a total halt. Her mind sat there, idling. Wasn't that what he'd wanted to do in the beginning? He'd wanted to get to know her over a cup of coffee.

And he had.

She wanted to leap to the quick conclusion that she'd been tricked. But it wasn't that simple. She'd been the one to bring the coffee in the first place. It was her coffee, her kitchen, her renovation project. It was her heart she had to hold on to as she took the other step through the door and closed Brice Donovan from her sight.

Chapter Five

Ava burst through the employee's entrance door in the back of the Corner Christian Bookstore. The big problem? Her oldest sister was heating a cup of tea in the break room's microwave and she had *that* look. The one where she frowned, shook her head slowly from side to side as if this was exactly what she expected.

"Oops, I'm late." Ava slid the bakery box onto the small battered Formica table. "My bad. But I brought chocolate."

"That doesn't begin to make up for it." The corner of Katherine's mouth twitched, as if she were holding back a smile. "What am I going to do with you?"

"Nothing. I'm your little sister and you love me."

"Not at much as Aubrey," she teased. "Aubrey showed up twenty-three minutes early for her shift."

"True." Aubrey appeared from the other doorway that led to the floor. "I smell doughnuts. The doughnuts that were missing from our kitchen this morning. I came back from the stables and had nothing to eat. You didn't have to take every last one with you."

"Hey, the real question is why would you walk by a kitchen full of boxed doughnuts and not take any in the first place?" With a wink, Ava shoved open the small employee's closet and dumped her bag on the floor.

"What could have possessed me, I wonder?" Aubrey flipped open the box and stole a chocolate huckleberry custard. "The construction dudes were—"

"Cool. Loved the doughnuts. Started beating down walls with their sledgehammer thingies right away." Ava grabbed a cup from the upper cabinet and filled it from the sink tap.

Don't think of Brice, she ordered herself. Too late. There he was in her mind's eye. Standing in her kitchen, looking like a good man, radiating character. Normally, she'd be *so* interested, but if she let herself like him, that would be just another huge mistake in a long, endless string of disasters.

Don't start wishing now, she told herself, letting her big sister Katherine take the mug from her hands and slip it into the microwave to heat.

"You look down," Katherine commented as she added honey to her steaming teacup, her engagement ring sparkling. "That can't be good. This is your first day of renovation. You should be excited. What's going on?"

"Uh-oh." Aubrey had a twin moment.

Great. Somehow she had telebeamed her thoughts to her twin; they seemed to share brain cells. Ava felt the humiliation creeping through her all over again. "Don't say it. Let's just not go into it."

Ava could sense Katherine's question hovering in the air unspoken between them, wanting to know what

was wrong and how she could help. Dear Katherine
meant well, wanting to take care of everyone and fixing what she could, but what do you do when you know
there's no solution to a problem?

*You refocus yourself, that's what, and concentrate
on preventing disasters.* There was Brice Donovan
again, flashing across her brain pan. Definitely disaster material.

Hayden, Katherine's soon-to-be stepdaughter, poked
her head around the door. "Hey, like, Spence is totally
freaking out. There's no one out there to ring up and
stuff."

"So? Our brother is always freaking out."

"I'll go," Aubrey said. "I'm supposed to be watching
the front anyway. I'll take this with me, though." With
a grin she slipped past the teenager with her chocolate-
covered doughnut in hand.

"Like that's going to make Spence happy." The kid
shrugged her gangly shoulders. "Maple bars, too? Cool,
Ava."

"I knew they were your favorite, not that I like you
or anything." Ava hid her smile, knowing she wasn't
so successful.

Hayden grinned, snatched a doughnut. "Thanks!"
she called over her shoulder as she disappeared back
into the stacks.

Talk about weird. "Are you ready to be a stepmom?"
Ava already knew the answer, but it was called a diversionary tactic. She *so* did not want to talk about her
shop, her dreams, and how it had all gotten tangled up
with Mr. Wishable. "You'll be marrying Jack in two
more months."

"I know. Time is melting way and it feels as if I'm never going to have everything ready for the wedding." Katherine waited for the microwave to ding. She opened the door, dropped a tea bag into the steaming water and left it on the counter to steep. "But I'm more than ready to be a stepmom. Hayden is a part of Jack. How could I not love her? Speaking of which, how are the designs for my cake coming along?"

Okay, another topic to avoid. "I'm working on it. Honest."

"I have all the faith in the world in you, sweetie."

Wasn't that the problem? "I've got some great sketches, but I've got a few more ideas I want to work out before we sit back down."

"Do you know what we should do?" Katherine pushed the plastic bear-shaped bottle of honey along the counter. "We'll all go out to a nice dinner, my treat. To celebrate."

"Celebrate what?"

Katherine shook her head, as if she couldn't believe it. "The first day of construction on your shop? This has been your dream forever, right?"

"I can't tonight. I have a consultation. Maybe later, though? Besides, you're just in a good mood because you've found Mr. Dream Come True. Not everyone is as lucky." She didn't mean to sound wistful, really. She was deeply happy for her sister. Katherine deserved a good man and a happy marriage. And, seeing that it had happened for her sister after all this time, it *almost* gave a girl a little hope it could happen to her.

Not that she'd go around praying for it, because she'd tried that route before. She had a gift for prayer.

She might make a mess of everything she touched, she might show up late for work and forget where she put her keys, but what she prayed for almost always happened. Hence her last relationship disasters with Mike, Brett and Ken. Before that, Isaiah, Christian and Lloyd. It was that old adage, be careful what you wish for. Which was why she wasn't, not even silently, wishing. Really.

"I know something isn't right." Katherine frowned as if she were trying to figure out what. "I know you've got to be under a lot of pressure getting your business off the ground, but you know you're not alone, right? You say the word and we're right with you. In fact, you might not have a chance to say the word before we barge in."

Was she blessed with her awesome family or what? Ava's eyes burned. She was grateful to the Lord for her wonderful sisters. "You know me. I know how to holler."

"Excellent." Katherine brushed some of Ava's wind-blown hair out of her eyes. "Whatever's got you down, remember you are just the way God made you. And that makes you perfectly lovable, sweetie. Trust me."

She didn't know about being perfectly lovable but she did know that her sister—her family—was on her perfectly lovable list. Blessings she gave thanks for every day of her life. Katherine's words meant everything.

The morning had been perfect. The construction workers were hardworking family men who were very happy with the box of doughnuts. And—surprise!—Brice looked like a good boss and a hard worker himself. She was confident that the renovation would be terrific when it was done.

She was the problem since she wavered on what she said she wanted. No, she wasn't exactly wavering. But she'd *almost* given in to wishing and that was just as bad. She had to be more careful. More determined.

A deep, frustrated huff sounded at the inner door. It was Spence, glowering. "There you two are. Ava, you're late. For, what, the fifteenth shift in a row?"

"Probably. Sorry." Ava couldn't argue. She upended the plastic bear over her cup and gave it a hard squeeze. "But I'm here now, so that's good, right? I mean, it could be worse. I could be even later."

That was the logic that always confounded Spence. His Heathcliff personality couldn't seem to understand and he stormed away.

She wasn't fooled. His bark was much worse than his bite.

"He's under a lot of pressure," Katherine excused him as she grabbed a cinnamon twist from the box on her way to the front. "Thanks for the goodies, cutie."

Alone in the break room, Ava took a sip of her tea, but the chamomile blend didn't soothe her. She dumped in more honey, and that didn't do the trick either. A big piece of sadness sat square in the middle of her chest, stronger after having been with Brice.

His words came back to her now. *You want a place where it feels as if wishes can come true.* He'd said what was in her heart.

How had he known?

At a loss, she headed out front. She had bills to pay and dreams to dream—and a no-man policy to stick to.

* * *

Ava had lingered in his thoughts all through the workday, all of Brice's waking hours and into the next morning. He hadn't looked forward to strapping on his tool belt this much in a long time. Though he liked his work, it was the prospect of seeing Ava that made the difference.

His commitment to this renovation project was about more than work. He wanted to do a good job with it—hands down, customer satisfaction was job one. But beyond that, he wanted to do his best to give Ava her dream. Listening to her talk about baking with her mom—the mom who had run off to Hollywood with the youngest daughter decades ago and had never been heard from since—was like a sign from above pointing the way to win her heart.

He wondered if Ava had any idea how purely her inner beauty shone when she talked about being happy like that? In wanting again, for others and for herself, a joy-filled place where wishes could come true?

She was a different kind of woman than he was used to. Whitney had been exactly what his mom had wanted for him. She was from a respectable family, from money older than the state of Montana. The right schools and the proper social obligations and charity work. But in the end, she'd been wrong for him. Wrong for the man he really was, not Roger Donovan's son, but a Montanan born and raised, who liked his life a little more comfortable and far less showy.

The shop had a decimated look to it, even gilded by the golden peach of the newly rising sun. The interior walls were bare down to the studs, which glowed like honey in the morning light. The white dip and rise of electrical wire ran like a clothesline the length of the room. Dust coated the windows, but he could see the promise. See her dream.

Rex romped to the front door, springing in place with excitement. His tongue rolled out of his mouth as he panted, and since Brice was taking too long, pawed at the door handle.

"Hold on there, bud. I'm eager to see Ava, too."

The retriever gave a low bark when he heard Ava's name.

Yeah, at least the dog liking her wouldn't be an issue the way it was with Whitney. Yet another sign, Brice figured as he picked through his mammoth ring of work keys, found the one for the shop and unlocked the door. Whitney hadn't been fond of big, bouncing, sometimes slobbery dogs. Brice was.

The second the door was open an inch, Rex hit it at a dead run and launched through the open kitchen doors. There on the worktable was a bright pink bakery box. That explained the retriever's eagerness. They may have missed Ava, but she'd left a consolation prize.

She'd come before his shift started, left her baking and skedaddled. Apparently, there was a good reason. Like maybe the comment he'd made about finally getting to talk with her over coffee. Maybe—just maybe—he shouldn't have pointed that out.

Right when he'd thought he was making progress with her, getting to know her, letting her know the kind of man he was, he'd hit a brick wall.

Apparently Ava wasn't as taken with him as he was with her.

Wow. That felt like a hard blow to his sternum. Here was the question: Did he pursue this or not? Sure, they'd gotten off on the wrong foot when she'd mistaken him for Chloe's groom, but even after that, she'd been determined to put some distance between them.

Face it, this was one-sided. He'd stood right here in this kitchen and got to know her, seen right through to her dreams. He was captivated by her. He was falling in serious like with her.

But now? She was missing in action.

Rex's bark echoed in the vacant kitchen.

"Okay, okay." Brice popped open the huge bakery box. "Only one, and I mean it this time. All this baked stuff can't be good for you—"

He fell silent at the treats inside the box. She'd promised muffins, but these weren't like anything he'd ever seen. They were huge muffins shaped like cute, round monsters. They had ropy icing for hair, big goofy eyes, a potato nose and a wide grin. Two dozen monster faces stared up at him, colorful and whimsical.

Ava made the ordinary unusual and fun. He liked that about her. Very much.

He'd been praying, to find a good woman to love and marry. Have a few kids. Live a happy life. That had been part of his plan for a long time, but it just hadn't worked out for one reason or another. In fact, it hadn't worked out for such a length of time that began to feel as if his prayer was destined to remain unanswered.

The front door swung open and heavy boots pounded against the floor, echoing in the demolished room. It was Tim, the electrician. "Hey, where are those muffins she promised?"

"In here."

"I gotta tell ya," Tim said as he dropped his tool bags on the floor, "this might be the best job we've done yet. The doughnuts yesterday were something. You think she's gonna keep bakin' for us?" Tim's jaw dropped in disbelief when he saw the muffins. "Look at that. Think anyone would mind if I took one home for my little girl? She'd get a kick out of that."

Brice realized that Ava had made five times the number of muffins they needed for their small work crew. "Go for it."

"Cool." Tim grabbed a mammoth monster muffin and took a bite. "Mmm," he said around a full mouth, as if surprised by how good it tasted.

Not that Brice was surprised by that. He flipped open his phone and dialed. While he waited for the call to connect, he took a muffin for Rex on the way out the back door. The sunshine felt hot and dry as he sat on the back step and unwrapped the muffin. The dog gobbled his muffin in three bites.

Ava picked up on the sixth ring. "Hi there. Is there a problem at the shop?"

Caller ID, he guessed. "A problem? You could say that."

"What's wrong? I was there and everything looked fine. Okay, it was like a total wreck, but it's supposed to look like that, right?"

"Right. That wasn't the kind of problem I meant." He leaned back, resting his spine against the building. He wondered where she was. A lot of clanging sounded in the background. "You left a box of monsters behind. Why didn't you stay and say hello?"

"I didn't want to be in the way."

"I hope you didn't feel uncomfortable with me yesterday. You know I like you."

"I'm trying to ignore that."

"Is there any particular reason for that?"

"Well, you're doing the renovation on my shop, for starters."

"Good reason. Look, I don't want you to feel uncomfortable. Not around me. Not around my men. Not when it comes to the work we're doing for you."

"Sure, I know that."

It didn't seem as if she did. She sounded as vulnerable as she'd looked yesterday when she'd been talking about her baking. Okay, so maybe what he felt wasn't a two-way street. "How about you and I agree to be friends. Would that make you more comfortable?"

"Friends? Uh, sure. Wait." He could imagine her biting her bottom lip while she thought, the cute little furrow digging in between her eyes. "You mean like platonic friends."

"I mean that whatever this is going on between us, let's put in on hold until your renovation is done. That way you don't have to come to your own shop before 6:45 a.m. just to avoid me."

"I wasn't necessarily avoiding *you*." Ava knew her voice sounded thin and honest. She was no good at subterfuge of any kind. Another reason she'd never understood men who had hidden agendas. "You see, it's not you. It's me. All me."

"You want to explain that?" he asked in that kind way he had, but he obviously didn't understand.

There it was, doom, hovering right in front of her, and its name was Brice Donovan.

"It's just that—" she blurted out, nearly losing hold of her grocery cart in the dairy aisle. "I have the worst luck dating. If there's a loser anywhere near me, he'll be the one I think is nice. I'm like a disaster magnet. That's why I have a policy."

"What policy? I don't understand."

She felt her heart weakening. She liked this man— and wasn't that the exact problem? She had to be totally tough. Cool. Focused. Strong. That's what she had to be. Strong enough to stick to her guns. "It's an ironclad, nonnegotiable no-man, no-dating policy."

"That's a pretty strict policy. There's a good reason for it, huh?"

Her throat tightened. When she spoke, she knew she sounded as if she were struggling. "Yeah. Nothing horrible, just disappointing. I don't want to spend my life believing in a man's goodness and being blind to any terrible faults that I just can't see until it's too late. You see, it's like being color-blind. I'm just…" She didn't know what to say.

Apparently Brice didn't either. No sound came from his end of the connection. Nothing at all.

"I'm sorry." That came out strangled sounding.

So she was never going to be a tough business woman. She wasn't a tough anything. Sadness hit her like the cold from the refrigerated dairy case. Was she disappointed?

Surprisingly, yes.

"Okay, then. I'll call you if we have any questions over here." He broke the silence, sounding business as usual, but beneath, she thought she heard disappointment, too.

Maybe it was best not to think about that, she thought as she closed her phone, dumped it into her bag and put the milk jug into her cart. She couldn't say why she would be feeling deflated, because she did the right thing by putting him off. She just had to stay focused on her goals and her path in life, she thought as she grabbed a carton of whipping cream.

Her phone rang again and she went fishing for it in her messy tote. Luckily it was still ringing when she found it. She didn't recognize the number on the screen. "Hello?"

"Uh, yes," came a refined woman's voice. "My name is Maxime Frost and I was at Chloe Donovan's wedding. Brice highly recommended you, and I just *had* to call. We simply must have one of your cakes for my Carly's wedding."

"I'm sure I can design something both you and Carly will love."

She wrote down an appointment time on the inside of her checkbook and ended the call. How about that? Brice had recommended her in spite of the mistaken identity incident.

Just when she thought she was sure she'd made the right decision to stick to her no-date policy, look what happened. He made her start wishing all over again—and reconsidering.

Chapter Six

Everyone was at the restaurant by the time she got there, seated in a big table at the back, between a cozy intersection of booths. Of course, she was late because she was time-challenged. From the head of the table, Spence spotted her first and his dour frown darkened a notch. He highly prized timeliness. Katherine sat between him and her fiancé, Jack Munroe. Seated next to her dad, the teenaged Hayden gave a finger wave.

Ava lifted her hand to finger wave back but the sight of the appetizers in platters placed in three parts of the table stopped her in her tracks. "I can't believe you ordered without me."

"You're twenty minutes late." Spence huffed. "The assistant manager wasn't going to hold the reservation just for you."

Personally, this was why she thought Spence wasn't married, but now was probably not the time to mention it. "Oops. Sorry." She didn't bother to explain the extra appointment she squeezed in, and that she'd left a message on Aubrey's phone that she'd be late, and there had been a major traffic snarl from some wild moose who was wandering Glenrose Street. It was easier to endure Spence's scowl.

She dropped into the empty seat next to her twin. "Do you check your messages?"

"I was out at the studio and lost track of time. I barely got here myself." Aubrey grabbed the platter in front of her and began sliding a stack of deep-fried zucchini slices onto Ava's plate. "Don't worry about Spence. It's that assistant manager who works here. The one that had that date with Katherine long ago and it didn't go well? He's always snippy with us. The construction—"

"Is going well." Ava paused to bow her head and gave a quick grace, since she'd missed Spence's blessing.

Aubrey spooned a heap of creamy dip next to the zucchini slices on Ava's plate. "And how's Brice?"

"Fine, I guess. I didn't see him today."

"And that wouldn't be because you're avoiding him?"

"I'm not avoiding him." It wasn't true but she wanted it to be. "Fine, I just avoided him for the day. Maybe I'll try again tomorrow."

"He's supposed to be this great guy. Wasn't he this year's most eligible bachelor or something?"

"Let's not talk about him." She glanced around the table to see if everyone was straining to listen. They were. "Later, okay?"

Katherine spoke up. "Didn't you do a wedding cake for Brice's sister?"

"Yeah. Just." Like she wanted to talk about it? *This* was the downside of being in a big family. Nothing was secret for long. "He's the contractor doing the renovation."

Spence leaned in. "You mean it's his *company* doing the renovation. He's not doing the actual work. He's an owner."

"No, he's like the on-site manager guy. Trust me, he had a hammer and everything." She hedged because everyone in her family but Aubrey was *way* too eager to marry her off. "Chloe recommended the company."

It didn't look like anyone at the table was fooled by that.

Katherine passed her hunky fiancé a platter of mozzarella sticks. "I thought Brice Donovan was engaged."

"No," Aubrey dragged a zucchini slice through a puddle of dip. "I read in the paper over a year ago that she called it off. The wedding was cancelled something like two days before it was supposed to happen. That had to be very hard for both of them."

Ava couldn't seem to swallow. The part of her that was afraid of getting close to him wanted to use this new piece of news as a reason to keep away from him. He'd already had one failed relationship. He was probably at fault, and she didn't need some flawed guy, right? On the surface, it sounded like the best reasoning.

But she knew it wasn't. Brice was a good guy—that much was clear. The real question was, how far down did that kindness go? Was it superficial, or the real thing?

The cracked pieces of her heart ached with a wish

she couldn't let herself voice. Brice had a lot of redeeming qualities, so what? She had to resist. What she had to do was clear every thought of him from her mind. His every image from her memory. No more thoughts of Brice Donovan allowed.

"Good evening, McKaslin family," said a familiar voice behind her. Brice's voice.

Of course.

Why did it have to be him? She felt as if she'd been hit with the debris from a fast approaching tornado. She couldn't outrun it, escape it and there was no hope of avoiding it as Brice Donovan stepped into sight.

To her surprise her brother stood, nodding a greeting. "Good to see you again, Brice. Would you care to join us, or are you here with your family?"

"With family. It's my mother's birthday, but thanks for the invite. I just spotted Ava and I thought I'd come over. Let her know a few things about the job today, if she's got time before her meal arrives."

Ava could feel the power of his presence, stronger than the earth's gravity holding her feet to the floor. "Do I have time?" she asked her twin.

"I ordered for you," Aubrey explained. "Take your phone and you two go talk. I'll call you when the meal arrives."

Okay, it sounded like a good plan, but there was a downside here—did she want to be alone with Brice? No. Was she mentally prepared to be alone with him? Not a chance.

She grabbed her plate and her phone and followed him to the more casual patio area, where there were plenty of tables available. Brice nodded toward one of the waiters, who gestured to a set of unoccupied tables along the railing.

"I was hoping to catch you tomorrow morning." Brice was entirely too close as he leaned to pull out a chair for her. "But seeing you charge through the restaurant a few minutes ago seemed like a sign. I hope you don't mind the intrusion."

"Nope." What she minded was being alone with him. How was she going to hold on to her policy now? She caught a hint of his spicy aftershave. "After all, we've agreed to be friends."

"Exactly." He smiled his killer smile, the one with the dimples.

Did he know what that did to a woman? It made every innocent, friendly thought vanish and the ones about sweet romance and marriage proposals surge forth like a hurricane hitting shore. That part of her, which always panicked when she got too close to anyone new, started to tremble.

There was no need to panic. This was only business, right? Except as he helped her scootch her chair up to the table, it definitely didn't feel friendly.

He took the chair across the table from her, and a girl might think that would be safer, with the span of the table between them, but somehow he seemed closer. Much too close.

Don't wish, she reminded herself and bit into a zucchini slice. "If it's bad news about the renovation, you can't just spring it on me. It's best to work up to it. Want some?"

"Sure." He grabbed a coated, deep-fried slice and

crunched into it. "I have some suggestions for changes for the finished woodwork. What Rafe drew up for you is nice, but it's plain."

"It's what I can afford."

"You can afford this, too." He took another slice. His manner was casual, his overall tone was friendly, but there was something intense beneath the surface, something that hadn't been there before. "I think you'll be happier with it. It won't add any time if I get started now. I mostly do the jobs with custom woodwork."

"I'm still trying to picture that. I know, I've seen you with a tool belt, but it doesn't still compute." She said this without thinking and watched his face harden. Not in a mean way, but guarded, like she'd struck a sore spot. "Don't get me wrong. There's a lot of integrity working to perfect a craft and doing your best. It's how I justify my baking. But I look at you and think, white-collar professional."

"It's a big issue in my family right now. My mom and dad have always just assumed I'd step into place at the family business and take over the firm when Dad's ready to retire. And he's starting to think about it, so they're starting to get serious."

"Aren't they supportive of what you're doing now?"

"They're tolerating it."

"I can't imagine that." Ava dragged a zucchini slice through the dip and bit into it. "My family is everything to me. I would be nothing without them."

"You seem tight with your sisters."

"Yeah. I'd never be able to open my own bakery without my family's help. I got my business loan from my grandmother—talk about fear of failure. I don't want to let her down. And Spence helped me with my business plan and buying the property. My sisters are helping me with the finishing stuff. Katherine took me to all the flea markets and swap meets and secondhand stores in the state, I think, and we got a bunch of bistro tables and chairs that Aubrey is refinishing for me in her studio. My stepsister Danielle has promised to make the window blinds and valences. That kind of thing. And that's not including the pep talks when I need them."

"So, they've got a lot of confidence in you. It must be nice to have the people you love most wanting what will make you happy."

"It is." Ava's eyes shone with emotion and she dunked her zucchini into the dip. "It's also a lot of people to disappoint. Something I could never stand to do."

He could see that about her. Brice's throat tightened. "I can't stand how much this has upset my parents either. It's been a huge strain on our relationship."

"They want the best for you, though?"

He could see from the hopeful trust in her eyes that she didn't understand. "They do. I know they love me, but the truth is, I'm not what they hoped for in a son. I wrestled with it for a long time. I tried things their way, but I'm not cut out for spending a day in an office, investing other people's money. I like the work I do, but they see it as too blue collar."

"And that would be wrong because…?"

He swallowed his embarrassment over his parents. They were too set in their ways and opinions to change. He tried to dismiss the pain behind it, and the weight of his father's disappointments. His father who was a good, loving dad. Love and family were always complicated. "Dad thinks I'm not going to be happy unless I have a white-collar career, but I think it's the appearance thing. They care too much what other people think."

"It's hard to know other people think you're a dope or a loser. It has happened to me too many times to count. I've become sort of numb to it."

He choked down a hoot of laughter. She said it with a twinkle in her eyes. She always surprised him. "Exactly. I've become a little numb on this subject, where my parents are concerned. My mom is still holding out hope I'll come to my senses and go to law school or medical school. Or into the seminary."

"I can't picture you doing any of that. I'm sure you'd be good at any profession you chose, but you can only be yourself. Who God meant you to be." She lowered her gaze and stared hard at the table's surface between them. "At least, that's what my older sister keeps telling me."

"She's right."

He considered the woman across from him, with her blond hair windblown and going every which way. She was lovelier every time he saw her. Today her cheeks were slightly flushed from what he guessed to be a busy day. She had that breathless look about her. Her words had been rolling around in his head all day. *It's an ironclad, nonnegotiable no-man, no-dating policy.*

He couldn't give up hope completely. Business first. And when the renovation was done, then he'd see where he stood with her.

At that exact moment her cell rang. She checked

it and turned it off. "It's Aubrey. Food's served. I'm sorry, but I'm starving."

He stood to help her with her chair. "You'll stop by tomorrow when I'm there so I can show you what I have in mind?"

"I can do that."

"No more drive-by bakings?"

"Now, I can't promise that." She swished away.

She was so small and fragile, so whimsical and feminine, that a vibrant, steel-like emotion came to life in his heart, overtaking him. He watched her go with a mix of care and affection. He really liked her.

She stopped at the end of the row of tables. "Oh, I forgot to ask about the muffins. Did the men like them?"

"The monsters were the hit of the day."

She flashed him her brightest smile, the one that showed her dazzling spirit. The one that caught his heart like a hook on a line and dug deep. The hook did not leave as she walked away with her gait snapping and her golden hair swaying across her back. Even when she was out of his sight it remained, inexplicably.

Without Brice Donovan anywhere around, it was like a thousand times easier to remember her policy. Later that day, Ava jammed her Bible study materials into her tote and heaved it off the floor. The classroom in the church's auxiliary building was pleasant and serene, but then she always felt peaceful after spending an hour in fellowship, studying her Bible. She was focused and calm and everything seemed clear.

Aubrey fell in beside her and they trailed the small

crowd filing out the door. "I'm in the mood for chocolate. Want to stop by the ice creamery and pig out on sundaes?"

"Like I would ever think that was a bad idea." Really. Did Aubrey even have to ask? She staggered under the weight of her mammoth bag. She was really going to have to find the time to go through it and clean it out—not that she was skilled at stuff like that. "I need sustenance if I'm going to be able to face my day tomorrow. It's jam-packed."

"You remembered we were going to babysit for Danielle, right?" Aubrey waited a beat before rolling her eyes. Their stepsister was happily married with two great kids. "It's okay. Don't even bother. I'll babysit and you'll do it next Friday. I've got that church retreat thing. So, tomorrow's packed?"

"It's just that I got this referral from Chloe's wedding. It was Brice, really—"

"Ex-boyfriend alert," Aubrey cut in, although by the interested lift of her eyebrows she'd caught the Brice reference. "It's Mike, directly ahead, in the hall."

They were still safely stuck in the doorway of the classroom, in a small queue, but she was definitely visible. Ava could feel his smug gaze sweeping over her. She didn't have to look to know he had some poor clueless woman hanging on his arm. Two years ago, she'd been there, believing the stories he told about what a moral Christian guy he was on the surface.

Unfortunately, his supposed values were pure fabrication, and every time she spotted him she felt beyond foolish. Yep, even years later, her nose was turning glowing strawberry red again. Why couldn't she have noticed right away that he wasn't what he seemed? It was her fault-blindness. She just couldn't see the big glaring signs of trouble that other people could.

"That poor woman," Aubrey said with sympathy and kindness. Good, gentle Aubrey never made a fool of herself and never made any mistakes at all, much less mistakes of gargantuan proportion. "I'm going to add both of them to my prayers. She's bound to be heartbroken one day."

Just like I was. Ava could still feel the crack in her heart from him. "I'll pray for her, too."

She purposely didn't look ahead down the hall, so she wouldn't have to see him. Or to remember she'd really fallen hard for Mike. Discovering who he really was had been tough.

"And there's Ken." Aubrey grabbed Ava's wrist and steered her toward the far wall. "No, don't look up."

Great. Ken was probably with someone, too. He'd been the chef who, on the third date, said he'd waited long enough and tried to take liberties. She'd accidentally broken two fingers on his right hand when she'd bolted from the passenger seat of his car and slammed his hand in the door.

Really, did she look like the kind of girl who said one thing and did another?

No—it was some men. See? It went right back to them. They needed to think faithful, pious thoughts. Study their Bibles even more. She was really starting to get disillusioned about men. *All men.*

What about Brice? a little voice asked—a voice that seemed to come straight from her heart.

What about him? So, he'd been a gentleman so far,

but wasn't that the problem? How deep did the gentleman thing go? She'd been fooled too many times by how a man *seemed*. So, he was Mr. Eligible Bachelor. Did that mean he was really good at fooling others? Or was he truly a good man, soul deep?

Well, if she was interested in him, maybe that was a sign right there. Ken and Mike were excellent examples of her flaw-blindness. What if she was doing the same exact thing with Brice? If the man was interested in her, as time had proved over and over again, there had to be something wrong with him.

It was as simple as that. And if the tiny hope in her heart wished for more, that he truly was what he seemed, did she risk finding out? Face it, she didn't have Aubrey's quiet beauty or her sister Katherine's classic poise. She'd driven her own mother away.

Don't think about that. She squeezed the pain from her heart. Erased the thought from her mind. Purposefully turned her thoughts from her failures and to her business. Her shop. She had more sketching to do tonight when they got home. And breakfast treats to bake for the construction dudes.

Maybe she'd do a batch of scones. She'd lose herself in the kitchen. Baking always made everything right. Baking made her problems and failures turn from shouts into silence.

There would be no dreaming. She'd lost too many dreams to waste them on what could never truly be. Brice had given her the perfect solution. He'd said he was happy to be friends. He didn't want anything to complicate their business relationship, and she was going to hold him to it, whether her heart liked it or not.

Pleased with that plan, she led Aubrey out of the church hall and through the parking lot, beeped the SUV unlocked and headed straight to the ice creamery.

Chapter Seven

Brice climbed out of his truck and into the morning. The hiss of the sprinkler system in the city park diagonally across the street provided enough background noise to drown out the faint hum of distant traffic. It was early enough yet that only an infrequent car motored down the nearby street. Birds took flight from the tree overhead when Rex hopped onto the sun-warmed blacktop. The parking lot was empty, except for them. He'd beaten Ava here. Again.

Ava. Spotting her in the restaurant last night had given him a chance to clear the air. The only problem was, nothing felt clearer. Their agreement to keep it to business, sure, that was crystal clear. But his feelings for her became more complicated every time he was around her.

Lord, You know I'm in over my head. Please, I need some help. If it's not too much trouble, show me the way.

As if in answer, he felt a shift in the calm peace of the morning. It was as if the nearly nonexistent breeze had completely vanished, as if the world stopped spinning on its axis. As if for one nanosecond, the rotation of the earth ceased. Brice felt an odd prickling at the back of his neck. When he turned around, there she was.

Or, more accurately, there she was in her yellow SUV driving straight toward him. The morning light cut at an angle through her windshield, illumining her clearly. Those sunglasses were perched on her nose again, and the bill of the baseball cap—pink, today—framed her heart-shaped face. She whipped into the parking space closest to the front door. Right beside his truck.

Her nearness was like taking an unexpected punch to the chest. Brice rocked back on his heels from the impact. He watched her through the windshield as she chattered on her cell while cutting the engine, pulling the e-brake and gathering up her things.

Knowing there would be more bakery boxes and careens of coffee and spiced tea, he moved to help. Rex bounded ahead, whining in anticipation of being with Ava.

"I know just how you feel, buddy." He scrubbed his dog's head with his knuckles.

Her driver's side door was open, but she'd turned away, still busy gathering her things and absorbed in her phone conversation. Her dulcet, cheerful tone was as soft as the morning breeze. "Yes, Madeline, I'd be happy to bring by my catalogue. If your client wants something unique, then I'm the right baker. I specialize in one-of-a-kind designs."

She backed out of the vehicle, dragging her enormous purse with her. The bulk of it clattered over the console and snagged on the emergency brake, which stopped her progress. No one was cuter. Captivated, he could not look away as she freed her bag from the snag. Once it was free, she hooked the big bag over her shoulder, absently, and went to slam the door. With the keys inside.

Suddenly it wasn't a mystery how she kept locking herself out. He caught the edge of the door.

"Goodbye, Madeline and—" She stopped, apparently startled to find him latched onto her door. For the tiniest part of a millisecond she gazed up at him unguarded, forgetting to finish her conversation. "Uh… thanks again, Madeline, for this opportunity. I won't let you down. Bye!"

She snapped her phone shut. "Thank you, too. You keep showing up right when I need rescuing."

"It's a knack of mine." He waited for her to step out of the way before he settled behind the steering wheel and snagged the keys from the ignition. He started fiddling with the remote.

"And now what are you doing?"

"Reprogramming this for you. So it won't auto lock. There."

He was starting to look more and more like a fictitious knight in shining armor…well, more like a knight with a tool belt. It was nice to be rescued by such a good guy.

"Who was on the phone?" he asked over a few electronic beeps that came from inside the SUV.

"That was Madeline from Madeline's Catering. She provided the food for your sister's wedding reception.

She asked me to make the desserts for a baby shower she's catering. The funniest thing, though. She said you had highly recommended me."

"I might have." He angled out from behind the wheel and closed the door.

"Thank you. I met with Maxime Frost yesterday, and her daughter Carly chose one of my designs. Also because of your recommendation."

"I'm just glad it worked out. If you want to head in, I'll bring in the boxes. Take a look at the plans. They're on the worktable."

"Oh. Well, okay." Ava tried so hard not to like Brice more, but found it impossible. Fighting her feelings, she accepted Rex's good morning jump up, hugged him and promised him his own scone. Thrilled, his doggy tongue hanging, he bounded ahead of her on the way to the front door as if to say, hurry, faster!

"It's too bad I really don't like your dog," she said, not quite comfortable saying the truth, of how very much she adored Rex.

"Yeah, I don't like him either," Brice said with a wink.

She ducked her head to dig for her office keys in the mess of her bag. Truth was, she didn't want to keep looking at Brice. And see more and more good things to like about him. But her attempts were futile. There was Brice's reflection in the glass as she went to unlock the door.

My, he was such a fine man. Her heart gave a little tumble—just the tiniest fall.

It's just business. That's all. That's what it had to be.

So, why didn't that rationale feel convincing? Best

not to think about that too much. She pushed open the door. Rex sprang in, expertly dodging the sawhorses and piles of fresh wallboard, and she lingered, turning to watch Brice. It was hard not to notice the powerful agile way he hefted the boxes, shut the back of the SUV and locked up.

He was a great guy—wait, rephrase that. He was a really awesome man. Why did that make her panic?

"It's starting to take shape." His voice and his boots echoed in the big empty shop. "You can see we've got the rewiring done. The inspector's supposed to be here in an hour. Once we get that okayed, the wallboard goes up. Do you like the cathedral ceilings? We were able to punch up a few feet higher than we'd first thought."

See? Just business. Ava managed to push aside the lump of feelings all wadded up in her chest. Did her best not to notice how she felt happy when he was near.

"I love the ceilings. It's better than I hoped for." She walked around, giving Brice time to head into the kitchen with the morning's treats, and to put space between them. "The guys have done a great job."

She could see her dreams of the new shop taking shape in the shell of the old. She'd have warm honeyed woods, cheerful yellow walls and the scent of happiness in the air. It was finally happening. For real. She thought of Madeline's call—was it a sign her business would boom? Maybe.

She had a business to build, not more mistakes to make. She caught sight of Brice unboxing the scones. A tiny question whispered inside her heart: What if he wasn't a mistake?

"Ava, you've topped yourself." He had one of the sunshine face scones in hand.

"I made a double batch, so the construction dudes can take some home to their families."

"Once you get this shop open, I hope you know that you're going to be in demand."

"From your lips to God's ears," she said, trying to stay focused on the business. The business. Not on Brice's kind words.

He took a bite. "Sheer heaven. You'll be open soon. Do you have hired help all lined up?"

"Are you kidding? I've got enough extended family to hire without even putting an ad in the paper. I'm just hoping this doesn't wind up being another failure."

"It won't be." Brice could see the burden of it weighing her down. "You have an excellent quality of product, and the decorating is top-notch. It's all I heard at Chloe's reception. I think you should believe in yourself a little more. It will turn out fine."

"You're just saying that to be nice, mister."

"That's the idea. I want to be nice to you. This is business, remember? We have this business relationship, but after that, I'm hoping you'll want more."

"Oh, that's scarier than starting my own business." She swiped a lock of golden hair out of her eyes, looking adorable. "It's that fault-blind thing. You look perfect to me, but it's just because I can't see the flaws. It's like walking blind into a tornado."

"Good. No man wants you to see his flaws."

"Some people are better at hiding them than others." She followed him into the kitchen where sunlight highlighted the drawings he'd set out beside the bakery box. "Take me, my flaws are totally noticeable."

"I haven't noticed any flaws."

"Sure you haven't. What about those accusations?"

"Those were perfectly understandable considering you were confusing me with a Darrin Fullerton."

Really, he was just trying to get her to like him, and it wasn't going to work. Absolutely not. The same way she *wasn't* going to notice how wonderfully tall he was. Solid. Substantial. How he looked like a man who could shoulder any burden. Solve any problem.

Okay, she was starting to notice, but only just a little. Really.

Rex, the perfect gentleman, was sitting there with his big innocent eyes showing just how good and deserving he was of a scone. Ava turned her attention to the dog because there was no reason why she shouldn't fall in love with Rex. She grabbed one of the cheerful iced treats. "Here you go, handsome."

Rex delicately took the scone from her fingertips, gave her a totally adoring look and sucked the sweet down in one gulp.

"He seems to like your baking," Brice said with a grin. "Can you stay for a while? I can pour you a cup of coffee if you want to look over the—"

"Oh." She was already looking at the drawings, and it was her turn to be utterly adoring. She couldn't believe her eyes. Could she talk? No. The penciled images had stolen every word from her brain. Her mind was a total blank except for a single thought.

Perfect.

He'd taken the photos she'd shown him yesterday

and transformed them into her vision. Into exactly what she'd imagined. There it was. Curlicue scrollwork and rosebud-patterned moldings and carvings framing the wood and glass bakery case. "There's no way I can afford this."

"Custom woodwork is built into the estimate you signed. This would be for the same price. We've agreed to it."

"How can that be? I love this, don't get me wrong, but this can't be what was on the estimate. I know it's not."

"Rafe doesn't do woodwork, so pricing it is a mystery to him. Trust me. I can do this for the same price as he quoted you."

"Are you sure?"

"Positive. There's no hidden costs and no hidden agendas. With me, what you see is what you get."

"Businesswise, right?"

"Always."

She loved the sincerity in his words. The honesty he projected was totally irresistible. Now she *had* to like him. But just a pinch. A smidgen. But not a drop more.

"I love this." She traced the drawn image of the bakery case with her fingertips. "This is my dream."

"That was the idea." He leaned closer to study the drawing, too, and to set a coffee cup in front of her. The steely curve of his upper arm brushed against her shoulder and stayed.

The trouble was, she noticed. She liked being close to him. She felt safe and secure and peaceful, as if everything was right in the world.

"If I have your approval, then I'll get started in the wood shop today. On one condition."

"Name it."

"Send two dozen of these scones to my office along with the bill." He moved away to take another treat from the box and broke it in half. Tossed one piece to the dog, who caught it like a pro ballplayer, and kept the other for himself. "Do you deliver?"

"For you, I could make an exception."

"Excellent. It's a pleasure doing business with you, Miss McKaslin."

"Anytime, Mr. Donovan." It was a good thing she had her priorities straight in life. Because otherwise, she could completely fall for him. Talk about doom!

She pushed away from the table, away from his presence and away from the wish of what could be. She grabbed her cup of coffee. "Later, Donovan."

"Later, McKaslin."

She gave Rex a pat and sauntered out of her shop like a businesswoman totally in charge of her life and her heart.

It was a complete facade.

Rex's high yelping rose above the grind of the radial saw. Brice slipped down his protective glasses and glanced over his shoulder toward the open workshop door.

Maura, his secretary, had walked the twenty or so yards from the front office and stood staring at him, her arms crossed over her chest, looking like a middle-aged spinster despite the fact that they'd gone through public school together. "The scones you ordered are here. Talk about amazing. We're all taking a coffee break. You want to come join us?"

"Ava was here?" He hadn't expected her to be by so fast. He'd figured she would have to make another batch, but she must have made enough originally. He hadn't planned on that, he'd been busy working on her molding and now he'd missed her.

Maura shrugged. "I didn't know you wanted to see her. I'll make sure she doesn't run off next time."

She gave him that smile that women have, the knowing one that means you aren't fooling them one bit, and he was floored. Just how many people had guessed about his feelings for Ava?

"I've heard her cakes are heavenly." Maura paused in the doorway, giving that smile again. "When you order next time, remember—we all love chocolate. Don't forget, now."

"It's a business relationship." It was the truth. For now. "What makes you think it isn't?"

Maura arched one brow and stared pointedly at the pile of wood. "You always take the summer months off, but it's now June and look, you're still here. You aren't fooling me. And for your 4-1-1, she's really nice. She goes to my church and we're in the same Bible study. I could put in a good word for you."

"I can handle it, thanks."

"It's just that I know what happened with Whitney. It wasn't your fault." Maura kindly didn't say more on that topic. "I hope you know what you're doing. You haven't dated in a long time."

"Thanks, Maura, but I have a plan."

"Well, if you need a woman's opinion, you can always run it by me." She hesitated again. "Thanks for the scones. They are wonderful." And finally she was gone, shutting the door tight behind her.

A plan? That wasn't what he'd thought to call it before now. He lifted the length of wood from the bench, a smooth piece of oak that would gleam like honey when he was through with it. He had a plan, of sorts. He intended to work hard. To deliver on his promise to Ava. To show her that he could help her with this dream. Maybe—God willing—with all her dreams.

The problem was, he didn't know if he could get her to go to dinner with him. It wasn't looking promising at this moment in time.

Based on his experience with her so far, he feared that Ava McKaslin might be the Mt. Everest equivalent of dating—a nearly impossible feat to accomplish and not for the faint of heart. A smart man would choose a much smaller mountain that required less effort.

He, apparently, wasn't a smart man, but he was a dedicated one and he recognized her value. He set his goggles in place, grabbed another length of oak from the lumber pile. He had long hours of detailing to do and he intended to bring this in on time. He'd work on this dream first.

Then he'd try to tackle the rest of them.

Chapter Eight

In the serenity of her oldest sister's snazzy kitchen, Ava piped careful scrollwork across the final dozen cookies in the shape of a baby's shoe. Madeline, the caterer, had subcontracted with her for six dozen specialty cookies for a baby shower and they were going perfectly. It was a good feeling, a relieved feeling. The first she'd had in two days. That's how long she'd gone without seeing Brice.

You'd think that would be enough time to get her feelings under control, right? But no, she thought as she piped the final curlicue on the last cookie and stretched her aching back. She had feelings for him, and she liked him. But that didn't mean she had to actually do anything about it, right?

She'd been avoiding seeing him. Oh, she'd continued to deliver baked goods for the construction dudes, but she arrived way early, well before Brice was supposed to show, and just left the box in the kitchen. *Drive-by baking,* as he'd called it.

She hit the off button on her digital music player and

plucked the buds from her ears just in time. Katherine was tapping down the hall, coming her way. Since she was in big, deep favor-debt to her sister, Ava snatched a ceramic mug from the cabinet and poured a brisk cup of tea she'd had ready, steeping. The instant Katherine stepped foot in the kitchen, she had the cup on the breakfast bar and was heating a monster muffin in the microwave.

"Wow, it smells amazing in here." Dressed in a modest summer dress and sensible flat sandals, Katherine slid onto a breakfast bar stool. The classy act that she was, she didn't even comment on the shambles of her ordinarily supertidy kitchen. "These cookies are too beautiful to eat. Your customer will be delighted, I'm sure."

Talk about a great sister. Ava rescued the muffin from the microwave and set it next to the tea. "Ta da! I promise I'll have this place spic-and-span by the time you get home today."

"I'm not worried about it in the slightest."

Katherine had so much faith in her, sometimes it was hard to get past the fear of letting her down. Ava went back to her cookies, boxing the ones that were ready, leaving the others to dry a few more minutes. The icing was still a tad tacky. Out of the corner of her eye she watched her sister bow her head and whisper a blessing over the meal. Her mammoth engagement diamond glinted in the overhead lights.

Katherine hadn't had the easiest time with things, but she'd made a success of her life. She'd become such a graceful woman. It was no wonder at all why she'd found a good man to fall love with her and promise her the real thing—true love—for a lifetime to come.

Katherine was the kind of lady true love happened to. Ava laid a sheet of waxed paper across the first layer of cookies in the box, not at all sure that true love would ever happen to her personally. She loved the dream, but all she had to do was to think of the long string of romantic disasters lying behind her like a desolate wasteland, and she knew, soul deep, it wasn't possible for her.

Or was it? Brice liked her. He had from the very start. Like he was either desperate, or maybe—*maybe*—this could be the start of something extraordinary. Something rare. Because she had to admit, what she felt for him was simply unusual. She had gotten to know him more, and he was a great guy—not just on the outside. He had a big heart, was an honorable character. He could see her dreams.

But was that enough to risk amending her no-dating policy? *That* was the million-dollar question.

"I love these." Katherine studied the muffin she'd bitten into. "Are you going to put these in your bakery? You'll have people beating down the door for them."

"From your lips to God's ears. Wouldn't that be something, if I actually succeeded at this? I've got a bunch of leftover muffins. Do you want to take some to the store? Maybe the early morning customers would like a muffin break."

"That'd be perfect. We have a reader's group this morning."

"Oh, and I've got the last of the cake sketches done. Do you want to see them now?"

"Are you kidding? Show me what you've got, sweetie."

Ava hauled out her mammoth sketch pad and removed the soft, pastel-colored drawings from the front. "I know you're going with a roses theme. Pinks and ivory. So I went with that."

She slid the drawings one by one onto the breakfast bar, carefully watching her sister's face for signs of dismay and abhorrence, but there was only a happy gasp of delight.

"Ava, these are so wonderful! I'm never going to be able to choose between them."

Whew. What a relief. The last thing she ever wanted to do was to disappoint her sister. Her family was all she had, and she loved them so much. "If you can't choose, maybe I should do a few more sketches. The right design should just jump out at you. It's something your heart decides."

"No, sweetie, you misunderstand. I feel that way about each one these. I love this rose garden theme. Can you really do this with frosting?"

"It's easy."

"I'm going to show these to Jack and see what he has to say. But…oh, the golden climbing roses on this ivory cake, with the leaves, that's stunning, too."

"I can amend any of this, too. That's not carved in stone, you know. A little erasing and redrawing and *ta da*, the wedding cake of your dreams."

Katherine gathered up the sketches with care. "Are you okay? You seem a little down this morning."

"Down? No, not me. I'm always in a good mood." As long as she didn't think about Brice, that is. She moved away—quick—before Katherine figured it out, and started assembling a second bakery box. "I've got a lot on my mind. The renovation is stressful."

"I've heard nothing but renovation horror stories. What problems are you having?"

Katherine was watching her carefully over the rim of her teacup, so Ava did her best to steer the topic away from her confused, tangled up heart. "None. Not a single problem. The construction workers are organized. They've got their schedule, they do their work on time, they've already got the inspectors lined up, so there's hardly any downtime. I haven't been by yet, but they are supposed to have all the wallboard up and taped. Can you believe it? My shop is going to have brand-new pretty walls and wiring that's up to code."

"I'm thrilled for you."

"I should be able to open on time. Danielle is going to help me set up my books. I've been throwing all my receipts into a shoe box in my closet. That's not going to work for a long-term bookkeeping solution, or so she tells me."

"No, sorry." Katherine smiled in that gentle, caring way of hers. "Now, tell me the truth. Something's bothering you. Is it the stress of getting a start-up business off the ground? You know you have us to help."

Ava nodded, slipping the last of the cookies into the box and snapping shut the lid. She deftly avoided mentioning her romantic confusion. "Tell Spence I might be a little late for my shift this afternoon. I have an ad to put into the church bulletin. The deadline's today. Oh, and I'm meeting Danielle for a bookkeeping session."

"Sure." She kept sipping her tea, assessing over the rim.

Ava knew what was coming. "Well, I've got a busy morning. See you—"

"Wait a minute. Don't run off just yet. You haven't told me what's wrong." Katherine was a sharp tack. "That leaves only one possibility left. You like Brice Donovan, don't you?"

"*Like?* That's a pretty strong word. Especially for a woman who has a brilliant no-dating policy." The smartest thing she'd ever done, hands down. Because without it, she'd be letting Brice charm her. Letting him close. Letting him into her heart. "I know you just want me to be happy, but I'm nothing but a country love song gone wrong."

"There's not one thing wrong with you. Maybe with some of the men you've spent time with, but you made the right decision in the end. Besides, you can't really get to know a man—any man, good or not so good—unless you spend time with him and get to know what he's really like."

That was the problem with Katherine. She always saw the good side. She believed that good things happened to good people, but she just didn't see the truth. Good men happened to *other* women, not her.

"Says the happily engaged woman. Get back to me on those sketches, right?" She grabbed the cookie box and her keys. If she left fast enough, Katherine couldn't say—

"Not every man is going to leave you, Ava. Not every man is going to let you down."

Too late. Ava stopped dead in her tracks, with her hand on the garage door. "I'm not going to give any man a chance to. I'll see you later, alligator."

Katherine said nothing, nothing at all, not that Ava gave her much of a chance to. She'd practically leaped into the garage and closed the inner door after her. Trying to shove out the words echoing in her head. *Not every man is going to leave you, Ava. Not every man is going to let you down.*

And Brice's words, *With me, what you see is what you get.*

Businesswise, right? she'd asked.

Always.

Would believing in him be the right thing? Heart pounding, she caught her breath in the echoing garage, feeling the pieces of her past rain down on her like soot and ash, willing away the sadness. It came anyway. Sharp and bone deep and in her mother's voice.

Why, after all these years, did she still feel like that seven-year-old girl, standing in their old backyard beneath the snap of the clothes drying on the line, watching the blur of their 1960s Ford disappear down the alley? Why did she still feel the panic of being to blame? Why did it feel as if every failure just added to that pain?

She'd prayed for as long as she could remember with every fiber of her being for a good man to come into her life. But unlike all her other prayers, that one had remained unanswered. Over the years, her wishes had faded in luster and possibility until she couldn't see them anymore.

And she was better off that way, really. Her no-man policy had been working perfectly fine. She'd already taken the leap to start a business. Already bought a shop and had placed advertisements, and already word-of-mouth recommendations were starting to come in. Okay, people weren't exactly knocking down her door, but it was a start, right?

She'd finally learned to stop spending her life with her head in the clouds and now what?

Brice.

She'd finally stopped looking for the one man whose heart was stalwart enough to love her through all time and accepted that he didn't exist. At least, not for her. And then what?

Brice. He came into her life like the impossible dream she'd given up on. But was he so impossible?

"Ava? Hel-*lo?* Earth to Ava." Aubrey slowed the SUV to a crawl. "You've been a space cadet all day."

"I know. Sorry." Ava blinked, focusing. She'd been trying to think of everything but Brice all day, and what was she doing? Looking out the window to see if his pickup was in her shop's parking lot. Pathetic, she thought, undoing her seat belt. It looked as if the coast was clear. "Just park here at the curb."

"Are you kidding? I'm coming, too. I've been dying to see this all week." Aubrey cut the engine and pulled the e-brake. She never forgot to remove the keys. "Just think, this time next week it will be done. Can you believe it?"

"No. Yes. I don't have to be too terrified of this venture failing until I open the doors, officially, for business." It wasn't the business she was terrified of, at the moment, but of not seeing Brice. Of turning down his more-than-friends offer to date, after the shop was done.

"You won't fail," Aubrey said with confidence. "You don't give yourself enough credit."

What did she say to that? Ava stumbled out into the stifling heat. The temperature was in the high nineties, and heat radiated off the pavement. She had to stop and dig through her purse to find her keys, no small feat. It gave her plenty of time to think over Aubrey's words.

She gave herself plenty of credit. But what did you do when you succeeded at attracting doom? Most of the time, she didn't let it bother her, but now....

Now, it was Brice. She could really fall for him, harder than any man she'd ever known. And that meant her heart could really be broken, right?

"Let me." Aubrey grabbed Ava's bag, plunged her hand in and pulled out the wallet so thick with debit and credit card receipts that it wouldn't snap shut. "There they are—at the bottom."

"I keep meaning to clean this bag out."

"I know." Aubrey dumped the wallet, papers and all, back into the bag and unlocked the door. She looked around the inside of the shop. "Wow, this looks *great*."

"Wow. It does." Ava followed her sister inside. The cooled air washed over her as she stared in awe at the tall cathedral ceilings and real walls. All the mess had been cleaned up. The cement slab was perfectly swept. The taped and mudded wallboard wasn't pretty, but it took no imagination at all to add paint and trim and flooring to see the airy, sunny result.

Footsteps boomed in the kitchen behind them. Heavy, booted steps. Ava heard her sister yelp, felt Aubrey's instant fear, but she *knew* the sound and rhythm of that gait. The instant she'd stepped foot into the building, she should have recognized his presence.

"Your dream is taking shape." Brice Donovan filled the threshold between the kitchen and the main room looking like her dream come true in a simple black T-shirt, black jeans and boots. He looked stalwart and easygoing, like a guy a girl could always depend on.

Her heart wished for him a tiny bit more. It was a sweet twist of pain that moved through her. She stepped toward him and her spirit brightened. "Your construction guys have done a wonderful job. It's just right."

"The finish work starts Monday. We'll be done before you know it."

She gulped, unable to speak. There was only the magnetic draw of his gaze. Of his dimpled grin. Of his presence that drew her like an unsuspecting galaxy toward a black hole. That couldn't be a good thing, could it?

"This must be your sister." Brice broke his gaze, releasing her, to hold out his hand to her sister. "It's good to meet you."

"Ava hasn't said a word about me, has she?" Aubrey's hand looked engulfed by Brice's larger one.

Oh, no. Ava held her breath, sensing what would come next. Knowing that, like it or not, Aubrey would *know.* It was that twin thing. Their brain cells would fire and she would guess the horrible secret Ava was keeping from everyone, including herself.

Yep, there it was. In the change in Aubrey's jawline, her stance, her voice. Aubrey withdrew her hand, but there was an "aha" glint in her eyes. "I know why she hasn't said anything about you. In fact, she's refused to do a whole lot of talking about this very important renovation."

"It's all the stress," Ava added. The stress of the construction, the financing, getting a new business started, of being afraid she was falling in deep like with a man who was entirely wrong for her.

"I understand completely." The way Brice said it, it was like he had unauthorized access to that twin brain cell, and that was impossible. "Ava and I currently have a business-only policy."

"Ah, so that explains it," Aubrey said as she backed toward the door. "I'm probably just in the way here. Brice, you probably have a lot of construction things to go over with Ava."

"As a matter of fact, I do have a few things to show her."

"Oh, *sure* you do." Ava couldn't believe it. That didn't sound very businesslike. She narrowed her eyes at him. "Why are you here anyway?"

"I spent all day in the wood shop, and I wanted to stop by and see the progress for myself. Make sure nothing had been overlooked before the painters show up at seven Monday morning. I want this done right for you."

When he smiled, she couldn't stop the rise of her spirit, the tug of longing in her heart. She'd come by because she'd wanted to see the progress of her dream, and Aubrey had wanted to see it, too. Now Aubrey was at the door, tugging it open. What kind of world was this when your twin abandoned you? Panic rattled through her. She'd feel better if Aubrey would stay—

"Aubrey, why don't you stay with us?" Brice asked. "Unless you two have other plans?"

"Not at all," Aubrey said so fast. "None that can't be changed. We were just going to barbecue supper."

"*What?* Wait one minute." Ava had a bad feeling about this. It was four-thirty on a Saturday afternoon. Not exactly business hours. "Brice and I have a strict policy to adhere to."

"True. But we agreed to excuse dating and romance from our business policy, right? That doesn't mean we can't be friends."

"Friends." Friendship did not begin to describe this swirl of confusing emotions she had for him. Emotions she did not want to analyze, thank you very much. What she wanted to do was to stay in denial about them. Denial was an excellent coping method.

"Sure, my business partner has been my best friend since kindergarten. Friendship and business don't have to be mutually exclusive. In fact, it can often be beneficial. If you two don't mind, come out to my place. I fix a mean steak. I was going to barbecue dinner tonight anyway, I'll just throw a few more steaks and shrimp on the barbie—"

"Shrimp?" Aubrey perked up.

Now there was no way to get out of this. Ava knew she *should* be sensible, like her sister Katherine. Stoic and self-disciplined like big brother, Spence. Be calm and think things through like her twin. Her problems always came from leaping before she looked, and right now looking at his dark tousle of hair, the curve of his grin and the steady hope in his eyes made her want to leap into agreement.

"Lots of shrimp," Brice promised. "I've got a shop behind my garage, so I work at home a lot when I'm doing custom stuff like this. Hey, while you two are there, I'll show you a few new ideas I have. Something for the display case."

"Now I don't believe there's an allowance for even more custom stuff in the contract I signed."

"True. This is just because. This is what I want to do for you as a friend. We start as friends. See where it goes from there."

Didn't that sound harmless? It was like a test-drive of a new car. You got to see if you liked it first before you bought it. It was the same situation here. If she didn't like him for a friend, she wouldn't date him and marry him, right?

Ava felt her heart fall even more. There it was, that terrible urge to leap. To just tell him yes. Friends first, and then let's see where this goes. What could go wrong with that?

Chapter Nine

"Did you know he lived up here?" Aubrey asked from behind the wheel as she negotiated the curving road that led into the foothills where the posh people lived.

"Nope. I had no clue."

Ava couldn't seem *not* to look at Brice. There he was right in front of them in his snazzy red sports car.

Aubrey followed Brice into an exclusive gated community. "If you're falling for this guy, you have to stop this destructive thing you do."

"I tried my best at all my other relationships. It's my fault-blindness. Maybe it's a good thing you're here. I need your help. You can watch for his faults that I can't see."

"You *definitely* need help." Aubrey rolled her eyes and turned her full attention back to the road. "Look at this place. This is really wow. How rich is this guy?"

"He's a Donovan. How rich are they?"

"Well, his grandfather knew Grandpop. They played golf together."

Grandpop had been pretty rich. "It still hurts to think about him, doesn't it?"

"Yeah." Aubrey paused a moment, the sadness settling between them. He'd been gone two years now and it was a terrible hole in the family. It was why Gran had moved permanently to their winter home in Scottsdale. She'd found it so painful to be alone in the house he'd built for her when they were a young married couple, that she simply stayed down south where there were fewer memories to haunt her.

The quiet stayed between them as they followed Brice through a gate and along a grand driveway to a private house tucked into the hill, surrounded by lush trees and lawn. Views of the Bridger Mountains backed up behind him, and views of the Rockies rimmed the entire western exposure.

Brice parked in the third bay of a three-car garage, and Ava was too busy looking around to realize Aubrey had parked the SUV and was already climbing out of the vehicle. Okay, pay attention. She joined her sister outside the wood and stone house that looked like something out of a magazine.

"That's nicer than Gran's house," Aubrey said.

True. Which only pointed out the plain truth. Brice was so wrong for her. He was going to look for the wife to fit into this house. Face it. It was such a good thing they had this friends-only policy.

He closed the car door and pocketed his keys. "C'mon in this way. I never use the front door."

"Not even when you entertain?" Aubrey asked.

"I never entertain. Having my folks over is about as elaborate as I get." There was that grin again, the inviting warmth, the good-guy charm that was so totally arresting.

He held open the door for them at the back of the garage. Ava saw a wide but short hallway with a laundry room to her right elbow and what had to be a huge pantry to her left. Ahead of her was an enormous kitchen with a family room off to the side, not that she noticed that. She was too busy salivating over the kitchen.

Gleaming, light maple cabinets and a gray granite countertop stretched for miles. She spotted a gas range, Sub-Zero refrigerator and a double oven. There were plenty of windows, a bay in a huge eating nook and then a row of them looking out to the green backyard. "This is better than Katherine's kitchen."

Brice went straight to the fridge. "Is that where you've been doing your baking?"

"Yeah. It's working out okay, but sometimes I know I'm in her way." Ava ran her hand over the expensive granite. "This is a nice work space you've got here."

"It's wasted on me. I don't cook much. What do you want to drink? I've got soda, iced tea and lemonade. Oh, and milk." He opened the door wide so she could see what was on the shelves.

Something pink caught her eye. "Wait one minute. You have strawberry milk?"

"Chocolate, too."

"I never would have pegged you for a guy who would drink pink milk."

"Hey, I like strawberries. Nothing wrong with that."

"No, it's just—" Did she tell him it was one of her very favorite things? "I'll take a glass of pink milk. Aubrey will, too."

"Do you always speak for her?"

"I'm just trying to be efficient. Where are your glasses?"

"Sit down. Both of you. You're guests, let me do the fetching." His words were deceptively light but when his gaze raked over her, tenderness charged the air between them.

Hmm. That didn't feel like friendship. It felt like "more than friendship" in the nicest way she'd ever experienced. She took a shaky breath. Whatever she did, she had to remember not to start reading things into his actions. *Friends only,* he'd said. But she knew he wanted more.

"Wow," Aubrey said somewhere behind her, and Ava turned.

"Look at that pool. It's bigger than Gran's."

Ava went weak in the knees. "There's my favorite guy."

Rex was lounging in the cooling spray of the pool fountain. He looked up with a start, gave a goofy grin and heaved himself up on all fours. Dripping wet he took off for a run and disappeared from sight around a huge sixteen-foot awning that shaded a patio set, chaise lounges and a built-in brick grill.

"Rex!" Brice called out a second before a big golden streak charged into the kitchen.

The sound of heavy dog breathing drew Ava's attention to the archway where the retriever streaked toward her. She caught a faint glimpse of a sleek dining room and a comfortable living room in the background before the oaf lunged toward her, both front feet wrapping around her shoulders. His tongue roughened her face and she started to laugh. The dripping heap of retriever stopped licking to give her a goofy grin and then started over again.

"Stop! Stop!" Ava was laughing, but it was kind of hard not to like such a good-hearted dog.

Out of the corner of her eye she saw Brice round the long span of counter, coming to her rescue, but it was too late. Rex dropped to the floor in front of her and gave a huge shake. Water droplets rained everywhere.

If she wasn't soaked enough down the front from his hug, she was now. The retriever dropped to his haunches looking from Brice's disapproving face to hers. Rex's eyebrows shot up, the goofy grin dropped from his cute face and the happiness faded from his chocolate-sweet eyes. His whine said, "Oh, no. I messed up again."

Ava's heart fell and she followed him to the floor where she wrapped her arms around Rex's wet neck. "I don't mind," she told him. "I know you didn't *mean* for disaster to happen."

"Speak for yourself," Aubrey commented on a laugh. "I was standing downwind and now I'm wet, too."

"But he was just excited." Ava kept one arm around the canine's neck. "I'm in love with this guy."

Rex gave a whine low in his throat and dropped his huge head on her shoulder.

"The feeling appears to be mutual." Brice. There he was, all six feet of solid male kneeling down, meeting her gaze with his. "Rex knows better than this. He just can't help himself sometimes."

"I think he's perfect."

"Another mutual sentiment."

Perfect, Brice thought, that's what Ava was. Dripping wet, her honey gold bangs tousled from wet dog kisses, sprayed with droplets, she'd never been more beautiful.

"I've always wanted a dog just like this, but Dad's allergic to dogs." She glowed with happiness as she hugged Rex, who looked like he was in heaven. "And then we've been in apartments and too busy for a pet. But one day, I want a handsome guy just like you."

Rex's eyes melted with adoration and gave Ava another swipe across the face.

"You are the best dog." She laughed, all spirit, all brightness and big loving heart.

Brice was enchanted. Tenderness blazed so strongly, it transformed him completely. His heart fell—a measureless, infinite tumble from which there was no return.

They were beneath the shady awning, seated at the poolside table with an impressive view of the sparkling azure water. Ava looked around, ignoring the full plate of food in front of her. The forest-like backyard and the rise of the Bridger Mountains spearing up to the sky were spectacular. She had to give Brice's home full marks.

But his cooking, wow. That deserved full marks plus. The juicy, flavorful steak was grilled to perfection. Talk about a total shocker. Who would have guessed that when Brice said he cooked a mean steak, he meant it?

He sat across the snazzy teak table, the breezes lazily ruffling his dark hair. He cut a strip off the fourth steak he'd barbecued—for Rex—and tossed it to him. Rex caught it neatly, gulped, swallowed and sat back down on his haunches.

The gentle waterfall of the fountain and the leaves rustling through the trees only added to the pleasantness of the evening.

Earlier, after readying the steaks in their marinade, Brice had brought their glasses of strawberry milk to the poolside and relaxed in the shade. Since their clothes were wet anyway, she and Aubrey did cannonballs into the pool, trying to see who could leave the biggest splash marks. Ava had won, but it had been an intensely close—and fun—competition.

Now, drying in the hundred-degree shade, she was just still damp enough from the pool to be comfortable temperature wise. But emotionally? Not so much. Brice dominated her field of vision. He was impossible to ignore.

"I read in the paper a while back that you were engaged," Aubrey said abruptly as she poked the tines of her fork into a cube of red herbed potatoes heaped on her plate. "Didn't the wedding get cancelled?"

What? Ava could not believe her ears. The fork tumbled out of her hand and fell into the three-bean salad. Hello? Aubrey did *not* just say that, did she? How could she stick her nose where it didn't belong?

Brice winced as if he'd taken a painful blow. "That's true. I was engaged to Whitney Phelps."

"Of the Butte Phelps," Aubrey nodded, as if coaxing Brice along.

Ava sank into the comfy cushions of her chair and

felt as if a hundred-pound weight had settled onto her chest. Sympathy filled her.

Brice put down his steak knife and took a long pull of strawberry milk. "It was one of those things. I'd just turned twenty-five. I had this plan. I had my business started and it was going well, and I was ready to get married. I figured we'd date for two years, get engaged for a year, be married for a couple more and then have kids."

"It sounds like a good plan to me," Aubrey said in the gentle quiet way of hers that made anybody want to tell her anything. "What happened?"

Ava knew. She could see it play across his face. Feel the resonance of it in his heart. He'd really loved this woman. The right way—heart deep and honestly. She wasn't surprised when he spoke.

"The moment I saw Whitney, I thought she was classy. Poised. Polished. Just what I was looking for." His tone wasn't bitter. There was no anger in his words. Nor was there any pining. Just the pain of regret. "I must have been what she was looking for, too."

"I imagine so," Aubrey answered.

Poor Whitney, Ava thought. She must have felt something like this. Overwhelmed by his million-dollar grin and honesty. Helplessly sucked in by the pull of those deep dark eyes. Enamored by his decency and strength and manliness. Lost in too many wishes to find her way out.

Brice stared down at his plate for a moment, as if gathering his thoughts. A muscle tightened in his square granite jaw. "We came from the same backgrounds. We seemed compatible. I cared for her, and she fit into my plan. Or, maybe I made her. I prayed for our relationship to work out. For it to progress. Sometimes I wonder if I imposed way too much too early when we were dating, instead of just trusting God to work things out for the best."

Oh, I so know what you mean. Ava felt the heavy pain radiate out from the center of her chest, into her throat, into her voice. "You have to be very careful what you pray for."

"Exactly." His gaze met hers, and she felt the connection, an emotional zing that opened her heart right up.

"I prayed," he said, "and while my prayers were answered in a way, I'll never know how much I messed up God's plan for me. Maybe He had someone better for me, a better match, and a better chance for happiness for both me and Whitney separately. I don't know."

I understand completely, Ava thought.

"I only know He answered my prayers, but I asked in the wrong way. Whitney and I would never have made each other happy in the end. It was hard, admitting that, because I cared for her deeply. I was a disappointment to her. She slowly became disappointed in me. These days when I pray, I ask for the Lord to show me the way He wants me to go."

You're not falling in total serious like with him, she commanded herself. She knew better than that. So, he was perfect in many ways. She could feel the weight of his pain and the honesty of his experience. Her heart tumbled a little more.

"It was a mess." He shrugged one big shoulder, looking vulnerable even for such a big, brawny guy. "My mom hasn't forgiven me completely for calling off the wedding. She was very attached to Whitney."

"Your mom still hasn't forgiven you?"

Brice studied Ava's dismay. "She'd come to love Whitney like a daughter and it was a severe loss for her. She loves me, but I'm different from my parents in a lot of ways. They just don't get me."

"You're talking about your construction company?"

"Yep. Like the dog. He's not a purebred." He cut another piece of steak for Rex. "Not that it's good or bad, I just was looking for a best buddy, and went to the pound looking for a puppy. Rex and me, we connected."

When his gaze met hers, Brice couldn't tell if she knew that's how he felt about her. There'd been something special about her right from the beginning, something unique and amazing and rare that made him look and keep looking.

And it kept him riveted now. She made him take this risky step toward another relationship. It was hard opening himself up. But he took the risk. "Ava, it's your turn to tell the real story behind your no-man policy."

"What? Oh, you so don't want to hear about that." Ava averted her eyes, dismissing his question. Then, as she cut a small bite off her steak, she appeared to reconsider. "Maybe it is a good idea. Then you can see what I mean and you'll understand how important being just friends is to me."

"Tell me."

"Where to start?" She looked to Aubrey for help.

Aubrey took a sip of strawberry milk. "The high-school boyfriend. It's classic Ava."

"True." Ava set down her fork, looking even more adorable with the way her hair was drying in a fly-away tangle. "Okay, here's the scoop. Lloyd was in my earth sciences class. Now, I'm totally not a science whiz but I had to take some kind of science credit, and it was like the easiest science class in our high school. So there I was, trying to figure out some weird earth crust layer experiment, I don't know, I never did figure it out. Lloyd was cute, he saw me struggling and came over to help me. I need a lot of help."

"I'm beginning to see that." Big-time. She clearly could take care of herself, but it didn't hurt to have, say, someone like him to look out for her. Help her find her keys, watch over her, make her happy. He was interested in that job. "Poor Lloyd. I bet he fell for you."

"Poor Lloyd," Aubrey agreed with a nod.

Just what he'd thought. Brice could picture it. The teenage boy probably had such an incredible crush on Ava to begin with, he'd been all vulnerable heart. "What did poor Lloyd do that made you dump him?"

"Oh, it wasn't me," Ava insisted. "I liked him. I mean, he was cute."

"Cute," Aubrey agreed, a mirror of Ava. "But clueless."

"He was like a big dopey puppy, sorry, Rex." Ava flashed him a smile and the big adoring dog tilted his head to one side, quirked his brows and gave a sappy grin. Totally besotted.

Yeah, Brice knew just how he felt.

"A girl wants a boyfriend with a clue. Aubrey, what was the first really nutso thing Lloyd did?"

"The utility pole."

"That's right, our first date. We were on our way for hamburgers at the drive-in, and he drove smack into a big light pole going twenty-five miles an hour. Not looking where he was going." Ava lifted both hands in a helpless gesture. "He wouldn't stop looking at me while he was driving. I kept telling him to keep his eyes on the road. I mean, even I know better than that. But his gaze just kept coming back to me and I said to him, 'Lloyd, turn. There's a utility pole.' But he just said, 'yeah, uh-huh' and didn't listen and didn't look. I was too smitten to notice that he didn't have a lick of common sense."

"He was nice, though. Unlike a few of your boy-friends." Aubrey began cutting her steak.

It was interesting, sitting with a view of both sisters. They were identical but the more he got to know Ava, the more different the two of them looked. Similar, but different. Aubrey was more composed and sensible, clearly the more responsible of the two, always there to watch over Ava. The way she studied him, as if he'd met with her approval, made him think she wouldn't mind handing over the caretaking of Ava to him. Good to know. It was nice feeling to have her sister's positive opinion.

"I didn't date for a while," Ava continued. "Until I was out of high school."

"That's because I had my accident," Aubrey added, setting down her steak knife. "I jump horses, and one day in the middle of a competition, my mare went down. On top of me. She broke her leg and I cracked my hip and back. It took us both a long time to recover. Ava was there helping me faithfully without complaint."

"It was my privilege to be there with you," Ava said.

There was no mistaking the affection between the sisters as their gazes met.

"Then there was Brett," Aubrey began.

Ava pealed with laughter. "Oh, Brett. He was the worst. He was like a stalker. But did I figure that out right away? No. We'd dated two years and he'd proposed. That's when he went really strange."

"Plus, he was mean to you."

"Yeah, but I was going to cooking school and working full-time at the bookstore. That was before Dad and Dorrie retired to Arizona, so I had to help out at home, I never had a spare minute to just sit down and think. Or I *might* have noticed it. It started out subtle at first."

"He was sarcastic right up front." Aubrey corrected. "Then it snowballed from there, especially after the proposal."

"Exactly." Ava rolled her eyes, adorable and sweet and as wholesome as the sunshine glittering on the spray of the fountain, a bright sparkle that he would never tire of watching.

Show me the way, Lord. He felt the conviction deep in his soul. *Do I have a chance here?*

"Well, he would get sharp or distracted or gruff, but he'd be tired. He was going to school full-time, too. But it kept getting worse and there's no excuse for that. So I gave him his ring back, and then he started turning up wherever I went. Apparently, he thought I had another boyfriend on the side. Like I'd want another one.

So it sounds like I've had boyfriend after disastrous boyfriend, but it hasn't been that many."

"Just that disastrous, but serious. Lloyd had proposed too," Aubrey commented. "This is why I don't date. Ava's experiences have scared me."

He watched the way the sisters laughed together, seeming amused and not traumatized by their experiences. "So you both have a no-man, no-dating policy?"

"Well, mine is more habit," Aubrey said.

"Mine is a philosophy. I date guys that *seem* great."

"You have a talent for it—" Aubrey started.

"—but then when I really get to know them, it's not the truth," Ava finished. "They're marginally moral at best. Or so-so, or have secret habits like gambling. What's a girl to do? The Mr. Yucks look nice on the outside. It isn't until you get to know them that you see them for who they are, and see the things they are trying to keep hidden. It's that fault-blindness, not a good trait to have in the dating world."

Ava shrugged, and there it was, the hint of sadness at the corners of her eyes, dimming the wattage of her smile. There was a lot of pain there. More than she was going to talk about.

"I'm not like that," he said. "I don't run off, I don't leave, and I don't have destructive habits. Just so you know. I'm respectful toward women, I'm not mean and I try as hard as I can to be one of the good guys."

Ava sighed. Yeah, she was noticing that about him, and his words made her soul ache with longing. He could capture her heart, if she let him.

And wasn't that the problem? Brice Donovan could be her downfall. The one thing she could never do was amend her policy, because if she dated him and fell in love with him, he could hurt her most of all.

He was like a dream man and too good to be true.

A few hours later, the sun was sinking into the amethyst peaks of the Rockies as Ava guided the SUV out of Brice's winding subdivision. Talk about gorgeous homes. She tried to focus her thoughts on the road, on how Rex had hopped into the driver's seat of the SUV when they went to leave, wanting to go with her.

She tried *not* to think of the man who'd grabbed his stubborn dog by the collar, kindly helping him down. He was a dream man. So where did that leave her? In more trouble than she'd been when she'd agreed to dinner. Now what? How was she going to resist him now?

"He's a great cook." Aubrey yawned. "I haven't had that good a dinner since Gran was up from Arizona."

One more thing to add to the growing list of the great things about Brice Donovan. Ava negotiated a corner, slowed to a stop and checked for traffic on the main road. "I know where you're going with this."

"He likes you, you like him. Why won't you go out with him? I wouldn't be surprised if he's asked you out and you turned him down."

"I never said I liked him."

"You don't have to. Do you know what your problem is?"

Ava stared extra hard at the road. "I don't need you to tell me."

"Yes, you do. That's why God assigned me to you. I'm telling you this for your own good."

"Please don't." Ava pulled to a stop at another stop

sign, staring in frustration at the city laid out like glitter in the twilight valley. "I know you mean well, but I've got things under control."

"You never have *anything* under control. You like Brice so much, you're afraid of it."

"Not that I'll admit."

"Ha! See? You're in the denial stage. Remember? Katherine was there after she met Jack, and she wouldn't admit it either, but she was."

"Denial is a very effective coping method. Except for the fact that I'm totally *not* in denial. I have a policy, remember? I'm dedicating my life to making the world a sweeter place. I'm on a mission. I will not be distracted by anything."

Even she could hear how those words were hollow— they were no longer the whole truth. No matter how hard she willed them to be, they fell short of what she now knew to be honest.

How had that happened? It was like sand shifting beneath the rock of her foundation and now she had to readjust everything.

Aubrey was only being caring, kind and gentle in that way of hers; and she was always right. Ava knew it, but she wasn't ready to admit this to herself. Because as long as she was in denial, then she wouldn't have to make a decision. She wouldn't have to acknowledge that caring about Brice was no longer her choice. Her heart was just doing it.

"Ava, do you know how great this guy is? He's wonderful. He really cares about you. He invited me to come along tonight, and none of the other guys you've dated ever welcomed me and included me the way

Brice has. The way he looks at you and the way he talks to you, it says one thing. He likes you. He didn't care that you drained half his pool of water with all your cannonballs."

"Hey, you helped with that."

"Yes, but I don't make as big of a splash. I lack your finesse and skill."

"True."

They smiled together.

"And what about the beautiful woodwork he's doing for you? Ava, he's working over the weekend. I don't think he has to work overtime to keep his personal budget in the black."

"Probably not." Did she tell Aubrey that Brice had wanted to give her this dream? And that was really starting to affect her?

"Ava, he had worked up two different scrollwork patterns for you to choose from. That's a big deal."

"Not if I don't think about it."

They had reached the outskirts of town, and the traffic was light. She concentrated on driving, which was a lot easier than concentrating on how Brice had brought her two two-foot lengths of wood, carefully detailed, from his home workshop. One had rosebuds and leaves, and the other had cabbage roses. He'd made no big deal about it, but she knew it was more. That was scaring her, too.

Aubrey hit her second wind when they turned into their apartment complex. "Okay, I have one more thing to say, and then I'm done. You've finally found a good guy. A man of substance who sees how special you are. He's not like the others."

"You mean, after I get to know him I won't see that he's not right for me, before my heart is broken?"

"At least you see the pattern."

"It isn't just me. We've all had such a hard time getting attached, I mean, Katherine's in her thirties and she's finally getting married. Spence? Well, look at him, he drives every nice woman away before she can say 'hi.' Do you think it's because Mom left us like that? We already know love ends."

"*Some* love ends. Mom wasn't happy. Don't you remember?"

Remember? Painfully. *You make a mess of everything. You ruin everything. I can't take it anymore.* Her mother's last words to her. Haunting her after all these years.

Ava maneuvered into their reserved covered spot and cut the engine. She even remembered to take the keys out of the ignition.

Aubrey didn't move to unbuckle her seat belt. "Not all love ends. Look at Dad. He stayed. He never left. He loved us enough to stick it out, even when things were devastating for him. After Mom left, he was so lost and overwhelmed with responsibility. Remember?"

It had been a tough time for all of them. Dad trying to hold it together, lost doing housework and cooking. His sadness was suffocating and Ava had felt the responsibility for their mom's leaving. Although what Aubrey said *was* true. Dad had stayed. He'd never let them down.

It hurt too much to dwell on that, too. She climbed outside into the stifling heat, the chlorine scent of the water from Brice's pool clung to her skin and clothes, reminding her. Of him. Of what her heart wanted. That Aubrey was right.

That still didn't mean it was the smartest thing to disregard common sense and believe in one man— to put all her heart and soul, and all the love she had, on the line. For some reason she felt that seven-year-old girl inside her, feeling small and alone and wishing she could be different, so that *everything* could be different.

The sun was setting through bright magenta and orange clouds, casting a mauve light that glowed on the ordinary asphalt shingle rooftops and changed them to shining satin. Rose pink glinted along the white siding of the two-storey buildings and reflected in windows.

The light cast over her, too, and she felt hope lift though her like grace.

Chapter Ten

The bookstore's after-hours' quiet made her little sigh sound like a hundred-mile-per-hour gust of wind, which wasn't her intention. Now everyone was going to stop their inventory work and come hunt her down and ask, "What's wrong, Ava?"

She could hear the question already—mostly because it was what they always asked. She was the kind of girl who had one kind of problem after another, and her family was slightly enmeshed in her affairs.

She crept forward a few inches on her rug-burned knees, ignoring the rough rasp from the industrial carpet. Did she remember her knee pads? No. She'd forgotten for the past four nights in a row straight. She'd been on the run, from sunup and well into the dark of night, working, trying to figure out the malicious concept of bookkeeping—to no avail—and baking. Running errands. Picking up as many hours here at the bookstore as she could, which was why she was helping with inventory. She hated inventory, but the sad truth was, she needed the money. Big-time.

She may have borrowed a chunk from Gran, but she'd only borrowed what was absolutely necessary for start-up, not for her wages or anything else. *A shoe-string start-up,* that's what Gran called it and while she'd offered more of a loan, Ava had refused. She'd appreciate the funds, but she wasn't out to take advantage of her grandmother, whom she loved very much. So, she was on a shoestring. She would just work harder to make ends meet, that's all.

The problem was, she wasn't as efficient as she could have been, and why? Who was to blame?

Brice Donovan. Thoughts of him were distracting her in a big way. Not that she'd seen him since they'd had dinner at his house. She'd run out of any hopes of actually seeing him. For four straight workdays she'd been by the bakery early every morning to drop off goodies. And every evening, except for today, she'd checked the work after the construction dudes had left. She'd been excited by the renovation's progress, but there'd been no sight of Brice. Sure, he'd left messages on her cell. And she'd left messages on his. But did they actually speak? No.

She'd even received a chocolate cake order from Brice's secretary for delivery to the office on Friday afternoon. Why hadn't he called with that? Or at least left a message? He'd given her the full-court press with his charm and his cooking and now when she was considering softening her policy, was he available to hear it? No-oo.

Ava halted in midrow and stared helplessly at the titles on the shelf and the clipboard on the floor beside her. Oops. Now she'd lost her place on the shelf, again. She stared down at the printout, and it started to blur. Probably because she'd been up since 4:45 a.m. that morning. It was now nearly nine—at night. She was totally beat.

"Ava?" Katherine rounded the corner of the history section, concern on her face. "What's wrong? You look exhausted. Why don't you take a break?"

Spence's voice sounded muffled coming from the other side of the row. "It's not time for her break. And she came in late. *Again*."

Katherine planted her hands on her slender hips and shook her head. She looked calm and classic, as always, even casually dressed for their late night work session in a simple butter-yellow knit top and black boot-cut jeans.

How did Katherine do it? She carried as much of the responsibility of the bookstore as Spence did, but with such serene, easy grace. No sharp words of frustration, ever. She looked gorgeous and totally put together and never missed her Bible study groups, had started a weekly woman's reading group program and found time to date, fall in love with Jack, get engaged and teach the teenager to drive.

"I don't need a break," Ava confessed, feeling so totally like a frumpy failure right then. She knew her hair was falling out of the comb holder thingy for the billionth time. Aubrey had talked her into wearing it this morning. She stood up to stretch and noticed that her linen blouse had wrinkled so much, it looked as if she'd been sleeping in it. "I need junk food."

"Pizza?" asked the teenager—more commonly

known as Hayden, Jack's kid. "Or how about French fries?"

"Nachos," Aubrey hollered from four stacks over. "With the works."

"No food near the books!" Spence sounded particularly annoyed. "And no breaks. I want this done before midnight."

Before midnight. Ava didn't want to think about how little sleep that meant she was going to get. But the good news was that she'd be able to make her next month's car payment.

"You look like a mess." Aubrey appeared and went straight to the comb clip thingy. "You didn't put this in right."

"I don't know how to put it in right." Ava rolled her eyes. "I'm so glad this is the last night we have to do this. Tomorrow night, I'm going to crash in front of the TV. The only time I plan on moving will be to answer the door for the pizza delivery guy. You, too, Aubrey?"

"No. I have plans, I know you forgot. I'm going to that singles church function in the valley." Aubrey ran her fingers through Ava's hair and gathered it up in a neat coil. "And you were going to babysit for Danielle, so she can go on a date with her husband? Remember?" Even the thought of those fried Tater-Tots made her feel perky.

"I'm too exhausted and hungry to remember anything. I think Mexi-Fries will help."

"There there's only one solution. We need junk food if we're going to last until midnight." Aubrey repositioned the Venus-flytrap-looking comb. "Spence, we're going to take another break."

"No breaks." He sounded angry, and there was a thud, like a few books tumbling from a shelf. He made an even angrier sound.

Aubrey took a step back to consider the comb's positioning. "He's extra crabby tonight."

"You distract him, and I'll slip out the back. Maybe he won't notice I'm gone."

"I'll notice," Spence barked, closer than they thought.

"Go." Katherine took Ava's clipboard. "I'll finish for you. Hayden, what do you want to order?"

"Uh…" The teenager poked her head around the corner. "I dunno."

"Hey, you come with me," Ava decided. "I'll need help carrying all that food. Katherine, I'm going to need money."

"I *knew* you were going to say that. Help yourself to a couple of twenties from my purse. Our late-night snack will be my treat."

Super-duper. It might not be the answer to her frustration about Brice, but there was nothing like a fast-food fix, right? If you order enough fried food, you could forget a lot of problems. Distraction, that was the key to coping.

After finding cash in Katherine's purse, she grabbed her own. The first thing she checked was her cell, already knowing what she'd see. One missed call. A voice-mail message.

She hit the button and waited to connect as she went in search of her keys.

"Are these them?" Hayden asked standing in front

of the open refrigerator. There they were, on the shelf next to the soda cans.

"Hey, you're pretty useful for a teenager," Ava winked at the girl while she listened to her one message.

Brice's deep baritone was a welcome sound. "Tag, you're it. Try me back when you're off work at the bookstore. I'll be up late."

Okay, at least there was hope. She dialed his number, pushed open the back door and held it for the teenager. Hayden bopped through with coltish energy and waited while Ava made sure the door locked after them. She didn't want the backdoor burglar to try to rob the place. Poor Spence had enough pressure without that.

She got Brice's voice mail. Big surprise. "It's your turn to call me," she said and turned her ringer to the loudest setting. For added measure, so the phone didn't get muffled by all the junk in her bag, she slipped it into an outside pocket. There. She was all set. "Kid, do you still have my keys?"

"Yep. I was kinda hopin' that you'd let me drive. You know, cuz I gotta practice so I can ace my driver's test."

"Deal." She opened the passenger's side door and hopped onto the seat. She was pretty exhausted and look, she had a chauffeur. Cool. "When Katherine marries your dad, I won't mind too much that you're my new niece. I mean, I could probably endure it."

"Like I guess I could, too." Hayden looked happy as she took control behind the wheel. "So, what taco place is it? And how do I get there?"

"You have much to learn. Lucky for you, you have me to teach you. We always go to Mr. Paco's Tacos.

They have the best nachos and Mexi-Fries. If you turn left out of the driveway, we can go past my shop on the way there. I want to see how the final coat of paint looks."

"You'll hire me when you open up, right?"

"Are you kidding? I thought you were going to work for free. I *could* pay you, I guess." Ava winked.

Hayden's smile was pure happiness. "You gotta teach me how to make monster muffins."

"In good time. Just drive, kid." Ava pulled out her phone just to check it.

No call. She knew that because she would have heard it ringing, but she had to check. Thinking of Brice at least made her feel a little closer to him when he felt so far away. Not that she wanted to admit it, but she missed him.

Big-time.

In the quiet of Ava's shop, Brice swiped the sweat from his forehead and uncapped a bottle of water. He downed half of it in one swig. He was hot, tired and hungry. But he didn't want to break until he'd installed the last of the ceiling moldings. He'd have to bust his hump tomorrow, put in a long day, to get this finished before the cleaning crew pulled up tomorrow—Friday—afternoon.

The week had gone by in a blur, too fast, and without Ava. He'd heard about the morning baked goods that she'd provided faithfully every morning. He'd heard about the free certificates she'd handed out to all the workers this morning along with the colorfully decorated little coffee cakes. He'd been busy in his shop, finishing the last of the intricate scrollwork.

He missed her. He knew she was working late shifts at the bookstore—she'd left a message on his voice mail telling him about it. They had been playing phone tag all week. The lack of contact frustrated him, but he had to get this right for her. It was her dream, which was important to him. Important for her.

The soft yellow walls had warmed like sunshine during the day and now, with the honey glow of the varnished woodwork, the place was better than any picture. He couldn't wait for her to see it, but he wanted everything done first. He wanted it perfect for her.

Which meant only one thing. Time to get back to work. He recapped the bottle, set it on the sawhorse next to his cell and noticed a green light was flashing. A missed call.

No. He'd missed her again. He'd either been hammering or running the saw—he hadn't heard it ring. He snatched it up, ready to hit the speed dial, but before he could, he glanced up and there she was. She stood on the passenger side of her SUV, closing the door, looking through the windows directly at him. There was surprise on her face and disbelief in her eyes as she remained frozen in place.

He crossed to the door in three strides and threw the bolt. The night air was balmy as he moved toward her.

"Oh, I can't believe this. Brice, this is wonderful. What are you doing here, working so late?"

His heart rolled over. She looked so dreamy, so precious. It was hard to believe that she was real and that he hadn't imagined her here.

"I didn't expect you to show up here like this." He studied her dear face. She looked tired, but happy. That's why he'd worked long endless hours in his shop. He wanted her to be happy. With the woodwork. With the shop. With him. "It was supposed to be a surprise for you. I wanted it finished before you came by in the early morning."

"But—" Her fingers caught tightly around his. "It's nine-thirty at night and you're still working. Were you going to work all night?"

"However long it takes."

"But that's so much work."

"It's my pleasure, Ava."

"But—" Her lovely eyes shone, as if she understood, finally. "This is my dream. It's like you could look right into my heart and know."

"Amazing, don't you think?"

Ava was starting to believe it. She could feel it in the marrow of her bones. Aubrey was right, okay, she was *always* right. *What about the beautiful woodwork he's doing for you? I don't think he has to work overtime to keep his personal budget in the black.*

This had to be so much work. This was such a big deal. This was more than business. More than friendship. This was everything that totally scared her.

"Want to go inside and see?" His hand was so strong as he guided her toward the door. He felt as invincible as titanium, like a man a woman could believe in.

She'd been fooled before, but those times faded like shadows to light. Looking at him—being with him—filled her with true hope. He awakened a part of her that had been never been wholly alive before—an op-

timistic part of her spirit. That positive force seemed
to fill her senses, overwhelming all common sense,
so that she couldn't think of anything else but Brice,
standing so tall and good.

It would be easy to lose perspective. She had to
move slow, be smart, think things through and not
rush into anything too fast. "Let's go inside so I can
see everything a little better."

"Sure." His hand moved to the middle of her back,
guiding her.

She turned at the door and gestured to the teenager
still behind the wheel. "Like I'm going to leave you
out here? C'mon."

"Who are you talking to?" he asked.

"My personal chauffeur. Brice, meet Hayden Munroe, my future niece, she's driving tonight."

"Good to meet you," Brice said politely, but Hayden
only stared at him in shock. "Munroe. Your dad
wouldn't be Jack Munroe, would he?"

"Yep. He's a state trooper. Did he like pull you over
and give you a speeding ticket?"

"No. I'm a faithful follower of all traffic laws. But I
met him at a charity golf match last month. To benefit
the children's hospital wing. He beat the socks off me."

"That's my Dad." Hayden gave a shy smile and
stepped through the open door.

Ava followed her, taking in the full effect of Brice's
work. Their footsteps echoed in the tall ceilings painted
the faintest shade of yellow, so that they looked white
as they angled upward. There were gaping holes where
the tract lighting was supposed to fit, but the ceiling
moldings were already mounted around half of the

room, separating the airiness of the ceiling from the warm buttery walls.

How many hours had all of this taken him? Ava could only stare in disbelief. The careful rosebud design was everywhere—not overdone, not ornate, but subtle and whimsical. Like something out of a country painting come to life.

His hand came to rest on her shoulder, a light touch, and a claiming one. She could feel the weight of it and his heart's question.

"What do you think?" His baritone rumbled dangerously close to her ear.

Dangerous because any amount of proximity was too close for her comfort. Panic beat with frantic, sharp edges against her ribs, but she held her ground. She stayed near to him instead of bolting away. "It's unbelievable. You must have worked so hard."

"True. And?"

"You know I love it." He'd done all this work, taken an infinite amount of care, done all of this. For her. How was she going to resist him now? She looked at the lovely work, the careful beveling, the meticulous detail, the perfection that glowed like varnished sunshine. "Thank you."

"You're welcome." His fingers curled into her shoulder, not bruising, not harsh, but tender. "You know what this means, don't you?"

A more-than-friends policy. "That's everything I'm afraid of."

"I know, but you don't need to be."

She could totally fall in love with Brice. Head over

heels, the whole shebang. She was already halfway there.

"Hey, this is so cool," Hayden said from the corner where she was tracing some of the lovely scrollwork with her fingertips. "There's a heart inside some of these roses. Do you have to like carve this or something?"

"Or something," he answered the teenager, but he didn't take his eyes from Ava, who went to the kid's side for a closer look.

Ava was endearing. Her golden hair was pulled back at the crown of her head to bounce in a curling fall down the graceful column of her neck. Her gauzy top could have been something a fair- tale princess might wear, and her modest denim shorts and rubber flip-flops made her seem even more wholesome and sweet. She traced the intricate scrollwork with her forefinger. Tears filled her eyes and did not fall. She stood still, studying the work, framed by the pale yellow walls and the dark rectangles of uncovered windows.

His heart filled with devotion for her. Afraid to scare her more with the seriousness of his affection, he waited, letting her have the time she needed to see what he'd done for her.

"This is amazing, Brice." Her smile was a little wobbly. "I love it."

She didn't say more. She didn't need to. The moment their gazes met, he could feel a rare, inexplicable connection forge between them. An emotional bond that was already so strong, what would it become if given more time?

He thought he knew the answer to that, too.

"I'm glad you like it," he said.

The niece-to-be wandered around, appraising. "I thought this was like supposed to be done tomorrow."

"We will be," he answered her but could not look away from Ava. From her violet-blue eyes silvered with tears and her heart showing.

He brushed at her tears with the pads of his thumbs, feeling as if he was ready for this.

He dropped a kiss on the tip of her nose. "Rex will be sad he missed you. He has a strict ten o'clock bedtime or he's grumpy the next day."

"I'll make an extra treat for him tomorrow. Will you be here?"

"To do the final walk-through with you. How does four o'clock sound? Will it work with your schedule?"

"I have no idea. Let me check." She pulled open the top of her enormous shoulder bag and began pawing through it. "No, no, no. Oh, here it is." She filed through a small appointment book and found the correct date. "It looks like I can make it at four. Will it take very long?"

"Not at all," he said. "I've got plans at five."

"Perfect." She ought to be done in plenty of time to babysit for Danielle. "This means that our business will be concluded. Done. Over."

"That's right." He flashed her that drop-dead gorgeous killer grin of his, full wattage, and showed both sets of dimples. "I guess it's time to work on amending our friends-only policy. I'll see you at four?"

"Four." Ava blinked, but that didn't help. Her mind had gone completely fuzzy. It was as if all her gray matter had turned into one big cotton ball. "If I could say thank you for the next decade without stopping, it wouldn't feel like enough."

"It's enough." He took a step back and held open the door. "Why are you two out and about this late?"

"The kid and I are on a fast-food run. It's our last night of inventory and we desperately need nachos to keep going."

"Let me guess. Mr. Paco's Tacos. One of my favorite places."

"Really? And here I thought after visiting your posh house and snazzy pool, that you ate only gourmet. Little did I know we share a love of Mr. Paco's nachos."

"The burritos, too."

"Don't even go there. My stomach is going to start growling and that would be so embarrassing." *Embarrassing.* That word hit her like a punch. She was gaping up at him like she was totally love-struck. How embarrassing was that? As if she'd let herself fall in love with him so fast. Not!

She was in total control of her emotions.

A distant ring penetrated her thoughts and broke the moment between them. Ava stepped back, fished through her bag again and came up with her cell. She saw the bookstore's number on her screen and she groaned. "It's Spence. I'm not going to answer this."

"Spence. He's a little wound up," Hayden said. She'd stationed herself by the door. "I don't like it when he's so mad. We better go."

"Yeah, or we'll be punished with that disappointed look of his." She dumped her phone back into her bag. Eventually it would stop ringing, but she had bigger concerns right now—and he was standing directly in front of her. Brice. "Should we come back with nachos for you? Or a burrito?"

"No, I'm good. Thanks."

"Okay." She took a step closer to the door, but she didn't want to say goodbye. She told herself it was the beautiful woodwork she couldn't tear herself away from. That wasn't the truth, but it was easier than admitting the truth.

She didn't want to leave Brice, because she knew she'd miss him. And in caring for him so much, she was terrified. "Good night," she said, as if she were in complete control of her heart, went up on tiptoe to brush a chaste kiss to his cheek and walked out of the shop. But when she'd settled in the passenger's side of her SUV, she realized she'd left something behind.

Her heart.

Chapter Eleven

Another drive-by baking. Brice had arrived just in time to see the back of a yellow vehicle far down the street, too far away for her to notice him. Rex seemed disappointed, too. He'd dashed to the kitchen only to find the box and a note on a star-shaped, bright yellow Post-it note.

Sorry, I promised the teenager monster muffins for her church thing today, so I'm running short on time. I've left gifts for the dudes and their families. And a special treat for my true love, Rex.

He wasn't surprised by her curlicue script or the fact that the note was written in glittery pink ink. There were a dozen medium-sized gift boxes set behind the regular baking box. One had his name on it, so he snooped beneath the lid. A small individually decorated cake and a gift certificate.

Rex whined with impatience, his tail thumping.

"You have one here, too." Curious, Brice peeked

into the box with Rex's name written in glittery gold ink. It was full of large, bone-shaped snacks.

Ava *would* have a recipe for fancy dog treats. He tossed one to Rex, who caught it in midair and gobbled it in two bites. It had to be delicious because his eyes brightened and he sat perfectly, the very best behavior ever witnessed. This dog obviously wanted another one.

Okay, he was a sucker. Brice tossed him one more before he went straight to work. He had a few touchups to do and the display case glass to pick up.

He was totally beat. He'd put in a hard week's work, but it was worth it. At exactly four-thirty this afternoon, their final walk-through would be complete and their business deal over. Then their relationship could get personal.

And he'd planned in a big way. He had reservations. A jet. A limo. Everything all lined up. By the time the jet touched back down at the local private airport tonight around ten-thirty, he hoped that Ava would have a better idea just what she meant to him. What he wanted to mean to her.

This might be the hardest thing he'd ever done. To lay his heart on the line. But what choice did he have? He loved her. No holds barred. No going back. All the way until forever—if that's what she wanted.

The hard thing about falling in love was that it took two to get to there. Ava had to make a decision now. He knew she was afraid, she'd been hurt. It was hard for her to risk again. He knew how she felt. He was scared, too.

With God's help, maybe they could take that risk together.

* * *

The late afternoon sun was in Ava's eyes as she screeched to a stop in front of the bakery. Wow, no one was around, just one green pickup parked in the shade. The brand-new windows were so clean they shone, and gave a perfect view into the cozy little shop space.

It was perfect, and her heart gave a little twist. She'd never dared dream as much as this. Even from the outside, the pale yellow walls warmed with the direct sunshine and seemed to invite a person right in. The empty display case sparkled, too, and the honey-colored wood was a comforting, homey touch.

Best of all, there was Brice, standing with his boots planted, wearing a knit black shirt and trousers, looking like a hundred on a scale of ten. There was no mistaking the intensity of his look or the reason why she felt joy light up in her heart.

It was his joy. His light.

Time to work on amending our friends-only policy, so think about the terms for our next agreement. His words had been troubling her since they'd talked last night.

So had Hayden's. Once they'd driven away, she'd said so innocently. "Wow, is that your boyfriend? Isn't he like rich and really cool?"

Yeah, so why was he interested in me? That was another insecurity that had plagued her every second, all day long. But seeing him coming toward her with his powerful athletic stride, knowing the gladness on his face was from seeing her made those insecurities whisper a little more quietly.

She grabbed her bag, tossed her phone inside and

hopped out of the car. The door slammed shut before she realized her hand was empty—no keys. But the locks didn't automatically set, so she could open the door right back up and grab the keys from the ignition—thanks to Brice.

"You are so handy to have around, I can't believe it," she smiled at him.

"Good to know." The look he gave showed her he was glad to see her.

Somehow she had to *stop* liking him more every time she saw him. Otherwise, she was going to be a total goner. She'd fall all the way in love before the evening was over.

"I dropped the check for the last half of the payment at the office on my way here. Along with a dozen monster muffins."

"I bet the office staff was happy. That was nice of you. You must be awfully pleased with the work. Everybody waits until after the walk-through and the punch list is finished before they hand over that much money."

"It just felt strange to give you a check, so I left it with your bookkeeper."

"Because you're past the business-only phase, too?" he asked.

Okay, she could officially admit it. "Just a little bit. Maybe."

"Me, too. Just a little bit. *Maybe.*" But when he said it, the words sounded as if he didn't have a doubt in the world. He took her hand, twining his big strong fingers between hers, holding on to her as if she mattered, as if she had so much value to him.

For now, that pesky little voice whispered inside her. That'll change. Just give him time.

It took all her inner might to silence that voice. To accept the cherished feeling of having him at her side, of his hand to hers, palm to palm.

"Let's get this over with because I have plans for you." His fingers tightened on hers, strengthening their connection. "Are you ready?"

"As ready as I'll ever be."

He held the door for her, a gentleman all the way. She tried to keep her emotions in check, but the sunshine spilling over her made her feel more than hopeful. Made her intensely aware of her blessings.

What if this was a sign that her luck in life was changing? This charming shop with wood-wrapped windows, cathedral ceilings and whimsical warmth had once existed only in her dreams.

Now it was real.

Maybe it was time to see if more of her dreams in life could come true.

"Four twenty-nine." Brice checked his watch and glanced over the top of Ava's head. No sign of the limo yet, but the driver still had another minute. "I'm glad you're happy with our work."

"Happy doesn't begin to describe it. I still can't believe this was so painless. And the work your men did here. I'm grateful to all of you."

He could see that this transition from friends-only to more than friends was hard for her, too. She was nervously glancing toward the front door. Trying to escape before he hit the serious questions? he wondered. Or being afraid that he didn't have any?

This was tough for him, too. He'd never been this nervous. He'd never felt as if he had so much on the line. Everything was riding on this—his heart, his hopes and his future. It was tough letting go and trusting God's will for him. Brice took a shaky breath, gathering his courage. He'd have to see how this worked out. It wasn't easy not knowing.

"There's the limo now." He set the clipboard aside to cradle her chin in his hands. "Remember I said I had plans for you?"

"Y-yes. I vaguely recall something to that effect."

"And that we needed to renegotiate our friends-only policies?"

"Yes, but why the limo?" Panic coiled through her.

He could feel her fear. "It's okay. I have plans. Nice plans, involving dinner and watching the sun set. It should be painless, maybe even romantic. Are you interested?"

"Tonight? I c-can't."

His heart took a blow. He'd really thought she felt this, too. He took a step back and released his hold on her. "Well, I had to ask."

"Wait—no, I'm not saying 'no.'" She looked tortured. "When you said you had plans, I was thinking more of that next step. You know, like you'd ask me out sometime soon. I didn't know that you meant tonight. Now you're mad."

"I'm not mad."

"I told Danielle that I'd babysit for her. Aubrey has this church thing, and everyone else is busy. Spence could do it, but we don't want him to scare the children. So there's nobody else but me. You're looking madder."

"No. I just…made…plans."

See? Already she was messing this up. How did she do it? And so fast. They'd been officially more than friends for two minutes, maybe three? She twisted around to get a good look at the limo. It was shiny white and one of the long ones with sparkling windows and it looked expensive. "What kind of plans did you make?"

"Nothing that can't be rearranged for another time."

There it was, the terrible sense of foreboding, that everything so wonderfully right in her life was about to go totally wrong. Doom would strike and then it would all be over. She would never know what it would be like to be cherished by this man.

"I'll be back." Brice strode away, shoulders set, spine straight, purposefully.

Oh, no. Every last one of her hopes plummeted. What plans had she messed up? She closed her eyes, took a deep breath and tried to get centered enough to pray. But she couldn't. She was all messed up inside, as if someone had taken a big stick to her vat of negative feelings and was stirring it hard.

The door opened with a faint swoosh. Brice's powerful, wonderful presence filled the room.

"C'mon," he said in his kind voice, the one that made all the fears inside her melt like butter on a hot stove. His hand settled on her nape, and his touch, his kindness, seared through her like hope. He opened the door.

"Okay, call me confused." She stared at the driver in his suit and cap, holding open the passenger door for her. "What about Danielle?"

"Rick is going to take you to Danielle's house. I'm going to borrow your SUV and swing through and pick up takeout so we all have something to eat. I'm coming with you tonight instead. My plans can change. Yours shouldn't."

"You mean...you're going to babysit with me?"

"Do you have a problem with that?"

She was vaguely aware her jaw was hanging open, but she couldn't seem to make it shut. She couldn't seem to move anything at all. All she could do was stare at this man—this perfect man—and feel even worse. How was she going to keep from falling 100 percent in love with him *now?*

Brice held out his hand. "Your keys?"

She went in search and found them in her pocket. Did he know what this meant to her?

"I'll see you soon." He leaned close, so close she could smell the faint scent of fabric softener on his shirt.

Her spirit lifted from simply having him near.

He pressed a sweet kiss to her cheek. "I know family is important to you. That means, since we're dating, your family is important to me."

She sank onto the leather seat, dazed. This wasn't a dream, was it?

Brice knelt down on the sidewalk until they were eye to eye. "We are dating, right?"

"Right." Her entire soul smiled.

* * *

"All right," Danielle said, dragging Ava into the kitchen. "When did you start dating Brice Donovan?"

"Officially about twenty minutes ago." Ava leaned over the counter to get a good look out the kitchen window. There he was, as gorgeous as a wish come true. He'd climbed out of her SUV and was now carting with him a box of drinks and several big food bags bearing the Mr. Paco's Tacos emblem.

"Why didn't I know about this? You girls aren't supposed to leave me out of the loop!" Danielle looked rushed as she grabbed her purse and rummaged around for something. She pulled out her cell and hit the power button. "You have my number, call if there's a problem. I just can't believe this. Brice Donovan. He's *wonderful*. Jonas knows him from the community of united churches charities board. They served on it together for a few years. He just raved about him. Oh, look, he's here. And I've got to go. I'm completely late."

"Don't worry. Tell that great husband of yours that it's all my fault. I was late in the first place."

"He expects it." With a wink, Danielle rushed to the door. "Madison's not to have sugar. Tyler will try to talk you into too much television."

"I know the scoop. Go. Before your husband holds it against me. It's okay that he's here, right?"

"Uh, yeah." Danielle grabbed her keys and rushed into the living room. After a final kiss to her little ones she headed to the garage door.

It closed the same moment there was a knock on the front door. She swung it open and wasn't prepared for how good it was to find him there. He could be anywhere tonight, but he'd chosen to be with her. Which worked out just fine since she wanted to be with him.

She took the drink box. "Come on in. The kids are watching TV. I like your choice of takeout."

"I figured we couldn't go wrong with tacos." He shouldered past her. "Do you want this on the table?"

"Yep. I'll round up the munchkins."

Brice set the bags of food on the table and glanced around. He wasn't surprised by the comfortable-looking furniture and pictures of cute kids on the wall. Several family vacation photos were framed in recognizable places like the Grand Tetons and Yellowstone. It felt like a real home. Cheerful checks and ruffles sparingly decorated the kitchen and what he could see of the living room. There was a TV in a cabinet tuned to a wholesome-looking cartoon. A couch faced it.

Ava knelt down to talk to the kids out of his view on the couch. She was pure tenderness, and his heart thudded to the floor. She was truly a kind woman. No doubt about it, she'd make a great mom. It was a side of her he hadn't seen but guessed was there.

A preschool-aged boy hopped up, stood on the cushions and threw his arms around Ava. The kid wore a plastic fireman's hat and the brim bonked her in the temple when he gave her a wet smacking kiss, which she pretended was gross just to have him laughing. Then she tickled his stomach, reminded him of the rule about the couch and standing and watched while he jumped down with a two-footed thud.

"Did ya bring lotza Mexi-Fries?" he asked as he charged Brice's way. "Aunt Ava says I gotta have lotza Mexi-Fries or I'll get shorter insteada taller."

Yeah, he could see Ava telling that to the little guy. Funny. "Don't sweat it. I got the largest tub of them."

"Whew." As if that had been a big worry, the kid pulled back his chair, climbed up and settled into his booster seat.

Brice wasn't around kids very much, but this one was cute. He started unpacking the food. "You like tacos, kid?"

"Lots." The preschooler rested his elbows on the edge of the table and propped his chin on his hands. "Are you a fireman?"

"No. Are you?"

"Yep. I put out lotza fires today."

"Good work." Brice pulled the boxed kiddy meal from the giant bag.

He felt more than heard Ava's approach. It was as if his spirit turned toward her, recognizing her and only her. She had a curly-haired little girl on her hip, and the sight did something to him. She had the little girl laughing, her chubby cheeks pink with delight.

"Aunt Ava! Aunt Ava!" The boy shouted, holding up three sticky-looking fingers. "I put out three fires today."

"Sorry, I can't hear you," she teased as she slid the little girl into a high chair. "I'm deaf from you yelling so loud."

"Oops. My bad."

Brice didn't need to wonder where the kid had learned that—his gaze landed on Ava again as she double-checked the little girl's lap belt on the high chair, and satisfied, straightened. "Brice, I hope you brought a lot of Mexi-Fries. We don't want anyone at this table to get any shorter than they already are."

"I brought the biggest tub."

"My hero. It's hard for a girl not to like a guy who knows what's important in life."

"Mexi-Fries are one of the real secrets to true happiness."

"Exactly." She peered into one of the food bags. "Nachos. Burritos. Tacos. I'm speechless with gratitude."

"Not hunger?"

"That, too. Let me get milk for the kids. If you want to start doling out the food?"

"Sure." As he got to work, the little tot across the table stared at him like she wasn't too sure she approved of his presence.

"Aunt Ava! Aunt Ava!" The boy twisted around on his knees and hung over the back of his chair. "I getta say grace! I getta say grace!"

"Okay, okay. But what's your mom's rule?" Ava asked from behind the refrigerator door.

"Umm." The kid appeared to be thinking extremely hard.

This was not his experience of a family, Brice thought as he put the tubs of Mexi-Fries in the middle of the table. His mom would have a coronary at the noise level. No laughing at the table. No yelling. Sitting like a little gentleman—always. Use our best manners all the time.

All that had its place, but this was better. Comfortable. Fun. That was one of the things he cherished about Ava so much. She could make the simple things in life, like settling down to the dining room table, feel like a refreshing and cheerful kind of heaven on earth.

Ava slid a plate and a cup of milk in front of the boy. "No hats at the table, Tyler."

"Oh, yeah. I forgot." He handed her the bright red fireman's hat. "Can I say the blessing now?"

Ava dropped the hat on the back of the couch and returned to hand out another plate. "Brice, do you mind if Tyler does the honors?"

He could tell by the twinkling humor in her eyes that the boy's blessing was cute. Call him curious. He took the offered plate. "Sure."

"*Now,* Aunt Ava?"

"Hold on a minute." Ava rolled her eyes as she slid a cup on the toddler's tray.

"*Now?*" The kid sounded as if he were about to spontaneously combust.

"Now." Ava dropped into her chair.

Before Brice had time to bow his head, the little boy started in. "*Thanks for the eats, Lord. God bless us every one!*"

"Dickens' *A Christmas Carol* has made an impression on him," Ava explained after they'd muttered a quick "Amen." "He keeps watching this wholesome cartoon version of the movie over and over and it's driving Danielle insane."

Before Brice could answer, the boy hollered. "Aunt Ava! Hurry, I need Mexi-Fries. I'm shrinking."

"We can't have that. Brice, you look a little shorter, too."

He held out his plate. "Load me up."

What else could he say? This was exactly what he

expected of an evening spent with Ava. Maybe not what he'd planned, but that didn't matter. All that mattered to him was being with her. For now and, he suspected, for his lifetime to come.

"I can't believe you're still talking to me," Ava said in the quiet of the warm night standing beside her SUV. It was dark out. Almost eleven o'clock. "Especially after Tyler squirted you with the hose."

"We were playing fireman, and it was an accident. I dried out pretty fast."

"You handled being drenched from head to toe in your snazzy clothes pretty well. Most men would have gotten really angry."

"I'm not like most men."

"I'm noticing that." It was hard not to.

Don't think about how perfect he is, she warned herself. That would just start making her nervous. *Look at him, Mr. Fantastic, nice, wealthy and kind.* He liked fast-food Mexi-Fries and went to church faithfully every Sunday. They'd talked about that after the kids had been in bed.

And after discussing faith, they went on to talk more about his family and hers. Chloe was still honeymooning in Fiji. His mom was ready to drive him nuts now that his sister was married off and she kept making elaborate plans for his upcoming birthday, and his dad was holding open a position at his investment firm, which Brice still didn't want.

She told of Katherine's upcoming wedding and all the planning that took, that she still hadn't picked a cake yet. She talked about their cousin Kelly who'd gotten married and was living in California on base with her marine husband. Then she mentioned the stress of owing her grandmother so much money.

Somehow they'd managed to avoid the more personal side of their conversation. Like, did he want kids? How many? She wanted children, but she had to find someone to get married to first. And wasn't that practically impossible? Certainly not a topic for a first date. If seeing her taking care of kids hadn't totally scared him off, talking about marriage and wanting kids would.

Then again, why risk it?

She dug through her purse for her keys. "It looks like you need a ride home."

"Nope, Rick should be arriving here in the next few minutes."

"Well, I don't want to leave you standing here alone."

"It's late. You've got to be tired from running after the kids. Go home." He smiled his billion megawatt smile with the double dimples. "I'll be fine. I want you to drive safely."

"That's always my plan. I might not be the best driver, but I've never hit anything. Except for Grandpop's St. Bernard. I didn't see him in the rearview mirror."

Brice burst out laughing. "Does anything normal ever happen to you, or it is always a circus with you?"

"Always a circus. You've changed your mind about dating me. By the way, I didn't hurt Tiny at all."

"Tiny?"

"The St. Bernard. Not even a bruise. He didn't want

us to leave and I couldn't see that he'd planted himself behind the car to stop us from going. He must have been in a blind spot because I checked the mirrors before I started backing up. There was this horrible thud. You should have seen the damage to Dad's bumper, though. It was the family car, and because they didn't want the insurance premium to go up, he didn't get it fixed. My family never let me live it down."

"And Tiny?"

"He learned to keep away from me when I was behind the wheel. I miss that guy. He passed away a month after Grandpop did." The pain of the loss still stole her breath. "Your grandparents are alive and well?"

"Thriving. They're vacationing at their home in Italy. They like to travel. They should be back for my birthday this week."

"I'm glad they are enjoying their lives. My grandparents always meant to do that, but they never got to travel much before they ran out of time to do it together."

"Our grandfathers were very close friends. I know he still advises your grandmother on her investments. Is she still living in Arizona?"

"She's stayed away since Grandpop passed. She said the house had too many memories of him, so she moved to their home in Scottsdale. They'd only had it for a few years, so I guess there weren't as many memories there. I think it helps her to be away, although we miss her. Dad's down there now, too, with Dorrie. They're all coming back at the end of summer for Katherine's wedding."

"My grandparents can't seem to breathe without the other. Were yours like that, too?"

"Gran said that losing her husband was like having her heart cut out. She's never been the same. They were very much in love. The real way."

"The way it's meant to be. My parents never managed to find that with each other." He shrugged. "They get along all right, they're compatible, but it's not what my grandparents have. They're tight."

"I know what you mean. Gran has always said Grandpop was her gift straight from heaven. She had all the best blessings in him." Okay, this was getting dangerously close to the topic she wanted to avoid, because she did not want to mess this up with Brice.

And yet, she couldn't seem to stop herself. "I've always thought they were the happily-ever-part of the fairy tale. You know, after Cinderella gets her shoe back *and* her prince, and Snow White is awakened by her prince, they end the stories. But I knew that kind of love was real because my grandparents lived for each other. They breathed together. It's what I always wanted."

Great going, Ava. She held her breath, *waiting,* just waiting, for him to start moving away.

But he didn't. "Me, too."

Headlights broke around the corner at that moment. It was Rick with his fancy limo and he pulled right up to the sidewalk, so Ava didn't know what else Brice had been about to say.

He brushed a kiss to her cheek. "Good night, beautiful."

Her soul sighed. "Wow, aren't you Mr. Perfect?"

"Oh, so it's working. Good to know I'm charming you."

"Only a tad. A smidgen. A pinch."

Okay, that was an understatement. If she could measure how much Brice Donovan had impressed her, it would be the distance from the earth to the moon and back six hundred times.

Then he was gone, leaving her there in the light of the moon, unable to stop the full-blown wishes rising up from her soul.

Chapter Twelve

With hopeful cheer midafternoon light tumbled through the new larger front windows of her shop. But was she feeling hopeful? No. *Astonished* would be one word. *Overwhelmed* would be another.

She couldn't stop staring at the two dozen yellow, red-tipped roses Brice had sent. What was a girl to do when her hopes were already sky-high, tugging like a helium balloon against the string? With every breath she took, she drew in the delicate fragrance of the lovely bouquet and tried to convince herself she wasn't scared.

The door behind her whispered open and there was Aubrey hefting a really big box. Ava caught the door, holding it as her twin tumbled inside.

"Whew, it's a scorcher out there. The air-conditioning feels nice." Aubrey slid the box to the ground. "Those flowers are gorgeous. From Brice?"

It wasn't exactly a question. And it wasn't exactly what Aubrey was asking. Ava could feel their shared brain cells firing. Her sister knew how she felt. She knew what those roses meant.

It was a shocker how calm her voice actually sounded. "Yes, they just arrived. Isn't it a totally nice gesture?"

"Nice, sure. But a bunch of daisies is nice. Roses say something much more. Like the *L* word."

"The *L* word is none of your business, nosy." No sense in getting into a blind panic. "Brice and me, we're in that awkward more-than-friends stage, but not totally committed stage. Who knows how it's going to work out? Doom might be lurking out there some-where, just waiting."

She had to be prepared for it, if it was.

"What doom? There's no doom." Aubrey went straight to the roses and inhaled deeply. "A man doesn't send something like this unless he's trying to sweep you off your feet."

"Yes, well, it's working."

"So, you called him to thank him, right? What did he say? Is he taking you out soon?" Aubrey pulled a pint carton of strawberry milk out of the box, still cold from the grocery store. She opened the spout and held it out for Ava to take. "What? You're just standing there not saying anything. You've called him, right?"

She took the milk. "Uh, I haven't got there yet."

"And you're procrastinating because…?"

"Okay, I can admit it. I'm a big chicken. Babysitting with him at Danielle's went so great. I mean, he was really Mr. Perfect. What if I mess this up?"

"Ava, Ava, Ava." Aubrey was using her gentlest voice, the one that was filled with so much uncon-

ditional sisterly love. It just proved that Aubrey was
blinded by flaws, too. "This romance with Brice is
totally new for you. You've finally found yourself a
perfect guy."

"And it's too good to be true, right? That's what I'm
afraid of." And much, much more, but could she admit
that to Aubrey?

No.

"You are perfectly lovable. Mom was wrong to say
that to you when she left. To blame you for her unhappiness. It wasn't true then."

"We're talking about men, not Mom."

"Okay." Aubrey's heart was showing. "Don't you
think the crazy accusations would have scared him
off if he was going to be?"

"I can't believe he helped me babysit. He said *my
family is important to me, so it's important to him.*"

"See? How many signs do you need?"

"I don't know if there could be enough."

Aubrey traced the pattern of the tiny intricate roses
carved into the trim of the gleaming, perfect case. "I
really think his heart is true. I think he's the right man
for you. Why don't you grab hold of this blessing the
Lord is placing before you? Brice might be the happily-ever-after I've been praying for, for you. Just believe that God is in charge and embrace this chance."

"I'm scared I'm going to mess this up. That he's
going to get a good look at me and see that I don't
fit into the right image. That's what Brice is looking
for. He wants someone from the same background and
compatible lifestyle. Look at me, I'm not exactly mink-

wearing, symphony-going material. You heard him talk about his fiancée."

"His ex-fiancée. Didn't you listen to him at all?"

"It's hard to hear really well with all this panic racing around inside my head."

"You're a nut." Aubrey rolled her eyes. "What am I going to do with you?"

"Not much. You're stuck with me."

"That's just my good luck." Aubrey smiled. "Call him. Take a deep breath and do it. Take the next step forward."

"Sure, what do I have to lose? It's only my heart at stake."

"Do you know what I think?" Aubrey knelt and began unpacking the box. "I think you're *more* scared this is going to work out."

"Uh, yeah."

"Go in the kitchen and call him. I'll watch the front. Oh, and I'll put up all this stuff I brought."

"Okeydokey. You're wonderful, you know that?"

"I do. Now go."

"Thanks, Aub."

Her cell was ringing as she streaked into the kitchen. Her heart jumped with jubilation when she saw Brice's name and number on her screen. Talk about perfect timing. Okay, she was scared, but this *had* to be a sign. She hit the talk button. "I love the flowers. Thank you."

"I know red roses are expected, but when I saw these in the florist's case, I thought of you. Bright yellow like the sunshine you are."

If he kept talking like that, he was going to scare her even more.

"What are you up to this morning?" he asked.

"No good, as usual. I just finished making a ballet shoe cake, it's for one of the construction dude's daughters."

"That was really nice of you, including certificates for a free birthday cake for everyone."

"It's the least I could do. My new kitchen is wonderful to work in. The question is, have you recovered from the trauma of babysitting?"

"No trauma to recover from. I'm made of tougher stuff than that. Remember how I said I had plans in place that we postponed?"

"You know I do." She heard a slight tinkle of chimes and peered through the open doorway. There was Aubrey hanging a beautiful ceramic bell over the door.

"I've been able to push those plans back a few weeks. I wanted to give you plenty of notice this time. I thought we could combine it with celebrations for the Fourth of July. You wouldn't be interested in spending that weekend with me would you?"

"Uh, did I hear you right? The entire weekend?"

"Now, before you start jumping to conclusions and questioning my morals, let me explain."

He was laughing, remembering their unforgettable first meeting when she'd told him to get some morals. At least he thought it was funny. That was a good sign, right?

"Okay, I'll wait for the explanation before I start firing insults."

"I have some property near Glacier National Park, and we won't be alone. I plan to invite my sister and her husband. My grandparents will be there, too. I was going to suggest that you invite Aubrey. We'll have a big cookout and watch fireworks over the lake. It'll be fun—and well chaperoned. What do you think?"

"Do you mean like going camping, or something? Because I try not to go too far out into the wilderness."

"Why? You're not a backcountry kind of girl?"

"If I tell you, then you'll stop dating me. Years from now you'll tell your friends it was a good thing you dumped me when you did."

"Not a chance, gorgeous."

She was in big trouble because her high hopes were rising higher than the galaxy. She was in bigger trouble because the logical part of her was drowned out by those rising hopes.

"Tell me about this story of yours, Ava. I gotta know."

"My dad loved to camp and he'd haul us all up to one of the national forests and we'd do the tent thing and the catch-trout-for-supper thing and cook over an open campfire thing."

"Uh-oh. I'm starting to see what might have been the problem here."

"I accidentally started a forest fire. It wasn't my fault. And it was only a little grass fire, but I never lived it down. Over the years the story has grown to gargantuan proportion and when Dad tells it now, you'd think I burned down half the western forests in the United States."

"And you started it how?"

"My marshmallow caught on fire. I was seven. I was afraid of flame, mostly, so I was sitting farther back than everyone else from the campfire. And Aubrey leaned over to say something to me and I forgot to watch the stick. It was sort of top heavy because I was holding the very end of it and it just sort of dipped into the fire.

"When I noticed that my marshmallow was turning black and spewing flame, I screamed and gave it a big shake. Blazing marshmallow fluff flew off the stick and onto Mom and Dad's tent. It caught fire, of course. It was a total disaster. Luckily, Dad followed the forestry rules of having so many buckets of water and dirt handy, whatever, and he got it put out with hardly any damage to anything but a piece of scorched earth where the tent had been."

"I'm beginning to see why your family calls you a disaster magnet."

"To this day, Spence will not let me be in charge of any fire-related thing. No barbecuing, no campfire, no lighting the Yule log in the hearth on Christmas Eve. It's embarrassing."

"You *are* a disaster."

"Don't I know it. You're going to hang up now, aren't you? You've changed your mind about me, about spending time with a big dope like me."

"Hey now, I don't think you're a dope."

It was his kindness that got her. His unending, constant kindness, even when he should be agreeing with her. Then it hit her. Duh. Could it be any more obvious? "Oh, no. I can't believe this. You have it, too."

"What do I have?"

"The flaw-blindness. Otherwise, you could see it."

"See what?"

He didn't know? That was only further proof. He

was as fault-blind as she was. Unbelievable. "My faults? You can't see them, can you? All six hundred thousand of them."

"Nope. You look perfect to me."

"Then we're doomed. This is only a matter of time." She rolled her eyes, trying to make light of things. But that wasn't how she was feeling. Not at all. Suddenly it was so clear. His devotion, his kindness, his affection and his romantic gestures would last only as long as it took for him to realize the truth about her. "We might as well accept it now. One day you'll look at me and decide you can't take it anymore. Then the more-than-friends aspect of our relationship will be done. A great big crash and burn. Ka-blew-y."

"No crashing and burning. No ka-blew-y. I like you exactly the way you are, Ava. I like *who* you are. Or I wouldn't be inviting you to my birthday party either."

"What?"

"You know I'm turning thirty-one on Tuesday. I've finally talked my mom into just having a small family dinner at home. My grandparents are coming. I want you there, too."

This was such dangerous ground. This was like the camping trip. Everything was great and happy. Everything finally looked promising, like it really was going to work out. And when you stopped expecting it, when you were sure it was smooth sailing ahead, *that's* when disaster struck. Like a category five tornado touching down right where you're the most vulnerable.

But what did she say? This sounded like the next step—a serious step. "Did I hear you right? You want me to come to your birthday dinner?"

"I'm asking you, right?" Brice adjusted his Blue-tooth headset before he slowed his truck to pull into the left hand turn lane at the red light. Rex was in the backseat, panting extra loud, as if he were in agree-ment. See how Ava improved their lives? Just talking to her lifted their spirits. "You'll come?"

"As long as I get to bring the cake."

"I'd love the dump truck cake."

"Anything else you want with it?"

"Nope. As long as you're there, what else could I want in this world?"

"Oh, you are totally Mr. Irresistible, aren't you? You keep saying things like that, and I'm going to have to start liking you."

"*Start* liking me?" Brice chuckled. "I thought you were already in that pond with both feet."

"You must be mistaken. I *hardly* like you at all."

He could just imagine her rolling her eyes, look-ing so sweet and sparkling, the way she did when she smiled. In his opinion, they were right in that pond with both feet together. It was scary, but nice. "I'll pick you up Tuesday at six-thirty—" His call waiting beeped. His mom. "Can I put you on hold for a few minutes?"

"Okeydokey."

Ava. She put a smile into his heart and made ev-erything better. The sun in his eyes was brighter than he'd ever noticed. The greens of the lawns and trees in his neighborhood more vibrant. Greener than he'd ever remembered.

He hit the garage door opener and switched over to answer the call. "Hi, Mom."

"Brice? Is that really you, or just my imagination. I can't believe I'm not getting your voice mail. *Again.*"

Uh-oh. She didn't sound happy. He racked his brain but he couldn't think of a thing he'd done. "I've been busy finishing up a project."

"Yes, your father mentioned that. For that baker. That friend of Chloe's."

He pulled his truck into the garage, not missing the disapproving tone in his mother's voice. "Ava McKaslin is a friend of mine, too."

"I know Chloe did her a favor by letting us overpay her for that wedding cake."

"Mom, you can't fool me." He cut the truck's engine and swung open the door. "Ava didn't charge Chloe— or you—for that cake."

"And how do you know this?"

He opened the door and waited while Rex leaped out. "I'm bringing Ava to my birthday dinner, and she's bringing the cake. You're going to be nice to her, right?"

There was silence. Frosty silence.

This was actually going better than he'd expected. That had to be a good sign, right? He unlocked the inside door and held it for Rex, who was yawning hugely and lumbered lazily inside. "Mom?"

"I'm carefully weighing my words and there doesn't appear to be anything I can say that you would deem appropriate."

"You have until Tuesday to work on that." He stepped around Rex who had collapsed in front of the nearest floor vent and opened the refrigerator. "I'm going to expect you to be on your best behavior."

"She's all wrong for you, you know that."

"It's not your decision who I date, Mom. Ava's important to me, and I want your word you'll be nice to her."

"I suppose I can try."

"Thank you. I'll call you and Dad later, okay? I've got her on the other line, so I need to go." He said goodbye, and he couldn't say exactly why there was a terrible sense of foreboding that settled dead center in his gut. He switched over to the waiting call. "Ava?"

"Yo. Danielle just walked in. She's taking the measurements for the shades she's making me. Hold on just a sec." There was a lot of cheerful talk in the background that grew fainter. "Brice? I've got a full house here. Spence just pulled up with the tables Aubrey refinished for me."

"Sounds exciting. I bet the place is looking more like you imagined."

"It is. I'm going to be officially open for business this weekend. There's a ton of stuff I still have do, and I'm totally excited *and* scared."

"I can understand that." Did he. "What can I do to help?"

"As if you haven't done enough with the woodwork. It still takes my breath away."

"Good. That's the idea."

Ava nearly stumbled at his words. Oh, she was so overwhelmed. So out of her realm of experience. Tender feelings for him just kept lifting through her, rising up until all she could feel was joy. Was it illusion? Could this possibly work out between them?

"I'll give you a call tomorrow," he said in that dependable, easygoing way of his. "See if you need any help hauling anything or helping with the set up. Okay?"

"Okay."

Ava leaned her forehead against the heel of her hand, listening to the click as he disconnected. Could this man be any more perfect?

It took her a second to realize that all the chatter in the front room had stopped. Her sisters were staring at her. Katherine's eyes were hopeful and sparkling. Aubrey looked as if she were going to start jumping up and down with glee.

This was another problem with a big family. A girl had no privacy. Ever. Even when you were grown and gone from the nest, you could not get away from nosy sisters, bless them.

Danielle shifted little Madison onto her other hip. "Did we hear that correctly? Are you going to a family birthday party?"

"Oh, this is *big*. Huge," Katherine added. "He's taking you home to meet his parents."

"See? What did I say?" Aubrey steepled her hands, as if in prayer. "This is the next step."

"Don't psych me out, I'm trying to cope here." Ava spotted Spence and his big gray pickup parked against the curb. He was glaring in at them. "He obviously needs help. I'd better get out there—"

"Was it my imagination or did you tell Brice about the camping trip?" Katherine asked, using the box Aubrey brought to prop open the door. "And he *still* asked you out?"

"The story just popped out. It wasn't intentional."

Ava shrugged. "I guess that old family stuff has been on my mind lately."

"I know how that goes, but you don't have to let the past affect your future. Good things happen to good people, and this is one of those times." Katherine grabbed a pair of sunglasses from the counter. "Take my advice. Leave the past behind where it belongs, and go live your future. You can do that, right?"

"Sure." Easier said than done. She didn't dare let herself believe it. Being with Brice was too important. She hoped that as long as she stayed right here, in this more-than-friends-only stage, then it wouldn't get serious. She wouldn't lose any more of her heart.

Chapter Thirteen

On Tuesday evening, as they headed up to Brice's parents' house in his red sports car, she felt as if they were driving heavenward. The foothills of the Bridger Mountains offered breathless views of the higher Rocky Mountain peaks and the deep, divine blue of the summer sky. As gorgeous as the view was, where were her eyes glued? On Brice, looking amazing in a black sports coat, shirt, tie and trousers.

Dazzled? Yeah, you could say that.

"We're almost there." Brice drove with confidence on the smooth, S-curving road that skirted private developments more upscale than the one he lived in. "You look a little pale. Are you okay?"

Okay? If she could survive the panic attack, she'd be just fine, thanks. There was a perfectly rational explanation for the panic. This couldn't be real. It was too nice to be real. Too wonderful. She tried to relax. Tried to pretend she wasn't terrified. She'd never felt like this, so vulnerable and so close to him.

Careful, Ava, she warned herself. *Don't start to believe in the dream.*

Brice pulled into a grand driveway that rivaled anything she'd seen on TV and that's when the nerves hit her. What had she been thinking? It was way too early in their relationship for her to meet his parents. Besides, she'd already met his mom. She'd been very dismissive of Chloe's choice of wedding cake designs.

"I don't suppose your mom is expecting a more fancy cake design?" She looked at the bakery box sitting on her lap.

"Does it matter?" He shrugged as if he couldn't imagine how she might even think it would.

Okay, maybe not. But as he pulled in front of a lavish Shakespearean-looking brick home with a turret and those diamond panel windows, she couldn't fight the strong feeling that her nifty dump truck cake might seem a little hokey by comparison. "You're sure about the cake?"

"Yep." He didn't look like he had a doubt in the world.

Okeydokey. Maybe it wasn't the cake she was worried about. Maybe Brice's family would take one look at her and think, not right for him. She smoothed the linen skirt of the dress she'd borrowed from Aubrey.

Okay, really, it was just her old insecurities flaring up like a big case of emotional warts.

He smoothly parked the car in front of a four-car garage and cut the engine. "You haven't changed your mind about coming in with me, have you?"

"Let me get back to you on that." Her voice wobbled.

"Don't be nervous. My family is going to love you."

"And if they don't?"

"They will learn to love you." He cupped her chin in his palm.

She focused her violet-blue gaze on his, her whole heart showing.

He got out of the car, noticing his grandparent's Land Rover was parked in the shade. Anticipation up-lifted him as he circled around to open Ava's door. He couldn't wait for his grandparents to meet Ava. He knew they would love her. His parents might take more time to accept someone new, but he knew they would come to adore her, too. How could anyone not fall in love with Ava?

He took the boxed cake and offered his hand to help her from the low-slung car. The brush of her hand to his renewed him, more every time.

Having her at his side was like a gift. She swept beside him with that buoyant walk of hers. Every-thing about her was bubbly. This evening, she wore a light purple summer dress that shimmered as soft as a dream. Matching lavender sandals clicked on the brick walk, echoing slightly in the balmy, quiet grounds. The purple gift bag she carried made a pleasant crinkling sound as she walked. Her hair was pulled back in one of those fancy braids and stayed in place thanks to a few little purple butterfly barrettes.

Cute. Whimsical. She was like a spring breeze and he could not get enough of her. Powerful affection filled him. He hesitated on the doorstep. "This is your last chance to bolt."

"How did you know that had crossed my mind?" She winked, and looked even more sweet and ador-able. "I'm as ready as I'll ever be."

"Super-duper." He said that to make her smile, and it worked. He opened the front door. "Hello? Anyone home?"

Their steps echoed in a mammoth marble foyer.

Ava looked around, a little afraid to step on the very expensive looking marble beneath her shoes. "Is this a house or a museum?"

"It always felt like a museum when I was growing up. Come all the way in. Don't worry. We don't charge admission. Not on Tuesdays anyway."

Her gaze went directly to an ornately framed watercolor, which was mounted on the wall directly ahead of her. It looked old. Ancient. Probably by some master—Aubrey would know which one. "That looks real."

"Mom likes to hang her expensive pieces where she can impress everyone who walks through the door."

"Me, too. We have a cross-stitch welcome sign hanging in our entry. Aubrey did it last winter. It's a total classic. We've had offers."

What was it about her that made even visiting his mother fun? He set the cake on the antique table against the wall.

"Did you really grow up here?"

There was that little furrow between her eyes again, a sign she was puzzled. So, he hoped, did she see what he wanted her to see? Most people who walked through the door were impressed by Monet and the imported marble. There were no family pictures framed and hung on the walls. No cross-stitched sign welcoming guests. No hints of love or comfort anywhere.

A maid in a black uniform hurried discreetly toward them. "Master Brice. Happy birthday! Let me take your things. The family is in the rec room. Dinner will be served promptly at seven."

"Thanks, Wilma. This is Ava. And here is the cake."

"Oh, well done. I'll get this to the kitchen." The tidy lady hurried off with efficient speed.

Ava knew she was gaping. Okay, call her intimidated now. What she had already seen of Brice's life was a neon sign they weren't compatible; *this* was a billboard framed in blinking red lights. "She took my purse and your gift."

"She's supposed to." Brice looked amused as he guided her through a cavernous formal living room filled with rich polished woods and upholstered velvet and toward a slowly downward winding staircase.

No way was this a *home*. It was too perfect to relax in, and there was no feeling of love or life. From the expensive imported carpets to the vase that looked like it came from ancient China. Where did his parents put up their feet at the end of a long day and watch television? And there wasn't a book anywhere. Not even a Bible. The rooms, stuffed with expensive furniture, felt vacant and hollow. There was no heart. No warmth.

This was Brice's childhood home? No way could she imagine children growing up here. Well, not the way she would want to raise children anyway. With noise and friendly chaos.

Their footsteps echoed in the coved ceilings overhead, just like they would in a museum.

"Everyone's downstairs." Brice took her hand, his gaze and his touch were more than tender. It felt as if he cherished her. Being cherished by Brice Donovan was just about the best thing she could wish for, but with every step she took, she wondered how this could possibly last.

Voices grew in volume as they descended the grand staircase and arrived in a slightly less formal version of the living room. Four people rose from stiff, uncomfortable-looking couches. Brice's parents and grandparents stopped in mid-conversation to stare at her.

During the few seconds of awkward silence, she felt Brice's hand tighten on hers. Tension rolled through her. The sudden silence felt uncomfortable. So did the hard way Brice's mother studied her.

Okay, she could see the mistake right away. She was wearing purple. Everyone else was dressed in sedate colors. Navy. Black. Beige. She stuck out like a grape Popsicle. Her dress wasn't floor length, her hair wasn't swept up and sedate. She wore her cross and not ten-thousand-dollar pearls—not that she had any or wanted to have any.

It was too late to rethink the wardrobe. The important question was whether Brice thought bringing her was a definite mistake?

"Everyone, this is Ava McKaslin," he said in that warm baritone of his.

Since her knees were a little wobbly, she took care stepping forward so she didn't trip as Brice introduced her to his parents.

"It's good to meet you." Brice's father, Roger, stuck out his hand.

She hoped her palm wasn't too damp. Oops. Nerves. She wanted her grip to be firm enough for him. She met his gaze, and she realized he had Brice's eyes. And they were warm and kind.

"I understand you designed our Chloe's wedding cake. That was beautiful. Everyone said so," Roger Donovan said stiffly, as if he were uncomfortable, too. "Chloe comes back from her honeymoon tomorrow. I'm sure she will tell you herself how happy she was with it."

"Thanks. It's very nice to meet you." Her voice hardly wobbled at all. Whew. That went pretty well. Considering.

"And this is my mom, Lynn. I know you've already met."

Lynn Donovan nodded once, a curt bob that was barely an acknowledgment. "I understand you're designing Carly Frost's wedding cake. Maxime and her oldest daughter were just telling me today how pleased she is so far."

"That's nice to hear. I'm glad they're happy."

"Hmm." The woman managed to make that sound seem judgmental, and said nothing more. She pursed her lips and stared hard at Ava, as if she didn't like what she was seeing.

Okay, this wasn't going as well. Ava took a rattling breath, feeling more and more unsure. Until Brice's hand engulfed hers, and his touch was a steady anchor of comfort and reassurance.

"Hello, to both of you." His grandmother looked elegant in her designer pantsuit. She crossed the length of the room, arms out, and pulled him into a quick hug. "Happy birthday, young man."

"I'm glad you could make it." Brice kissed her cheek. "How was your flight home?"

"The usual. Lines. Customs. Only one lost piece of

luggage. An improvement from the trip over." Merriment twinkled in her eyes and she grasped Ava by the hands. "Ava, dear girl, how is your grandmother? Mary and I have been playing phone tag for the last few months."

"Gran is fine, or so I hear. I haven't spoken to her for the last few weeks, but she's scheduled to call soon. I'll tell her that you were asking after her."

"Tell her I demand she calls me."

"I'll tell her. It is good to see you again, Ann. And you, too, sir."

Brice couldn't believe it. He curled his hand around the nape of her neck, tenderly pulling her closer. "Okay, how do you know my grandparents?"

"We met at my Grandpop's funeral, although it's been a few years now," she explained. "I'm glad to see you are both well."

"As right as rain." Gram clasped her hands together as if in prayer. "How wonderful that you are with us here tonight, dear. To think you and Brice are dating."

"I'm afraid that's just a rumor. I suppose it will never stop if I keep hanging out with him."

"Oh, you have your grandmother's sense of humor." It was plain to see that Gram already adored Ava. "I hear you've brought the cake tonight. Something special for our Brice. Now, we'll know just how much she's fallen in love with him when the cake is unveiled. What fun."

"I'm afraid it's not what you're expecting." Ava rolled her eyes in that way he loved so much. "Brice requested the cake, so if you don't like it you have to blame him. I'm the completely innocent baker."

Ann and her husband, Silas, laughed pleasantly, as if they understood completely. Except for the fact that Brice's parents were staring at her as if she were their worst dream come true, the evening was going great.

The maid lady chose that moment to announce the salad was ready and to come to the table. She caught Lynn's coolly assessing gaze and thought, uh-oh. But the minute his big hand closed over hers, she felt cherished all over again.

"See? They love you," he whispered in her ear.

She might not be so sure, but he looked happy and she wouldn't jeopardize that for anything.

"Did I tell you how beautiful you look?" he whispered again, hanging back to let the others head upstairs first.

"Not recently."

"On a scale of one to ten, you're a two hundred. A definite Miss Perfect."

Whatever you do, Ava, she warned herself, *don't fall in love with him.*

But it was too late.

Seated at his place at the mammoth dining room table, Brice couldn't believe how great dinner was going. Okay, Mom wasn't as warm to Ava as he would have wished for, but she was doing pretty well considering. There had been no comments, bold or veiled, that could hurt Ava's feelings. It mattered to him that his mom was keeping her promise.

His dad, he could tell, thought she had it together. He'd quizzed Ava about her business plan, while

Granddad had added his advice, and they both pronounced her plans financially sensible and well done.

Ava smiled in that sweet way of hers, winning his heart all over again, thanking Wilma as the maid cleared her plate.

Powerful love for her hit him like a punch to his chest. He couldn't breathe, couldn't feel his heart beating. He could see only her. Be aware of only her. Seconds stretched into eternity and it was scary, this all-consuming love for her. Scary, but right.

He knew she was the right woman for him. The real question was: Did she feel the same way about him?

"Excuse me," Ava said in her cheerful way, "but I'd better help set up the cake."

"Oh, the cake!" Gram clasped her hands together in anticipation. "This I have to see."

"I hope it's chocolate, like Chloe's wedding cake," Granddad commented.

His mother's lips pursed tight; but thank the Lord she kept her opinions to herself. Brice's heart swelled with love for his mom. He was proud of her. He knew how hard it was for her to keep her promise to him. Catching her gaze, he nodded his silent thanks, and some of the tension eased from around her mouth. He knew it was going to be okay.

"Yes, it's chocolate." Ava bounced up from her chair. "But this is a different recipe than I used with Chloe's cake. This is more like fudge. I call it my triple chocolate dream cake."

Granddad grinned. "I like the sound of that."

"He has a terrible sweet tooth." Gram shook her head, as if in great disapproval, but there was no mistaking the depth of love alight in her eyes. "What am I going to do with you, Silas?"

"Just love me for who I am, I guess," Granddad grinned at her.

Across the table, Brice recognized that loving glance his grandfather gave his grandmother and understood it for what it was truly, for the first time. Not merely love, but a breadth of love that happened to a man, if he was blessed, once in a lifetime. And he had to be brave enough to grab hold of that rare blessing and not let go, no matter how scary it was.

Opening himself up to love and hurt and rejection again was tough. But truly, Brice realized as Ava pushed in her chair, her purple skirt swirling, his heart had already made the choice.

Ava was his everything. He knew it, soul deep. He wanted to spend the rest of his life loving her, protecting her, cherishing her.

She took two steps and then turned to give him a death-ray glare. "From your chair, I think you can see part of the kitchen, and you are not supposed to see the cake until it's ready. No peeking. Got it?"

"Yes, ma'am."

"I see that twinkle in your eye. You're thinking about peeking."

"If I was, you've made me change my mind."

"Oh, *sure* I did." Was it so wrong that she wanted this to be a surprise? She'd worked really hard on his cake, just for him. She'd wanted him to be happy with it. As she headed to the kitchen, it occurred to her that making him happy was taking top priority on her list of the most important things in life, and how scary was that?

With every step she took through the magnificent house, she felt more and more out of place. Sure, his family had gone out of their way to extend their warmth to her, and she was grateful for that, but did that help all the bad feelings that kept wanting to bubble up like lava into a volcano's dome?

No. Not a bit. The pressure was building, and there was nothing she could do about it. She smiled at Wilma, who was busy setting down the cake plates in a totally fancy china pattern, and fetched the bakery box from its spot on the counter.

"Let me set out the cake," the maid lady said, as if possessive of her job.

"Oh, I want to make sure it's perfect. I'll just unbox it, then."

"Very well."

As Ava carefully picked up the box and moved it out of Brice's sight, she felt the tangible stroke of his gaze like a tender caress to her cheek. Pure sweetness filled her heart, and she did her best to hold back every feeling. Every caring emotion. Every piece of growing affection she had for this man.

She stood frozen, his loving glance holding her in place like a tractor beam.

Don't let yourself fall any more in love with him, Ava. She gulped hard and forced her foot forward. It took a few more steps and then she was safely out of his sight. But out of the tractor-pull of his feelings?

Of course not. She felt the pressure building in the center of her chest, like the rising dome of that volcano about to blow. She felt little and plain and very purple in her dress, in this enormous kitchen that was roughly the size of her apartment. She could see into the next room—some kind of solarium thingy, with rich-looking imported carpets and antiques and more paintings on the walls—probably from some master she knew nothing about.

This was Brice's life, she realized. This was where he grew up, this was his childhood home, he'd had maids and probably nannies and, as she heard the conversation drift in from the dining room, he was intelligently discussing the summer symphony series.

She felt the first crack in her heart as she lifted the lid of the box. Even so, there was no way to stop her love for him as it brightened in intensity. No way to hold it back. She didn't even know she could hold so much love inside her, but there it was, an infinite amount, welling up right along with the building pressure of the truth. The truth she could no longer deny.

Brice *was* Mr. Perfect. But not *her* Mr. Perfect.

The first stroke of agony burned like fiery lava licking at the edge of her heart. Who knew doom would fall so quietly? The only sounds were the muted clink of Wilma counting out the silver-and-gold-plated dessert forks and the pleasant murmur of voices discussing Beethoven from the next room.

All she had to do was to lean a little to the right, and she had a clear view of him. Of Brice, looking like a magazine cover model in his designer suit, the Ivy League educated, successful son of one of the oldest and richest families in Montana. Mr. Eligible Bachelor, who looked comfortable in this museum of a house.

This wasn't the Brice she'd come to know and, sadly, to love.

Ava felt another crack slice through her heart. She lifted the cake carefully onto the counter. She looked at it now through different eyes. She'd put her heart into doing her best job for Brice.

The big blue and red dump truck was parked in the middle of the cake board she'd decorated to look like a dirt and gravel road, made of sugar paste and crumbled chocolate cookies, tacked with sugar glue and sprinkled with edible gold sparkles, to jazz it up. A construction driver was tucked behind a steering wheel. D&M Construction was spelled out in silver script on the door. The bed of the truck was mounded high with gray boulders, which were individuals bites of iced cake.

Her best dump truck cake ever, and it didn't seem that way now. It wasn't right.

She wasn't right.

Brice's mother tapped into the kitchen and blinked, as if she were totally confused. "That's a cake?"

Yeah, just as she'd thought. Ava took a steadying breath and wished she was centered enough for a quick prayer, too, but she wasn't. "It's what Brice wanted."

"Yes, I can see that."

"I know, it looks really close to the real toy, doesn't it? But trust me, everything is edible."

"It's certainly…interesting." Lynn was apparently struggling for something complimentary to say.

But there was no denying the truth, not anymore. She lovingly slid the elegant white candle that had been laid out by Wilma into the center of the cab's roof. Just one candle, that was all, and it looked out of place on the cake.

She thought of the bright yellow number three and one candles she'd brought for the cake, and decided to leave them where they were—in the back of the bakery box. Lynn Donovan didn't look as if she'd ever used novelty candles. Only classy all the way.

Which was probably why the woman had such a pained look on her face. "Brice will be pleased with this, I'm sure," she said stiffly.

Ava caught sight of Brice through the archway, leaning to speak with his grandfather. Her heart cracked a third and final time. She'd been right all along. There was no way this could work.

"You see it, too, don't you?" Lynn said quietly. "He's really a good man. He deserves the very best of everything, don't you agree?"

Yes. Her entire soul moved with that word. She wanted the best of everything for Brice, too. But the man she watched could have been a stranger. Sure, he looked like the Brice she'd fallen for, but the man she knew was a craftsman. He made beauty with wood with skill, discipline and heart. He loved fast-food nachos and drank strawberry milk. He had a sometimes well-behaved dog, an easygoing manner that made her feel comfortable with him, and a sense of humor that made her feel lighter than air.

But *this* Brice, he was the real thing, honest hardworking guy and the most eligible bachelor all wrapped up into one. He was so perfect, that was his flaw. She'd finally found it. She'd known all along this relationship couldn't work, didn't she? But did she listen to her experience, to that little voice inside her head, to the ironclad no-man, no-date policy that was supposed to keep her from being hurt like this again?

No. She was foolish to think that there could be a Mr. Perfect for her. She always fell in love with the wrong men, and there was no man more wrong for her than Brice Donovan.

She was vaguely aware of Lynn ordering Wilma around, of being herded back to the table, of seeing the anticipation on Brice's handsome face as she slipped into her chair. But her mind was in a fog. Her heart was a total mess. Somehow she had to hold it together.

Ann gasped when Wilma entered, carrying the cake. "Oh, that's delightful. Simply *adorable*."

Her praise felt like a blow from a boxer's glove, as kind as those words were. Ava swallowed hard against the lump rising in her throat. She had to hold down her negative thoughts and keep them from blowing over.

"That looks like the real toy," Silas said in wonder. "I can't believe that's a cake. Is it really a cake?"

"It's a real cake, Granddad," Brice spoke up. "And I bet everything on it is delicious."

"That's not real dirt, is it?" Lynn asked in distress.

"It's crumbled chocolate cookies," Ava explained gently.

His beautiful, precious Ava. He saw all the love she'd put into his birthday cake. The D&M Construction logo on the door. The dog seated beside the driver inside the little cab. The detailing that had to have taken hours. She'd done this for him.

One look at her and he was hooked like a fish on a line. He loved her without condition, without end. She sat across from him, and the expanse of the table might separate them, but he could feel the connection of love strengthening between them.

"I've never seen anything like this," his dad said from the head of the table. "You have a talent, Ava."

"It's not hard at all. You'd be surprised how easy it can be. And fun, too."

"Can you make other things, besides trucks?" Granddad asked.

Ava bit her lip, looking as sweet as sugar icing. "Well, I just did a ballet shoe the other day. That was a first for me, but I've done all sorts of things. Everything from football cakes to a medieval castle."

"I'll ask for the medieval castle for my next birthday," Brice told her.

She beamed her beautiful smile at him, the one that gleamed like a little dream.

I'm in big trouble, he thought. Just when he'd thought he was so in love with her, he'd fallen as far as he could go, he fell a little more in love with her. As his dad started the first notes of "Happy Birthday" and everyone joined in, he didn't have to wonder what he would wish for: Ava.

She was his dream come true.

Chapter Fourteen

Brice pulled the car to a stop in a spot marked for visitors, in the shade of tall poplars that lined the grassy lawn of her apartment complex. Ava knew he was going to ask her what was wrong, and what was she going to say? That she'd done it again. It was all her fault. She'd brought this misery down on herself.

"Thanks for coming," he said, breaking the silence between them. "I hope my mom wasn't too much. She comes across a little sharp, but she's a softy down deep. My grandparents love you. I think you've got lifelong customers. Granddad wants to order a cake for his birthday next month. You might want to start thinking up something with a golf theme."

"I'll get right on it." Her voice sounded strained, but it was harder than she thought to hold back so much pain. The thing was, when you'd been struck by misfortune as much as she'd been, you learned to cope. There was that first initial hit that hurt deep, but then shock set in and it didn't hurt so much. You could figure out how to cope until the shock wore off. And she was just about there. She could feel the press of hot, sharp emotions slicing through the defensive layers of her heart. The burn of tears gathered in her throat, rising up, too.

"Why do you look so unhappy?" He studied her, leaning closer, his gaze tender with concern.

"I'm not unhappy." That was the truth, she told herself stubbornly. She wasn't unhappy; it was much, much worse. She'd known better, but here she was with the wrong man. And here she was, exactly where she tried to avoid being, clutching every shard of her broken wishes. Why had she done this to herself? She'd known from the start this would happen. She should have listened to the fears inside her heart and resisted his kindness and his charm and his affection.

Then again, how would she have resisted caring for Brice? He was perfect. A thousand on a scale of ten.

"Did something happen I don't know about? My mother was unkind to you." He said it as if he'd expected her to be.

"No, she was fine. The problem is all me. It's me. Just like it always is."

"How could that be possible? You're perfect to me."

His words were the final blow, echoing around the damaged chambers of her heart. Agony clawed through her, so sharp and deep she squeezed her eyes shut against the physical tangible pain. How could a feeling hurt so much?

"Perfect? *That's* the problem. You just can't see it yet. You can't see me yet. And if tonight didn't do it, then I don't know what will."

"What are you talking about? Whatever it is, I can fix it. Just tell me."

Wouldn't you know it? She'd finally found a good man, a more-than-stellar man, and he was still the wrong man for her. How was he going to fix that? He couldn't see, yet, that this wouldn't work out. It couldn't. There was absolutely no way.

She was never going to be anyone other than someone who lost her keys, who liked the color purple, who liked cross-stitch on the wall instead of fine art. She didn't belong in his world.

She was doing them both a favor, cutting their losses now. Before they fell even more in love. Think how devastating that would be, right? Because every day she spent with him, she loved him more. So think what he would come to mean to her in a year. In two. How much more would it hurt her heart then, when it finally hit him that she wasn't the woman he'd made her out to be?

He deserved the right woman. The woman he thought she was. The woman he expected her to be. Since her vision was blurring, she released the seat belt while she could still see. The thunk of it sliding into place behind the seat hid the sob that caught in her throat.

"Are you crying?" Brice sounded distressed.

"Nope." If she could blink the tears away, then she *couldn't* be crying. Really. Even if the burning behind her eyes was getting worse.

"You look like you're crying."

"L-looks can be d-deceiving." She groped to find the door handle.

His hand caught her wrist, holding her in place. Why did the affection she felt in his touch feel like the final straw? The tears she'd held back so carefully leaked one by one down her face.

"Okay, I might not know what's going on," he said, "but this isn't right. Did I do something?"

She shook her head, more tears rolling down her face.

"Did I say something?" She shook her head again, leaving him at a total loss. He felt his chest crack with pain for her. "Ava, please tell me what's wrong. I can't fix it if I don't know what is broken."

"Oh, see how awesome you are?" She choked on a sob. "You just don't see it, do you? This just can't work. I mean, hello? I told you from the start. I'm a romantic disaster. I always pick the wrong man, and now there's you. What am I going to do about you?"

His thoughts were going in different directions, and his guts were telling him she was about to break up with him. It was his experience that women who were happy with you generally didn't sob like that. He could feel her emotionally pushing him away, although she hadn't moved a muscle. "Wait a minute. I'm not the wrong man. Why are you saying that?"

"B-because it's the truth."

"It can't be the truth." Tenderness filled him, and a love so deep that it couldn't be measured. "Because I *know* this is right."

Did she have any idea all the vulnerability he saw in her big violet-blue eyes? That he could feel the worry and fears in her heart? That he could hear the unspoken agony she hadn't spoken aloud? He thought not, so he said it for her: "I love you. Just the way you are. I love that you forget your keys and know how to make a dump truck cake and that you always make the sunshine seem brighter, the world better, *my* world better."

She didn't answer. It didn't look as if she could, her hand at her throat, her eyes bright with emotion. He knew what she needed to hear. He knew he'd been holding back the truth in his heart, and now was the time to lay it on the line. He knew how much his reassurance meant to her. They were linked emotionally, spiritually; he'd known she was special to him from the beginning. She was heaven sent.

It was hard to find just the right words, so he went with what was in his heart. "I love you, Ava. This is the real thing. I'm very serious about you. You have to know that I'm in this forever. That one day, I'm going to get down on one knee and ask you to be my wife."

Her eyes widened in unmistakable fear. Fear. He hurt for her. Yeah, he understood exactly how that felt to be so terrified, but he was taking the risk. "This is the only way to get past the panic. You have to take that leap, Ava. You have to look at the man I am, and the promises I've made and have already kept and believe that I will be that man for you. Forever."

Her lower lip trembled. "See, that's what scared me. And if I'm this scared, it has to be a sign, right? That this is never going to work. Love ends, and I have to be smart about this."

"No, you're being scared. I can feel it, Ava. I can feel your heart, and right now, I'm sure in a way I've never been. Because I can feel how much you love me and how terrified you are."

"Yeah. I'm afraid for a reason. This is all wrong, and my heart is going to be totally devastated when you figure out that I'm just me. Just Ava."

"Just Ava? See, that's where you're wrong. You are my everything. My dream come true."

"*That* is why it can't work." She pulled away from him, when everything within him longed to draw her closer. Misery marked her face and shadowed her eyes. Sobs tore apart her words. "But this is better than you deciding down the road that I'm not what you want. That's what happened to my parents, you know. I watched it happen. I m-made it happen. Love isn't always enough."

"But—"

"No, don't say it." She stumbled out of the seat to get away from him, but he was saying it anyway.

"I want *you*, Ava."

She truly believed that he loved her. She only had to look at him to know that his love for her was deep. She felt so close to him she could sense his soul as if it were her own, and she could feel his love for her there, a love without measure.

But without end? That was the question. And she feared it had a different answer. If only she could peek into the future and know for sure, then she could find a way to think clearly past the fear overtaking her.

Love wasn't always enough.

That's why she did what she had to do. To be smart about this. To be logical. To hold it together. She could keep calm, hold her heart still, and keep her emotions frozen. She *would*. Really. She just had to make it as far as her apartment—she was almost there—and *then* she could fall apart. Into a hundred thousand tiny pieces, but not here. Not now. Not in front of Brice.

How did she put all that he meant to her in a few parting words? She was clueless. Panic blinded her. Fear gathered like a hurricane in her stomach. It felt like disaster striking one more time as she took a step away from the car. How could the action meant to save her from pain—to save them both from terrible pain—feel like the worst mistake ever?

Because you're afraid, Ava. She took another step back, not at all sure if she could keep going. What she knew for sure was that she could not reach out to him. The hurricane of fear in her stomach began to gust, like the edge of the storm hitting shore.

The plea in Brice's dark eyes, the sadness settling into his handsome face, the sincerity of his good soul, felt like the summer heat on her skin. It just went to show the power of this bond—at least on her side— and how much she stood to lose, to be hurt.

Walking away was the best choice. There would be no happily-ever-after ending for her. True love didn't exist for a girl like her. And if it did, would she take the chance to find out?

That made her step falter. There was Brice, climbing out of his car, coming for her. And she could feel his love for her—he was sincere. He did love her. But how did she tell him she was afraid it wasn't enough? That one day he would look at her and see a disappointment.

Lord, please help me, here. Show me that I'm doing the right thing. Please, I'm begging You. She took another step back, she'd chosen a direction and she had to stay on it. She needed the strong safety net of her faith, of her stable life, of the path she'd stepped off of when Brice had walked into her life.

Her cell chirped and vibrated in her little pocket-book. Saved by her family. The Lord worked in mysterious ways. She dug the phone out and flipped it open without even looking at the screen. She could feel that it was one of her sisters. Hopefully not calling to ask how the dinner with Brice's parents went.

"Ava?"

She didn't recognize the woman's thin and strained voice. She glanced at the caller screen. It was her step-sister's cell number. That couldn't be right, could it? The woman did not sound like Danielle.

"I—I'm so glad I caught you." Danielle choked out a sob. "Katherine's up hiking in the mountains with Jack, and she's out of range. Aubrey isn't picking up. I know you're probably in the middle of dessert or something, but c-can you come?"

"Absolutely." Ava felt her strength kick in. Now she knew why she'd felt as if doom was about to strike. "Come where? What's wrong?"

"It's *J-Jonas*. He's been sh-shot."

"Shot?" Shock washed through her. Jonas was shot? That didn't seem possible. She thought of her tall, kindly brother-in-law who always seemed so invincible. "You mean he was working tonight?"

"Y-yes. He's c-covering for someone on vacation, and—" Another sob broke her voice. "I'm at the hospital and there's no one to t-take the k-kids."

"I'll do it. Is Jonas going to be okay?"

"They d-don't kn-ow. Please c-come."

"I'm on my way." She snapped shut the phone. Okay,

talk about a sign. There was Brice, watching her with concern in his eyes. So big and strong, everything within her ached for his strong arms around her. She longed for the safe harbor of his love.

How did she know that his promises were real? That she wasn't letting her fears rule her life? How did you know if a love would last? Well, she'd asked for the Lord to show her the way, and this was it. Her family was what mattered, the people she'd been able to love and trust all of her life. Not some romantic dream.

For a breathless moment their gazes met and she felt his empathy, his concern for her never wavering, steadily pulling her closer like a tractor beam.

How did she give in? How did she walk away? Panic crashed like a storm, stealing her breath, leaving her ice-cold in the brazen heat. As afraid as she was to walk away and lose him forever, she was more terrified of really leaning on him. Of really trusting him.

"This is for the best," she said. "Family is everything. I think that when you love someone, you truly love them. That it's like the Bible says: *'Love never gives up, never loses faith, is always hopeful, and endures through every circumstance.'* That's not what I think we have."

She watched the pain fill his eyes, and she hated that she was hurting him. But it was for the best. It was the right thing to do. You couldn't go into a serious relationship already knowing it couldn't work.

And if that was her fear talking, then maybe that was for the best, too. Because how could a man as truly wonderful as Brice love her that way?

"Did you say that Jonas was shot?"

Somewhere in the dim recesses of her brain she remembered Danielle saying Jonas and Brice had volunteered together once. So it was only normal human concern behind his question. Somehow, she made her voice answer. "Yes. He was covering someone's shift tonight, I guess, and that's all I know. I promised my sister. I have to go."

"I'll drive you." He held out his hand, palm up, looking as valiant as a knight of legend, one of good deeds and of good heart and she was hopeless.

Never in her life had she wanted something so much as to place her hand in his. To throw caution to the wind and trust that everything would be fine. That he was right—twenty years down the road they would be together and happy. That they could survive the rift of his mother's disapproval, unlike her own parents could have done.

But it wasn't logical. It wasn't smart. It wasn't safe. She took another step back. *It will only end in heartache,* that little voice within her said. And if there was a part of her that knew she was really afraid, she couldn't listen to it. "I'll drive myself. I can't be with you. You are great, you have made such a difference in my life, but I think real love is like a special kind of heaven on earth. It shouldn't hurt like this. It just shouldn't be this frightening."

"Ava, wait. You wanted to know if this was the real thing, if we had a shot at a real happiness together. I'm pretty sure we do. But we'll never really know if you walk away. Don't you want to find out?"

"I already know." She hauled her key ring out of her purse and the first deepening rays of the setting sun brushed her with a rare magenta light, that shone like heaven's light. "Goodbye, Brice."

He couldn't say anything. He stood there like he was made of granite, despair filling him, watching her hurry the rest of the short distance to the covered parking. She slipped from his sight, and he felt the first fall of grief. The hard ball of it burned in his throat. Was he really losing her? How could she be so sure?

There was no way. Because he could see a different path. A different outcome. As intimidating as it was to be given this singular blessing of true love, he was more afraid of spending his life without her as his wife. Without her sparkle and her life and her brightness lighting the rest of his days.

He couldn't believe he'd lost her.

Chapter Fifteen

After saying about ten prayers for Jonas on the drive over, Ava couldn't keep thoughts of Brice away. He might be out of sight, but not totally from her mind. His words kept troubling her. *You wanted to know if this was the real thing, if we had a shot at a real happiness together. I'm pretty sure we do. But we'll never really know if you walk away.*

Hey, it wasn't her fault, she thought as she drove up to the parking garage and snapped a ticket out of the automatic dispenser. She dropped the ticket on the dash and waited for the red-and-white-striped arm to lift. If her vision was blurring again, it was just from being so tired. Really.

Not because she felt as if there was an enormous void in the center of her rib cage, where her heart used to be. And as she pulled into the closest space by the doors and took the elevator to the main lobby, that void began to fill with bleak misery.

You did the right thing, she told herself as she took another bank of elevators to the intensive care floor.

She wasn't going to set herself up for more doom. She wasn't the right girl for Brice. No matter how much she wanted to be.

As soon as the doors opened she popped out into the echoing corridor and headed down an endless hall with closed doors. She followed the directional signs, struggling to keep tight control of her feelings. She was here for Danielle, she was here for her family, where she belonged, where she was accepted, where she was safe.

Safe. That was the word that was haunting her. She felt the tangle of emotions ball up tight in her chest, growing tighter and tighter, sheer misery. Pain throbbed between her ribs, making it hard to breathe. Almost as if she were sobbing, which she wasn't, of course. Really.

She could do this, she could hold everything down, because if she didn't, she wasn't sure she was strong enough to hold back the tidal wave of sheer agony. How could she feel so alone without him? She'd been alone before, she'd managed just fine without Brice Donovan by her side. And if she needed him, then she'd learn to get past it.

Pain arched through her as if she'd broken a rib. It was only heartache. Although nothing like she'd ever known before. Because she'd never loved any man before the way she loved Brice. The way she still loved Brice. She didn't want to love him, she didn't think it was smart to love him. She didn't fit into his life, not really, and why start on a road you knew would end?

Okay, so she didn't *know* it would end. She was just terrified, but wasn't Brice right? If she could see through the blur of panic long enough to think clearly, she had to admit he was totally right. You didn't know unless you gave something a chance.

The truth? He terrified her. Absolutely. Positively. Without condition and without end. She was too chicken to hand over her heart to the one man who really wanted it. Because she was too terrified that he might get a really good look at her and stop loving her. That he'd see who she was deep down, at heart, at the bottom of her soul, he'd stop loving her.

Love ends, she knew it. Wasn't that the lesson of her childhood?

Yeah, that frustrating little voice inside her argued, *but it's not the only lesson, right?*

Right. She was afraid because she'd never been here before. Brice wasn't just Mr. Perfect, he was *her* Mr. Perfect. Exactly like a dream the angels had found in her heart and made real. She didn't have any reason at all to find fault with him and push him away. She was out of excuses. Out of options. Had she been picking boyfriends who weren't good enough so she didn't have to be right here, where it was so scary? Because the relationships had always ended, she'd be able to retreat back to her safe life, with her sisters and her lifelong job at the family bookstore. No risks. No failures. No pain.

Brice was different. That's why he made her feel all these things she hadn't had to experience before. Like being so vulnerable it was as if she were inching out onto a tiny little limb hanging way out over the Grand Canyon. With every move she could feel the limb sinking downward, getting ready to snap beneath her weight.

And like the scared little seven-year-old inside her,

she'd jumped right off that limb onto the safe earth. Brice was right. If she stayed here, she would never know if the limb would break beneath her weight or if it would support her across the void.

Then she saw Danielle in the intensive care waiting room, her elbows on her knees, her face buried in her hands, sobbing, and Ava forgot everything but comforting her sister. Her heart broke at the strangled sound of Danielle's muffled sobs. As she came closer, she noticed a smaller room off to the side, where a volunteer was trying to read to the munchkins.

Tyler saw her first. "Aunt Ava! I wanna go home."

"That's why I'm here, cutie." As heavy as he was, she scooped him up and gave him a hard hug. She didn't even want to think about what would happen to this little boy if his daddy wasn't okay. Madison was fussing in the volunteer's lap, a pleasant-looking grandmother type who had a sad smile as she put the book away and stood, taking care with the miserable little girl.

"You go help the nice lady with your sister, okay?" Ava set Tyler back down and smoothed his hair. "I gotta talk to your mom for a sec. Then we'll go by and get pepperoni pizza because you know that helps to make anything a little better."

Tyler nodded, swiped at his eyes with his sleeve and bravely went to help his sister like the good big brother that he was.

Ava's heart broke when she knelt down beside Danielle. She'd never seen her stepsister like this, her hair was tousled and her face streaked with tears. She simply wrapped her in a hug, feeling her heartache and terror. She couldn't bear to think about what Dani's future would be like without her beloved Jonas. With her great love lost.

Okay, she wasn't going to *take* that as a sign from above, because it wasn't. Really. She released Dani and fetched a full box of tissues, since the box on the table beside her was empty. "Any word?"

Dani shook her head. "He's still in surgery."

"That's gotta be good, right? He's hanging in there. And he has you and the kids to fight for. I've been praying on the way over. Do you want to pray together now? You'll feel better."

"Praying is all I've been doing. I feel terrible interrupting you tonight. Where's Brice?"

That was Dani, always thinking about everyone but herself. "Don't worry about that. I want to know what I can do for you. To make this easier for you."

"Oh, Ava." Dani wiped at more tears. "Nothing but Jonas being just fine is going to make me okay. Do you know what I've been thinking about? I can't get out of my mind how I complained at him this morning. How he wasn't home enough, he wasn't supporting me with the kids enough, that I didn't feel as if he were really listening to me about the hedges needing trimming, and I was so *mad* at him. Just mad. How stupid was that?"

At the misery on Dani's face, Ava's heart broke even more, impossibly, as if there was enough of it to break again. "I know you. You weren't that bad. You couldn't have been. You adore Jonas."

"I do. But if he passes away, then the last thing I said to him was selfish and unkind. And I was just tired, that was all, but it doesn't change what I said. That when I should have reached out to him, when I should have asked how he was feeling, why he was preoccupied, if there was something I could do for him, I pushed him away. And—" a sob tore through her words "—I just can't bear it."

"Shh, he knows how much you really love him. Dani, don't cry harder. We'll put it in prayer, all right?" She took her sister's hands, so cold, and cradled them in hers. *"Dear heavenly Father, please—"*

Even in prayer, she could feel Brice's presence, washing over her like a sign from above. *"—please watch over Jonas in surgery and let him know that we love him, especially Dani, who is hurting so much. Please ease her worries, and bring Jonas back safe to us. In Your name, Amen."*

Like grace, peace washed through her. She opened her eyes to see Brice, with Madison cradled in one strong arm and Tyler's hand tucked trustingly in his much larger one.

He was such a good man. At heart. Of character. Decent to the core. Seeing him again made every vulnerable piece of her spirit long for his love. She wished she could go back and find the clue that would show her this relationship between them would have worked out right.

That was the real issue, wasn't it? That she was terrified that she wasn't enough. That any man—even one as sincere and incredible as Brice—could love her enough to weather any storm to come. She'd watched her parents' marriage crumble, and she never wanted to feel like that again. But how was the pain of not being able to love him, of not ever having the chance to be his wife, any better than never being able to love him at all?

"If it would help you out, I can take charge of the kids," he said. "Get them home and some dinner in them. Ava, I know you were going to do this, but no one else is here to be with Danielle. You should stay with her and let me do this for you."

Was she capable of speech like a normal person? No-oo. She just stared at him, falling in love with him all over again. Was it smart?

No. Was it sensible?

No. But could she stop it?

No.

The strength of her love for him overwhelmed her, filled with the blazing light of a hundred galaxies, so bright that it changed how she saw him. She now looked at him in a way she'd been too afraid of before. Through the eyes of her heart, through her deepest dreams and into her future. Where there was only a love for him so strong, that it felt as if nothing could defeat it. Nothing could break it.

She could see that happily-ever-after dream of hers, and it was within her reach. All she had to do was to accept it. She'd never realized how terrifying it was to be so vulnerable and to have a dream come true. It was so much to accept. So much to treasure. So much to lose.

So much to lose.

She understood better Danielle's agony. From a deeper place. Life was uncertain; anything or everything could change in a moment. She'd spent her life being afraid of that moment, of losing everything, that she'd lived her life to protect herself from what Danielle was feeling at this moment.

But was that how she wanted to live? To spend her years protecting her heart and her life from loss? How could there be any goodness in that? There would be no love and no joy. What if Brice was right? His words came back to her, and she knew, when their gazes met and held, that he was thinking this, too.

If she walked away now, she would never know. Maybe never knowing would be a greater sorrow than finding out what could ever be.

"Thanks, Brice. That would be great."

He didn't need to say anything, she knew he understood. They had things to say to one another, but not here. Not now.

"Let me give you my house key." She pulled her ring out of the pocket and removed the key with trembling fingers.

When she handed it to him, their fingers touched and peace filled the empty places in her soul. It was love, his love, that made her believe.

"Thank you," she whispered, because she had no voice.

"Anything for you, sunshine."

She believed him. She watched him walk away, remembering the Scripture she'd quoted to him. *Love never gives up, never loses faith, is always hopeful and endures through every circumstance.* It was all him, she realized. He was the man who embodied that verse. Who had a heart big enough and a character true enough to never give up, never lose faith and endure through everything.

And then, she realized, so did she.

"Brice is such a good man," Danielle said on a sob. "Sometimes you just don't realize exactly how blessed you are."

"And sometimes you do," Ava said, and knelt down to stick with her sister through the wait ahead.

Brice headed down the hallway, finished checking on the sleeping kids. Although it was nearly six in the morning, he'd been pretty much up all night. He hadn't been able to get a wink of sleep with so much on his mind. With so much left unsaid.

Ava had called around two in the morning to say that Jonas was out of surgery and was touch and go in intensive care. She would be by as soon as she could leave Danielle.

He'd just put the tea water on when he heard the front door creak open. Ava was in the entryway, dropping her purse and keys on the little table there. Exhaustion haunted her face and bruised the delicate skin beneath her eyes, but not outright grief. "He's doing better. Danielle's still with him.

"Good. I've been keeping him in prayer."

"Thank you." She moved aside, and it was hard to read what was in her eyes, what she intended to say, and then he knew why. They weren't alone.

Aubrey stepped in, holding a grocery bag. "Hi, Brice."

"Good morning. Would you two like some tea?"

"That would great, thanks." Ava answered for both of them, taking the sack from Aubrey. The twins exchanged glances and without a word Aubrey slipped down the hallway to check on the kids. Or, more likely, to give them some privacy.

Ava came toward him. "Katherine is at the hospital now, and we're taking turns with Danielle. It was really great of you to do this. It meant she didn't have to worry about her kids, and she wasn't alone until the rest of the family could get there."

"It was my pleasure." Brice came toward her and took the grocery sack from her arms and set it on the counter, so there was nothing between them. Nothing to hide behind. Only the truth of their feelings. "Do you know how devoted to you I am? How sure of my love for you?"

"I'm starting to get the picture."

He would always be devoted to her. Always 10,000 percent committed. Love moved through him of a strength and breadth that knew no bounds. That would never know a limit or an end. "Here is something you should know about me, something I haven't told you yet, but I intend to spend the rest of my life proving this to you. I will never give up on you. I will never lose faith in you. I will never fail you. Even if you ever give up on me, I will still be here. On your side. Come what may. I love you, Ava."

Her heart took a long tumble. Could he be any more wonderful? And wasn't that the scariest thing of all? Because right here standing before her, was every kind of heaven she could dream of having on this earth. Every blessing of love and faith and commitment she could ever wish for, and she would spend the rest of her life cherishing.

Totally scared, and yet more scared of not reaching

for him, she pressed her hand to his, trapping the big curve of his palm against the side of her face. "I love you, Brice. Forever and ever."

"Then you'll marry me, when I get around to asking you properly?"

"Consider it a guarantee. You are my Mr. Wish Come True."

"And you, you are perfect for me, just the way you are, and that is never going to change. Can't you see that?" He looked so vulnerable for such a big man. All heart. All honesty. "You are the sun come into my life. I was in the dark before you."

He smiled. Not the dazzling one she'd so fallen for. Not the one that made his goodness of spirit show in his eyes. But a better one, a deeper one. One she'd never seen before. It was serious, too, and sincere, soul deep.

He leaned closer and then closer still until his mouth slanted over hers. Slowly, his lips brushed hers with a brief, tender reverence. She was so in love all she saw was him. He filled her every sense and every thought. He was the reason for the beat of her heart now and forever. Her Mr. Wish Come True.

Epilogue

The first customer to officially walk through the newly opened bakery door looked very familiar. Ava squinted through the fall of light from the cheerful windows to the broad-shouldered handsome man closing the door behind him. Was he Mr. Perfect or what? Her soul sighed. She closed the cash register drawer, and her engagement diamond glinted in the bright sunshine.

"May I help you?" she asked courteously.

"I sure hope so." Brice Donovan carried a vase of yellow and red rosebuds and placed them on the counter between them. "I've come to check on the progress of my cake."

"Lucky for you, Mr. Wonderful, I just finished boxing up your order."

"Say, you wouldn't want to go get a cup of coffee after all this, would you?"

Call her happy. Why wouldn't she be? She was engaged to the best man in the entire world. Okay, she might be just a little biased when it came to Brice, but only a tad, a dash, a smidgen. "I'll have you know that I'm engaged to be married."

"Lucky guy."

"No, lucky me."

His kiss was the sweetest heaven. The way his love filled her was the best of blessings.

The bell on the door chimed, and more customers tumbled in. Aubrey and Katherine, dressed for work at the bookstore. "It's a little quiet in here," Aubrey said.

Katherine took a look at the two who'd quickly stepped apart and smiled. "And for a good reason. Ava, after you finish my wedding cake, you'd better start on your own."

"I know." They hadn't set a date yet, with Jonas still recovering in the hospital, but they weren't in a serious hurry. They had the rest of their lives together. How amazing was that? "Wait, does this mean you've decided on a design for your wedding cake?"

"Yes. Finally." Katherine beamed her own happiness.

Wasn't this a wonderful world? Okay, so it wasn't perfect, but look at the blessings the Lord gave every day. Love and families and sisters. Hope, dreams to come true and chocolate cake. Lots of chocolate cake.

"The climbing roses design, right? I knew it." Ava rolled her eyes. The door chime rang again.

More customers? Then she recognized Brice's grandmother, Ann, and his mother, Lynn, who was *almost* actually smiling.

"We thought we'd stop by and support your business," Ann explained, pausing to press a kiss to Brice's cheek. "And to pick up some treats for our garden club meeting this afternoon."

"You came to the right place." Delighted, Ava went

to box up a chocolate dream cake, only to have Aubrey step in to do it.

"Go," her twin shooed her away. "Mr. Perfect needs you. I can help out until the teenager gets here."

"Cool. Thanks, Aub." Did she mention what a great blessings sister were? They were absolutely wonderful.

"Come with me," Brice said, taking her by the hand and pulling her into the kitchen. He wanted a moment with her all to himself. He waited until the door swung closed and they were alone before he pulled her into his embrace. It was going to be a long day and would probably be a busy one, and he wanted to say this while he had the chance. "I'm proud of you, sunshine. You know how much I love you, right?"

"Sure, but a girl always likes to hear it on a daily basis."

"I do love you." He cradled her face with his hands, sheer tenderness.

She kissed him sweetly, so happy she was floating like a big helium balloon, but this time there was no doom in sight. How could there be? They were in this together, a team. Between the two of them and with the Lord's help, they could solve any problems that came their way.

"I love you, too," she told him, this man who was her idea of heaven in this imperfect world, and would always be.

Wow, was she turning into an optimist or what?

With joy in her heart, she thanked the good Lord before giving her husband-to-be another sweet kiss.

* * * * *

Dear Reader,

Thank you so much for choosing *Every Kind of Heaven*. I hope you enjoyed Ava's story as much as I did writing it. Ava has learned to expect doom—she's dated a few too many less-than-stellar men. But when Brice walks into her life, his steadfast goodness and caring make her rise to the challenge of changing her view of herself and embracing the heavenly blessing of true love in her life. I hope Ava's story reminds you of how gracious God is and the wonderful gifts He sends into our lives every day.

Wishing you heavenly blessings,

Jillian Hart

EVERYDAY BLESSINGS

Put on a heart of compassion.
—*Colossians* 3:12

Chapter One

Aubrey McKaslin didn't know if she was coming or going. All she knew was that her eighteen-month-old niece was crying in agony, holding her fists to her ears. The little girl's cries echoed in the coved ceiling of the dining nook of her stepsister Danielle's home. To top it off, her almost five-year-old nephew Tyler was refusing to eat his dinner.

She was running on four hours' sleep at the end of a difficult day that came at the end of a very bad week, and she was at her wit's end. And she wasn't the only one. Tyler, always a good and dependable boy, gave his plate a push away from him at the table and shot her a mulish glare.

"I want Mommy. I don't want Mexi-Fries!" He choked back a sob, his eyes full of pain. "I want my d-daddy. I want him to come h-home."

"I know, but he can't come, pumpkin. He's still in the hospital." Aubrey ran a loving hand over his tousled head. "You know he would be here with you if he could."

"But why?"

"Because he's sick, honey." Aubrey's heart broke as she bounced the weepy little girl on her hip, to comfort her. With her free hand, she knelt to brush her fingertips down the little boy's nose. It usually made him smile, but not this evening. No, it had been a rough day for all of them.

On days like this, she wanted to know why so many hardships. She'd take it to the Lord in prayer, but she knew that life was like this, sometimes difficult, sometimes beyond understanding. All she could do was make the best of such an awful day.

"But why's he sick?" Fat tears glistened in Tyler's sorrowful eyes. "Why?"

Tyler's dad, Jonas, wasn't sick. He'd slipped into a degenerating coma, as the doctor had told them this afternoon. Jonas was a state trooper who'd been shot ten days ago when he'd stopped a speeder, who apparently had an outstanding warrant for his arrest and didn't want to be caught. The man was still at large.

"When I'm sick, I hafta stay in bed or quiet on the couch." The boy's soulful eyes were filled with such innocence. "Daddy can, too?"

How could she explain this to him so he'd understand? Aubrey was at a loss. She loved her nephew; in the end, that's all she could do for him. Love him through his pain. "Your daddy is so sick he has to stay at the hospital."

"N-no?" Tyler choked on a sob. "I w-want my da-daddy. He's gotta have M-Mexi-Fries."

So, that's what this was about. She'd picked up fast-food Mexican meals on her way here to take turns sitting with the kids. Aubrey knew now why Tyler was so upset. It was a standing jest in the family that Mexi-Fries, which were seasoned, deep-fried Tater Tots from a local taco place, could solve a host of problems. Being sick was one of them. "How about I ask your aunt Ava to take care of that? Will that make you feel better?"

"Y-yes." Tyler was sobbing so hard he choked.

Poor little boy. Aubrey's heart broke all over again for him as she wrapped her free arm around him. He clung to her, crying as hard as the baby in her other arm. How their mother handled this on a daily basis, Aubrey didn't know. Talk about a tough job.

But an important one. A job she'd given up hope on ever having as her own, considering the way her life was going. She pressed a kiss to Tyler's temple. "Are you feeling better now?"

"Y-yeah." He hiccuped and let go to rub his tears away with his fists. "I'm a big boy."

"Yes, you are. A very big boy. You're doing a terrific job, champ."

"Y-yeah." He gave a sniff and stared at his plate. "Do I gotta eat the Mexi-Fries?"

"Try to eat something, okay?" She rubbed her free hand over Madison's soft, downy head. The antibiotics she'd picked up earlier hadn't kicked in yet, or at least not enough, and she was still in misery. "I'm going to try rocking her again. I'll be right over here if you need me."

"O-kay." Tyler hiccuped again, wrestling down his own misery, and stared halfheartedly at his plate.

Madison wrapped her little fists in Aubrey's long

blond hair and yanked, at the same time burying her face in Aubrey's neck.

Poor baby. Aubrey began humming a Christian pop tune, the first thing that came into her head as she ambled over to the rocker in the corner of the living room. The instant she sank onto the soft cushion, Madison let out a scream of protest. She must be missing her mom, too.

"It's all right, baby," she soothed, and Madison's cries became sobs.

Lord, please show me how to help them, how to comfort them. She closed her eyes and prayed with all her heart, but no answer seemed to come as the air conditioner kicked on, breezing cool air against her ankle.

Life had been so dark the past week and a half that she'd forgotten there was a beautiful, bright world outside the house. It was a gorgeous summer evening. The trees were in full bloom. Thick streams of sunshine tumbled through the dancing green leaves of the young maple trees in the backyard and glinted over the sparkling surface of the in-ground pool. The tabby cat stalked through the shadows of the perimeter shrubbery, and Danielle's flower baskets on the deck shivered cheerfully in the warm night breezes.

How could such a beautiful day hold so much sorrow?

Her cell began to chime, startling Madison even more. Red faced, the little girl slumped like a rag doll against Aubrey in defeat, her fingers fisting in the knit of Aubrey's summery top. She leaned her cheek against the little girl, willing as much comfort into her as she could while at the same time inching the phone out of her front shorts pocket. She checked the screen, just in case it was a call from family.

Ava's cell number came up—her twin sister. Thank God for small miracles. "Tell me that you're on your way over. Please."

"Sorry, I wish I could." Ava's voice sounded thin and wavering, and Aubrey's stomach squeezed in a painful zing of sympathy. She knew what was coming before her twin said it. "Things aren't good here. Danielle's not okay. That's her husband in there, dying, and I can't leave her. Is that Madison?"

"You can hear her, huh?" No big surprise there. Aubrey kept the rocker moving and tried to comfort the baby, but things were just getting worse. Now Tyler was sobbing quietly at the table. "Have you heard if Dad and Dorrie's plane has landed yet?"

"No, but when they get here, I'll race straight over to give you a hand with the munchkins."

"Thanks, I'll take whatever help I can get."

"I'll hopefully see you soon and, in the meantime, I'll send a few prayers of help your way."

"Great, I'll take 'em."

The doorbell rang, the sound a pleasant chime echoing in the high cathedral ceilings overhead. Tyler looked up, tears staining his face. Madison ignored it, keeping her face buried in Aubrey's neck. It was probably a thoughtful church member dropping by another casserole. "I gotta go. Someone's at the door."

"Who?"

"How can I tell? I'm not near the door. It's not family, because they would walk right in." Somehow she managed to straighten out of the chair without jostling

Madison or dropping her cell phone. "Call me if anything changes, okay?"

That was all she could say with Tyler listening, all
ears, trying to figure out what was really going on.
But he was too little to understand, and overhearing
it was not the right way to explain what was happening with his daddy.

"Understood," Ava said. "The doctor is talking with
Danielle right now, so I'll let you know."

Aubrey flipped her phone shut. The doorbell pealed
again, but she wasn't moving very fast. Neither was
Tyler.

He slid off his seat and landed with a two-footed
thud on the linoleum floor. He rubbed the tears away
with his fists, smearing them across his pale cheeks.
"I can get the door, Aunt Aubrey. I do it for Mom all
the time."

"Go ahead, tiger." She followed him through the
hallway to the front door, where the door's arched window gave her a good view of the newcomer standing
on the porch. She caught the impression of a tall man
with jet-black hair framing a stony face before Tyler
wrenched the door open.

"Who're you?" he asked with a sniffle.

Aubrey stood up behind the boy, staring at the
stranger who took one look at them and rechecked the
house number tacked on the beige siding.

"I'm looking for Jonas Lowell." The man said in a
gravelly baritone. "Do I have the right place?"

He had dark eyes that met her gaze like an electrical shock. He had an intense presence, not dark and

not frightening, just solid. Like a man who knew his strength and his capability.

Aubrey couldn't find her voice, so she nodded, aware of Madison's baby-fine curls against her chin, the warm weight of the toddler, and the blast of dry summer wind on her face.

Tyler leaned against her knee, tipping his head all the way back to look at up at the man. "You're real tall. Are you a fireman?"

"No." The man came forward, and with the sun at his back shadowing him as he approached, he looked immense. His dark gaze intensified on hers. "You're not Danielle, right?"

"No, I'm her stepsister." He definitely was not a close friend of Jonas's, Aubrey decided. But there were friends who still didn't know. She opened the door wider. Not a lot of crime happened in this part of Montana, in spite of what had happened to Jonas.

"Maybe you didn't hear, I…" She paused. How did she find the words to say what had happened, with Tyler listening so intently? Danielle hadn't wanted him to know the whole truth yet. It was so violent and cruel. *Too* violent and cruel.

"I'm sorry to show up like this," the big man apologized. "I've left a few messages on Jonas's voice mail, but he hasn't gotten back to me."

"No, he's not going to be able to do that right now. He's in the hospital. If you want, I can have Danielle give you a call to explain." That might be best. Tyler was frightened enough as it was. She could feel his little body tense up, board-stiff against her knees.

"In the hospital?" The man looked stricken. "I'm sorry. I didn't know. You said you're Danielle's sister?"

"Yes, I'm Aubrey. Let me get a pen so I can get your number." It was hard to concentrate with Madison sobbing. She was gently rubbing the toddler's shoulder blades with her free hand. "Tyler, would you run and get a pen and the notepad by the phone for me?"

"Wait—" The man's rough baritone boomed like thunder. "Obviously this isn't a good time. I'm sorry for intruding. I'll leave my card with the gift—"

"Gift?" Okay, call her confused. She had no idea who this man was or what he was talking about. "I'm sorry. Run that by me again."

"Sure. Jonas bought a gift for his wife. An anniversary present. He was going to come by and pick it up, but since I hadn't heard from him, I thought I'd bring it by. Where do you want it?"

She felt her jaw dropping. Her heart cinched so tightly there was no possible way it could beat. "An anniversary gift? For Danielle?"

The man nodded warily, watching her closely as if he were afraid she was going to burst into tears or show some emotional reaction. Maybe it was his size, or the awkward way he'd taken a step back, but he seemed like the type who was easily panicked by an emotionally distraught woman.

Not that she was emotionally distraught. Yet. "If you could put it in the garage, maybe? I'll hit the opener for you. I'm sorry," she said as Madison began a more intense wave of crying. "This is really a bad time."

"I see that." He studied the little girl, his ruggedly handsome face lined with concern.

"It's an ear infection. The medicine's starting to work. I just have to rock her until she falls asleep."

"All right, then." Stiffly, he took a step back. "Is Jonas going to be okay?"

No. But could she say that in front of Tyler? All she could do was shrug her shoulder. Tyler had frozen in place, ears peeled, eyes wide, trying to absorb any detail.

As if the stranger had noticed, he nodded in understanding. Sadness crossed his granite face. With a single nod, he turned and strode down the walkway, taking the shadows with him.

Immeasurably sad, Aubrey closed the door and sent Tyler into the garage to hit the button that activated the door opener. Madison was crying anew and there was nothing Aubrey could do but rock her gently back and forth, quietly singing the only song that came into her mind.

She wasn't even sure if she had the words right, because all she could think about was Jonas. Thoughtful Jonas. He'd gotten an anniversary gift for his wife, but would it become like a message from the grave? A final goodbye? Aubrey choked back her own sorrow. It was too horrible to think about.

Life could knock your feet out from under you with a moment's notice, she thought. You could have it all, do everything right, pray diligently and live your faith, and tragedy could still happen.

She tightened her arms around the little girl who might have to grow up without her daddy, and she tried not to wonder what awaited her family, the people she loved.

* * *

William Corey could see the woman—Aubrey—
through the garden window. His opinion of women
was shaky these days, due to his experience with the
gender. But he could see how this woman was different.

Maybe it was the soft, thick, golden fall of sunlight
through the glass that diffused the scene, like a filter
on a camera's lens. That soft brush of opalescent light
touched her blond hair and the porcelain curve of her
heart-shaped face, making her look like rare goodness.

Or, maybe it was the child in her arms, clinging to
her with total trust and need. Whatever the reason, she
looked like innocence, pure and sweet.

Stop staring at the woman, William, he told himself and shook his head to clear away all thoughts of
her. He popped the crew-cab door of his truck. Sweat
dampened the collar of his T-shirt and the black knit
clung to his shoulders as he lifted the wrapped frame
from his rig. Across the street, a miniature dachshund
came racing down from its front porch to bark and
snarl, teeth snapping. It halted at the edge of the curb,
glaring at him with black beady eyes. Someone shouted
for it to shush and the little fellow kept barking, intent
on driving William away.

"Yeah, I know how you feel, buddy," he said to the
dog, who only barked harder in outrage. William didn't
like strangers, either. He'd learned how to chase them
with off with a few gruff words, too.

As he circled around to the open garage, he caught
sight of the woman in the window, framed by the honeyed sheen of the kitchen cabinets. Washed with light,

caught in the act of kissing the little toddler's downy head in comfort, she looked picture-perfect.

His fingers itched for his camera to capture the moment, to play with light and angle and reveal this pure moment of tenderness. It had been a long time since he'd felt this need to work—since Kylie's death. It took all his will to drag his gaze from the kitchen window and force his thoughts away from the woman. His days of holding a camera in his hands were over.

"So, mister." The boy stood in the open inner door between the garage and the house, a lean, leggy little guy with too-big Bermuda shorts and a shocking-green tank top. His brown hair stuck straight up as if he'd been struck by lightning. Tear tracks stained his sun-browned cheeks and had dampened his eyelashes. "That's a present, huh?"

"For your mom." William softened the gruffness in his voice. He liked little kids, and he figured this one had enough hardship to deal with.

He leaned the framed photograph, carefully wrapped, against the inside wall safely away from the garbage cans and the lawn mower. "I'll just leave it here, all right? You make sure your mom gets it, okay? With all you've got going on in your family, it might be easy to forget this is here."

"I never forget nuthin'." The little boy said with a trembling lip. He gave a sigh that was part sob, sounding as if he were doing his best to hold back more tears. "My daddy's sick in the hospital."

"I'm real sorry about that."

"Me, too." The kid sniffed once.

William had questions, but he didn't know exactly

what to ask. An illness? That didn't seem right; Jonas was the type of guy to hit the gym three times a week without fail. Not that William knew him well.

The little boy looked so lost, holding on to the doorknob with one hand, as if he were hanging on for dear life. What on earth should he say to him?

William stood in the shadows of the garage, as still as the boy, feeling big and awkward and lost. He'd been alone too long, out of the world so long that he wasn't used to making small talk with adults, much less a little boy.

"I miss my daddy. You haven't seen him, have ya?"

"No. Sorry." William could feel the kid's pain—it seemed to vibrate in the scorching heat. The silence stretched until it echoed in the empty rafters overhead. "How long has he been in the hospital?"

"A l-long time." The boy scrubbed his left eye with his free hand. "For-ev-ever."

William had a bad feeling about this, a strange reeling sense of the present lapping backward onto the past. "How old are you, kid?"

"I'm gonna be this much." He held up his whole hand. "Daddy'll be well, cuz he's takin' me to the f-fair. He prom-mised."

William studied the fat gleam of two silver tears spilling down the boy's cheeks and felt the sorrow of his own past. Things didn't always turn out well, stories didn't always end happily, and ill loved ones didn't always recover.

Maybe that wouldn't be the case for Jonas.

Faintly, from inside the house, came the woman's—

Aubrey's—voice. "Tyler, close the garage door and come try to finish your supper, okay?"

Tyler hung his head and didn't answer. His pain was as palpable as the shadows creeping into the garage and the heat in the July air.

"You'd better go," William said, ambling toward the cement driveway, where birdsong lulled and leaves lazed in the hot breeze and the dog across the street was still yapping with protective diligence.

"Mister?"

The little boy's voice drew him back. William stilled. Even his heart seemed to stop beating.

"You could p-pray for my daddy so he can come ho-me." Tyler scrubbed his eyes again, took a step back and closed the inner door.

Leaving William alone in the heat and the shadows with an ache in his chest that would not stop.

Chapter Two

Aubrey breathed a sigh of relief when she saw the inside door snap shut and Tyler plod across the linoleum. One problem down, and now she'd move to solving the next.

"Just eat something," she said softly to him, brushing her fingertips through his hair as he wove past her.

"Okay," he said on a sigh and halfheartedly climbed back up onto his chair.

Madison gave a hiccup and relaxed a little more. Good. Aubrey stood in place in the center of the kitchen, gently rocking back and forth, shifting her weight from her right foot to her left. The stinging tracer of pain fired down her left femur, as it always did when her leg was tired, but Aubrey didn't let that stop her, since Madison's breathing had begun to slow. She became as limp as a rag doll. Her fingers released Aubrey's shirt, so the collar was no longer digging into her throat.

Aubrey sent a prayer of thanks winging heavenward and pressed another kiss into the baby's crown of fine curls. Somewhere outside came the growl of a lawn mower roaring to life. Aubrey didn't know if it was cruel or comforting that the world kept on turning in the midst of a tragedy. That lawns still needed to be mowed and housework done. The gift Jonas had ordered for Danielle—now *that* was getting to her. She tried to swallow down the hot tears balling up in her throat.

The lawn mower was awfully loud. Either that, or awfully close. Aubrey eased forward a few steps to peer outside, careful not to disturb the sleeping toddler in her arms. The lawn had gone unmowed. Since everyone in the family was so busy juggling kid care and sitting with Danielle at the hospital, there wasn't any time left over for much else.

Not that she minded at all, but she hadn't been to the stables to ride her horse or able to work on her ceramics in her studio. There hadn't been time for normal living—only working at the bookstore and helping Danielle out afterward. But now that her dad and stepmom were flying in, they wouldn't all be stretched so thin.

Then she saw him. William. He was wrestling with the mower at the far end of the lawn, lining it up for the next pass. Dappled sunlight gilded his strong profile and broad shoulders as he guided the mower out of sight. For a moment she didn't believe her eyes. He was mowing the lawn?

She *knew* he was, and yet her mind sort of spun around as if it was stuck in Neutral. She could only gape speechlessly at the two strips of mowed lawn, proof of a stranger's kindness. A tangible assurance, small but much needed, that God's goodness was at work. Always.

Don't worry, Aubrey, she told herself. *This will work out, too.*

She took a deep breath, watched William stride back into her sight, easily pushing the mower in front of him, and she knew what she had to do.

William wiped at the gritty sweat with his arm, but it still trickled into his eyes and burned. He upended the final, full lawn-mower bag into the garage waste bin. It was hot, and although the sun was sinking low in its sky, the temperature felt hotter than ever.

All he wanted was to get into his rig, turn on the air-conditioning full blast and stop by the first convenience store for a cold bottle of water. He gave the heavy bag a shake to make sure all the cut grass was out and a dust cloud of tiny bits of grass and seed puffed into his face. He coughed, and the tiny grit stuck to his sweat-dampened skin. *This* was why he had a riding mower, not that it would be practical for Jonas's patch of lawn.

Jonas. In the hospital. It had to be an extended stay, since William had been leaving messages for the past week and a half or so. Which meant it was a serious deal. Sick at heart, William reattached the bag to the mower and wheeled it against the far wall, out of the way. Every movement echoed around him in the car-less garage. There was the photograph, wrapped and propped carefully against the wall. The photograph he'd sold to Jonas for practically nothing.

He closed his eyes, and there was the memory, as vivid as real life. Jonas grinning, still in his trooper's uniform after a long shift. He was standing in front of the Gray Stone Church, where the united church charities in the valley met for their monthly meetings. He'd produced a hardback book of William's photographs for his signature.

"I really appreciate this, Will," Jonas had said in all sincerity. "My wife loves your work. It's a gift for our anniversary. It'll be seven years."

"Seven years," William had said while he'd scribbled his signature on the title page. "Isn't that said to be one of the most critical years?"

"Sure, I've heard of folks talking about the seven-year itch or whatever, but I don't get it. I've got the best wife in the world."

William had remembered, because he'd believed Jonas. The man had actually planned for his wedding anniversary a month in advance. He'd been telling the truth about his feelings for his wife. That was rare, in Will's opinion. After all, he knew. Once, the blessing of marriage had happened to him.

Maybe that's why he'd offered one of the photographs from his personal stash. He liked to think that the things he'd lost in life still existed somewhere. That there was a reason to hope, although he'd lost that hope right along with his faith, and a lot of other things.

Standing in the baking heat of Jonas's garage, William pulled out his wallet and searched through it until he found a battered business card, which he tucked around the string that held the brown paper wrapping in place. He thought of the little boy's sorrow, his request for prayer, and vowed to honor that request tonight. It had been a long time since he'd said a nightly prayer.

As he turned to go, the inside door opened. The sister—Aubrey—stood framed in the doorway, one slender hand on the doorknob, poised in midstep. She hesitated, as if she were a little shy, and she made a lovely picture with the child asleep in her arms.

The painful lump was back in his throat. A ghost of memory tried to haunt him, but he wrestled it down. The trick was to keep your heart rock hard.

"Oh, good. I'm glad I caught you," she said in a voice as soft as grace. "It's ninety-six degrees out there in the shade. I have a bottle of cold water, or lemonade. I didn't know which you'd prefer."

Sure enough, she'd managed to wrap her fingers awkwardly around two plastic bottles, and still cradled the sleeping baby lovingly against her.

"Water's fine." Somehow he got the words out.

"Thank you for doing this." She stopped to deposit one of the bottles out of sight and breezed toward him with a careful step. "You have no idea how much we appreciate it. You must be a good friend of Jonas's."

"He's a good man." William glanced behind her at the open door, knowing his voice might carry to the little boy inside. "I didn't know he was sick."

"He's not. That was the best way to explain to Tyler." Her answer came quietly. "He was shot on duty."

While it hadn't occurred to him, the possibility had been there, in the back of his mind, William realized.

"He was doing better, but he suffered something like a stroke a few days ago and now he's in a deep coma."

"Not good."

"No." Pain marked her face and weighed down that single word. She said nothing more.

She didn't have to. He knew too much about comas. Wished he didn't. "Is there anything more I can do for his family?"

"Prayer. God's grace is the only thing that will help him now."

What could he say to that? It was the truth, and from his experience, a deep coma was a death sentence. William moved forward to take the bottle of water she offered. He tried not to brush her fingers with his or to notice the stunning violet-blue of her eyes or the shadows within them. He would not let himself think too much on the soft feminine scents of shampoo and vanilla-scented lotion or her loveliness. It wasn't something he ordinarily noticed anymore.

"Thanks." He held up the bottle, ice-cold from the refrigerator, and kept moving. "Be sure and turn on the sprinkler after I leave. Oh, and I left my number with the package. If his condition changes, will you call me? Leave a message on my machine?"

"Yes, I will. Thank you again."

He didn't look back or acknowledge her as he strode straight to his vehicle, all business, and climbed in. He didn't look at her as he backed into the residential street or lift a hand in a goodbye wave as he drove away.

Aubrey watched the gleam of his taillights in the gathering twilight and couldn't help wondering who was this Good Samaritan? He hadn't exactly been friendly, but clearly he'd thought enough of Jonas to have pitched in with the lawn mowing.

He seemed distant and not exactly friendly. She felt as if she'd seen him somewhere before, like in church or in the bookstore her family ran. The look of him was familiar—though not the personality he radiated. That hard steel and sorrow would be memorable.

At a loss to explain it, she went to hit the button to close the garage door and noticed the bright yellow SUV whipping down the curve of the cul-de-sac and into the driveway. Behind the sheen of the sinking sun on the tinted windshield, she could see the faint image of her twin sister busily pulling the e-brake, turning off the engine and gathering her things, talking animatedly as she went, which meant she had to be yakking on her cell phone.

Aubrey kept an ear to the open inside door, where she could hear the drone of the cartoon version of *A Christmas Carol* that Tyler watched over and over again. Knowing he was safely riveted in front of the television, she waited as the bright yellow driver's-side door swung open and Ava emerged. Her sister Ava was chaos as usual, her enormous purse slung over her shoulder, thick and bulky and banging her painfully in the hip. Yep, she was definitely on her cell, and judging by her shining happiness, she was talking to her handsome fiancé, Brice.

Madison stirred drowsily between wakefulness and sleep, and Aubrey patted her back gently and returned to rocking again. She watched as her sister gave her a welcoming wave, shut her SUV's door, then opened it and extracted her keys from the ignition.

"Oops." Ava grinned, keeping her voice quiet as she shut the door. "You've got Madison half-asleep."

"Working on it." Aubrey kept rocking, full of questions that would have to wait for later, she thought.

Even if Tyler was momentarily distracted, any long discussion would have the little boy hurrying to come listen. But not all of her questions had to wait. "I take it that Dad and Dorrie are with Dani?"

"Yep, so the rest of us figured we'd let the parents stay with Danielle through the night, and we'll take turns relieving them tomorrow." Ava dragged her feet in exhaustion as she came closer. "Brice said he can take the kids in the morning, so at least that's taken care of."

"See? I told you. You've got a great guy."

"He's the best guy." She said it with confidence, as if she no longer had a single doubt.

And why would she? Brice was absolutely perfect. Happiness for her sister warred with the sadness she felt for her family and the odd aching sorrow that William left behind. Which reminded her. "Do you know a friend of Jonas's named William?"

"Nope. Then again, why would I? I can't keep my own name straight some days." Ava rolled her eyes and leaned close to reach for Madison. She transferred the sleepy child into her arms. "I'm taking over. You're officially off duty."

"When it comes to family, there's no such thing as off duty."

"Stop being stubborn and go home—"

"To an empty apartment?"

For a moment they both paused in their lifelong habit of interrupting each other and finishing the other's sentences. Aubrey knew what Ava stopped short of saying. They'd spent their whole lives together. Even when they'd pursued different career paths after high school, they'd still been practically attached at the hip.

They talked throughout the day, all day long, thanks to the invention of cell phones. They met for lunch and dinner, and they shared an apartment. They spent their free time together as they always had. But Ava's marriage would change that.

Aubrey loved her sister with all her heart, and there was nothing more important than her happiness, but she knew she was going to miss spending so much time with her twin. When she looked into the future, Ava would have a home and a husband, children. That's where her time and energy should lie. Absolutely. But all Aubrey saw for herself was a long stretch of lonely evenings and weekends. Even now, without Madison in her arms, she felt lonely.

Not that she was going to be sad for herself for a second, because look at all the wonderful blessings the Lord put into her life with each and every day. But still, it was a change. And a big one.

"Tyler's watching one of his DVDs," she said with the most cheerful voice she could muster under the circumstances. "Maybe I'll just crash with him on the couch."

"Hey, what's that?" Nothing got past Ava. She pointed with her free hand to the wrapped gift.

"No idea. That William guy I mentioned dropped it off. It's an anniversary gift from Jonas to Danielle."

Ava looked sucker punched. "That's just about the saddest thing I've heard today, and it's been a day with a whole lot of sad in it."

"Tell me about it," she said over the sound of the ga-

rage door ratcheting closed. She stared at the package
wrapped so neatly and noticed, for the first time, there
was a business card tucked beneath the intersecting
twine. "It's hot in here. Maybe I should take that in."

"Good idea. It's probably something really nice,
knowing Jonas."

A beat of silence passed between them when they
said nothing at all. Aubrey knew Ava was thinking,
too, of how devoted Jonas had been to their stepsister.
Now what would happen? She could tell by Ava's face
that whatever the doctors had told them tonight hadn't
been good, which could only mean one thing. Danielle
would need her family more than ever.

"I'll see to this." Aubrey broke the silence. "You get
Madison inside."

"Ten four." Ava looked on the brink of tears as she
dragged her gaze away from the gift, which was clearly
some kind of a wall hanging. "Did you get anything
to eat?"

Aubrey shook her head. Not that she was hungry.

"I'll heat something up for both of us," Ava decided as she headed inside. The snap of her flip-flops
echoed in the empty garage, leaving Aubrey feeling
sorely alone.

Okay, call her curious, but she snatched the business card from its secure place beneath the string. The
name William Corey was printed in small letters in the
lower right-hand corner, in block script. Photographer.

Jonas's friend was *the* William Corey? *That's where
I've seen him before,* Aubrey thought, a little shocked.
She'd shelved so many of his books at the bookstore
over the years, she should have known him on sight.

His picture was plastered on the back jacket of his best-selling collections of inspirational photography. How did Jonas know the famed photographer? And why had someone of William's stature mowed the lawn?

No, that couldn't be right. Could it? Aubrey tucked the card back into place and carefully lifted the wrapped package. It certainly felt like a framed photograph, she thought as she shut the garage door and headed down the hall. It was a good-size picture. Not that Jonas could afford an original, but William Corey *was* Danielle's favorite artist. She had a book of his in the house.

Aubrey took care with the package and leaned it against the wall in Danielle's bedroom. There was a small wooden bookcase in the corner with a collection of devotionals and inspirational books.

There, on the bottom shelf, Aubrey found what she was looking for. A hardback book with William Corey's name on the spine. She tugged it from its snug place and turned the volume over. A man's image with jet-black hair and dark eyes stared up at her.

Yep, it was the same high cheekbones and ruggedly handsome look. William Corey.

It was a nice photograph, she thought, but it didn't look like the man she'd met tonight. His features were the same, yes. His look was the same. But the man in the picture seemed at ease, with a relaxed half smile on his face, standing in a mountain meadow with rugged peaks in the background. He was vital and alive and full of heart. Not at all the man who'd stood in the garage, looking lost in the shadows.

"Aunt Aubrey?" Tyler came up to stand beside her. "I'm lonesome. Will you come watch TV with me?"

"Sure thing, pumpkin." Aubrey put the book back on the shelf, but she couldn't put away her thoughts of William Corey as easily.

She took her nephew's small, trusting hand and let him lead her down the hall.

In the stillness of his mountain retreat, William was comforted by the echoing scuff of his slippered footsteps. He was back in his space, where he was safe from life and the way it made memories tug at the sorrow in his heart.

Hours had passed since he'd driven away from Jonas's house. He'd slapped a sandwich together and called it dinner, then hopped on the internet to scan through the online version of the local paper. He found a small article saying only that Trooper Jonas Lowell had been shot at a routine traffic stop and was in critical care. Nothing more. He'd tried the hospital, but they weren't releasing any information.

Maybe tomorrow, he'd try harder to see what he could find out and if there was anything he could do to help. After what Jonas had done for him, it was the least he could do.

Troubled, William watched the sun turn bold crimson in the hazy dusk and told himself he didn't long for his camera. He had no desire to capture the light of the sun and the haze of descending twilight. Really. Or, that's what he told himself as the long-dead desire grew razor sharp.

It was that woman Aubrey's fault, he decided as he

bent to turn on the lamp at the bedside table. There had been something about her, probably just the trick of the light, that made the dead place inside him come to life. For a moment, he wished for the things that would never be for him again—like innocence and trust and hope.

It had been a long time since he'd prayed. His knees felt stiff as he knelt beside the bed, resting his forearms on the soft, cool percale of the turned-back sheets. The shadowed darkness in the room seemed to deepen and grow; the low-watt bulb in the table lamp wasn't strong enough to keep it at bay.

Maybe it was the shadows within him that seemed so dark. He thought of Jonas's little boy and the promise made. William might have given up believing in nearly everything, but he was not the kind of man who went back on his word, especially to a child. So, he bowed his head and, while no words rose up prayerfully from his forgotten soul, he did find the words that mattered.

"Help Jonas to recover, for his family's sake. Please."

It felt as if he were talking to no one. He was certain he was alone in the room, that God wasn't leaning down to listen to his prayers. That only made the darkness bleaker and the iron-hard place inside his soul harder.

William climbed from his knees, sank onto the mattress and buried his face in his hands. Unable to make sense of the broken pieces his life had become, he lay in the dark, alone.

Chapter Three

In the antiseptic scent of the hospital's early-morning waiting room, Aubrey searched her father's face for signs of the latest news on Jonas's condition. Even in the harsh fluorescent lighting, John McKaslin looked suntanned and robust for a man in his sixties, but there was no smile in his violet-blue eyes.

"Dani's in with him. There's no good news." Heavy sadness weighed down his voice. "You've lost weight, pumpkin. You look tired."

"It's nothing." And that was the truth. Doing what she could for her family wasn't a hardship, it was a privilege. What was a little sleep lost compared to that? "I stayed to help Ava with the kids, and Madison had a rough night."

"I'm so glad to be here to help out. I'll take over to-night, dear." Dorrie wrapped Aubrey into a caring hug and then held her at arm's length to appraise her. "Your dad's right. You look exhausted. If only we could have come back sooner. John, the girl is exhausted."

Dad shook his head. "We should have come sooner.

Spence said Jonas was doing better and to keep on with our cruise."

"He had been." For a little while, it seemed as if Jonas would be fine, and they had all breathed a sigh of relief. Dad and Dorrie had been starting a cruise and Danielle had convinced them to stay on it. That had been before the coma, of course. Aubrey thought the long trek standby from St. Barts and the night at the hospital had to be taking a toll on her parents. "I'll stay here, if you two want to head home."

"All right, then. I'll get some shut-eye." Dad leaned to kiss Aubrey's cheek. "You call if there are any changes, you hear?"

"Yes, sir." It was good to have her parents back in town. She'd missed them both so much since they'd moved to Scottsdale. "You're okay to drive? You must have been up most of the night."

"I got a few *z's* in, don't you worry about me." Dad gave his wife a kiss. "Are you coming? By the look of you, I'd say you've made up your mind to stay."

"Dani needs me, no matter how tired I am."

"You need me to grab you breakfast before I go?"

"No, dear, but how about I walk as far as the cafeteria with you?" Dorrie turned to Aubrey. "I'll be right back. You'll keep an eye on Dani?"

"You know I will."

Aubrey watched her parents amble down the hall, hand in hand, shoulders touching. They had found a good marriage, and it had deepened over the years. Somehow, watching them made her heart ache with loneliness, and what kind of sense did that make?

None. Absolutely none. She ought to be feeling less lonely because her parents were back in town. She wasn't sure what that said about a woman in her late twenties, that she was used to spending so much time with her parents. But she was a homebody. Her family had always been her life and she knew they always would be. It wasn't as if eligible bachelors were exactly knocking down her door. In fact, not one had ever knocked on the door for her.

For Ava. Yes. Absolutely. Her twin had that adorable charisma that made everybody love her. But Aubrey, well, she knew she was a wallflower, the kind of girl men passed by.

It was simply a fact that she'd learned to deal with. Besides, she had so many wonderful blessings in her life, how could she feel right about asking for more?

There was hot water for tea next to the coffeepot in the pleasant little waiting room, so she started in that direction, but something stopped her. A movement out of the corner of her eye. She recognized the gentleman far down the hall at the nurses' station. A tall, broadshouldered, austere-looking man dressed all in black. Why did she know it was William Corey without him having to turn so she could see his face?

Maybe it was the way his wide, capable shoulders were set, as if he were confident he could handle anything. Perhaps it was the shadows that clung to him in the harsh fluorescent light. Whatever the reason, her attention turned to him automatically, as if she had no say at all.

One of the floor nurses pointed her way, and Aubrey

watched William turn toward her. Recognition sparked in his dark eyes, and something else—something she couldn't name, but she saw his guard go up. His entire being, body and spirit, stiffened. He marched toward her like a soldier facing a firing squad.

He didn't seem comfortable. He didn't look happy to see her again.

"I was going to give you a call later this morning," she explained. "You didn't need to come down."

"I wanted to." He jammed his hands into his jeans pockets. "They wouldn't give me any information because I wasn't family, but I wanted to talk to Jonas's wife, when she has a minute."

No welcoming greetings. No small talk. He wasn't the most extroverted man. Maybe that's why she automatically liked him. She was introverted, too. "I'm not sure when that will be."

"I don't mind waiting." William shielded his heart with all his strength. He wasn't going to let himself remember being in the same place in another hospital. In another time. He knew coming here wouldn't be easy, but the antiseptic smell was more powerful a reminder than he'd anticipated. So were the echoing halls magnifying every movement and the sad shuffle of relatives waiting for news.

Enough, he told himself. He had to wipe his mind clean and not let a single thought in. That seemed to take all of his effort, and Aubrey was looking at him as if she wasn't too fond of him.

He wasn't coming across well and he knew it, but this was the best he could do. He couldn't be the only one in this hospital with bad memories. Surely he could handle this better. He had to try harder, that was all.

"I don't know if anyone thanked you," Aubrey was saying.

It was hard for him to focus. The past welled up no matter his best efforts to blot it out. He felt as if he were traveling down an ever-narrowing tunnel and the light at the end of it was blinding him.

"That was really nice of you to mow the lawn."

"Nice?" The sincerity in her violet-blue gaze startled him. He wasn't being nice. He was doing what needed to be done. It was so little to do when he owed Jonas so much. "No. It took all of twenty minutes, I think. No big deal."

"It was, believe me, and bless you for it. We're simply swamped trying to keep everything together for Danielle's sake and the kids."

That only brought back the memory of her holding the small child, awash in light. He might not have been able to capture that extraordinary image with his camera, but apparently he had with his mind. "Danielle. Is there a chance I can see her?"

"She's in with Jonas and he's failing and she doesn't want to—"

He held up one hand, the emptiness inside his soul splintering like fragile glass. "I'll wait until she has time."

"It might be a long wait."

"I don't mind." He nodded once as if the matter was settled and strode to the first chair he came to in the waiting area. He folded his big frame into it and pulled a paperback book out of his back jeans pocket.

Aubrey watched him flip the book open to a marked page, tucked the book marker at the end of the book and bow his head to read.

Okay, so call her curious and a little protective of Danielle. Her feet seemed to take over, and on auto-pilot she wound up beside his chair. "Would you like something hot to drink while I'm up?"

"No."

He didn't look up from his book. Not the most talkative of fellows. Aubrey wasn't at all sure she should like this guy, but there was something about him sitting there all alone, his entire body tense, and he didn't look comfortable being here. Somehow the overhead light seemed to glance off him, leaving him lost in the shadows.

Her hand trembled as she reached for the hot water carafe on the heating plate. Why did this man unsteady her? He had a powerful presence and his gaze was sharp enough to cut stone. That ought to be enough, but it wasn't the whole truth. Just as it wasn't only curiosity that had her watching him out of the corner of her eye as she dunked the tea bag up and down in her little foam cup of steaming water.

The volunteer at the desk looked up from the newspaper she was reading, glanced in William Corey's direction and gave Aubrey a knowing kind of smile as if to say, *he is a handsome one.*

Aubrey *had* to admit that she'd already noticed he was extremely handsome. It was a purely objective observation, of course.

He lifted his focus from his book and studied her

through the curve of his long dark lashes. Microseconds stretched out into an uncomfortable tension as his eyes locked with hers. She couldn't tell if he was annoyed or angered, then the left corner of his mouth quirked up into a hint of a grin.

Who knew the man could actually smile?

"What?"

That was sort of an invitation to talk, right? Aubrey dropped two sugar cubes into her cup and headed toward him. "I was wondering how you know Danielle and Jonas."

"I only know Jonas."

"Then why do you want to see Danielle?"

"It's personal."

That's all he had to say. Aubrey stared at the man. He'd gone back to his reading. "I see you're a very forthcoming type. And talkative."

"I can be."

"Talkative? I don't believe that." Did she detect another hint of a grin?

He shrugged one big shoulder. "I'm not here to talk to you."

The corner of his mouth quirked into a definite, one-sided grin, not an amused one, but enough so that it softened the granite features of his face and hinted at a man with a good-humored nature behind the hard stone.

"I owe Jonas a favor, that's why I'm here." His eyes darkened with a terrible sadness.

Sadness she could feel.

He went on. "I want to know what I can do for Danielle. How I can help. Make a difference in their lives." He paused. "The way Jonas had once done for me."

"Jonas helped a lot of people in the line of duty."

"I imagine." He gave a curt nod, as if it were all he could manage. He swallowed hard, and his sorrow was a palpable thing drawing her closer. "I'm not handling this well. It's the hospital. I've spent a lot of time in them."

"In this one?"

"Yes."

She slipped into the chair in the row next to him, leaving an empty seat between them. "Your story didn't end well, did it? I'm sorry."

He didn't know why he was telling her this. What had happened to his resolve to keep this buried? "Four years, five months and twenty three days ago, no, twenty four days ago, my wife died in this hospital. One moment we were riding bikes on the shoulder of a country road, and the next, she was bleeding to death in my arms...."

He could feel the woman's silence like a touch, her gaze on his face, her sympathy as soft as dawn's light. The title on the front of the book he held began to blur. "Jonas answered the 911 call. He was going off duty, but he came to help. The paramedics were right behind him, but I'll never forget what he did. He drove to the hospital and he sat with me while my wife was in surgery. I had no other family. No one else."

That was all he could say. But there was more that Jonas had done, things that had made all the difference. A difference William could not face, much less put into ordinary words. He hung his head, willing the pain down and forcing his vision to clear.

Her hand settled on his arm, her touch light and comforting. He couldn't explain why a sense of peace cut through the well of pain gathering deep within him. Or why she made the agony of an endless sorrow ebb away like low tide on a shore. He only knew how dangerous it was to open up to anyone, to let anyone in, and he jerked his arm away.

"Uh, there's Danielle now," Aubrey said in a startled voice, hopping to her feet, acting as if he hadn't embarrassed her.

He was too overwhelmed to do anything more than close his book and try to find the will to stand, to greet Jonas's wife with a voice that wouldn't betray his own inner turmoil. He closed off everything else from his mind—even the bit of peace Aubrey had brought to him.

It was just about the saddest thing she'd heard. Aubrey ached for the man as she watched him amble down the hallway toward the elevators. Now that she knew what had happened to him and the loss he'd suffered, she could see that he was walking around broken down to the quick of his soul.

"I can't believe this." Danielle sank into the nearest chair in the waiting room and stared at the business card she held in her hand. "I'm too tired to think."

She looked beyond exhausted, Aubrey thought as she eased into the chair beside her stepsister. Coincidentally, she discovered she had a perfect view of the elevator bank where William was waiting, head bowed, staring at the floor.

He'd jerked away from her. She'd meant to comfort him, and he pulled away as if she were hurting him more. She was embarrassed, yes, but it was nothing compared to the hurt she felt on his behalf.

"That man was William Corey. The photographer." Danielle stared at the card. "I didn't even know Jonas knew him. Wait, maybe I did. My brain is a total fog."

"Did he tell you about the gift?"

"Oh, you mean he wanted to contribute to Jonas's medical fund, except there isn't one." Danielle rubbed her hands over her face, so weary. "I told him about the funds we're accepting for charity in his name. Oh, and I mentioned the auction fund-raiser thing you and Ava are coordinating with our church."

Should she tell her about the anniversary gift? Aubrey wasn't sure at this point that Danielle looked strong enough to take one more blow.

"Mr. Corey was interested in writing a check to Jonas's medical fund, but I told him I wasn't able to think about that much right now." Danielle shrugged. She seemed frayed at the edges, at wit's end, as if her heart had stopped beating. "I've got just about all I can cope with."

Aubrey put her arm around her stepsister. "Did you get some sleep?"

"I'll be fine. I—" Danielle shoved the business card in Aubrey's direction. "I told him you or Ava would be in touch about that donation. It was nice of him, don't you think?"

"I do. And don't worry, I'll take care of it." Aubrey took the card, wrapping her hand around her sister's. She willed all the sympathy she had into a prayer.

It was hard to know what exactly to pray for. For Jonas to miraculously recover? For Danielle's marriage and family to be whole and happy, as before? To turn back time so that Jonas would not have been shot? Some things not even God could change. The past was one of those things.

Please, Father, make this come out all right.

But she didn't see how. All she could see was her sister's tenuous act of holding things together, and the remembrance of William Corey's sadness. She could still picture the steel-straight line of his spine and the inherent sorrow that made him seem so distant and impersonal. But his story clung to her like skin.

How sad is this? she thought, wanting to push it all away like an empty plate. If only she could get this ordeal out of all of their lives. She hated dealing with this constant sorrow and sadness. She liked to look at the positive side of life. She hated the heartbreak and woe that had permeated their family and stolen Jonas from his wife and children.

"Are you all right?" Danielle asked in concern; Danielle who always thought of others even when her world was unraveling at the seams.

"Don't worry about me. I'm just overwhelmed." Aubrey shrugged. "You know me. I hate that things like this ever happen. I would want there to be no hurt and loss in the world. Just goodness and sunshine for everyone."

"Sounds like a good deal to me. If only that were true." Tears brimmed in her dark blue eyes. "What I'd give if we could make that true, but life is a mixed bag of blessings. Some days it's more than I want to face, but that doesn't change the fact that I have to."

A faint bell dinged at the end of the hallway, echoing against the long empty corridor. The light above one of the elevators came on and William Corey moved toward it.

Sympathy tugged at her heart. William looked deeply alone. She watched him wait while a few passengers in the elevator disembarked—Dorrie was among them. She carried a drink carrier and a covered plate, tapping quickly in their direction. But it was the man, lost in shadows, who kept Aubrey's attention as he entered the elevator and disappeared from her sight.

The impression he'd made on her heart remained.

William listened to the echo of his step in the hospital's chapel and wondered why he was here. It was as if he had followed his feet. He couldn't remember making the conscious decision. The chapel had been noted on the main-floor directory and he'd followed the arrows without thought. Now that he was here, he didn't know what he could possibly do. There was no prayer on earth that could comfort him.

Candles flickered in the front of the nondenominational sanctuary, candles that had been lit in hope and prayer. The stillness of the simple place felt as if it still held the memory of decades of deepest prayers whispered in sorrow. Maybe his were still here, earthbound and unheard, from that dark, desperate night long ago.

I shouldn't have come here.

He'd thought he was doing the right thing, but now he wasn't so sure. The online article about Jonas's shooting was sparse, and he'd come thinking there was some difference he could make. Sure, Aubrey had told him enough of Jonas's current medical situation to prepare him, but hearing it was another reality entirely. Seeing the look of it on Jonas's wife's face was too bleak a reminder.

William knew that look too well, the appearance of exhaustion and desperation. Of what it took to put life on hold to stay at a loved one's side. There wasn't enough sleep, not enough hope, not enough love, no matter how hard you tried to will that loved one well.

The day's blazing sunshine spilled through two arched stained-glass windows, and the colorful spill of light might be a sign to some who sought comfort in this solemn place. But that comfort and hope had been elusive for him. William's hand felt empty, as empty as his soul, and coming here had been a mistake. He'd been unable to make any sense of life, or reason behind it. It wasn't what he wanted to believe. It was simply all he was left with.

The scent of flowers placed on the altar became cloying, a scent-related memory of when he'd knelt here, praying for mercy to save his wife.

It hadn't happened.

He turned his back to the altar and the cross on the wall, feeling devoid of faith, like a pitcher empty of water, but the pad of approaching footsteps made him hesitate. It was as if the light slanting in thick, nebulous rays through the stained glass brightened when she stepped through the threshold and into the sanctuary.

Aubrey. She recognized him, and their gazes locked. With the way she was haloed by the jeweled light, a hopeful man might think this was a sign that heaven was listening after all.

Chapter Four

"William." Aubrey blinked but couldn't quite believe her eyes. The man seemed darker somehow even as he stood in the light. "What are you doing here?"

Okay, duh, obvious. Was there any question why she was twenty-seven and single and doomed to stay that way? Her conversation and social skills *could* be better. She took a quiet step forward, careful not to disturb the reverence of the sanctuary.

He didn't answer or acknowledge her obvious question.

"I guess we had the same thing in mind. Prayer," she added when he continued to look at her without saying a thing. "I didn't mean to intrude. I can come back later—"

"No." His baritone boomed like summer thunder. "Don't go. I was just leaving."

"Okay." She remembered how he'd jerked back from her touch in the waiting room. Maybe he was on his way out; maybe he was trying to avoid her.

Way to go, Aubrey. This was where being her twin

would come in handy. If she could clone her sister's personality, she'd know exactly what to say to this man who looked slightly panicked and out of his comfort zone.

She moved aside to give him plenty of room to escape. "I always turn to prayer, too, when I feel lost."

He held out his hands, palms up, in a helpless gesture. "I didn't pray. Couldn't."

She noticed his gaze slide lower. She put her hand where he would be looking, at her throat, and felt the small gold cross their maternal grandmother had given her. Gran was a deeply religious woman, and that had always given Aubrey courage. "Danielle gave me your card. My sister and I are trying to handle all the donations that are coming in. Jonas is fortunate to have extensive insurance after all, so we're designating a few charities to donate to in his name. If you're still interested, then just let me know."

A single nod, that was all. His face was stone hard, but now she knew the reason he ambled past her as if he didn't have a heart. No, she thought, a man wouldn't who'd buried his wife.

"I'll get back to you about donations, then." At least she thought that's what his nod had meant. "This had to be pretty important to you for you to come here in person."

He hesitated in the doorway. Turned. He didn't look at her but above her head at the windows radiating light. "It was. I owe Jonas a great debt. Whatever else I may have lost, I still believe in the Golden Rule. In doing right by others."

He left in silence, without a goodbye. Even the pad

of his black-soled shoes hardly made a noise, as if he were more shadow than man. Aubrey knew it was just the artistic part of her, thinking of him that way. In the sanctuary filled with God's light, she knelt and said a prayer for him first.

Whatever reason God had brought William into their lives, and into her path, she hoped she could do the right thing by him. But as to what that could be, she was clueless. She left that up to the angels as she bowed her head and began to work her way down her prayer list.

"I don't know if I'm coming or going."

Aubrey looked up from shelving new inventory at her parents' Christian bookstore to see her twin dashing down the main aisle toward her. "Ava, you're twenty-three minutes late. Again."

"I know it. My bad!" Breathless, she skidded to a stop beside the book cart, dressed in neon-pink from head to toe. "But on the good side, I remembered to bring lunch for you. I did a drive-through at Mr. Paco's Tacos. Is Katherine in yet?"

"No, she's staying with Danielle at the hospital this afternoon so Dorrie can get some sleep. Oh, and Spence got a call from Rebecca."

"Is our wayward stepsister finally on her way home?"

"After a month of missionary work, she says she's looking forward to the creature comforts of indoor plumbing and air-conditioning."

There was a lot they didn't say, but Aubrey knew what Ava was thinking. So many serious issues were hammering hard on their family right now. Spence and Katherine, who both had spoken to their grandmother Whitman on the phone, had concerns about her health. Gran was their mom's mom, who had decided to snowbird in Arizona and wound up staying there for the past few years. So far away, it wasn't as if they could be there to help her out.

Then there was this thing with Jonas, and it had all of them running as fast as they could to help Danielle and the kids get through it.

And then there was Rebecca and her not so nice boyfriend, Chris. It had been a good thing for her to be away in Mexico for a chunk of the summer without phone service. But now she was coming back and Aubrey had real concerns—and so did Ava. She could tell by the dark look.

"What happened to boring?" Ava asked as she snatched an armload of books from the cart. "Remember when our lives were so boring all we did was yawn?"

"If I remember correctly, you were complaining you were bored and kept praying for something exciting to happen."

Ava slid the first book onto a place in the shelf. "I've learned my lesson. I'm never praying for something to break up the doldrums again."

"Be careful what you pray for, huh?" Aubrey teased as she sidled close to her twin and pulled out the book she'd just shelved in the wrong place. "I guess that means this is all your fault."

"What's your fault?" Spence strode toward them,

glowering, but he was more bark than bite. "And you're late. Again."

"I know." Ava shrugged as if it was no biggie. "I'm just lucky I could make it at all."

Spence's left eyebrow shot up in a furious arch. "We're truly lucky you graced us with your presence. Aubrey, did she misshelf that book?"

"Not now." Aubrey easily slipped the volume in where it belonged. "Ava's holding down two jobs, and helping out Dani. You could be more flexible."

"I could be, but I'm not going to." He almost said it without a hint of humor.

She wasn't fooled. "Go back to your computer. We've got it covered."

"You'll watch the front?"

"There isn't a single customer in the store. Stop worrying." She often thought that instead of giving her worries up to God, she'd just give them to Spence. He wasn't happy unless he was worrying over something. "Ava brought Mr. Paco's Tacos nachos."

Not amused by the rhyme, Spence jammed his hands into the pockets of his perfectly creased trousers. "No food near the books." He scowled extra hard as if to make up for the ghost of his smile and stormed off.

They watched him go. Aubrey didn't know what to do with their taciturn older brother. She knew Ava didn't, either.

Ava was the first to speak. "Do you know what he needs?"

"Exactly. A girlfriend. But how impossible is that?"

"I've been praying." Ava had an undeniable gift for

prayer. "Just like I've been praying for you, too, so brace yourself."

"Ha-ha, very funny. I can't imagine some guy falling for me."

"What kind of talk is that? If I can break my date-only-duds pattern, then you can break this no-dating-ever habit you've got going." Her two-carat engagement diamond chose that moment to sparkle as she shelved a book. "It's all about positive thinking. That, and a lot of prayer. Oh, and the right man coming along at the exact same moment."

"We both know how hard that is to accomplish." Aubrey didn't mind that she didn't have a boyfriend who was so deeply in love he couldn't wait to marry her. Really. Okay, so she did. "Anyway, I love my life the way it is."

"Okay, but that's not going to stop me from praying hard for you." Ava's cell chimed a cheerful tune and she abandoned her shelving to search through her pockets for her phone. She studied the screen and brightened like a star in the heavens. "It's Brice."

Her fiancé. Aubrey pulled the book Ava had misshelved and whispered, "Go into the break room. Go on."

"Thanks. I owe ya. Hello, there, handsome." Ava's smile was 100 percent pure joy as she skipped away, answering the call. Her voice, filled with love and happiness, faded away as she disappeared from sight.

Aubrey hated to admit it, but no amount of Ava's praying was going to help. She was looking thirty in the face and had never been on a date. It wasn't as if she was likely to start now. She was a wallflower and doomed to stay that way. She didn't mind, really. Think of all the blessings she already had in her life. A big loving family. Her left leg, which had healed miraculously enough for her to walk. She had her art and her horse and a good life. She didn't have any business regretting the blessings she didn't have.

And why did her thoughts return to William?

Call her curious. She happened to have a few books to shelve in the next aisle. She'd been in such a hurry, she hadn't taken the time to check out whether they had any of William's photography books in stock. Maybe now was as good a time as any to see, with her lunch break coming up and no one in the store.

She knelt down and found two of William's books. One was a big coffee-table type collection full of rich, colorful photos. She took the other, a smaller collection with text from Scripture, and stacked them on the cart. After all, she'd need something to read while she ate lunch, right?

By the time she'd shelved the first row of books on the cart, Ava had come back into sight, grinning from ear to ear. It was a good thing to see amidst all the sadness and worry in their family.

"Brice is going to do my afternoon deliveries. Whew." Ava was working two jobs to keep her bakery business afloat. "Oh, how about that? You pulled one of William Corey's books."

"I was curious. I mean, I've seen his stuff before." Aubrey shrugged as if it was no big deal. The question was, why did it feel like a big deal? She hardly knew the man. "I just wanted to look again, after meeting him."

"Danielle said he came to the hospital." Ava stopped to flip open the book. "I had no idea. I guess Jonas knew him from some distant tie to the united churches charities. He's a big donor, I guess."

"I'm not surprised." Aubrey thought of the story William had told her, and the truth he'd trusted her with. He'd struck her as a deeply private person, and she didn't feel comfortable saying anything to Ava.

She looked over her twin's shoulder. The first photograph was one of his most collected works, a subtle sunrise scene over the craggy amethyst mountains in Glacier National Park. She recognized the scene because she'd been to Glacier a few times. The lake beneath the mountains glowed as if each rippling wave of water had been painted with rosy, opalescent paint. The photograph seemed to glow with a life—and hope—of its own.

It was hard to reconcile with the man in the chapel. A man who looked as if he'd had all the hope torn out of him. She didn't know why she ached with sympathy for him. Maybe because tragedy had hit her family, too. Maybe. But somehow her sympathy for William felt more powerful than that. As if by sharing his story, she'd seen more of the private man, the tender places within that no one knew.

"Talk about beautiful stuff." Ava turned page after page. "It's a shame he doesn't work anymore. I've heard it's hard to get hold of some of his prints. They're all limited editions or something."

"I didn't know he'd retired." Aubrey thought of the man shadowed and lost. She didn't have to wonder whether he'd put down his camera because of his grief.

Of course he had. "I didn't tell Danielle about Jonas's gift, did you?"

"I couldn't bear to, so I talked Katherine into doing it since she's older, but I guess she tried and broke down in tears, so she hid the gift. Maybe Jonas will get well and be able to give it to her himself. Miracles happen."

Although Ava tried to say it with conviction, Aubrey knew Ava didn't feel it. Neither did she.

Okay, that was about all she could take of all this sadness. Maybe she wouldn't look at his pictures after all. It would only make her hurt for William, and she needed to do something to counterbalance it. Make a positive in the midst of all this darkness. She had her laptop in the employee closest. Maybe she'd start to answer all the emails from the church members about the fund-raiser for Jonas.

Ava snapped her book shut with an echoing thud. "Your lunch is getting cold, hello? Go eat. Put your feet up. Shoo."

"Will you promise to double-check the books you're shelving? Or I'll just have to do it all over again."

"Sure I will. Really."

Aubrey ignored Ava's eye roll and headed toward the back. There was no better fast-food pick-me-up than a chicken burrito and nachos, and boy, did she need one.

William had made his trail ride a long one, stabled Jet, and as he shouldered through the back door to his home, he still couldn't get Aubrey out of his mind. She stayed there the way a half-forgotten dream hung on through the day, with glimpses and images that would not let him forget or push thoughts of her aside. Images of her gentle and luminous beauty had seemed so genuine and, like the pull of his awareness in his heart, remained.

Nothing had been right since he'd first spotted her. He couldn't deny this, not even to himself. He went straight to the fridge and let the cool air wash over him as he debated the choices on his sparse shelves. Finally, he grabbed a bottle of sweetened iced tea, twisted the cap as he closed the fridge door, and took a long pull.

The icy liquid cooled him from the inside out, but did it get rid of that unsettled, sore feeling in his chest? The one that had worsened after he'd told Aubrey about his wife?

Of course not. Not even his strength of will had been able to get rid of that. He wasn't sure what would.

Why had he told her of his most private pain? Maybe he'd felt overwhelmed with Jonas's wife's sorrow and fears, because he knew exactly how she felt. He'd been there, too. Maybe he'd talked about it because the memories had been so near to the surface.

Or, he wondered, was it because he knew it wasn't likely that he'd be seeing her again? She'd been so kind and sincere the story had just tumbled out.

It was too late to change any of it, so he had to stop working it over and over in his heart and in his head. He had to let this go. He headed for the built-in desk in the corner of the huge kitchen. The best course was not to think of it again—or the lovely Aubrey. Then the weight sitting in the chambers of his heart would fade.

It was dark, so he flashed on the lamp on his desk in the corner. The fall of light illuminated a stack of unopened mail, bank statements, fat envelopes from his investment firm, colorful postcards and envelopes signifying junk mail, and his answering machine. There was no blinking light. Pretty typical. He didn't get a lot of calls these days.

Still, he'd hoped for good news from Aubrey.

Aubrey. Just thinking of her made him remember standing in the hospital's chapel and feeling shadows of the past that could not let him go—or that he could not let go of. He didn't know which.

He only wished things could go back to the way they were, where he was numb inside and content enough to be that way.

In the quiet of Danielle's house, with both kids finally asleep, Aubrey found herself on her hands and knees scrubbing the soap ring off the side of the kids' bathtub. Did she know how to spend a Friday night or what? For an exciting follow-up, she planned on scrubbing the toothpaste gunk off the sink.

She heard the click of the front-door key in the lock and the whisper of the door opening.

Her twin, she guessed as she squirted more soap-grime-killer stuff onto the fiberglass. Whatever Madison's bubble bath was made of, it left a stubborn rainbow-colored coating at the water line.

Lucky me, she thought and kept scrubbing. At least she was able to concentrate on the soap ring and *not* William Corey. At least, that's what she was struggling to do when she heard quiet, slow-moving footsteps padding down the hall—definitely not her twin after all. Then who?

She pulled herself off the side of the tub and gri-
maced. Her muscles were all kinked up from the complicated twisting positions she'd been in so she wasn't
exactly moving fast by the time she poked her head
out the door.

Danielle's bedroom door was open, light spilling
into the hallway.

It was probably Dorrie, come to get a fresh change
of clothes for Danielle. She wasn't supposed to be staying over in the room with Jonas, but Dani had vowed
a class-five hurricane wasn't going to move her from
her husband's side and the nurses didn't have the heart
to try.

Aubrey peeled off the rubber gloves only to find
her fingertips were all wrinkly. She hesitated outside
the door. "I have clothes in the dryer— Oh, you're not
Dorrie."

"No." Danielle stood in the middle of her room like
a ghost, she was so weary. "Mom made me come home.
She told me to get some sleep."

Okay, call her confused. Why had Danielle left her
husband's side? "Dorrie's staying with Jonas?"

Dani nodded vaguely and pushed open her closet
door. "I'm going to hop into the shower. H-how are the
kids? I've b-been a terrible mother." She pressed her
hands to her face, on the verge of tears.

The toll this was taking on Dani wasn't right and it
wasn't fair. She laid her hand on Dani's bony shoulder.
She'd lost so much weight—too much. "Why don't I
run a bath for you? You can sit and relax? I'll bring up
some munchies and some of that strawberry soda you

love. I hid a can at the back of the refrigerator for an emergency like this one."

"You should go home. I should be taking care of my own kids. I just—oh, I can't do everything and I'm too exhausted to even try."

"Then how about this? Grab your robe, and I'll start the bathwater. Deal?"

"You are a blessing to me, you know that?"

"Impossible. You're the blessing to me." She headed toward the master bath. "Tell me you didn't drive home this tired? You know drowsy driving is just as dangerous as being intoxicated—"

Dani gasped. "What's this? I don't remember putting anything here?"

Oh no. The anniversary gift. Aubrey mentally groaned. She'd forgotten it was hidden in the closet, and that was one more emotional hit Danielle might be too fragile to take. "Don't worry about it. Just grab your robe."

Aubrey popped back into the room, but it was too late. Danielle was already kneeling down to read.

"There's a business card from William Corey. How strange is that? He was at the hospital. I had no idea Jonas had helped him when his wife had been in a coma."

"Spence knows William, too. Spence caught me looking at one of William's books in the break room and had a major meltdown over the expensive book being near a large order of Mr. Paco's nachos."

"Sounds like Spence." Danielle's eyes were already filling. "Is this a picture?"

"William came by to leave that for Jonas. It's an anniversary gift for you."

Tears brimmed Dani's eyes but did not fall. Her jaw dropped as she let the realization settle in. "Jonas planned this. He…"

She said nothing more, but the tears started to fall, soundlessly, one after another rolling down her face. "What was Jonas thinking? This can't be an original. He knows we can't afford something like that."

Aubrey didn't know what the picture was, only that her sister was falling apart. She gently took the robe from the hanger. Her heart was breaking. True love, once found, should not be torn apart like this. "I imagine Jonas would think you were worth every penny that picture cost him."

Dani tugged at the string bow and drew the paper away from the simple black frame. Even in the shadows, the photograph glowed with light.

Staring at the work, her hand to her heart, she thought she'd never seen anything so arresting.

It was no ordinary snapshot. It *lived.* She felt overpowered by the emotional pull. It was a simple shot of a snow-covered evergreen bough, green needles fighting through the mantle of pristine snow. The bough reached upward, like an arm to the sky. A sky where thin, gold and peach rays of sun broke like hope through dismal storm clouds.

The image settled in her heart and in her soul. And it tugged at her spirit like a little reminder of faith.

William Corey, with his artist's eye and poet's soul had been able to capture, for a brief microsecond in time, the divine shining out of the ordinary.

Whatever the man's sorrows, he'd had a gift.

"It's my favorite work." Dani swiped at her eyes. Her fingers came away wet. "It's called *Hebrews 11:1. Now faith is being sure of what we hope for and certain of what we do not see.* One of my favorite passages. And a good reminder."

"It's lovely. Jonas went to a lot of trouble to get this for you."

"I see that. The doctors spoke to me about letting Jonas go. They say he's probably not going to come back. They think he's already gone. That's why I came home. To think over what they said. To figure out what to do. Or at least be prepared if his coma worsens much more, for then there'll be no hope at all." Danielle stared at the photograph, silent for a long time. "But this, it's like a sign."

"What do you mean?"

"I came home too weary, I just am burned-out and worn-out and out of hope." Dani rubbed her eyes again. "This was just the sign of faith I need to go on. When you talk to William Corey, tell him thank you for this. Tell him this has made all the difference."

Aubrey suspected he already knew.

Chapter Five

The ring of the phone echoed through the dark corners of the great room, shattering the tense stillness of the gathering thunderstorm. William squeezed his eyes shut, but the image of the black storm clouds closing over the sunset's crimson glow remained, along with the desire to capture it on film. A desire he'd thought long gone.

He knew why. Aubrey. For some reason, seeing her had started this. She'd thawed a frozen part of him just enough to feel. Or maybe he'd simply been ready. It had been over four years. They say time heals all things, even, he supposed, a loss so deep.

The phone's insistent ring continued. He checked the caller ID; it was her. His heart skipped from fear that she was calling with bad news—also an unease that she was calling at all. He'd said too much to her. He'd let the vulnerable truth spill out as if it was nothing, nothing at all. He'd opened himself up too much, and now there was no way to pull back his words. No way to hit Delete, rewind and try playing it differently.

He would, if he could. So, why did his hand shoot out and grab the cordless handset?

Because he couldn't stand to sit in the growing darkness any longer. "Hello?"

"William? I'm glad I caught you. This is Aubrey McKaslin."

Yeah, he knew. There was the image of her, graced by the light in the chapel, all purity and sweetness. He'd learned long ago that looks were deceiving, or at least that's what he reminded himself of, so he wouldn't start believing in anyone again. "Hi, Aubrey. How's Jonas doing?"

"He's still in a coma and unresponsive. We're not sure what's going to happen next, though. We're just trying to take it one step at a time."

"That's a nice way of saying they don't expect him to come out of the coma, right?"

"No one wants to actually say that, but; yeah. The chances aren't good."

He squeezed his eyes shut again. He knew what it was like to wait and wonder and pray against all odds.

"William, I have to let you know. Danielle found the photograph you brought over the other night. It made a real difference for her. She said it gave her hope. We have you to thank for that."

"Not me." No one seemed to understand that.

"It was a good thing you did for Jonas. You have no idea what a difference you made."

"It was sitting in a closet, gathering dust."

The warmth in Aubrey's voice told him she wouldn't be fooled. "You did a lot of good for Danielle, and that's making a lot of difference to my family, William. You did that, and I'm so grateful. I wanted you to know."

William watched the black turmoil of the storm clouds crush out the last spears of dying sunlight. He tried to do the same to Aubrey's words. On one level, he'd had a lot of this over the years since he'd been a widower. Whether women meant well or not, too many of them had not been sincere. They'd thought he would be a financially advantageous man to marry.

He knew in his gut that Aubrey meant what she said. Her family mattered to her, the way his once had to him. Maybe that's why she'd seemed to inspire that innate, soul-deep need to pick up a camera again. He was able to see her heart, and it was not so different from his own.

As for the work, what she didn't know was what no one understood. The beauty he found with a lens didn't come from him, but through him. All things good came from God. But it wasn't a discussion he felt up for. He said what was easier.

"If it helped her, I'm glad. How about you? Are you still taking care of your sister's kids?"

"Not as much, now that my dad and stepmom are up from Arizona to help out."

"It must have put a dent in your social life."

Aubrey rolled her eyes. Had she heard him right? "That *is* my social life. I pretty much babysit for Danielle most Friday nights anyway, and my big plans for Saturday night are usually with at least one of my sisters. That's it."

"That's it?" He didn't believe it for a minute. "If

you're not engaged and you're not seriously dating, then you must have come off a breakup. Right?"

"Where did you get that idea? I'm not the dating type."

"I don't believe that."

"Sure you don't, because nobody is more boring in this entire world than I am. Wait, there might be someone up in, maybe, Alaska, far up in the tundra, if there is tundra in Alaska—what do I know? Whoever that poor person is has probably expired from inactivity. Everyone else on the planet has a more exciting life than me."

"Now, I might have to disagree with you. My life could be more boring than yours."

"Impossible. For example, I'm about to do my favorite thing, and it tends to outbore anyone."

"Let me guess. You were reading a book."

"How did you know?"

"I know about the family bookstore."

Okay, it wasn't a sign or anything, Aubrey thought, but coincidence. She'd always wanted to find a man who understood her love of reading, although clearly William wasn't the answer to that prayer. As if! "I think there's nothing more exciting on earth than reading, but my sisters say that's the real reason I'll never get a date. I think books are the epitome of excitement, but not many guys do."

"Well, I don't know about those other men, but I say it's a good way to spend time. What are you reading?"

"Anthony Trollope. And before you say, who—"

"A popular English author who was a contemporary

of Dickens. I'm in the middle of reading *A Tale of Two Cities*. It's my evening entertainment."

"No. You're kidding me."

"Nope. You're not the only one with a love of old and very thick books."

What did she say to that, other than it made him just about perfect?

"How do I tell you that I'm reading my way through the entire Penguin Classics library?" He chuckled. "You're speechless. See? It's true. I make you look like a social butterfly."

"That's a picture." One she couldn't imagine. "Me, a social butterfly? I don't think so. That would be my twin. She's got the gift. She's always been extroverted, so I've always let her—"

"You're a twin?"

"Yep. I'm the oldest by three minutes."

"Are you two identical?"

"Yes and no. We look exactly the same, but our personalities couldn't be more different."

"Then I *might* be talking to your sister right now and think it's you."

"No one has *ever* mistaken me for Ava, unless they didn't know us at all. Trust me, even if we'd wanted to deceive someone like that, as wrong as that would be, no one would believe it."

"Are you two really that different?"

"Night and day. Where Ava got all the social ability, I got all the common sense, which isn't thrilling depending on your point of view."

"Common sense is an admirable quality."

Aubrey rolled her eyes. Notice how he wasn't *inter-*

ested in her, as in a romantic thing? That's how men saw her, she'd learned, as the plain and practical one. Sure, it was always good to have basic common sense, but was she the one with an engagement ring on her finger? No. "Easy for you to say. I thought someone who proclaims himself to be boring might understand."

"You see, I like boring. It's not a liability."

"Says the man who spends his Friday evenings reading."

"I have my reasons, but I still don't see why a woman like you is home alone on a weekend night."

An arrow to her heart. Aubrey scanned the apartment's living room. Although she'd tidied up, evidence of Ava was everywhere. A right-footed yellow sneaker—who knew what happened to its mate?—was sitting lonesome and haphazardly beneath the coffee table. A stack of books, listing to the north, had been shoved onto one of the end tables—Ava's books for her premarriage counseling program at the church. Why was she alone tonight? "Because my sister is off with her fiancé having dinner with his parents."

"Fiancé? Then I suppose that means she'll be getting married."

"Yes, in April, and leaving me. I can't believe my luck. I'm finally getting free of her."

William heard the warmth in her words, and the truth behind them. It was tough facing a change, no matter how good it was. "And what about *your* fiancé?"

"My *what?*" There was humor in her words, a lightness that reminded him of the gentle light of a summer's dawn. "I thought we established that I was single—"

"I still can't wrap my mind around it. It can't be true."

"It's true, because I'm dull. I've been passed over by every appropriate man at my church's singles' groups."

Passed over? He doubted that. "You don't sound unhappy about that."

"As my sister would say, at our age, most of the good men have already been snatched up and married off. And who wants the leftovers? They've been leftover for some very good reasons. Besides, I've watched my twin date and that's been enough for me. I don't have to experience them myself to learn from her disasters."

It was her tone that made him smile and brightened him up inside. It had been a long time since he'd enjoyed talking to anyone so much, and he had to know more. "Disasters?"

"There was the guy she dated before she met Brice, her fiancé. On the third date he behaved inappropriately and in her attempt to escape him she accidentally slammed his hand in the car door and broke two fingers. That's only one of more examples of dating gone wrong. I wisely try to stay as far away from those situations as I can."

"Smart move." It hit him like a blow to his chest that he was laughing. He couldn't remember the last time he'd truly laughed. The odd rumble of it vibrated through him and as the first drops of rain drove at the window, the storm didn't feel as ominous. "I have a fair share of dating gone wrong, as you put it. I stay out of the game."

"Me, too. The entire ballpark. Why try when you know you're going to strike out? My older sister, Katherine, is getting married next month—if she doesn't postpone the wedding because of Jonas—and she said she was lucky enough to find the real thing, but it took her well over a decade of looking. That idea totally exhausts me. I lack the strength and the will. I'm happier sitting at home watching a storm move in, or reading a book, or watching a movie on the classic movie channel."

Okay, he was going to ignore that she said that. He'd been watching the storm move in. He spent evenings between a classic work of literature or a classic movie. Best not to read anything into the fact that they liked the same things. "So, how did your twin find a fiancé and you didn't?"

"We don't do everything together. Well, we did when we were little and all the way through high school. But every year that we get older, we spend more time apart."

He heard the warmth in her voice, and although her tone was light and cheerful, he knew what she didn't say. "It's hard to know she's leaving you behind."

"Not behind."

There was love in her voice—the real thing, like a light that never dimmed, like the light he searched for with his camera's lens. Well, before he'd put his work down for good. It was the light that drew him now. He felt himself leaning toward it, toward her, although she was nearly an hour's drive away. Distance vanished as he listened to her words fill with honesty, another rare thing.

"A wonderful blessing has come into my twin's life," she was saying. "I've been praying for Ava's happiness every day since I was old enough to pray. I'm the one who talked her into trusting this guy she's going to marry, and he's good to her. He really loves her, and he gets her. I know I can hand over the job of looking after Ava to him, and believe me, she *needs* looking after."

"Relieved to hand over that job, are you?"

"No kidding."

He wasn't fooled. No, he'd heard a lot of untruths and falsehoods and full-out lies to know the real thing when he heard it. "You love your sister."

"More than my own life. I have the greatest family. I am deeply blessed. I appreciate them and love them with all my heart. I know a good thing when I see it."

William felt his frozen heart crack a little. The squeeze of pain that followed confused him. He'd kept his heart ice-cold for a reason. Despair had done that all on its own. But now, he felt as if something were struggling to the surface, trapped beneath the ice.

"Here I am, babbling on."

He cleared his throat, but emotion seemed stuck there. "No problem."

"I have another reason for calling. I wanted to make sure you're okay."

It had been a long time since he'd heard that in such a caring way. Her warmth and honesty captivated him and he squeezed his eyes shut, his mind spinning. He remembered how he'd left her in the chapel, how she'd looked like loveliness and hope.

It seemed impossible for him to feel anything again, but real emotion, alive and strong, flared in his chest. Emotions of a deeper nature, beyond the casual simple small talk they'd been sharing. He liked her, but Aubrey McKaslin was getting too close.

That meant only one thing: time to end the call. "I'm fine. Getting along. I'll keep Jonas in my prayers."

"Everyone's prayers are sure helping, I—"

"I've got to go." It wasn't easy to interrupt her. To stop the gentleness of her voice and the bright way she made him feel. Lightning strobed through the roiling black sky in a blinding flash from sky to mountaintop. Thunder crashed as loud as an avalanche rolling downhill, and William didn't know if it was divine help or simple coincidence, but he was grateful for the excuse.

"You shouldn't be talking on the phone. I could hear the thunder from here. William, I'm keeping you in prayer—"

"You take care now."

"You, too." The line went dead the same instant the overhead light winked off. Hail slammed against the windows and the roof overhead. Aubrey set down the phone and went to the living-room window. The storm had drained the last of the light from the evening, and it looked as dark as night outside, except for the brilliant jagged bolts of lightning crackling across the sky. Everything went black, including the other apartments in the building and the entire residential block she could see from her perch.

Maybe she should go in search of a flashlight and some candles. Who knew what Ava may have done with the matches? The chances of finding them had to be next to none. Aubrey felt the edge of the coffee table press against the back of her calves. She'd try the kitchen drawers first, then decide what to eat if the electricity stayed out.

About the time she found a flashlight at the back of the sixth drawer she'd searched, the door flung open with a gust of wind and hammering hail. A faint, familiar shadow filled the entryway and wrestled the door shut.

"Whew!" Ava leaned against the door, looking utterly exhausted. "Talk about a storm. I pulled into the parking lot as the lights went out, or I'd probably be snarled up in a long traffic jam somewhere. The streetlights are out, too. Guess what I brought?"

Aubrey squinted at the brown paper bag. Could it be? "Leftovers?"

"Yep! I didn't forget ya, and good thing, too. And guess what? It's still warm. What have you been up to, besides hunting for a flashlight?"

"It would have helped if you made it a habit to put things where they belong."

"I had technical difficulties."

"What a surprise." Aubrey pulled a knife and fork from the silverware drawer and a length of paper towel from the roll. "I never thought I'd ever be lucky enough to marry you off. I can't believe there was a taker for you."

"I know. It just goes to show that true love doesn't find you until you've given up your last shred of hope." Cheerfully, Ava padded into the living room. "I heard from Dad, who'd talked to Katherine who heard from Danielle that Jonas is holding his own. He's not better, but he's not worse. That's a miracle enough for now."

"And something to be very thankful for." Aubrey

slid onto the middle cushion of the couch and stood the flashlight on end on the coffee table. She opened the brown bag Ava had brought her. "Ooh, chicken manicotti. Garlic bread. Onion rings."

"And chocolate fudge brownies are on the bottom." Ava dropped into the reading chair and tilted her head to one side as if she were focusing on something on the shadowed edge of the coffee table.

Right where she'd left the phone, Aubrey realized. And William's card! She reached out to snatch it.

Not fast enough. Ava slapped her hand down on it. "Well, now, what have we here?"

"Nothing. And if it was, it's not your business."

"You have that wrong, Aub. Everything is my business." If Ava grinned any wider, she was going to sprain a jaw muscle. She snatched up the card and kept it protected against her palm, so that it would be impossible for Aubrey to grab. She squinted in the bad light. "William Corey. Imagine that."

"Danielle asked me to keep him informed of Jonas's condition."

"Sure she did." Ava rolled her eyes, reading far too much into that simple, innocent request.

"Don't even go there." Oh, Aubrey knew exactly what her twin was thinking. Her twin with no common sense whatsoever had an imagination that always got her into trouble. "It was totally nothing."

"If I remember right, didn't I say the same thing when I met Brice?"

"Yes, but this really is just business." Not that she'd remembered to tell him much about it. How could she have forgotten? "He wants to make a donation, too."

"Okay sure, but I said it was just business, too, and look at me—engaged to be married to Brice and having had an *almost* successful dinner with his parents."

"No, when you met Brice, you thought he was a yucky man with no morals, propositioning you. Nothing could have been further from the truth."

"Oh, yeah, well, so I was wrong. It worked out."

It was Aubrey's turn to roll her eyes. Ava was wrong all the time, but she wasn't about to argue with her. That would only keep the conversation focused on William, right where it didn't belong. Ava *so* had the wrong idea about poor William. Time to redirect the conversation. "Why was the dinner with Brice's parents *almost* successful? What did you do this time?"

"It's always me, isn't it? Okay, so it was." In good humor, Ava laughed at herself. "Brice's mom had just got this new vase kind of thing. I guess it was worth beaucoup bucks. Do I look like an art expert? No-oo. I decorate cakes and work part-time in a bookstore when there aren't enough bakery orders. What do I know about porcelain or china or whatever antique vases are made out of? So, I said that it was nice, but our sister had one like it she found at a flea market and Brice's mom about had an aneurysm. She choked right there in the dining room on a bite of manicotti. Brice's dad had to give her the Heimlich."

"Sounds like a typical dinner with you."

"It was a disaster. The vase was some priceless collector thing. How did I know? Although it made Brice and his dad howl with laughter for a good ten minutes. It was even funnier than the time I mistook their conversation on Schubert for the guy who owns the candy store in town. Do I look like a classical music expert?"

"You look like a nut." Aubrey couldn't resist. She loved her sister.

"Don't I know it. I'm waiting for Brice to tear the engagement ring off my finger and run for the hills as fast as he can go, but he says he loves me just the way I am."

"Go figure."

"There is definitely something wrong with that man." Ava sparkled with happiness. "Okay, it didn't work."

"What didn't?"

"Diverting me. I haven't forgotten about this guy." She waved the card in the air for emphasis. "Dorrie said he was so gorgeous, she gave him a nine point five on a scale of ten."

"Why didn't she give him a ten? I would have." The words were out of her mouth before she could stop them. How on earth could she have admitted something so personal? So ridiculous? So not true?

Okay, it was true. But was she prepared to admit that? No. She had to do some backpedaling and fast. "Not that I was really noticing or anything. But if I were a different sort of girl, one who was looking for a great-looking guy, I might rate him a ten."

"But since you're not the kind of girl who is looking for a great guy, you didn't notice," Ava said reasonably. "I understand perfectly."

"You do?" That didn't sound like her sister. Panic shot through her stomach. "Wait, you aren't planning any matchmaking schemes are you? Remember what happened when you tried to set up Katherine with the copier guy?"

"It didn't work out."

"Didn't work out? The copier at the bookstore was broken for three whole weeks because Katherine didn't want to call the repairman to get it fixed. She was avoiding him. I was the one who had to run to the copy shop down the street and get stuff copied. You are a terrible matchmaker. Look at Rebecca."

"That's not a good example. I set them up accidentally."

"You set our little stepsister up with a mean guy."

"I didn't know he was mean. The chef I was dating at the time knew him from a Bible study group. He seemed real nice. How was I to know to he'd be a disaster?"

"Maybe the clue would have been that on date number three you slammed the chef's fingers in the car door when he tried to—you know. Here's a hint. He wasn't a nice guy."

"For the record, I realized that after I set Rebecca and Chris up. And I never meant to break the chef's fingers. It was an accident." Ava rolled her eyes. "What happened to forgiveness? Besides, I wouldn't dream of trying to fix you up. I know that you don't mind having to live alone forever after I get married. I know you like being a single, happening kind of girl."

"That's me." Not. Aubrey rolled her eyes. "I hope the lights come back on. I wanted to start reading my new copy of *Phineas Finn* tonight. And before you say it, I know I'm not going to get a husband sitting home reading an old, thick book, but I like old, thick books and I don't want a husband."

"I don't believe that for a minute. That's dishonest."

It was, technically, because she intended to make it the truth. She would work at it until it was the whole truth, that she didn't mind the feeling of an empty home or looking ahead to a future without a good man to share it with. What were the chances of finding a man who would fall devotedly in love with her? Nil. Men did not fall 100 percent in love with girls like her. It was just a fact of life. And one day, she'd be able to face that fact without it hurting so much.

Not that she wanted to admit that truth, either. Or that her thoughts went automatically to William. "I'm happy with my life. And I love being an auntie. You know I adore Danielle's munchkins and one day, I'll have yours to spoil."

"Scary thought, huh? Can you imagine? That's a disaster waiting to happen." Ava rolled her eyes, but she was beaming joy again. "Well, in good time. I'm not in a hurry. We've got to get Katherine married off first—"

"If she doesn't cancel the wedding because of Jonas's condition. I think she's pretty sure she's going to."

"—then we have to get Jonas well and back on his feet. Then there's my wedding to plan. Then the actual wedding. I want to just enjoy my new life with Brice first before we start a family, so you'll have a couple of years to prepare yourself for the challenge of babysitting my munchkins."

"I can't wait. I'll need that long to gather my strength."

"Oh, here's your book. I'm going to call Brice." Ava

pulled the book off the cushion where she was sitting. "I wonder if William likes to read, too?"

"Don't even go there," Aubrey demanded, but she wasn't sure if she was telling that to Ava or to herself.

Too bad, because William was definitely off-limits. And she liked him. Very much. Wasn't that just her luck?

Chapter Six

She'd been tricked. Duped. Deceived. Days later, behind the wheel of her sensible beige Toyota, Aubrey tried to keep her frustrations at her sister down *and* at the same time keep her eyes peeled for the right driveway, but she'd probably missed it. Nothing surrounded her but wilderness and mountains. The town was nearly an hour away. The directions Ava had scribbled on the back of her bakery's napkins were confusing at best. No surprise there.

What was a surprise? That she'd let her twin talk her into deliveries this afternoon. Now that Dad and Dorrie were in town to help out, she actually had a free afternoon. She'd planned on working in her studio or updating her website or any of the numerous errands that had been put off for too long.

Instead, she'd let Ava, who'd been suddenly overwhelmed with cake orders, talk her into making a few deliveries. She did this all the time for Ava, so why would she suspect that there would be anything out of the ordinary? And there wasn't, until she got to the fifth invoice piled on her front passenger seat and realized that the next delivery was not only way out of town, but it was probably more than an innocent delivery. Ava and Danielle must have concocted this scheme together.

Was that nice, or what? It was a loving thing, that her sisters wanted her to be happy, but they were off the mark. In fact, Ava's harebrained matchmaking schemes were always a sign of sure disaster, so this meant there wasn't the remotest possibility for romance. It didn't matter if she liked William or not, it wasn't as if he were interested in her, right? Besides, she wouldn't allow herself to like him like *that*. End of story.

According to her odometer, she'd already driven the two miles from the end of the maintained county road. Since there wasn't a soul in sight, only trees and an empty gravel road, she pulled to a stop in the narrow lane and went back over the directions. Then she saw it, the unadorned driveway flanked by old-growth cedars, and nosed her sedan down the gravel lane.

But was her mind on her driving? No. It was on William. Would he be glad to see her? She'd tried calling to warn him of her arrival, but there had been no answer. Hopefully, he wouldn't take her showing up with a chocolate cake the wrong way. She steered carefully around the bend in the road. The evergreens were so thick and stretched so high it blocked out all but the smallest dapples of sunlight and most of the sky above. The world and its troubles seemed so far away, and she knew exactly why William had chosen to live here.

The evergreens gave way to a large lush clearing

of land. When had she driven off the edge of the earth and into paradise?

Acres of white board fencing, picture-perfect, framed green pasture. Under the shade of a copse of maples sat an upscale stable, made of log and stone. A stable? Did that mean William had horses? She felt her pulse still when she spotted a sleek gray gelding grazing in the green paddock.

William did have horses. That came as a total surprise, but an exciting one. Okay, so there were a lot of horse owners in the world, but it seemed cool that they had this in common, too. It was always great to meet a fellow horseman, right?

She pulled to a stop in a gravelly area beside the three-car garage. Right in front of her, neatly hung from the light pole was a very large No Trespassing sign.

Oops. Well, she might not be invited, but she had legitimate business. She pocketed her keys and grabbed the bag from the front passenger seat. The minute her foot hit the ground, she took a moment to breathe in the crisp, clean mountain air and feel as if she could brush her fingertips across the iridescent blue sky. In the background, mountain peaks speared up with such force and closeness, she felt as if she could reach out and touch those craggy, amethyst peaks. There was nothing but miles of green wilderness to explore.

The ratchet of what sounded like a round being chambered in a rifle echoed in the heavenly stillness. Larks silenced. The wind stilled. Then she heard the telltale metallic clunk of a gate latch falling shut. She turned toward the stable and there he was, William, astride an impressive, midnight-black Thoroughbred. Why did that suddenly make her nervous?

He halted his horse and leaned slightly forward, resting his fists on the saddle's pommel. He looked rugged and masculine in a black T-shirt and jeans. High astride the tall, impressive horse he seemed, somehow, as distant as the shadows. The dappled shade from the tall grove of trees shifted over him, hiding all but the hard, lean lines of his disapproving face. "Seeing you again, Aubrey, is a surprise."

"A good surprise or bad surprise?"

The hint of a smile strained against the line of his mouth. "Depends."

"I brought cake." She lifted the bakery bag as proof.

"Chocolate?"

"Is there any other kind?"

"Nope." At the subtle brilliance of her smile, William felt the protective walls around his heart buckle a tiny bit right when he needed them the most. She was like a refreshing summer morning, radiating innocence and light, and he couldn't pinpoint why. There was simply something innately good about her beyond the image of the golden hair framing her face and ruffling in the mild mountain breeze and more than the sweetness of her smile.

Drawn to her, he pressed Jet into a walk to close the distance between them. "Why did you bring me chocolate cake?"

"It's not from me. I'm just the delivery person." She held the bag so he could read it. There was a smiling cartoon sun on the side of the bag with the bold script, Every Kind of Heaven Bakery. "I'm on a delivery for my sister. Danielle ordered this for you. As a thank-you."

Realization sucker punched him. "What for?"

"Do you really want me to make a list? There's the lawn mowing and the picture delivery. I guess she also found the book you'd autographed for her. You stopped by the hospital to offer to donate to his medical fund. Your photograph gave her hope when she'd hit rock bottom. Isn't that enough?"

"No." He didn't need anything from anyone—how did he explain that to her? That he might not be happy alone on his mountain, but he wasn't unhappy, either. "I hate to ask how Jonas is doing."

"You know how serious this is."

"My wife's coma continued to degenerate. That's a very distant way to say it, right? Like a line descending on a graph somewhere, as if it isn't about the slow, painful loss of human life. Is that what's happening with Jonas?"

The brightness seemed to fade from her. Aubrey shrugged and concentrated on setting the bag on the top of the low stone fence that separated them. "Actually, he's holding his own. He's responding to deep pain stimulus, or something. Some of his signs have improved. I have no idea what that means or what they are, but Danielle is convinced his vitals change when she's in the room with him. So, maybe between a miracle and her love, it'll make a difference."

In his experience, love hadn't been enough but that didn't mean Jonas would suffer the same fate. "I've been keeping him in prayer."

"I know it helps. Thank you." She gulped in air, as

if willing away the sadness. "So, change of subject because it's too hard to deal with."

"I understand. It's why I live all the way out here."

Her gaze met his, full of heart, and he felt the connection zing through his spirit. She did understand. He didn't feel as sorely alone. It was a nice change.

Unaware he'd nudged Jet forward on the lawn, suddenly they were closer to her. The distance between them was no longer yards but less than two feet with only the decorative stone fence between them.

"Hello there." Aubrey lowered her gaze to the gelding. She held out her hand, palm up, for Jet to sniff. "You are one handsome guy."

William's throat tightened, and he dismounted, hardly aware of the horse's low welcoming nicker as he snuffled at Aubrey's slender hand. He didn't need to ask if she liked horses; he figured Aubrey liked everything. William's every sense, every brain cell was captivated by her. Unable to look away, he watched Aubrey smile when Jet offered his nose for a pat.

"How did you know I'm a softy for a good-looking guy like you?"

The tightness in William's throat expanded until it felt as if not even one atom of oxygen could squeeze past. Emotions he couldn't name, and didn't want to if he could, seemed to sit there right behind his Adam's apple. He couldn't talk or breathe. He could only watch as the big black gelding lowered his head and began to lip at Aubrey's jeans pocket. She must have candy.

Jet stomped and huffed, clearly demanding.

"William, your horse is spoiled."

"Guilty."

"You don't sound one bit sorry about that."

"Nope. He's my best buddy."

"I'm sure he's a good one. And a charming guy." Aubrey could feel the weight of William's focus.

The line of his mouth crooked a little higher in the corners. "Jet seems charmed by you."

"I think it's the roll of butterscotch candy." She slipped it out of her pocket and Jet nodded his head as if he was agreeing.

"It's his favorite."

"I can tell."

Aubrey noticed the kind twinkle in William's eyes. It was hard to notice anything else as she kept the roll out of the horse's reach and unwrapped the candy. If she kept watching William like this, he was going to leap to the wrong conclusion.

She turned her attention to the beautiful gelding. "I'll have you know that my girl's an Arabian and butterscotch is her favorite, too."

She held the buttery candy on her palm for the gelding to lip up. Jet's mouth was velvety warm and his whiskers tickled her skin as he took the offering and crunched away contentedly.

"An Arabian? For pleasure riding or show?" William asked.

"We used to compete when I was in high school, but now we jump for fun. She's one of my best buds, too." Aubrey knew William understood. "My Annie and I have been through a lot together. This is probably the only time in my life when I've been too busy to see her much."

"You miss her."

"I do. Life can't get much better than when you're galloping with your horse."

"I know that feeling."

Caring snapped in the vicinity of her heart. It would be really easy to like William, to truly like him, in a way that could only be one-sided. Whatever she did, she'd have to be careful, very careful, not to let that happen.

Perhaps she'd better concentrate on the horse. He'd finished his candy and had started to nudge her hand, wanting more.

As if she could say no. She was all marshmallow fluff inside, so of course she unwrapped another candy to feed him. She waited until he was munching away before she offered William the roll. "Would you like one?"

"Sure." He moved a step closer and took a candy from the top of the roll. "You've been riding most of your life?"

"Of course. My gran taught me when I was little." Aubrey took a candy for herself and slipped Jet one more butterscotch before pocketing the roll. "She owns a ranch east of the city. She had a serious love for horses. I got that from her."

"Sounds nice to have shared that with her."

"Her and Grandpop. They used to take all of us kids for wonderful long trail rides. It was some of our best times together as a family. Our mom left when I was seven, and that helped get us through. I was the one who spent even more time at the stables."

"Do you still trail ride?"

"Not with my family anymore. Everything changes,

doesn't it? Grandpop passed away a few years ago, and Gran hasn't ridden since. But I'll always have a lot of good memories I wouldn't trade for anything."

William leaned closer, and the empathy on his face showed that he understood. "You know, there's a lot of good backcountry riding around here. Trail riding. Hiking. Canoeing."

Okay, that was too much of a coincidence. "You like canoeing, too?"

"It's one of my very favorite things."

That shouldn't have surprised her, but it did. They had so much in common. She could just picture him paddling through a serene mountain lake, alone, of course. That's how she essentially saw him. She took a step back on the path. "I've intruded on you long enough. Before I go, I've got news on what Danielle's decided to do."

"You mean the medical fund?"

"She doesn't want to take people's money. So many people have offered. It was the first thing the church started to do. But Jonas seems to have great insurance and they aren't hurting at this point. She'd rather donate the money, in Jonas's name, to the widows and orphans fund for the state's lawmen."

"She doesn't believe she's going to lose him."

"If she can, she'll will him well."

He knew what that was like, too. "It's a good cause. I'm still interested in donating. It's the least I can do for Jonas. If there's something else I can do to directly make things easier for Danielle, then you'll tell me?"

"There's more about that than you're telling me, and that's okay. I'm not prying." There was only compassion and concern on her face as she took another step back. "Just ready to listen if you need it. I've put the information for the fund-raisers in the bakery bag."

"I'll take a look at it."

"I'm keeping you and Jet from your ride. I'd better go."

"We're in no hurry." He was at a loss as to why he didn't want to let her go.

She retreated a few more steps into the shadows. "You might want to put the cake in the house first. I'm not sure about the frosting melting or whatever, but it's still, what, in the high nineties?"

"Gotcha. I'll take it in, first." Somehow the words escaped, although the emotion remained lodged tight in his throat, a sharp stubborn tangle he couldn't swallow down or dislodge. He told himself it was because of what he'd told her that day in the hospital, private information he'd kept intentionally buried. That's what this had to be. It was the only thing that made sense. Those had been his truths, his past, times that hurt too much to remember.

He could feel the dark within him, and yet it was not all that he felt. He was aware of the brilliant sunshine, the vibrant summer's heat, the whispering of the green leaves overhead and the warm life of Jet's coat as he nickered after Aubrey. And Aubrey…she made him feel less alone. Every step she took away from him made that lonesomeness return.

She lifted her fingers in a little wave. "Take care, William. Jet, it was nice meeting you, handsome."

The gelding nickered while William stood glued in place, once again unable to speak. Why was it that once again in her presence he longed for his camera? That suddenly he was able to see more of the world and feel his faith?

She moved with elegance and presence; flawlessly except for the limp in her left leg. He'd noticed it before, but he focused on it now. What had happened? He wanted to know more about her. He didn't mean to call out to her. He didn't know he was asking her until he heard his own voice. "Aubrey. Do you want to go riding with me sometime?"

She spun on her heels, one hand lifting to shade her eyes from the glare of the sun as she studied him. For a moment he feared she was going to turn him down, think him a fool for asking.

So, even more impulsively, he added, "Jet wanted me to ask you. He said he'd like the company."

A beaming smile lit up her lovely face. "I'd like that. I'll talk to Annie about it and see what she thinks."

"Then I'll be in touch."

The sunlight seemed to follow her as she turned and picked her way across the rocky border between the mowed grass and the gravel driveway. Even the trees seems to quiet as she passed beneath their boughs, as if they, too, were charmed by her.

She kept her head down as she opened her door and slid behind the wheel. With the sunshine full strength on the windshield, William could see her clearly—every freckle, every curve of her soft petal complexion and her subtle frown of concentration as she buckled herself in and started the engine.

He would never love another woman again. Love had brought him nothing but pain. And it was a moot point anyway, considering that his heart was broken beyond repair. So, why couldn't he turn away from her? She swiped the fringe of golden bangs out her eyes with slender artist's fingers. Light caught on the tiny gold cross at her throat with a quick flash of brilliance that blinded him.

Unmoving, he listened to the crunch of gravel beneath the tires as her vehicle backed up and away. For one brief moment, their eyes met through the driver's-side window. Across the bright sunlight and deepening shadows, William's soul stirred. He watched the road until there was nothing more of her than a glint of sunlight reflecting on the vehicle's rear window. Then only a plume of dust. Then nothing.

Nothing at all.

Chapter Seven

Jet wanted me to ask you. He said he'd like the company. William's words stayed on her mind through the rest of the afternoon and into the evening, even when she was supposed to be concentrating on her Bible study class. Or rather, the lessons of her Bible study class, since it was now over.

Her sister was in the desk across the aisle from her, jamming books into her book bag. "Great class. Hey, so we haven't had time to talk yet today. How did the delivery go?"

"Fine. Just like all the others." She could see her sister coming from a mile away. She gathered up her Bible study materials and slid them neatly into her tote. What she should be doing was not thinking about William, right? Ava wasn't helping. "Will you need help with deliveries tomorrow?"

As if she hadn't heard the question, Ava kept right on talking as she hopped to her feet and wrestled her enormous tote onto her shoulder. "Was he glad to see you? Did you get a chance to talk with him? Did he like my cake?"

"I don't know if he did, since I delivered the cake and left."

"Ooh! You're avoiding telling me stuff on purpose. I know it."

Aubrey settled her book bag's strap on her shoulder. The last thing she wanted to do was encourage this behavior. "You left the keys on the desk, Av."

"I did?" Completely unaware, Ava pivoted in the aisle, spotted her keys, scooped them up and led the way to the classroom door.

Aubrey fell in beside her and they trailed the small crowd filing into the hall. It was fairly crowded for a July evening, and other classes were getting out, too. The hallway echoed with so much commotion. Was it her imagination or did it seem louder tonight than other nights? Louder because of the absolute stillness and peace she'd found on William's mountain.

There she went again. Wasn't she trying to *stop* thinking about the man?

Ava turned to her, eyes full of mischief. "Okay, I need the scoop."

Uh-oh. It was a twin thing. She could tell exactly what her sister was thinking, and there was no way she wanted to talk about William. She wanted to *avoid* discussing William, and the reasons were ones she didn't want to examine too closely. So she went on the offensive. "I hear Spence scared away another prospective girlfriend."

"Sorry, but like that's gonna work. I am the master of distraction. I was trying to get to the bottom of this William thing."

As if she needed help thinking of William. "There is no William thing. Honestly."

"Yes, but you want there to be."

How was she going to deny that? "Have I said anything? No. Not one word. You're reading too much into this."

"Okay, you might not have said anything, but it's there at the back of your mind. Admit it."

"I'll do no such thing. You have romance on the brain."

"I know. It comes from being deliriously happy. You should try it."

"I think I'll skip, thanks." Really, a woman didn't need a wedding ring to be happy. Wasn't her life perfectly fine the way it was?

Yes. So that wasn't the reason she kept thinking about William and his offer to ride together. He had looked good astride his midnight-black horse. Powerful. Essentially masculine. As if hewn of rock, like the mountains that had dominated the horizon behind him. Tender feelings rose through her, but they were *only* protective feelings. She thought of all she knew about William, of his losses and his remoteness. She wasn't interested in him; she wasn't the kind of girl who went around knowingly making mistakes. And how big of a mistake would it be to let herself care deeply for a man who wasn't interested in her? It'd be huge. Enormous. Catastrophic.

"Change of subject," she told Ava, and meant it. There was only one thing that was going to help her put aside every thought of William. Every sigh of admiration. Every ounce of sympathy. "I'm in the mood for chocolate. Want to stop by the ice creamery per usual and pig out on sundaes?"

"Have I ever said no to that?" Ava boldly led the way along the crowded hall, her mammoth bag weighing down her left shoulder. "Hey, I'm kinda tight right now. How about you buy the sundaes, and I'll get 'em next week?"

"Deal."

Poor Ava. Aubrey kept behind her in the hallway, because no one was better than plowing a path through a crowd than her twin. She wondered how on earth she could help her sister more. Business wasn't exactly beating down her bakery shop's front door, but in time Aubrey knew that would change. Jonas was at the forefront of her family's energy, and that's why the bakery had been operating on limited hours. She opened her mouth to offer to man the shop on her days off, but something held her back.

William's invitation.

Wasn't she going to stop thinking about him? Frustration rolled through her. Why was William sticking in her mind like glue?

Because he wasn't in her mind, but her heart. It was hard *not* to have sympathy for him. He was a nice man; it was impossible not to like him. But that was all. She wasn't romantically interested in him. Talk about a totally out there idea.

She was just glad to think about trail riding again. It wasn't safe to ride alone in the backcountry, and she'd lost her trail-riding friend years ago when September's job transferred her north to Whitefish. So, the idea of having a buddy to ride with into the wilderness sounded like a wonderful opportunity.

Oops. What was it going to take to stop thinking about him?

"Okay, what's on your mind? I can tell something's going on." Ava led the way out the doorway and into the hot, bright evening. "I've never seen you so spacey."

"It's been a long day." It was called a diversionary tactic, but it was also the truth. She'd been up early to help Dorrie with the kids, then a shift at the bookstore after which she helped with Ava's deliveries, then Bible study and it wasn't over yet.

A shout rose above the din of conversation surrounding them. "Hey, you two!"

It was Marin, the youth pastor and a family friend, making her way across the parking lot, hurrying to catch up with them. "Look what I have for you. More donations for the auction."

Aubrey could tell by Marin's excitement that it was something good. She crowded close to see the computer-printed sheet Marin was holding. There was an image of a framed work of art—by William Corey. What were the chances?

"Wow." Ava pushed close to see, too. "That's amazing. We have two other originals, you know."

"I know." Marin was nearly hopping in place. "This is phenomenal. One of my kids just brought this to our youth group meeting. He said his family wanted to help, that Jonas had helped them out once. See? Goodness always makes the world a better place. Aubrey, you can upload this onto your website, right?"

"Sure." She saw that the email address of the kid

and his family were printed on the sheet, so she could contact them for more information. The trick was going to be keeping her no-William-thoughts vow. Especially with the gorgeous photograph of his in hand.

Aubrey folded the page in half and carefully stuck it in her book bag. "Thanks, Marin. I know you've been behind a lot of the fund-raising ideas."

"Danielle can stay in denial, maybe that's better for her, but she's going to need help."

"She says she feels guilty."

"It doesn't change the fact. It's a generous idea to give the proceeds in Jonas's name to the fund. It's also something we're praying hard she won't need herself."

"Us, too." Aubrey had never doubted her church family was a blessing. Now she knew how very much. "I can't believe how big this auction is getting."

"The donations still keep coming in," Marin agreed. "Oh, I was supposed to tell you two something else, too. When I remember, I'll email it to you. Let me know if there's anything else I can do. Anything, okay?"

"Have a good evening, Marin." Aubrey tugged her little notebook from her bag and slid the folded page into it for safekeeping.

"You two have a safe trip home. I'm keeping your family in prayer."

Something they'd heard too many times to count since they'd stepped foot inside the auxiliary hall this evening. And not just this evening, but since the moment the news about Jonas's shooting had broken.

"We are so blessed," she said to her twin when they

were alone in the SUV. "Sometimes you never take a look to really see it."

"And sometimes you do." Ava started the engine and, when the warning bell dinged, remembered to buckle her seat belt. "Now, are you going to spill? I have to know what's bothering you."

"It's William. And before you leap to conclusions, it's not for the reasons you think. He's had a hard time of it. Not everyone is as blessed as we are, with family and friends and a community."

"That's true. You know, Spence mentioned to me that he thought William was a good guy."

"Does Spence know everyone?"

"Our brother is apparently cooler than we think he is. Weird, huh?" Ava put the SUV into gear and checked for other cars. "Spence said William is a decent man, high praise from our critical brother. William gives heavily to the united churches charities. Who knew? Anyway, he's handsome and totally a Mr. Wishable and he likes you."

"Right." Aubrey shook her head. Ava. What was she going to do about her sister? Ava was so not in touch with the real world. Her head was always in the clouds. "Trust me, it's not like that, and I wouldn't want it to be. He's not head over heels over me."

"Why not you? You're a cutie."

"You have to say that. I look just like you."

"Yes, but you're not a disaster like I am. That ought to make you a much better catch than I ever was. So, it only stands to reason that you'll find an even more awesome dude to fall in love with you. Why not William?"

"There's something terribly flawed with your reasoning abilities."

"Okay, that's true, but I'm sure about this. Really." She checked the mirror again and eased out of the parking spot.

William. Why did her thoughts zero back in on him? But it was more than simple thoughts, she realized. She cared about him. Really, truly cared. Whatever hardship came her way, she had family around her. Loving, supportive family to cushion her. When hardship came to her family, she had a loving extended family in friends and in the church. But what did William have?

Alone on his mountain, he had no one. No one at all. Her heart ached for him, and ached in a way that it never had before.

William left his riding boots in the mudroom off the back door and wandered through the house to the echoing kitchen. Early-evening shadows crept through the corners of the room, but the bakery box Aubrey had brought him sat square in the center of the island like a bright pink beacon. Earlier, he'd pushed Jet far into the high backcountry where there was no single sign of civilization, where the wilderness was breathtaking so he would have some chance of getting Aubrey out of his mind.

No deal. He'd been unable to do it. Aubrey's wholesomeness had reached right in and taken ahold of him with such force that he could still feel it hours later. Nothing could make it fade.

She was unlike any woman he'd even known. She was true goodness. It was as obvious as the sun in the sky and how easily Jet had trusted her. How easily *he* had trusted her.

Had he made a mistake asking her to ride with him? He didn't know. But he hoped that she was exactly what he needed.

In such a short time, she had changed him. She was like a little drop of goodness falling into his life, and she made him aware of the automaton he'd become. He'd survived by putting one foot in front of the other and just counting the days go by. That's how he'd been living, empty of hope, faith, everything. And he couldn't do it anymore.

He'd never forget the way she'd looked holding Jonas's little girl in that kitchen the first time they met, or in the chapel with the light gracing her. He'd never forget how she'd looked earlier today dappled with sunlight, lovely as a summer's dawn. That's what made him sit down to the computer at the built-in desk in the family room.

It was the hope for hope that made him begin to type—the hope that his life wouldn't always be like this.

It was a rare night home in their apartment and Aubrey was thankful for it. At the kitchen table, she savored the rich chocolate sundae they'd picked up on the way home and checked off things on the daily to-do list. The kids were accounted for—Dad and Dorrie were watching them tonight. Danielle was at the hospital. Jonas was reported to have incrementally improved, another small victory.

All she had left to do was email the donors Marin

had given her tonight. She glanced at the time on her computer screen. That would mean she'd have just enough time to squeeze in a few minutes of reading before prayers and bedtime. It had been another long day, but the days were getting a little easier. She was grateful for that.

As she waited for her modem to connect, she caught sight of Ava in the living room, her feet up on the coffee table, chatting away to her fiancé. She looked so happy, and Aubrey was thankful for that, too. Her twin had had a long string of unhappy romances, so she totally deserved the great guy who'd fallen in love with her.

What was it like to be that much in love? Aubrey didn't know. Sure, she loved reading inspirational romances and a good wholesome romantic comedy and those wonderful classics where true love always prevailed, but that wasn't the same as actually experiencing her own happily-ever-after.

Not that she *had* to have one, but it sure seemed nice. She'd watched so many of her friends find it, and now her sisters. But she'd never come close. She'd spent many of her high-school years recovering from a bad riding accident. Through her early twenties, she'd walked first with a walker, then hand crutches and then a cane. She'd sported a serious limp through her midtwenties. While the limp had faded, her shyness had not. Not dating had become such a habit she didn't even know how to go about breaking it.

Still, seeing her sister so happy made a girl start to wonder just a little. Would there ever be that kind of happiness for her?

And no, that was impossible, she ordered herself before her mind could automatically go straight to William. All she had to do was remember how remote he was, how mantled in sadness to know that he wasn't looking for anyone. He'd lost his heart. It wasn't as if that was something you just got over. Ever.

The computer beeped—she had two new mail messages in her in-box. One from Katherine—a quick checklist for next month's wedding shower she wasn't supposed to know about. So much for that secret. Aubrey mentally rolled her eyes.

And the second message was from William. Talk about a surprise. As she clicked to open it, her heart didn't tug. Really.

Aubrey,
Wow. That was the best chocolate cake I've ever tasted. I owe you a big thank-you for going to the trouble of bringing it out all this way. That's dedication to your sisters. Then again, I think your sister's bakery has a new customer for life. I'll stop by her place the next time I'm in town. Anything else you care to recommend?

And yes, I'm still interested in making a donation. Plying me with chocolate was an excellent idea.
William

Aubrey blinked at the screen. Simply thinking of him was all it took for a lonely ache to come into her heart. Her fingers moved to the keyboard and before she'd made the decision to answer, she was already typing.

William,

While plying you with chocolate wasn't the intent, I'm glad you liked the triple chocolate dream cake. Appropriately named, right? Check out the auction's website, I'll put the address beneath my signature. By the way, we just got a generous donation tonight from one of our parishioners. It's an original from an inspirational photographer named William Corey. He's amazingly gifted.

How was your trail ride?

Blessings,

Aubrey

She hit Send and her heart gave a final, resounding thud. She felt as if she were standing on crumbling ground, as if she could see the pebbles and dirt give way beneath her feet right before she fell into the unknown. Not exactly the most comfortable feeling. Not at all, and she didn't know why William affected her like this.

She didn't want him to.

Now that she'd answered William, she might as well answer Katherine. She was just finishing up that message confirming that, yes, they'd remembered to invite everyone to the shower. Katherine didn't want any of her friends to be forgotten, since it was a "surprise," bless her. One day, Aubrey hoped to be as organized and as together as her older sister. She was ready to hit Send when a new note popped into her in-box.

From William. Really, she wasn't affected by him. And that's the way she intended to keep it.

Hi, Aubrey,
William here. I just popped onto the website. You
have a lot of donations. Count me in. (I'm ignoring
the comment about my work—it's nice of you.) I was
surprised to see items on the site from a certain tal-
ented Miss McKaslin. You should have mentioned you
were an artist. One more thing we have in common.
I can email you the images for your website, or drop
off the originals. Let me know.

Jet and I had a great ride. We hit the summit of the
Lone Tree Mountains. It was a long ride, but worth it.
We could see all the way to Yellowstone Park. Not a
bad way to spend a summer's afternoon. Have you
ridden that far?

What did Annie have to say about Jet's suggestion?
William

Okay, she was seriously going to ignore that *one
more thing we have in common* comment of his. They
had an awful lot in common.

William,
No, I've never ridden that far south. Could you really
see all the way to Yellowstone? That sounds like a
great way to spend an afternoon to me. Did Jet have a
good time, too? Or wasn't he very talkative? I haven't
had the chance to stop by and ask Annie her opinion
yet. I'll have to get back to you on that.

As she was typing away, she heard a distant, very
vague sound but kept typing.

But I think she'd be amenable to it. Her best friend, before he moved away, was a Thoroughbred, too—

"Oh, so there is no William thing, huh?"

Ava's words jerked her out of her thoughts and brought her back into the kitchen where she sat, plain old Aubrey. Apparently, Ava had finished her nightly phone conversation with her fiancé and now she didn't have anything better to do.

"You could be doing your share of the housework," she couldn't help suggesting, but Ava merely scoffed.

"Housework? Please. I am not going to be thrown off the trail, now that I know what's going on. You like William, don't you?"

"William's not *interested* in me."

"What kind of answer is that? You're dodging the question."

"I am, but the answer is obvious and you know why. I have this no-dating habit going, and it's a habit I don't want to break."

"That's not right. You're keeping something from me."

Aubrey hung her head. This was the first time she'd had a real secret from her sister. If Ava knew what William had told her in the hospital and if she'd seen the man's pain when he'd tried to pray in the chapel, then she would understand. But William deserved to keep his pain private. "Trust me, he's just interested in helping with the auction. That's all."

"He must really care about the auction." Ava rolled her eyes, as if she didn't believe any of it, and dropped to her knees to read over Aubrey's shoulder.

As if! "Hey, this is private."

"A trail ride, huh? Very interesting. Don't worry. I didn't see a thing."

Aubrey mentally groaned. How was she ever going to convince her sister that she was fine being terminally single? It wasn't optimal, but she could be happy either way.

Of course, that was easy to say since she'd never met William before. Men like him were no everyday, ordinary occurrence.

Ava climbed to her feet. "I'll lay off, but I want you to know how hard I'm praying for your happiness. I can't go and marry Brice and leave you to fend for yourself."

"You are a nut, you know that?" Aubrey shook her head at her sister, bless her. "Do you have an early start time at the bakery tomorrow?"

"Uh, yeah. I have this huge order of monster muffins for a customer pickup at seven. I'll try not to make any noise when I get up at four-thirty."

"I'd appreciate that."

"Get back to your email. You don't want to leave William waiting. Good night."

Aubrey watched her twin head down the hall. Deep down, she knew that Ava was right. There was a William thing, but it wasn't what she thought. It was friendship, nothing more. Maybe that's why she felt so comfortable with William. Because she didn't have to worry about all those pressures and insecurities and expectations that came along with dating.

What she had to do now was finish the email before her server got impatient and ate it.

—so I think Annie will say yes. Let me know when Jet would like us to come up. I'll hitch up Annie's trailer and we'll hit the road.

Oh, you can drop off any donation at the bookstore or Ava's shop. Or I can always send someone out to pick it up. Let me know what's convenient for you. I'll keep you in prayer,
Aubrey

She waited till the message was sent and then logged off. Had she ever felt so comfortable with a person of the male persuasion? Only with family. It was telling. It was a relief.

She and William really could be just friends. They had a lot in common. They were both alone. They were both without riding buddies. With him, she didn't feel like plain, average Aubrey, and it was nice. Very nice.

When she said her prayers tonight, she would remember to put William in them, not only as someone to pray for, but as a friend she was thankful for. What could be better than that?

Chapter Eight

As she pulled into the small strip mall's parking lot and into a shady spot, Aubrey wasn't sure what mood she was in. It had been several days since she'd exchanged emails with William and vowed not to think of him, but had it worked? Not as well as she would have liked.

The minute she stepped out of the air-conditioned car, she started to melt. It was another blistering Central Montana summer day, and everything was crackly dry. She did her best not to think of how refreshing the green foothills outside of town looked, and the mountains—and William—beyond them.

She hitched her bag higher onto her shoulder, locked the car and started toward the bakery. The newly renovated shop glistened with charm and newness. The long row of front windows were shaded by a cheerful yellow-striped awning and soft white shades that made the storefront look picture-perfect.

The chimes she'd made trilled overhead when she opened the door. The cool whoosh of air-conditioning bathed her hot face and she sighed. The cheerful sun catchers she'd made that hung along the stretch of windows began to dance as she shut the door.

"Hey, stranger." Ava was on the other side of the display case already pouring two large glasses of strawberry milk. "I saw ya comin'."

"Bless you." Something cold was exactly what she needed. It was another long day and not over yet. If she stayed busy enough, then it was easier not to wonder why William hadn't gotten back to her about their ride. "How's business today?"

"About the same." Ava nodded toward the seating area where a dozen bistro tables sat without a single customer. Everything was spotless and lovely but sadly empty. "Except for an early rush for the monster muffins and sunshine scones, it's been like this."

"Okay, so business isn't exactly booming. That doesn't mean that it won't pick up this September. All those college students will be back from summer break, and you're not too far from campus."

"Yeah, I know. I got another wedding cake order, so that part of the business will keep me afloat. Hey, I got all of Katherine's reading group goodies decorated. Want to help me box 'em up?"

"Sure. Did you get her text-message reminder about the final wedding dress fitting?"

"I don't think so. I haven't looked at my phone for a while. I've misplaced it. Jonas is doing a little better, so that means the wedding is still on?"

"Danielle told her not to cancel it, and it's Danielle's call." Aubrey took a long sip of the cold, sweet milk. It hit the spot. She followed her twin into the kitchen.

"What's the plan with the munchkins today? Are they with Rebecca today?"

"Last-minute change. Dad came in to get monster muffins for him and the kids for breakfast. I guess Rebecca was supposed to take them all day, but she has a date with Chris tonight." Ava donned a little pair of plastic gloves and went back to work at the kitchen's big table. "So that means we have to take them shopping with us. Dad's pretty tired, and Dorrie is staying with Danielle."

"Okay." See? She had enough to keep her busy between her job and her family. She studied the rows and rows of decorated cookies spread out over the worktable. "You've outdone yourself. Katherine is going to love these."

"I hope so. I was bored of the usual, so I thought, why not make cookies shaped like books for the reading group? It's been fun. Tomorrow's your day off from the store. Do you have any plans?"

"Nothing in particular."

"Aren't you going to go riding?"

Not so subtle. Aubrey took another sip of milk and headed to the industrial sink to wash her hands. She dropped her bag on the counter next to the sink. The second she turned on the water, the door chime rang.

"It's probably Rebecca with the munchkins," Ava said on her way through the swinging door.

Rebecca was seeing Chris. Again. It was another worry for the family, but was she thinking about that?

No. She soaped and rinsed, but was she thinking about her niece and nephew? Her imminent shopping trip and what to buy for Katherine's upcoming shower?

No. Her mind returned to William. To wondering how he was doing alone on his mountain.

As she reached for the paper towels to dry her dripping hands, two black boots came into her field of vision. Then long, strong legs encased in worn denim.

William. The paper towel slipped from her fingers. She turned toward him, and when their gazes met, everything within her stilled. It was good to see that he was well.

When he spoke, his baritone moved through her as sweetly as a summer wind. "Don't look so surprised. You said I could come by."

Did she look surprised? Aubrey fumbled with the fallen paper towel and managed to make her fingers work well enough to pick it up off the counter and toss it into the nearby can. Her voice sounded almost normal when she spoke. "It's good to see you again, William."

The hard line of his mouth softened in the corners. "I thought you might say that. Your sister sent me back here to fetch you. She's looking over the stuff I brought. Come see."

"Sure."

So, it was all business. Whew. Aubrey couldn't exactly pin down why that was such a huge relief, but it sure made it easier to act as if everything was totally normal.

She followed all six feet plus of him through the sunny kitchen and into the cheerful dining room. Light slanted through the window and sparkled in the sun catchers, but he was shadow, stalking like a giant panther through the sun's brightness. He jammed his fists on his hips and stopped short of where Ava stood at the display case, examining two large frames side by side.

Aubrey saw the closest photograph first. The visual impact hit her like a punch to the soul, dragging the breath from her lungs. There was a golden eaglet, his downy feathers gleaming like gossamers of gold. He was surrounded by a background of dawn's gentle colors. Peach, gold, rose and lavender painted the streaks of clouds. The fragile baby eagle was caught perfectly as he hopped from the rim of his nest and seemingly onto a bed of clouds ready to cradle him. Light shimmered in those clouds like a blessing. She forgot to breathe as she stared at the image in wonder.

William broke the silence. "It's not technically one of my best, but one of my favorites. Maybe because I was rock climbing when I spotted this little guy across the way. I was hanging almost upside down under an outcropping. I nearly dropped my camera trying to get the shot."

"You rock climb?"

"I've been known to do it without falling." His mouth curved upward to show a hint of a dimple.

Sure, and he had probably leaped buildings in a single bound, too.

The second photograph was even more amazing. It was a winter scene of solemn snow and forest, of hillside and frozen stream at first light, when the world was more gray than bright, more sleepy than awake and tinted in a deep lavender glow. The ribbons of clouds had halted in the sky to admire the rising sun.

It took every bit of Aubrey's effort not to admire the photographer standing at her side.

Ava broke the silence. "How do you do this? You make the light glow like you've put glitter on it."

"It's called waiting for the exact moment to take the picture. That, and having a really good filter."

Aubrey wasn't fooled. This was more than craft, it was a calling. A calling he'd turned away from. One that had made him a lot of money, she supposed, since she had no idea what these pictures would go for in a gallery. But it had to be a lot. This donation of William's was substantial. "Are you sure about this?"

"Yeah. It's for Jonas. And maybe there's a miracle waiting for him. I hope he gets well." Sorrow passed across his face, the way a storm fell across the granite face of the mountains.

Aubrey could feel what he didn't say.

William started to walk away. "I can't walk out of here without taking a look at your desserts. That was some chocolate cake you sent to me."

Aubrey's twin dragged her gaze away from the pics. She beamed at him. "Aubrey told me that you liked it. If you're in the mood for chocolate, I baked some fudge brownies this morning that are totally to die for. Interested?"

"How about a half dozen?"

"Super-duper. I'll be right back. It'll probably take me a while, you know, so, Aubrey, why don't you keep our favorite customer company?" She gave Aubrey a telling look and hurried out of sight.

So, the twin had the wrong idea about them. He waited until he heard the door to the back swing shut and they were safely alone before he focused his full attention on Aubrey.

She was still staring at his pictures. Sunlight dappled her with a green and blue glow from the stained glass, and she looked amazing. What made her so infinitely lovely to him wasn't only the way she looked. Sure, she had delicate cheekbones and a small sloping nose, and brilliant violet eyes, but he saw more when he looked at her. Something deeper that shone quietly from inside. She made his guard go down and made him relax. She made him understand how alone he'd become.

"William, you've gone beyond anything we could have expected. I'd say thank you, but it's way too small a word for this."

"They were just sitting around gathering dust."

"Oh, sure they were." She rolled her eyes, not one bit fooled.

She seemed to understand, and he didn't feel comfortable saying more. He'd looked behind and into the past too many times lately, and he couldn't stand to keep revealing it. Some things hurt too much, and always would. He knew if anyone could, Aubrey would understand.

He managed to clear most of the emotion from his throat. "It's the least I can do. It's all I can do."

"It matters, believe me. Would you like something cold to drink? We've got milk, soda, juice, iced tea." She circled behind the counter, reaching for glasses as she spoke. "I'd offer you butterscotch candy, but I'm all out."

That almost made him laugh. "Wouldn't mind some tea. If you're out of butterscotch, does that mean you've been riding?"

"*No.* Life has been too intense. I board Annie at an equestrian stable just out of town. It's just easier. I think this is the first time since our mom left—I was seven—that I've missed so many days of riding in a row." She deftly grabbed a pitcher out of the case behind her and headed his way, balancing two plastic tumblers and a pitcher full of iced tea and lemon wedges. "Annie's always taken care of, regardless if I show or not, but she's my bud. We've been together a long time."

"I understand. You miss her if she's not around."

"I do."

It was strange how he already knew the slightly off rhythm cadence of her gait and the whisper of her movements as she set the glasses on the table in front of him and poured—his glass first. As he watched the golden liquid spill in a perfect waterfall from spout to glass, he wanted to believe that he'd come here to deliver his donation and be done with it.

But it wouldn't be the truth.

"You couldn't live in a more perfect place to trail ride." Her voice shone with wistfulness as she filled the second cup.

Wistfulness. Maybe that's what he was feeling, too. His gaze froze on the line her arm and wrist made holding the pitcher in midair. The tiny, delicate gold chain at her wrist was so airy and elegant, it seemed exactly right for her. He studied the perfect contrast that airy strand of gold made shimmering against the slender, feminine curve of her wrist and hand. Light caught on the glass of the pitcher and transformed the scene.

William itched to have his camera, but he didn't carry a camera with him. He gritted his teeth, frustrated and helpless. He wanted to capture the moment. With the way the slanted sun cut through the catchers, painting separate rays of light in vibrant, royal colors as a backdrop, it made the simple act of a woman pouring a glass of tea ethereal, touched by grace, sheer heavenly innocence.

He forced his attention away, took a sip of the tea and tasted regret.

She set down the pitcher and slipped into the chair across the small table from him. "One day, I want to find my own place out of town so Annie and I can be together. I stayed at one of the rental houses on my gran's property when I was in college, and it was great having Annie so close. She used to poke her head in the windows during the summer. It was fun. And there were a lot of trails to ride."

"A few weeks ago, Jet and I were up in the mountains behind my house and I saw the very fresh tracks of a grizzly bear along a stream. I turned Jet around and put some distance between me and the creek."

"I'm glad you two got away uneaten."

"Me, too." William took another swallow of the sweet tea, unable to stop noticing her. It was his artist's eye, of course. She made a lovely picture. The way she swept at a few escaped strands of her light blond hair was pure grace. Surrounded by sunlight, she looked like goodness itself. The kind of goodness even a man as lost as he was could believe in.

Behind her, the row of sun catchers winked and twinkled. He recognized the whimsical, intricate scenes from Aubrey's website. There was a tiny hummingbird hovering above a honeysuckle bloom. A shaft of sunlight through clouds. The first bloom of a single wild rose.

Those scenes—for some unfathomable reason—reminded him of Aubrey, lovely and simple. Honest. Emotions he would not allow himself to name rolled through his chest.

"The mountain meadows are just starting to bloom with wild roses." He said it without thinking. "When's your day off? Jet and I'll show you."

She narrowed her eyes and studied him, and it was hard to tell what she was really thinking. "I suppose Annie would like that. How long of a ride are we talking about? I have a few hours free tomorrow. Otherwise, we'll have to wait until Friday rolls around."

"This'll take more than a few hours. Jet likes to take his time when we're on the trail. Friday, then, around ten?"

"Sure, but only if Jonas is doing better."

"I understand."

"Tell Jet I'm looking forward to seeing him again. I'll make sure I pick up plenty of butterscotch candy at the store."

"Tell Annie we're looking forward to it, too." He got up. He couldn't help feeling awkward. It was a lot easier blaming all of this on Jet. William didn't want to think about what was really behind the invitation. He wasn't sure he knew.

He pulled his wallet from his back pocket and tossed a twenty on the table. Aubrey was gazing up at him wide-eyed, ready to protest his paying for his drink, but she didn't have a choice. He cleared his throat. "You'll keep me updated on Jonas?"

She nodded, but any answer she may have been getting ready to say was cut off as her twin popped into the room with a small pink bakery box in hand.

"With our thanks," the other sister said as she slid the box onto the table. "I still can't believe what you're donating to our cause. It's totally super-duper. Jonas will be awed by this when he wakes up, of course."

William could hardly nod in acknowledgment. He heard the women's words, but he wasn't capable of ripping his gaze from Aubrey. While the women were identical in looks, he saw the difference. The one wearing the apron bubbled like a mountain creek, while Aubrey was a quiet stream, running slow and deep. She drew him like the stars to the heavens, and, if he was going to reach out to improve his life, there could be no one better to trust.

She didn't appear to be as captivated by him, thank the heavens. Maybe that's why he felt comfortable with her. Calm. At peace. She was getting ready to argue about the twenty, but he stopped her.

"I've got to get back before the storm hits." It was the truth, but a convenient excuse, too. He took the box and headed for the door. "I'll see you and Annie Friday."

"Yes, but—"

"Unless you've changed your mind about riding with us?"

Aubrey couldn't seem to get the right words out. She didn't want him to seriously overpay for the brownies—or to pay at all. "Uh, no, a twenty's too much—"

"Then I'll take one of these, too." He stopped short

of the door, where the sun catchers glinted and swayed. He lifted one neatly off its hook.

"I'll see ya around," he said on his way out the door. The bell chimed, and he was gone.

Aubrey blinked. She knew her mouth was still hanging open—out of surprise or disbelief, she wasn't sure which. She could only stare at the sight of William making his way across the sun-bright parking lot. Dressed in black, he was an odd contrast to the lively green of the trees lining the lot. He paused in the shade beside a top-of-the-line charcoal-gray truck. He drew a set of keys from his pocket and opened the door.

There it was, that raw hurt in her heart, not one of sadness or pain, but because she felt too much. No, correct that. *William* made her feel too much.

She was hardly aware of Ava at her side until her twin spoke. "He's definitely wow. A twenty on a scale of ten. A real Mr. Wish Come True."

Yeah, she'd noticed and she was starting to wish a little, too. That was walking on dangerous ground, so she forced down all the quiet new wishes within her heart until they were silent. It was best to be practical.

"Ava, I think you have marriage on the brain. It must come from decorating so many wedding cakes. It's warping your sense of reality." She said it gently, to tease, to hide the more serious things taking root in her heart. Plus, it made her sister laugh.

"Sure. Right. That's me. But I have weddings on the brain because I'm happily engaged. You know how misery loves company?"

Aubrey nodded, watching as William backed his truck out of the spot.

Ava kept right on chattering. "Well, it's like that but the opposite. Happiness loves company, too, and I want you to be happy."

Me, too. Aubrey felt the power of that wish with all of her soul. William's truck zipped away and turned out of sight. She was a realist, she wasn't the kind of girl who wished on first stars of the night. She had to be real about this, too. She whipped around and started clearing the table. "What time was Rebecca going to drop off the munchkins?"

"Any second. So, how does it feel to have a date with William?"

"Date? I don't think so. He's lonely. I don't have a trail-riding partner. You know September and I used to ride together, but she moved. That's all there is to it."

Aubrey refused to wonder why William had bought one of her sun catchers. She refused to let Ava's hopes divert her from what she knew to be true. "William is alone. He's gone through a lot of hardship all by himself without the blessings of family and friends and the support that we have around us. That's all this is. You're making too much of it. Really. He needs someone to reach out to him."

"Then I'm glad it's you."

Rebecca chose that moment to drive into sight, and Aubrey was grateful for the interruption. She couldn't find the right words to explain what she felt. Before, Ava had always understood, but now…everything was changing from the way it had always been.

As for William, she knew he needed help. She could *feel* it, but she didn't tell her sister that, either.

She said nothing, watching through the windows as

Rebecca, tall and slender and very tan, heaved Madison from her car seat and onto her hip. Rebecca settled a heavy diaper bag on her shoulder and closed Danielle's minivan's side door with the remote. Then, checking for traffic, she took Tyler by the hand.

"Rebecca looks good, doesn't she?" Ava asked.

"Time away from Chris was good for her."

"If only it would stay that way."

They said no more. Everyone in the family had tried to help Rebecca see, but it had only driven her away from them. And now, they had a tenuous peace and at least some closeness.

The kids looked better, too. Tyler seemed more like himself as he charged into the shop. His damp hair spiked straight upward, as if he'd been swimming. "Aunt Ava! Aunt Aubrey! I gotta have some pie. Can I? Pleeease?"

Aubrey let her twin handle it. Emotion still seemed wedged in her throat.

"Sure, thing, kiddo, but only a very tiny, itty-bitty piece." It was their personal joke, which meant a huge slice.

"All right!" Tyler's thongs beat the tile floor in a bee-line to the display case as Rebecca let the door swing shut behind her.

"I'm totally in need of chocolate. It's the only thing that got me through two hours of public swim." Rebecca looked tired, but she was still smiling—always smiling.

Although they weren't related by blood, they were more alike than not. Aubrey reached to take Madison from Rebecca's arms. "You sit down. I'll take charge of our prettiest girl and wrap you up a few treats to go."

"Thank you so much." Sweet as could be, Rebecca gave Madison a kiss on the cheek and slipped into the closest chair. "Let me hand over the keys to Danielle's minivan. I just need to give Chris a call. He said he'd pick me up."

Over the top of Madison's downy brown hair, Aubrey caught Ava's worried look. See, this was what Aubrey should be focusing on—her family and their troubles and how she could help even more. But what was at the back of her mind and lurking in her heart?

William. Her attention shot to his pictures that were all hope and heart and soul. She doubted that he knew she would not be able to stop thinking about him. At least she knew better than to tread on dangerous ground.

He was a good man, soul deep. Maybe it was admiration she felt. Yes, that's what this was, admiration. And if it was more, then she didn't *have* to think about it. It wasn't as if there was some rule or law saying she had to examine these feelings and impossible wishes, right?

Right. She could simply deny those feelings and wishes. In fact, denial was a traditional coping method in her family. Who was she to buck tradition? She was a realist. She had to stay in control of her feelings.

With Madison on her hip, she went into the kitchen to box a few chocolate cookies for Rebecca.

Chapter Nine

An entire week had nearly spun by in a blur, but Jonas had improved and so that meant Aubrey was on her way to see William again. She pulled into his driveway with the trailer in tow, and there he was beneath the shade of the trees where they'd talked before, adjusting Jet's cinch. Dust swirled around her as she stopped the SUV and hopped out, coughing, into the quiet summer's morning. In a navy T-shirt and jeans and boots, he looked ready to ride. A Stetson shaded his face.

William straightened and led Jet by the ends of the reins in her direction. He was actually smiling. "I could see you coming a mile away."

It was an exaggeration, but Aubrey knew what he meant. She squinted against the bright yellow paint job that seemed to attract sunlight and amplify it. "This belongs to my sister. It's shockingly bright, isn't it?"

"I suppose your sedan doesn't have a towing bar?"

"Exactly." Okay, this was going to make her look even more sensible and he was bound to notice. "I wanted a new SUV, but they're fairly pricey, and when

Katherine bought a new car, she sold me hers at the balance of her loan, which was way below blue book. I couldn't refuse."

"Practical."

"Yeah, that's me." Not exactly a compliment, but if she'd even had a smidgen of a doubt—the tiniest drop of doubt—then this cinched it. William, like every other guy she'd come across, saw her as sensible, practical. And in guy talk that meant dull. Plain. Boring.

Yeah, she knew. Not that this was anything more than friendship, but for once, she'd like to be thought of as classy and together and remarkable, like her older sister. But maybe that was never going to happen and if that stung a little, she tucked that down, too, right along with all the other unwished hopes gathering in the bin marked "denial." "Since Katherine's fiancé already owns a house, she has this awesome condo she's not going to need anymore. I'm going to take over the payments, I think."

"Sounds good. Probably close to the bookstore?"

"Yeah. And Ava's bakery."

"I noticed. I stopped by the bookstore while I was in town last week. Ran into your brother."

"He didn't mention it, then again, he's not much of a talker. I was surprised to find out that you knew him."

"From the united charities. Seems like aeons ago." He came into the full sunlight and he looked good. Healthy. Better than she'd ever seen him. There was something snappy to him. Well, maybe *snappy* wasn't the right word, but he definitely seemed to be thriving. His smile came easier as he unlatched the back gate to the trailer. "Spence is a good guy."

"That's what we keep telling ourselves." There was no point in boring William with the details of her family dynamics. Jet was close enough that he nosed toward her pocket. "Okay, I'm glad to see you, too, handsome, and yes, I brought candy for you, but you have to wait. Annie hates being stuck in her trailer and missing everything."

A muffled whinny from inside the trailer seemed to say that Annie agreed. Aubrey politely excused herself to the gelding and slipped past William and into the stall. A few quick minutes later, Annie was backing down the ramp, trying to get her head up to look around.

"She's obviously a well-mannered lady." William's baritone was pure rumbling admiration. "Unlike Jet, who has no manners. He kicks and squeals and refuses to load."

"Annie and I are well-traveled girls." She kept a tight rein on her energetic mare until Annie had all four hooves on solid ground.

"You would have to be if you two competed."

"Annie and I liked to travel."

"You miss it. I can see it on your face."

"We do, don't we Annie?" The mare nudged her with her velvety nose, so Aubrey gave her ears a scratch. They'd been together for almost fourteen years. If William thought she was so sensible, he might as well know all of it. "We took a bad fall during a competition. Really bad."

"That's why you limp?"

"I'm lucky that I walk at all, and Annie almost didn't survive. She shattered her cannon bone and it didn't look as if she could make it, but she surprised all of us." Aubrey took a rattling breath, grateful, always grateful. "But we're still together and we're both fine now."

"Annie couldn't compete?"

She nodded. "And while I could, eventually, I couldn't do it without her. We're buds."

"I see that."

Aubrey knew that probably made her look even more dull. Who knew how far she could have gone with her riding? But that wasn't the important part. Her idea of success was the life she lived right now, with her close ties to her family and friends, and Annie, who had been a loyal horse friend. Those blessings were worth more to her than all the money in the world.

"I understand." It was all William said, but his words came so warmly, she knew he did.

"It was a long time ago."

"It must have been pretty severe."

"There are worse things."

She avoided William's gaze and the concern she knew warmed the cinnamon flecks in his eyes. She turned around to fetch Annie's gear but William was already pacing up the ramp. If she leaned to her left side, she could just see him in the dim recesses of the trailer's second stall, hefting the Western saddle and blanket from storage.

How had things gotten so personal between them? She gulped hard to keep all the things she shouldn't be feeling down in the denial bin in her heart. William needed a friend, not more. And she needed…well, she was happy with her life. She had to be sensible. To see this for what it was. If she didn't, then she'd only get hurt.

Just look at him. He was all substance and character, and it was as obvious as the ground under her feet. He emerged from the back of the trailer, handily carrying the saddle and blanket. He was helping her without even asking first. Ava was right. He was definitely a Mr. Wishable. But not hers.

His shadow fell across her as he halted at her side.

"She is beautiful," he said of the horse. He waited for her to take the blanket laid over the saddle. "Her confirmation is excellent. She won a lot of blue ribbons, did she?"

"She has her share." Aubrey carefully grasped the light saddle blanket by the hem. She didn't notice at all how her heart sighed, just a little, from being so near to him.

Focus, she told herself. The point is the trail ride, right? She gently laid the soft fleece across Annie's sun-warmed withers, her sorrel shining red in the direct sunshine. "Annie and I made the Olympic equestrian team, but that was before the accident. She would have won. There isn't a better horse anywhere."

"So I see." So much love, William thought. For her horse, for everyone around her, for her life. Maybe that was what drew him so strongly to Aubrey. It wasn't only her goodness, but she was everything missing in his life. Everything missing within him. It had been there once. He could see so clearly how he'd stopped living, stopped loving and stopped giving thanks.

It was a good thing he'd invited her. His chest gripped tightly, as if his entire spirit were in agreement. He needed this—a real friend—more than he'd realized.

As soon as Aubrey had carefully smoothed Annie's lavender blanket, he eased the custom Western saddle onto the mare's back. He liked the care Aubrey took with her horse, her every movement steady and calm, her voice low and warm. When she tightened the cinch, her mare didn't fight the tightening of the belt around her middle. The Arabian simply reached around to try to grab Aubrey's hat by the brim.

When Aubrey laughed, it was the softest, warmest sound. It reached deep inside him and made him feel renewed. Not a bad thing at all, he decided. Since Jet nickered his unhappiness with less attention, he turned his attention to his buddy.

Everything was going to get better now. William could feel it deep to his soul.

Aubrey couldn't catch her breath. Beauty was everywhere she looked, in every direction. Complete, flawless beauty. God's nature was an incredible place from the Rockies' proud, rugged peaks holding up the western sky to the offshoot mountains and foothills lifting far above the valley floor. Tall, peaceful evergreens crowded together, arms raised to the infinite sky. Wildflowers peeked their purple, yellow and red heads out from between fern and moss to face the sun.

And the wildlife. She'd seen a hawk stroking the sky in large gliding circles, wings held seemingly motionless. Smaller birds, larks and finches and even a few jays flitted away from their perches in tree branches.

She'd missed this. In her saddle, Aubrey felt deeply

content. The stillness was incredible, the indefinable sense of calm that stretched from the bottom of the valleys to the silent profiles of the mountains. Only the occasional creak of leather or the jangle of a bridle was a reminder that they were in the backcountry. Even the plod of horse hooves on the sun-baked earth seemed a part of the great stillness.

But the best part of the ride? It was William. He was an excellent riding buddy. He led the way along the trail, an old logging road grown nearly over, and set a leisurely, easy pace. He had a sharp eye, too. It was the photographer in him, she supposed. When he spotted fresh cougar tracks, he'd pull up and gesture but didn't break the majestic quiet. His gaze met hers in understanding as she bit her bottom lip to hold in the sigh of awe. An hour into the ride he drew Jet to a halt at the crest of a rise. She reined Annie in beside him and hardly noticed what lay beyond. All she could see was William.

He seemed at peace here. It was in his posture as he twisted a bit in the saddle to look at her, in the straight relaxed line of his shoulders and the easygoing, kind smile that transformed his rugged face. It was an arresting combination that was all substance. Even the shadows were gone from his eyes, as if he'd been able to leave his sorrows behind. She could feel it in the bright air between them.

Definitely wow. It was hard to force her attention to the meadow stretching out before her as quiet and as lulling as a lake. It was one stunning softly pink carpet creeping over the rise of the mountainside and disappearing out of sight. So many roses, there wasn't a single blade of wild grass to break the fragrant, heavenly beauty. She breathed in the sweet wild scent. "Oh, it's like a secret blessing just waiting here to be found."

"I figured you'd like it."

"Like it? I could just sit here forever."

"I thought you'd feel that way." He paused, as if he were going to say something more, something personal, but changed his mind. "I noticed you use a lot of wildflowers in your artwork."

"I do." Okay, she was a little pleased that he'd taken the time to notice that about her. He was a thoughtful man, and it only made her like him more. "Do you mind if I take a few pictures?"

"We've got nothing but time."

When she smiled, William knew he'd done the right thing in bringing her here, in showing her this tiny piece of paradise. He knew how it was, wanting to capture emotion right along with that creative inspiration. He dismounted when she did. He took Annie's reins so Aubrey could wander along the edges of the meadow without disturbing the beautiful flowers. He watched while she knelt and clicked away on the little digital camera she'd had in her saddle pack. He watched her wander along the field's perimeter, stopping to look, consider and kneel again to snap more images.

Perfect. That's what she was. Complete, modest beauty. Never had he seen so clearly. The graceful way she smoothed a fingertip lightly over a fragile velvet petal. She was sweetness itself. Sunlight played in her windswept hair, and the summery top she wore was the exact shade of the roses. Feeling flooded him, hurting like light in a dark place that had been left untouched for too long.

"I've got the best idea for my next project." She glowed with happiness as she rimmed the meadow, heading back his way. "I've been wanting to do more rain chimes, with the fall rains a few months away, and this will be perfect."

"Rain chimes? Never heard of them."

"You'll get the first one for the season, how's that?" She must have enjoyed leaving him to wonder as she stowed her camera in the small saddle pack. "They're like wind chimes, but instead of the wind, they catch the rain and chime."

Sun catchers, wind and rain chimes, he could see the way she took the ordinary and made it a little lovelier. They had that in common, the appreciation of what was right in front of them, and it broke down his reserve, the careful space he kept between himself and other people. He felt revealed as the warm mountain breeze swept over him. Aubrey came close, too close, but he didn't move away.

She pulled a new roll of candy from her jeans pocket. Annie tried to grab it and Jet whinnied a demand, but she only laughed softly as she tore off the wrapper cap. "You two will have to wait. William, you're first."

As William took the first disk of butterscotch, Jet nosed him in the shoulder. The gelding's impatience made Aubrey laugh again, so he gave Jet the piece of candy. The gelding crunched away, causing Annie to lift her lips back from her teeth in protest.

"You're next, you." Kind, always kind, Aubrey slid

a butterscotch onto her palm. The mare lipped it up fast, apparently territorial over what she considered to be her roll of candy.

He could see how it was between the woman and her horse. Close friends. They'd been together through a lot. "How long ago was the accident?" he found himself asking without thought of intention. He just wanted to know more.

"I was sixteen, so, what's that, eleven years ago."

"Most horses don't survive a fall like that."

She stroked Annie's sun-warmed cheek. "We had a top-notch vet and a team of specialists, and God was gracious. Annie got through it."

"Pretty well, by the looks of it."

"We rehabilitated together. It was a long haul, but we made it. We have some of our best blessings in our family. My stepmom was—is—amazing. She made sure both of us were okay." Aubrey could sense there was something William wanted to say or ask, and the furrow across his forehead seemed to confirm it. She pulled two small bottles of tea from her pack and handed him one. "My family has weathered a lot of storms together. Our mom took off one day and never came back. Dorrie had a bout of cancer. Katherine had a very hard time. Annie and I had our accident. And now this with Jonas. Up until now, we've come out all right, maybe because we're all together. When something bad happens, and all turns out right in the end, it's not the same as, say, what you've gone through."

William visibly swallowed, as if he were wrestling with his emotions.

"Were you alone?" she asked.

He winced, as if he'd taken a painful blow and turned away to lay his hand on Jet's neck. Aubrey felt her stomach fall. Maybe she shouldn't have asked. Maybe he wasn't ready to talk. Maybe he never would be.

Then he spoke. "Yes, I was alone. My wife was the only close family I had left. My parents had already passed. They'd been told they could never have children and for one reason or another, adoption didn't work out for them. I came as quite a surprise rather late in their life. Mom said she went to three doctors before she believed the diagnosis of pregnancy. They were in their late fifties when I graduated high school. In their sixties when I married. I still miss them."

Aubrey waited while William paused, feeling the stillness of the mountains become more solemn and the caring for him grow stronger. She didn't only hear the love for his parents in his voice, she could feel it in the air between them, in the silence, and in her own heart. He was, beyond a doubt, a big-hearted man. Sympathy filled her, and she waited, wanting to reach out and not knowing if she should.

He gathered the knotted ends of Jet's reins from where they'd fallen in the grass. "In the end, it was just me watching Kylie waste away in a coma. Knowing there was a little bit less of her with every day that passed until she was gone. The accident happened around the time we'd been talking about having kids. So, we never had the chance. When I buried Kylie, there was no one close to me. That's why I owe Jonas so much. I was too numb to deal with anything, and he helped me with the funeral and all the arrangements.

On his own time. That was beyond the call of duty, and I never forgot what he did."

She heard what he didn't say. There was no one close to help him through his grief. No one near to help ease that unquenchable loneliness and drowning grief. "What about friends? The church?"

He shook his head, as if he did not have the heart to say more.

"I am sorry." She could feel his pain as tangible as the earth at her feet.

"Home was Chicago. We were on vacation. I'd spent time here before, but I was always working. We were bike riding along some of the country roads that parallel Lewis and Clark's trail when an elderly driver lost control and hit her. I was knocked into the ditch and barely bruised, but Kylie, she—" Pain broke in his voice and he fell silent. The saddle creaked slightly as he mounted up. "I couldn't leave her grave to go back home, so I stayed here in Montana."

Alone. Aubrey had never hurt for anyone as much as she did for William. "But you had friends. Extended family. People you could trust who cared?"

"Yes, and no. I pulled away." Settled in his saddle, he spun Jet away from her, keeping his back to her.

But he couldn't hide a thing. She could feel the broken pieces of his heart in the deepest core of her being. A pain too deep to measure. A loss too huge to ever overcome.

"I pulled away," he said with a hollow voice, "because it seemed like everywhere I turned there were people trying to take advantage."

"Like reporters? I don't remember anything in the papers."

"It didn't merit a lot of attention at the time. In Illinois it did. I'd gone back home at first to make the arrangements, to have the funeral there, but I was inundated. Overwhelmed. The reporters were part of it, but to this day it still surprises me that there were some women approaching me every time I turned around. Women who basically thought the grieving widower might be an advantage to them. They were gold diggers, and I couldn't believe their nerve. I'd lost everything; and then I lost my illusions about people, too."

"*Some* people," she corrected him.

When he didn't answer, she mounted up, too, not at all sure if she should. They were surrounded by such beauty, by God's grace in every flower and tree and rock. This did not feel like the right place for such darkness and sadness. "If only there was something I could do for you."

At first, William didn't move. Not a flinch, not a tensing of a single muscle, not even a breath. Maybe he hadn't heard her, she thought. Then he spoke.

"You already have." He pressed Jet into a quick walk and headed east, as if into the rising sun.

"There's one more thing I want to show you." William broke the long stillness that had settled between them. It wasn't easy. What he wanted to do was to retreat back into his silence and withdraw. To put distance between them and keep it there. He hadn't revealed so much of himself to anyone since he'd lost his wife. He'd been without reason or purpose or heart ever since, but something had changed standing at the edge of the field of roses.

Maybe it was being able to see the world so clearly again, or maybe he was starting to live again. Something that had been so hard to do, because real love was everything. He did not think he could find meaning in a single breath otherwise. And now Aubrey's friendship had made him begin to see and feel with his heart again. He hadn't even realized how long he'd been standing as if in utter dark, and the world, in contrast, was so blindingly bright.

Aubrey moved alongside him, quiet and serene on her gleaming red horse. He'd probably been along this trail a hundred times, but he'd never seen the lake shine so brightly, as if a hand had reached down from heaven and polished it until it gleamed. The deep greens of the trees, the softer greens of the grass, the gray granite of the rocks and the lavender faces of the mountains were all so vibrant it hurt his eyes—and his heart—to see.

"It doesn't look real." Aubrey's whispered words were an awed hush. "It looks like someone laid down a mile-long sheet of perfectly hammered pewter."

"It's the light. In an hour's time, the sun will be higher in the sky and it will turn blue like an ordinary lake. It's the mountain's reflection that makes it look gray."

She nodded as if she understood. "This is where you canoe."

"Yes." He let silence settle between them again, and he wanted to press Jet into a walk. He felt safer with distance, but distance wasn't what he really wanted. Old habits died hard. He'd developed a scarred psychological skin and had worn it for so long, keeping people away was his natural MO these days. It took conscious effort to take a deep breath, let it out and stay where he was. His heart beat thick and hollow. "Would you like to go canoeing with me sometime? Maybe something a little more exciting than a placid lake?"

She let the silence settle, too, and he couldn't help but think they were more alike than different, the two of them.

When she answered, she sounded as if she understood what he was offering. Not just a chance to go out in a boat on the water, but friendship. Friendship and nothing more. "I haven't been canoeing in so long I've probably forgot how to row."

He chuckled. "Then that's a yes?"

"Annie, what do you think?" It was hard to tell exactly what Annie was thinking, but Aubrey's smile said it all. "It would be wonderful."

Wonderful? Yep, that was the word. William wasn't ready to end their ride just yet. "There's a forest service road just down the way. I'll take you back on it, if you want. It takes longer, but it's the scenic route. Might come across some deer, maybe some elk. We'll have to see."

"Then it's a good thing I have my camera with me."

That's what he wished he had, his camera with him to capture the morning. No, not the morning, he realized, but her. Light filtered through the evergreens to burnish her, like liquid gold, highlighting her light blond hair platinum, softening her lovely features until she was too good, too sweet to be real and not a dream.

It was like seeing her for the first time, all of her spirit's beauty that was so rare.

"Hand over your camera." He reached out, and her eyes smiled at him as she laid the small camera onto his palm. He could read her face, so honest. She was unaware of his feelings and of what she meant to him. She probably had assumed he wanted a few stills before the light changed and the lake became ordinary, for she turned to watch the water a moment longer. And, so revealed, he snapped a single shot of her.

"Hey!" She scowled at him, but only Aubrey could make a scowl look cute. "No fair. I am *so* not photogenic. You have to erase it."

"If that's going to be your attitude, I'll have to pocket this."

"William. You can't keep my camera."

"Watch me." Sure enough, he slid it into his shirt pocket and wheeled Jet toward the shore, once again leaving her to follow.

She knew he wasn't truly going to keep her camera, but why had he taken a picture of her? Her hair was windblown, her face was probably a little pink from the sun, and her riding hat's wide brim always made her cheeks look chubby.

Fab. Just what she wanted recorded for posterity.

"Are you coming?" he said at the lake's shore, twisting in his saddle to look up at her. His eyes were sparkling; his grin was relaxed and genuine. He looked like a whole new man, a man without shadows as he rode into the full light. "If you want your camera back, you'll have to come with me."

He needed her friendship, this man who had lost everyone he'd loved. She could feel it as surely as if he'd said the words. Okay, it was nice to be needed. She felt her heart fill and her spirit brighten. She braced her feet in the stirrups, ready for the steep, downhill ride to the shore, where William was waiting.

For her.

Chapter Ten

Talk about a fabulous ride. The effects stayed with Aubrey through the rest of the late afternoon and into the supper hour. Nothing could dim her joy. She'd spent the afternoon running errands for Danielle and now she nosed her car through Danielle's subdivision.

It was hard to keep her thoughts from going over the morning spent with William. After all, she'd had a lovely time. She felt bright from the inside out. Wasn't it always a wonderful feeling to find a real friendship? She signaled and turned onto Dani's street. She liked William. She enjoyed spending time with him, but her family was not going to understand that. She knew the parameters of the relationship, but they were all going to leap to conclusions. She'd just have to set them straight, right?

Right. She spotted the dozen cars parked in front of Danielle's house. She managed to wedge the SUV into a spot curbside and, after grabbing the shopping bag with her contribution to tonight's supper, she faced the blistering heat of the July evening. Still one hundred degrees in the shade, and she felt every degree as she made her way up the cement walkway to the front door.

Why was she remembering how temperate it had been on the mountainside with William? Surely it was the sweet, soft, wild wind she was wishing for because it had felt so pleasant. Not scorching and sticky and oven hot. Which was the reason she was wishing she was still up in the mountains. It wasn't as if there could be another reason, right?

Right.

The front door swung open and Ava bopped down the porch steps with Madison on her hip. "Okay, tell me. I gotta have the scoop. How did the ride with William go?"

Aubrey stopped to give Madison a kiss on the cheek. "Thanks for the use of your SUV. Annie and I had a great time."

"Oh, of course you two did. I'm sure being with William had nothing to do with it."

"He has this gorgeous Thoroughbred." Diversion, that was the key to keeping Ava distracted. "How's Dani doing? Was she able to leave Jonas today?"

"She's afraid he's going to wake up any minute and she has to be there when he does."

"Yeah, I get that." There was still a lot of doubt about the extent of Jonas's brain injuries, but it was too scary to think about. "Is Dorrie staying with her?"

"Yep."

Ava said nothing more, but Aubrey knew what she meant. While it was miraculous enough that Jonas was becoming more and more responsive, there were still so many worries.

Unaware, Madison leaned trustingly against Ava's shoulder and held up her chubby arms. "Ay! Pap-op."

Aubrey melted, as she always did for her little niece. "Hello, pretty girl."

Madison's pure blue eyes sparkled. "Ah! Nah-no-gup."

"Really? Well, me, too." She gave a kiss to Madison's baby-soft cheek and received a wet smack in return. "Good girl."

The thud of little-boy feet thumped in their direction. Tyler raced into sight, his fireman hat askew. "Aunt Aubrey! You gotta come see! Uncle Spence 'n' me, we're fightin' fires!"

"Wow, cool. I can't believe you left Spence all by himself. He needs your help, buddy."

"Yeah, I know!" He raced off again, making siren sounds that echoed in the cathedral ceilings.

Aubrey dumped her purse and bag in the entry closet and stood in the cool draft of the air-conditioning vent. That's what she needed. And, since she was back to thinking about William, it was amazing that the serenity she'd felt on his mountainside was with her still. "Seeing Tyler like that is heartening. He's doing better, too."

"It feels as if life just might go back to normal, right?" Ava led the way into the kitchen, where Katherine was busy at the stove tonging ears of corn from a bubbling kettle.

"Hey, there." Katherine looked up from her work. "And exactly why are you so late?"

Aubrey winced. She could tell by her sister's warm smile, that she already knew the answer. She set the bag on the counter and pulled out two loaves of French bread. "I had to get Annie settled in, and I had a hard time leaving her. I haven't been spending as much time with her."

"I see. The horse. Is that the story you're going to stick to?"

"With all my might."

"Okay, I understand the importance of denial. But for the record, great choice. This is *the* William Corey. Spence sings his praises, so that has to mean he's a great guy. And that's exactly what you deserve, sweetie."

See? She'd known this was coming. She had to set the record straight. "First of all, it was a trail ride, not a date. It was *so* not a date. And, Ava, I know that look—"

"What look?"

"That one. It's pure mischief. Don't even go there." Oh, she knew what was coming next. How this was about romance, this was about falling in love with Mr. Perfect, and Ava couldn't be more wrong.

Really. If they knew what *she* knew about William, they would see that very sensibly.

Ava rolled her eyes on the way through the kitchen to the dining room. "I can't believe this. You got to tell me when I was trying not to date Brice, how he was so right for me. And so good for me. And now I don't get to do the same to you?"

"Uh, no-oo. This is not the same thing. I need you both to drop this. It's not like that with William. Really."

"Okay, *sure*." Ava didn't look convinced as she slipped Madison into her high chair, deftly corralling the little girl into place despite her attempts to escape. "And here I thought it was your one chance to break that no-dating habit you've developed."

"Not all habits are bad or need to be broken. For instance, daily flossing can be a very good habit."

"But chronic nonsocial behavior isn't."

"I'm not nonsocial. I'm just shy, which is something you will never be able to understand." But William did.

Ava rolled her eyes. "Okay, so I'm not shy. You don't have to be, either."

"Sure, I'll just toss this personality away and grow a new one."

"That's the spirit!" Not an ounce of mischief had faded from Ava's face.

Apparently, Aubrey would never be able to convince her twin of the obvious.

"Aubrey." Spence strolled into the room, drenched as if he'd taken a hit from the sprinkler. Little Tyler loved to pretend he was a fireman and play with the garden hose. But being a preschooler, he didn't have the best coordination with the nozzle. "I hear you had a date with William Corey."

"Not a date. How many times do I have to say that?"

"Well, whatever it was, I hope you thanked him for those pictures he donated. I took them over to the gallery and the owner nearly had a coronary. I guess they're worth huge bucks. You should ask him if he wants to help more with the auction. Not with more donations, but to volunteer. He's big on that, and it might be good for him."

Uh-oh. Even Spence? "We're only friends. Just friends. I'm not going to explain it again."

"Oh, sure." Spence didn't look as if he believed her, either. "Still, he might want to help out. Anyway, did you remember to bring your laptop?"

Now there was the Spence she recognized: all work. "Yes."

"Okay, then." He gave her a very appraising look, as if he were trying to figure out this William thing, and stormed off.

"With him it's all work, work, work." Ava shook her head. "I don't think we can have a family get-together without him having a purpose behind it. Tonight it's work-on-the-auction stuff. On Sunday it will be to start taking down Katherine's rose trellises so he can transport them to Jack's house. What are we going to do with him?"

Katherine poured the kettle water into the sink with a steamy whoosh. "I tried fixing him up with a friend from the reading group, but he refused to even consider it. He said she was too flighty."

"He says that about all women." Ava adjusted Madison's high-chair tray and handed her a sippy cup.

"It's just a defense." Aubrey could see her brother so clearly. Sometimes it was better not to get involved beyond a certain point, especially when you knew you would get hurt.

It was better to be smart and practical in life and in love. That, in her opinion, was a good habit to follow. Not even a wonderful trail ride with such a good man was going to change that.

William stared at the image on his computer screen, the image he'd downloaded from the digital card in

Aubrey's camera before he'd returned it to her. At the time, she'd made a comment about images of the field of roses and the lake and he'd said nothing. He didn't want to tell her that he wasn't interested in those shots. That wasn't the reason he'd taken the camera from her.

This was. He stared at her image on the screen, framed by light, taken in a quiet moment. Her beauty shone from the inside out, and he was thankful he'd caught her with the lens the way he truly saw her. With his heart.

You know what that means, man. He felt fear thud in the chambers within him. In all the years he'd been tucked on this mountain away from civilization, from people and anything that would remind him that he had no life, he'd never been able to do this. To see once again with faith and hope and capture it.

Even if he'd wanted to.

He had Aubrey to thank for that. Her friendship had made a difference in his life. So much so that he still felt the peaceful aftereffect in the evening hours. The sunset spilled through the wide picture windows of his study and hit the royal colors of Aubrey's sun catcher. Light and color glowed like a promise.

He reached for the phone. He couldn't say why. He did notice that the loneliness bothered him, and wasn't that a change?

The phone rang twice before she answered. "Hello?"

"Aubrey. Bet you're surprised to hear from me so soon."

"Something like that." She sounded happy and bright. "We were just talking about you."

"We?"

"I'm at Danielle's house with my family. I forwarded my home phone to my cell," she explained over the background noise. "We're updating the auction's website. Spence says hi, but I really think he's annoyed with you."

There was humor in her words, and that made him curious. "Why, what did I do?"

"As much as we love that you donated your pictures, do you know how many emails this has generated in three days? Two hundred and eleven. Spence has answered thirty-six, so it's going to be a long evening."

Now he hadn't considered that. "I should help."

"As if you haven't done enough? You don't need to volunteer, too."

In the background he heard a man—probably her brother, Spence—say, "Tell him yes."

Aubrey kept going as if she were ignoring the comment. "Although you're welcome to volunteer, you shouldn't feel obligated."

"I know. And I'm still offering."

"Really? Well, we'd love to have you."

She eased the lonesomeness within him. He studied her image on his computer screen. "Of course, it's not really a generous offer, now that I think about it. It's after eight and it takes an hour to get to town from my place. You'll probably be done for the night by the time I get there."

"There's always tomorrow."

"That, I can do."

"Great." Aubrey felt bright from the top of her head to the tips of her toes. "We're meeting—ah, where are we meeting after church?"

She looked at the expectant faces of her nosy family—bless them—gathering around Danielle's kitchen table to listen in as she talked with William. Why couldn't she remember their plans for tomorrow?

"My condo," Katherine said in that calm way of hers. "Remember?"

That did sound vaguely familiar. Then it hit her. Yikes, she was starting to sound like her twin. This was so not her, forgetting everything. She wasn't behaving like herself. That could *not* be a good sign.

"Ask William if he likes barbecue," Katherine urged.

Ava added her two cents from the kitchen counter. "Tell him I'll make something chocolate if he comes to dinner."

Aubrey felt her cheeks heat. She knew William had to be able to hear them, since no one was bothering to lower their voices.

Spence leaned close. "Invite him to church. Hear that, William? You should come. It's the early service at the Gray Stone Church."

Hayden, Katherine's soon to be stepdaughter, looked up from playing a learning video game with Tyler. "Is that, like, Aubrey's boyfriend?"

She listened to William's warm chuckle. At least, he thought this was amusing, because she didn't. Embarrassment was creeping across her face. Her nose was turning strawberry-red. Another bad sign. Could it get any worse?

Before it could, she got up and walked away from the table. "I'm sorry about that boyfriend comment, William. My family is getting very carried away. You are invited to come over tomorrow, as a friend of the family, if you still want to meet them. They can be scary, but only in the nicest way, of course."

"How about I look for you at the service and we'll go from there."

"That would be perfect." It meant everything to hear the understanding in his voice.

"What can I bring for dinner?"

As if he needed to do one more thing for her family? "We've got it covered. Just come."

"I guess I'll see you tomorrow, then."

"I guess so. Goodbye, William."

She waited to hang up until she heard the click on his end of the line. When she looked up, she realized that she'd wandered all the way to the back deck, just for a little privacy. There, through the large living-room window, she could see her family watching her and debating among themselves just exactly what kind of friend William was.

This was wholly private, what she felt. Friendship, yes. Admiration, yes. Respect, yes. And anything more than that, she didn't have to acknowledge. Just like she didn't have to acknowledge the brightness shining se- cretly in her heart.

Determined to keep feet firmly on the ground, Au- brey pocketed her phone and went back inside. There was more computer work waiting and dessert to help serve and kids to get into bed. She would concentrate on that. Not on William.

William set the phone in the cradle. The sun had sunk lower toward the western mountains, and the spill of light through the window came lower, beneath Aubrey's sun catcher so that it no longer glowed and winked. The simple rose in the glasswork made him remember how she'd looked beside him at the edge of the field, and how she'd made him feel.

It had been a long time since he'd really trusted anyone. He'd glossed over the devastation he'd felt after losing Kylie. For so very long, he'd been alone and glad to be. Trusting no one had been easier. Staying away from others, trustworthy or not, had saved him from caring. And from caring, getting involved. Because love hurt too much.

But Aubrey, she was different. Simply talking with her affected him. He could feel the warmth in his heart like the gentle new glow of the first star of the night. Not romantic, no, it wasn't that kind of glow. Deep down he was so hungry for the ties of family and friends that, as scared as he was, he needed this. He needed Aubrey's friendship. She was one woman he could trust with that need.

While she stood in front of Danielle's pantry shelves with a notepad in hand, Aubrey listened to the sounds of Katherine's, Jack's and Hayden's final goodbyes to Dad and Dorrie at the front door. It had been a good evening with her family, with the excitement of the growing interest in the website's auction items, and the call from William. Danielle was still at the hospital, refusing to leave Jonas, and the strain of it, according to Dorrie, who'd spent all day with her, was starting to take its toll.

She recognized Spence's footsteps behind her in the

quiet kitchen. She didn't turn as she scribbled down another item on the list. "I'm almost done."

"No hurry. I'm waiting for Dorrie to pack a new overnight bag for Danielle. I've got some casserole dishes to return to a few of the church ladies, and I'm swinging by the hospital, too." Spence had that tone in his voice. The seriously serious one. "Did I hear Ava right? Did she try to set you and William Corey up by having you deliver a cake to him?"

"The cake was a thank-you from Danielle, and a setup only works if the two people are interested in being set up." She noticed the peanut-butter jar had nothing but a few scrapings in it, and she added that to the list. "Don't worry, Spence. I'm not looking for an engagement ring from William."

"You're a sensible girl, unlike some others I can name in this family." While Spence looked gruff, Aubrey wasn't fooled. Not a bit. Not at all. She couldn't help adoring her big brother who had taken care of them all through tough times and good. He'd always been there, grumbling, sure, but he'd never let one of them down.

He was simply trying to take care of her now as he lowered his voice. "No one knows William real well, but I know this. He gives heavily to the united charities and he's done it for years, and he's never wanted anything in return, not even a mention of it anywhere. Whenever the soup kitchen is running low on funds, all one of us on the board has to do is call him and there's a check when we need it. He's a reliable and upstanding man, and if he's interested in you, maybe you should take down a few of your defenses."

"You know something about defenses, do you?"

That actually made him smile. "Not me."

"I didn't think so." If anyone had impenetrable defenses, it was Spence. She knew why. He'd been hurt the most after their mother left. She schooled her face, kept her emotions steady and all while adding macaroni and cheese to the grocery list. "You don't have to worry about me, okay? I'm just friends with William. We're riding buddies. He's all alone, and I hadn't been riding in the forests since my old riding buddy moved, you know that."

"Sure." Spence nodded as if he saw her clearly. "Just think about what I've said."

She didn't have to. She ripped the list from the pad and handed it to her brother. "The list is arranged by aisle, if you start at the vegetable side of the store."

"That's very practical of you. You're great, Aubrey. Thanks." He walked away, pocketing the list. "Good night."

"'Night." She closed the pantry door and waited a moment in the empty kitchen, letting the emotion settle.

Dorrie padded into sight. "Aubrey, are you all right?"

"I'm good."

"Are you sure, dear? You look terribly sad."

"It's nothing, really. I'm all right. Did you need something?"

"Tyler's asking for you to come read his bedtime story. Would you mind? I know you wanted to get home."

"You know I can't say no to my nephew."

"I thought you might say that." Dorrie's loving smile

said it all. She came and gave Aubrey a hug. "I've got the book all set out. Tyler's prayers are said and he's tucked in."

"Then you go enjoy a little unwinding time in front of the television. There's a new series starting on Masterpiece Theatre."

"I might do that. Thanks, dear. Are you sure you're all right?"

"I am."

Dorrie didn't look as though she believed her.

Aubrey felt very plain and practical as she turned out the kitchen light and headed down the hallway. She'd told Dorrie the truth. Everything *was* all right; nothing was hurting but her heart.

Chapter Eleven

There she was. The instant William found Aubrey in the crowded sanctuary, his uncertainty faded. It was hard taking this step, harder still to stand with his guard down in the resonant church loud with the sounds of rustling movements and conversations as families settled onto the long pews. Hardest of all was to let in just a little hope.

"William." When she looked up to find him at the end of the row, her smile seemed like a confirmation. "Believe it or not we've been saving a spot for you. If I can get Ava to move all her stuff. Ava."

"I'm hurrying." Her twin, beside her, was busily trying to stuff numerous items back into an enormous tote. "I can't find my Bible anywhere."

"It's probably right where you left it last," Aubrey said patiently. "Like on the nightstand at home."

"Oops." Ava sounded as if she wasn't all surprised. Apparently this was a frequent occurrence. "I'll just share with my handsome fiancé."

William recognized Brice Donovan from the many

times he'd made donations to the united churches board. After saying hello and shaking hands, he nodded to Spence, who was much farther down the row with the rest of the family.

Aubrey scooted over to make room for him next to her and he settled in awkwardly. Church was a place made for feeling, and letting any emotion move through him had been something he'd fought so hard against for so long. It overwhelmed him now. He held back as hard as he could and still he felt, hurt with the newness of it.

Aubrey's smile made the stinging sharper. Her low alto drew him closer.

"I'm glad you came," she said in that gentle way of hers. "I sort of thought that it would all be too much, with my family and everything."

Remembering the boyfriend remark he'd overheard should be enough to keep him away, but he could look into Aubrey's violet-blue eyes and see her honesty. She understood. Gratitude moved within him like light through the stained-glass windows, transforming him just enough so that he could stay. Relax. Feel comfortable at her side.

As for her family, he understood. They were close-knit and protective of her. Something he'd once known and lost, so he got exactly how precious it was. "Don't worry. I understand."

When she smiled, his heart did, too.

She leaned closer. "How long has it been since you've been to a service?"

"Years. It hurt too much to go alone. My wife and I—" He shrugged, unable to say more. He didn't have to. It was a comfort to know that he didn't have to say some of the hardest things out loud. She simply understood him.

The music started. Since everyone was standing and reaching for the hymnals, he did the same. Aubrey's soft, perfect alto didn't surprise him, but what did was the sense of closeness he felt to her.

It felt good, not to be so alone anymore. He was glad he'd come. He had a lot to give thanks for.

Poor William looked lost, Aubrey thought as she peered out Katherine's front window. He stood in the condominium complex's parking lot holding a shopping bag in one hand and studying a piece of paper in the other. A laptop case hung by a strap from one strong shoulder.

"You'd best go save him," Katherine said, as she carried the covered bowl of marinating chicken from the kitchen to the back patio door. "I'll take care of setting the table so you don't have to worry about it. Just go help him."

Yeah, her sister *so* had the wrong idea. Aubrey rolled her eyes, wishing she knew what to say that would make them believe her. The truth wasn't working; only time would show them. She headed straight to the front door. She hurried not because her heart took a dive at the first sight of him, but because the units weren't uniform and the directions could be a little confusing.

She hardly noticed the blistering heat radiating off the blacktop as she headed out the door and onto the front step. Did she notice the sweet honeysuckle scenting the air? Or the kiss of sunlight on her skin?

No. There was only William and the way his face lit up when he saw her. The shadows were gone, and a lot of his reserve. Once, she'd thought him as remote as the mountains and now he was her friend.

"Hi, stranger," she called out, shading her eyes with her hand.

"I guess I'm not lost after all. I was just getting ready to call you." As he walked toward her, his smile widened to show real honest dimples.

Not that she should be noticing that or how handsome he looked in his black trousers and matching shirt. Or how self-conscious she felt in her best lavender dress and matching sandals.

He fell in beside her and said nothing.

A huge silence grew between them. *Quick, Aubrey, think of something entertaining to say. Something engaging. Funny.* She searched her brain, which had gone totally blank. Well, she shouldn't be surprised. She'd never been full of interesting things to say.

William broke the silence, bless him. "This is the place you're going to buy?"

"Yeah. It's like home anyway, since we—I mean, I—spend so much time here. Ava and I are always imposing on Katherine. Well, that was before she got engaged. She had more time on her hands before Jack popped the question, so we helped her fill it. It won't even feel like a real move. I think half of my things are in the guest room."

"Then it sounds like a real sensible purchase."

Yep, that's me, she thought. It was a good thing to be

sensible. Really. That wasn't what was bothering her, if she were honest with herself. No. If she were honest, then she would have to admit she'd been holding on to a tiny hope that William might see her differently. That he might see more in her, beyond the plain and the sensible woman, to the real Aubrey McKaslin.

It was best not to think about all that. "Spence and Dad were just getting ready to barbecue. I hope you like chicken."

"I like everything. I've never been a picky eater. Which reminds me." William held up the large bag. "I stopped by the farmer's market and got some fresh corn."

On the cob. Sure enough, the bag was full of green husks of corn, the tassels a perfect light gold. "You get full marks."

"I'm not done yet." He said nothing more, but his dark eyes were warm with a secret. His smile, so relaxed and bright, made him seem like a whole new man. He stepped into the shadowed foyer after her. "I brought my laptop. I figured it might help out with the online stuff."

"Great. After dinner, we plan to have a huge email session. Even more messages have come in since late night, so we should be busy. Oh, and Ava brought dessert. Her triple-chocolate dream pie."

William had a hard time focusing on much of anything aside from Aubrey. She was all he could see. From the soft shine of her golden hair to the sweet way she talked and moved and smiled, she drew him like the stars to the sky. At peace, he followed her into the large gourmet kitchen. "Where do you want me to put the corn?"

"Oh, on the counter is fine. Would you like something cold to drink?" She opened a stainless-steel refrigerator, and the wide door engulfed her as she began rattling off the choices.

All he could see of her was the hem of her lavender dress and her matching shoes. Cute. Perfect. Nice. Not that he was supposed to be noticing.

"Lemonade," he decided, managing to get the word out of his tight throat. Maybe it was the aftereffect of the service that was weighing on him. Once his guard had gone down, it had been slow going back up. He felt too full of feeling—emotion he wanted to ignore instead of analyze—and eagerly took the glass Aubrey had filled and set on the counter. The icy coldness eased some of the ache in his throat, but not the big one dead center in his chest.

"I have something for you." He set the glass aside and opened the laptop case. Inside was the eight-by-ten he'd matted and framed. "I thought you might like this."

"Oh no, it's not of me, is it?" She didn't cut her gaze to the picture but instead her eyes met his. It was impossible to read what the shadows in them meant. Impossible to understand why she looked troubled. "I *knew* I should have stolen my camera back sooner."

"I wouldn't have let you. Aren't you even going to look at it?"

"I hate to look at myself in pictures."

"Sorry. I want you to look at this one." He felt like

saying more, something about how beautiful he thought she was, or telling her how amazing she looked today. He wanted her to know he had nothing but respect for her.

The thought of saying any of those things, well, it made him feel uneasy. It would suggest a deeper closeness between them that didn't exist.

Or *if* it did, he couldn't acknowledge it.

Her fingers brushed his as she took the frame from him. Peace filled him, and he didn't want to acknowledge that, either, or the fact that he couldn't take his eyes from her. Still, she had not looked at the image. He had to ask. "What do you think?"

Then she looked. She didn't react right away.

Why did that make him nervous? It wasn't like him to hang on what other people thought, but he *had* to acknowledge that her opinion did matter to him. This photograph meant something to him.

Seconds ticked by and she didn't move. She didn't blink or seem to breathe. She didn't smile to say that she liked it, or frown to say she didn't. Nor did she hand him back the photo. His heart began to beat hollowly. There was no way watching her that he could guess at her feelings. He'd never known anyone else who'd been able to keep thoughts and reactions so private. They had that in common, too.

Finally, he broke the silence. "I thought you'd like a picture of you and Annie."

"You thought right. This is incredible. Annie looks—" She didn't finish. "She looks like the champion she is."

"I got a lucky shot."

If that were true, Aubrey thought, then William had been lucky every time he clicked the shutter. This was no exception. How he'd managed to capture the exact moment when Annie had lifted her head to scent the wind, Aubrey didn't know, but somehow the mare was sheer, frozen motion. The fluid ripple of her red mane, the flowing texture of lean muscle beneath sun-warmed satin, and the gloss of sunlight on her sorrel coat made her shine like a dream against the background of blinding blue sky, polished lake waters and rough-cut amethyst peaks.

As for the image he'd caught of her, she didn't even know what to think. She was mostly suffused with the fall of sunlight falling over her. She would have been washed-out had anyone else taken the picture. But, instead, she looked surrounded by light, as if the sun had deigned to lean low to touch the earth and she happened to be in the way. She'd been watching the lake, her hair spilling down from beneath her hat and rippling in the wind at the same angle as Annie's mane.

She didn't look like herself. Sure, it *was* her, but she wasn't plain or ordinary. The woman on horseback did not seem overly sensible or practical. She looked opalescent, tranquil and self-possessed.

Katherine spoke; Aubrey hadn't even been aware of her coming into the kitchen. "This is amazing, William. It looks just like her."

"I think so." William's baritone rumbled with sincerity.

"That's how you see me?"

When he nodded, her heart fell and didn't stop. How perfect was he?

Don't fall in love with this man, Aubrey. But how did she stop the emotion rolling through her with the power of all her unacknowledged hopes and most secret dreams? Wishes that went beyond friendship. Dreams of happily-ever-after with this man who could see her.

Was it possible? Not as things stood now. What was she going to do? How was she going to keep these new, uncertain affections private? Was it on her face, and, if she said one single word, would her voice give it away?

Spence saved her. He marched into the kitchen as if he owned it and placed the marinade bowl into the sink with a *clunk*. "Corn? Great. I'll get this husked. Katherine, you'll boil some water?"

"Sure."

Katherine's moving around and Spence's departure were background because, as hard as she tried, she couldn't seem to make her brain jump out of Neutral. Only one thing was clear. She was in deep jeopardy, and William, he didn't even know he was so dangerous to her.

She propped the frame on the counter, so the rest of her family, who were sure to make their way into the kitchen, could admire William's work.

She wasn't falling in love with him, really. As she headed toward the arched doorway, she tried to convince herself she was in perfect control of her feelings. "C'mon, William, I'll show you the backyard. Katherine has done a gorgeous job with it."

William said nothing as he followed her. They walked in companionable silence, neither saying a word.

It was safer that way.

William had retreated into silence behind the screen of his laptop; it was the most distance he could create between himself and the McKaslin family without actually getting up from the dining-room table and leaving. He wasn't sure what that said about him, that he fought a jagged-edged panic being so near to anyone.

But the truth was, as much as he wanted to get away, he also wanted to stay. He'd had the best time. He hadn't realized how hungry he'd been for an evening just like this one. He liked Aubrey's family. He liked their ties of caring and connection. The shared history. It made him remember his own.

Aubrey sat beside him at the oval table and leaned close to speak low, so only he could hear. "How are you doing? Are you ready to run away from us yet?"

"So far so good." He winked. "You know, now that I have access to your server, I can help out during the week from home."

"That would be wonderful. I want to say that you've done more than enough, but on the other hand, we really need the help."

Wasn't that just his luck?

From across the table, the oldest sister was watching them approvingly. William hoped she wasn't reading more into his presence here than there was, and it made him a tad uncomfortable. He knew it was well intentioned, but love was the last thing he ever would want again. He was glad Aubrey understood, and that was what mattered.

Katherine spoke above the hubbub of the other family members working away behind laptops at the table. "It's a comfort to know that there have been so many people who have wanted to help. People we don't even know, who Jonas has touched in some way through his job or the church. It helps balance out the tragedy. Don't you think?"

Her words, while they weren't directed at him, troubled him. He wasn't sure what to say, because that wasn't his view of life. He wasn't sure what to say.

"That's what everyone says," Spence muttered as he tapped away at his computer. "It's a trite cliché. Nothing makes hardship better. We're just supposed to say that, but it's not true."

The other twin, Ava, made a face. "Yes, we've all heard your tough view of existence. Life is hard and then you die. Do you know what you need, Spence?"

"Is there any way to stop you from telling me?"

"Nope, sorry." Ava sparkled with mischief, apparently living to torment her older brother. "You are a terrible pessimist. You need to turn that around and start thinking optimistically."

Spence frowned, but there was a hint of humor in his voice. "I don't believe in optimism. William, you're a sensible sort. Maybe you can explain life to my little sister who has been hunting and pecking at her keyboard for the last hour, unlike some of us who've actually been *working*."

William still didn't know what to say.

"Hey!" Ava defended herself. "I don't know how

to type. Really. Oops. I think I did something wrong. Aubrey, how do you get something back you've sent?"

"This is a disaster. Let me see what you've done." As always, Aubrey sounded patient and amused.

Why was she so revealed to him? Why could he see so much of who she was? He'd never been able to see anyone so clearly. The depth of love for her family, her commitment, her values, her spirit. When he looked at her, it was as if he was back at the lakeside, holding a camera in his hands and seeing through the lens, seeing all of her, seeing what mattered.

That panicked him. A whole lot. What he should be doing was packing up. It was getting late and dark would be falling. He had a long drive home and chores waiting. So, why wasn't he eager to head out the door?

Everyone at the table broke out in laughter; he'd missed what had been said, but he didn't miss the fact that these people stuck together, regardless of tough times. On the wall behind Aubrey was a collection of framed photos, some in collage mats, some in single frames, and all of family. They'd welcomed him in their midst today, and he was glad. It made the lonesomeness inside him fade.

The sound of the front door opening silenced everyone. Aubrey's twin popped out of her chair, engagement ring gleaming. "It's Brice back with the ice cream. I'll better go help him, he was going to pick up—"

That was as far as she got. A golden blur streaked through the archway and into the room. Ava dropped to her knees and the streak became a golden retriever who gave her a few swipes of his tongue and barked in greeting.

"—his dog, Rex!" Ava finished, and the rest of the women abandoned their work to pet the dog.

"Too bad he can't type," Spence muttered from behind his computer screen.

Yeah, William knew what he meant. It was hard to open up at all. He found it much easier to stay tough and stone-cold.

This was his only defense.

He closed up his laptop and reached for the case he'd left behind him, against the wall. He wasn't keeping track of Aubrey, really, he wasn't, but he couldn't come up with any rationalization to explain why he kept her in his sight. He noticed the moment she became aware of his packing up. She didn't turn to look at him but tilted her head slightly to listen to the zip of the computer case. Tension slipped into the slender line of her shoulders.

The oldest sister spoke first. "William, you can't go yet. Not without a second round of dessert."

"I've got livestock to feed."

"That's right. You and Aubrey are both horse lovers. I suppose you aren't boarding your horse?"

"No, I have enough land. I don't mind doing the stable work."

Katherine nodded slow and sure, as if she approved of him completely now.

Yeah, he knew what she was thinking. Aubrey was right. Her family was kind, but they didn't understand. They wanted the best for her, of course. They looked at him and saw a single, Christian man who happened to be well-off. Wouldn't that be a good situation for their beloved Aubrey? On the surface, he looked marriageable. But underneath, not so much. Underneath there were the broken pieces of his heart that had no pulse, no life.

Aubrey came to him. "Did you want a piece of pie to go?"

"No, I'm too stuffed from dinner. That was some barbecue. Thank you, all."

"C'mon," Aubrey said in that quiet way of hers that drew him so. "I'll walk you out."

"Thanks for the help, William," Spence called out. "I'll email you."

"Good."

Everyone called out wishes for a safe drive, a good night and thanks, as if he'd done something extraordinary. No, coming here had been terribly selfish, he realized as he stopped on the way out of the room to pat the retriever who was grinning so widely he drooled.

The truth was, William had come here tonight to save himself. He didn't realize it until he stepped out into the evening. Twilight hovered like a promise at the edges of the eastern horizon, and the air and sky were mellow. He was finally alone with Aubrey.

She fell into stride beside him. "I can't believe you made it through the entire day with my family."

"Why not? They're great people. It's a special blessing, to have the gift of such a family."

"I'm grateful for them every day."

The blacktop was still radiating heat, and the air was hot, but there was the scent of cooling in the wind that rustled the trees lining the parking lot. It was only the hush that came with the gathering twilight, but to Aubrey it felt like more.

William had fit right in. He'd helped Spence and Dad and Jack dismantle some of Katherine's gorgeous trellises, and when that work was done, he'd tried to help with the dishes, although Katherine had refused to allow such a thing. He'd bantered right along with the family through the email-answering session. It seemed as if William belonged with them.

Even now, her steps and his steps tapped in synchrony and their gaits fell into rhythm while they wandered along the sidewalk toward the guest parking area.

William's pace slowed as his truck loomed closer. "We didn't get a chance to talk about that canoe trip I've promised you. I'll even pack a picnic. Not just bologna sandwiches, but a real nice meal. How about this week sometime?"

"Sure," she managed to say as if it wasn't a big deal. But it was. Huge. Enormous.

Don't think about how perfect it feels to be standing with him like this, making plans, just hanging out. Because that would be acknowledging the worst possible thing that could happen. It would make her admit, even to herself, how much she had fallen for this good man when she had no business doing so.

William fished his keys out of his pocket. "Then it's a plan. I'll call you."

"Sure. Anytime. Except for tonight, I'll be sitting with Jonas for part of the night so Danielle can get some much-needed sleep. Wait, and Monday I'll be babysitting the munchkins. And Tuesday, I've got a late shift at the bookstore. Well, I'm busier than I thought."

"I've never met anyone busier."

"I know, it's the price of being in an enmeshed family. I'll leave my cell on. Please call whenever. I'll manage to find time for you. *Maybe.*" Her tone said otherwise.

He *did* like her. There was no point in denying it. He hadn't given thanks for his life in a long time, but spending the day with Aubrey and her family had inspired him. The blessing of friendship was nothing to take for granted. He popped the locks and opened the door. He'd never found it so hard to leave her before, but she stood there, blond hair rippling in the breeze, looking like everything good in the world. And it was an image that stuck with him long after he'd driven away. He couldn't explain why.

Or why he felt a little bit more like the man he used to be.

It started the instant she walked back through Katherine's front door. Her sisters were being way too sisterly, bless them. Ava was radiating joy as if she were a star shining under its own power. Katherine was looking pleased as she sliced perfect pieces of chocolate pie and slipped them onto dessert plates.

"This is super-duper!" Ava burst out as she poured iced tea into a row of tumblers. "I mean, he's so totally in love with you."

"In love with me?" That was a hoot. The last time she'd looked, "friendship" was an entire universe away from "romantic love." "You're out to lunch as usual, Ava. William doesn't see me like that at all. Trust me."

"Oh, *sure* he doesn't." She'd made up her mind and

apparently nothing was going to change her mind. "Katherine, what's your verdict?"

"Well, isn't it obvious?" Katherine licked a dollop of chocolate icing from her thumb as she carried the knife to the sink. "Did he look at any of us the entire time he was here?"

"In some kind of vague way." Ava spilled tea and put down the pitcher to grab at the roll of paper towels. "I don't think he noticed much of anything with Aubrey in the room."

"At last we've found a man who can see all the lovely qualities in Aubrey the way we do."

"Enough, you two." She tried to keep it light, but the truth was, this wasn't cheerful, it wasn't fun, it wasn't true. What she'd give for their words to be true, she wasn't sure, but it would be a whole lot. What could be more wonderful than for William to love her?

Talk about impossible, though. She gulped air past the pain gathering in her chest. She was the sensible one. She had to be practical. "William is a friend, nothing more. Besides, I'm not his type, and he's not my type."

Katherine shook her head stubbornly. "Sweetie, just look at the picture he took of you."

There it was, still sitting on the counter. Okay, she wanted to read everything into it, but that would be foolish. "He's a master photographer. You know we've had email bids on his work in the six figures and there's no official bidding yet. He makes everything look good in his pictures. Even me."

"No one believes you, sweetie." Katherine grabbed

two loaded dessert plates and headed toward the dining room with them. "Ava, do you believe her?"

"Nope, but then she's in denial."

"No, she's in love. Look at her. She's shining."

They'd guessed? She hadn't even allowed herself to think the truth, but there it was, out in the open. She couldn't argue with them. Her feelings for William, as new and as unwanted as they were, were a fact. She could deny it all she wanted to, but it didn't change her heart.

What was she going to do now? Had William guessed, too? The phone rang, and Ava dashed to get it, leaving Aubrey alone at the island where William's picture stood, a masterpiece of light and joy. She hadn't noticed it had a title before, but there it was, like all his others. *Peter 3:4.*

It wasn't one she automatically knew. Where was Katherine's Bible? Aubrey glanced around and spotted the little flowered book bag tucked in the window seat of the casual kitchen nook, where Katherine did her daily study. What luck. Aubrey went straight to it, hardly noticing Ava's excited screeching. Their maternal grandmother was on the phone. But did that distract her?

No. The Bible's leather cover was worn smooth from use and the pages whispered open as she flipped to the Book of Peter, then the chapter and, her heart jackhammering, to the verse.

You should be known for the beauty that comes from within, the unfading beauty of a gentle and quiet spirit, which is so precious to God.

That was it. The final falling. She couldn't seem to

stop her affection for William from intensifying. Every dream rose up from her soul, and the wish that some-day, maybe, William might feel this way for her, too.

Chapter Twelve

As she tried to get some work accomplished in her studio on her grandmother's property, the only thoughts she had were of William. He'd been stubbornly at the front of her mind since she realized she was falling in love with him. This made it impossible to concentrate properly on anything, including her work. The sketches she'd come up with for her new rain chime designs were not making her happy.

Probably because she kept glancing at her watch every two seconds. William was on his way. He was supposed to be here in a while so they could go canoeing. It seemed as if she couldn't think about anything but him. Or all the things she liked about him. It was a long, long list. So long, that she would probably sit staring into space until she was in the utter and complete dark and not even notice.

The last thing she should be doing anyway, was daydreaming about the wonderful attributes of William Corey. She shouldn't be daydreaming at all, right? Well, she wasn't sure, since she'd never been prone to daydreaming before. She'd always been levelheaded, but she'd never been secretly in love before.

Her sisters had guessed. What if he had? That thought sent her into total panic. Probably, if he thought she'd fallen in love with him, he wouldn't be coming with a canoe and a picnic, right?

That lessened her panic, but she had a greater problem. Somehow, she had to keep her feelings for him secret. That meant, she had to keep the affection out of her voice, out of her words and expressions. While, at the same time, trying *not* to wonder if he was feeling this, too.

William. She knew he'd arrived a moment before she heard the pad of his shoes on the cement outside. It was as if her soul turned toward him in acknowledgment. That's how deeply he affected her.

He filled the open doorway. "This is a nice place you've got here."

"It's my grandmother's property, although she doesn't spend a lot of time here anymore."

"Who keeps up the garden?"

"Spence, mostly, and I tend things when I can. Lately, it's been hit-and-miss, but I usually spend a lot of time here. Since Gran won't accept rent, I work it off unofficially."

"That doesn't surprise me." It was the only word William could think of to say. Seeing her again was like coming home. It was like watching dawn rise and knowing you had the whole sweet day ahead, full of possibilities. It felt right to walk right in, to stand beside her and look over her shoulder at her work on the long, scarred table. There was a big sketch pad and a careful row of descending-sized bowls, lake-gray and textured as if hammered pewter but, instead, it was glazed ceramics.

"From the lake," he realized.

"This is my prototype. You're early. It's only eleven-thirty. Let me close up and find my tennies." Like a morning breeze, she slipped from her stool and landed on her bare feet. She made no sound as she bent to drag a pair of pink sneakers from beneath the table. She slipped her feet into them and grabbed a baseball cap and sunglasses from the organizer against one wall.

How did he tell her that he hadn't intended to be thirty minutes early, it had just happened? Probably because he'd been eager to see her, to talk to her, simply to be with her. It was a comfort, he told himself, the same way it had been a comfort to sit with her family on Sunday. To feel as if he were a part of something again, even if on the outside looking in.

She had a nice setup here, a potter's wheel, an oven and a sink against the far wall. Wide wood-framed windows looked out at views on three of four walls, showing a riot of green garden, a long slope of meadow where quarter horses and paints grazed, and a wide span of gleaming river. But he was only noticing these things so intently because it gave him something to do besides focusing on Aubrey.

He followed her outside into the heat and brightness and wind, and it was as if she were leading him by the heart.

"You won't guess what I've got for us," she said over her shoulder as she traipsed up the pathway toward the gravel driveway where he'd parked. She stopped by the shade where a cloth-covered basket was tucked up against the outside wall of her studio.

"I picked them from Gran's garden and washed them. They should be dry and sun warmed." She knelt to peek beneath the cloth. "Yep. I hope you like berries."

"I've been known to eat my share."

"Excellent." Her smile made his soul sigh.

"Where's the launch?" He hadn't spotted it when he'd come in; mostly he'd wanted to find her first. He opened the passenger door for her and as she brushed close, bringing with her the scent of fabric softener and strawberries, his senses filled with her. Her beauty, her gentleness, her graceful movements, her peaceful presence.

"Thanks for doing this with me," he said, his voice gruff with emotion, raw with honesty. "It means a lot to me to have you here like this."

"For me, too."

She eased onto the seat, and their gazes met. Locked. William realized he felt renewed. The morning seemed more joyful, the sun more cheerful and the wind more refreshing when he was with her. He was simply glad it was. It had been a long time coming, but he was finally out of the dark of his life, starting to live again. While he would never be the same or forget what he'd lost, it felt good to appreciate this life. This day.

This friendship.

Perfect peace. That's what it was like floating the river with William. Aubrey tried to take it all in and memorize each detail—the clear, gurgling river, the amber grasses drying on the riverbanks, the rustling cottonwoods stretching overhead and their dappled shade. But really, all of that was background. William was seated behind her on the board seat. The sun was behind them and she stayed in his broad-shouldered shadow. And felt protected.

Was she dazzled? Yes. One hundred percent.

"Look up ahead." William leaned close to speak against her ear. "The canyon's coming up around this bend."

His nearness brightened her. She squeezed her eyes shut to keep the secret love she felt down deep and hidden, where it belonged.

"Would you do me a favor?"

Anything, her heart answered with sheer devotion. Why couldn't she hold back these feelings?

"Would you mind digging into the basket? I've got my camera in there. I want to take a few shots."

"Sure."

Their fingers touched and she felt it all the way to her soul—and pretended she didn't. She tried hard to concentrate on the music of the river lulling them around a wide sweeping curve and offering an even more breathtaking view. A sweeping green meadow dotted with cheerful yellow sunflowers, vibrant cone-flowers and crimson Indian paintbrush swept up the reaching hills on either side of the river.

"Look." William eased the paddle out of the water and leaned so close she could feel his heart beat. "Up there, near that stump."

She was overwhelmed by him. So out of her realm of experience. Tender feelings kept rising up until all she could feel was joy. All around her sunlight gleamed on calm waters and smiled down on the flowers. She still didn't see what William had spotted until he brushed his hand with hers and gestured. There, barely taller than the fat seed-heavy tips of the wild grasses, was a tiny fawn. Soft and downy, the delicate creature lay perfectly still. Its soft brown coat was sprinkled with snowy-white speckles. Its dainty ears pricked in their direction. Big chocolate eyes studied them with innocent wonder.

Aubrey felt William behind her and heard the board seat creak with his weight as he leaned in for the shot. The man-made click of the shutter, as quiet as it was, was a shock in the peaceful lull. The fawn didn't move, but another had risen up out of the grass to stand and stare beside its twin. Identical little faces studied the intruders. William's shutter continued to click until a soft sound came from the edge of the meadow, and the fawns blurred into motion. In three bounds they were gone from sight, disappearing into the shelter of the trees.

"Breathtaking," William whispered, his camera silent.

Yes, breathtaking was the word. The connection she felt with him was not superficial, but deeper—one of the soul. She'd never felt like this before in her life. It was a terrifying combination of complete vulnerability, peaceful companionship. Being with William was like having all her best blessings rolled up into one. William was the man she'd always hoped to fall in love with—a strong, kind man who saw her, who accepted her and respected her, and who would never let her down.

She was so in love with him. And if she wasn't careful, then it was going to show. William would know. And, what if he didn't feel this, too? What if he never would?

William panned with his camera for a few more shots but didn't take any. He studied her over the viewfinder. "Good thing I brought this. I almost left it at home."

"You got both of the fawns?"

"Yep. Talk about perfect timing, huh? You know, I'm taking pictures again."

"I noticed." There was so much she didn't dare let herself say. She held back all the feelings in her heart with every last ounce of her might. "You have to be glad to be working again."

"It's all because of you."

The ability to speak completely left her. All she could do was manage a nod. Did he know how amazing he was? Graced by light, guarded by the silent trees like loyal sentries behind him, he dazzled her. He was everything good and decent and right in a man. Everything a girl could dream of.

Everything she had ever dreamed of.

"Aubrey, you've been real quiet. Are you okay?"

She twisted around and there it was, the concern on his handsome face. Why did that make pain slice through her heart? "I'm good. It's just hot. I didn't expect it to be quite this hot."

"It's a scorcher. Want some water?" He pulled a small bottle of water out of his pack. "Here."

She reached to take it, doing her best to avoid his

fingers with hers and his smile. "Just what I need. Thanks."

"Sure thing."

William eased back on the bench and watched as she took a sip of water. Having her with him today was like a gift. She improved his day. She was becoming his inspiration, apparently, since he had his camera with him again. Powerful affection filled him. Overwhelmed him. Carried him away like the current guiding them. He didn't know where this strong caring was coming from or why. Perhaps it was gratitude that she was here.

He reached for the little bucket of berries she'd brought. "Do you mind?"

"It's why I brought them."

Her smile did him in—made his world shift and blur. It was like changing a lens—there was that flash of a moment before his eyes adjusted as he brought a scene into crisp focus. When he saw clearly again, he had a handful of ripe, juicy strawberries and Aubrey bent close. Her silken strands of hair had escaped her ponytail, brushing his jaw.

He was distantly aware of the sides of the small canyon rising up around them, and the echoing sound of the water against the tall, ever-rising walls.

Concentrate on the scenery, Will, he told himself, but even his own thoughts came distantly, for there was only Aubrey. She was all he could see. Her rosepetal-soft skin and gentleness and heart. Her fingertips brushed him as she took a berry from the few in his hand. He could smell the sweet strawberry scent on the air between them and, without thought, he cupped her chin with his free hand. He'd surprised her; her violet-blue eyes widened and searched his.

Overwhelming tenderness for her pummeled him like a blow to his chest. Or maybe that was simply his heart unbreaking. Crisp, keen-edged affection overwhelmed him, pulling him along like gravity to the river. He leaned close and then closer, unable to stop this new, all-consuming feeling for her. His mouth hovered a scant inch over hers. "Okay?"

"Yes." The river's current quickened, and the moment he brushed his lips to hers, the canoe began a slow, graceful spin. Aubrey closed her eyes. This was her first real kiss, and it was perfection. His kiss was soft and reverent and real. This was real and it was happening.

He loves me, her heart whispered. Sweet devotion filled her until he was all she could see. Her head was spinning—no, that was the canoe. William broke the kiss, but neither of them moved. The canoe was drifting and scenery was going by. She had no idea what to say. Gratitude filled her when he smiled.

He poured the berries into her palm. "I think I'd better right this boat before we crash into the bank."

"Crashing would be bad." It was all she could think of to say. She watched as he slipped the oar into the water. She should help him. She was perfectly capable of paddling, but she was frozen in place, so filled with rising hopes that she felt higher than the sun shining in the sky.

Sometimes dreams really did come true, she thought, but her cell began to ring. Here? In the canyon? Then she realized they had drifted safely through.

William had straightened them out and the main country road was in sight.

Katherine's cell number was on the display, so she answered it. "Hello?"

"Jonas opened his eyes." Katherine's voice sounded rushed. "Dad said we should all get to the hospital."

That couldn't be good news. Aubrey flipped her phone shut. "I'm sorry. Jonas—"

"I heard." William's face had shuttered. For a moment, he looked as granite-hard and remote as the canyon walls, then he smiled at her, and the look he sent her was pure warmth.

How could he have done such a thing? The weight of it nearly destroyed him as he rowed back to the launch and hurried straight to the hospital. William couldn't even guess at what Aubrey was thinking of him; strain showed on her face. Of course, she had Jonas and her family on her mind, but beyond that, was she mad at him? Disappointed in him?

Why wouldn't she be? He was angry and disappointed in himself. Kissing her like that. What had he been thinking? That was the problem. He hadn't been thinking. He'd acted on pure tender feelings he didn't even know were there. He liked her, sure he did. He cared for her very much.

Maybe too much.

Now, had he ruined everything good in his life?

They were at the hospital. He swung into the half circle to let Aubrey out.

"I'll park and be up," he said, knowing it wasn't the time to say more.

"All right." She avoided his gaze.

Did he blame her? No. Not one bit. He couldn't stop the heavy weight of regret from settling on his chest like a two-hundred-pound barbell. He didn't know what to say as he watched her unlatch her seat belt and open the door. Again, she didn't look at him when she closed the door. Walking away, she seemed so somber. Alone.

No, maybe it was *his* loneliness he felt. The sobering knowledge that he'd messed up the best blessing he had in his life—Aubrey's friendship.

He parked and hiked through the echoing corridors of the hospital to the waiting room he'd visited before. He kept going over and over in his mind how he could fix this. How he could reassure Aubrey that he had nothing but respect for her and how important their friendship was to him. She was a sensible woman. She was bound to understand, right?

Right.

The moment he saw her, he could read it on her face. The news about Jonas was good. There was only relief and joy sparkling in her clear violet-blue eyes. She shone with gladness from the inside out; he could see all the love she had for her family. She was hugging an older woman, and talking with Katherine at the same time. Their excited conversation, while low, resonated through the solemn corridors like sunshine.

A sunshine that seemed to dim when Aubrey spotted him. "William."

Yeah, that's what he thought. Kissing her had been the wrong thing to do. The elation filling her up had dimmed, and his heart right along with it. Stiffly he headed in her direction. "I take it Jonas is going to be all right?"

"Danielle says he's foggy and confused, but that's not out of the ordinary. They'll know more after some testing, but he's awake and he's out of danger. He'll be able to go home."

Sometimes stories ended happily, and William was thankful that this was one of those times. "What a relief for Danielle. What about the kids?"

"Ava's fiancé, Brice, is watching them so we could all be here." She said nothing more and silence fell between them. "I'm sorry our canoe trip was cut short."

"There couldn't be a better reason."

He seemed so distant, Aubrey thought. The hard look was back. He was stony with no hint of emotion. The tenderness she'd seen on his face, after their kiss, had faded slowly. The shadows returned to his eyes.

It *could* be because of the hospital, she realized and her heart broke for him. There was no possible way for him to be here and not to remember his losses. That had to be part of it, but she knew without words that he was moving emotionally away from her. His heart felt more and more distant from hers. She felt those shining dreams within her fade a bit.

"Are you uncomfortable here?" she finally broke the silence to ask. "We could go down to the cafeteria. Or the chapel."

"No, I just need some air." He jammed his hands into his pockets and looked over her shoulder at her family clustered together, now that Danielle had emerged from her meeting with the doctors. "You belong with your family. I'll wait for you out front."

A muscle twitched in his tensed jaw. It worried her. "I can catch a ride back with one of my sisters. I don't want you to be hurt by too many memories here."

"That's not it. Not solely." The tendons in his neck tightened. When he turned his focus on her, he could have been a stranger. His defenses had gone up and the shields around his heart. "I'm sorry about the kiss. I shouldn't have done it. I had no business—"

He fell silent, and in that silence shock washed through her like ice water. Had she heard him right? "You're sorry that you kissed me. You're *sorry.*"

"You have no idea how much." William looked tortured. "It's my fault. I was overwhelmed, and I don't know what came over me."

He didn't know what had come over him? He didn't want to kiss her? Aubrey took a step back, too shocked to react or feel. One thing came through the shock clearly. He didn't love her. All this time, when she'd been falling in love with him, he had not been falling in love with her.

The first swipe of pain sliced through her heart.

He kept talking. "This is one thing you probably won't understand. What I did wasn't sensible. It wasn't planned out. I just wasn't prepared for how much your friendship means to me. How can we be friends after this?"

Friends. There was that word again. The one that slit open her unsuspecting heart like a serrated knife. The one word that she'd never known could hurt so much.

"I know this isn't the time or place to discuss this." He winced. He was clearly hurting, too. "But I can't let this go on. I'll wait for you outside. I'll take you home when you're ready. You should be with your family right now."

"Yes, sure." Too numb to move a muscle, she stood there, probably looking as foolish as her heart had been. She'd known all along that William wanted friendship. He apparently hadn't guessed her true feelings, which was a saving grace. She didn't want him to figure it out now. She gulped in air and took a shaky breath. "I think you should go home, William. I'll probably be here a long time, and I don't want you to wait. Not when it's in the high nineties outside."

"But I—"

"Goodbye, William."

For the first time in her life she didn't feel sensible. She pressed a hand over her heart, amazed that a part of her could hurt so much when there was nothing physically wrong.

Before the dam of feelings could break loose and he could see it, she turned on her heels and walked away. Leaving him standing there, alone.

The way he wanted to be.

Chapter Thirteen

The moment she stepped through the hospital's main doors with Katherine and into the oppressive heat, she knew he was waiting for her. No matter how much she was hurting, her heart seemed to turn toward him like flowers to the sun. She looked and, sure enough, there he was, leaning against a bench in the shade. Waiting to talk about friendship with her.

No thanks. Not right now.

Katherine leaned close to speak low, so her voice wouldn't carry. "See what a fine man he is? How much he loves you? He's been waiting in the heat for two hours."

"Lucky me." The last thing she wanted to do was face him. But she'd never been a coward. "Kath, why don't you go on without me."

"Sure, I understand. William wants to drive you. Don't forget we're meeting tonight at the dress shop. The wedding is on for sure." She was beaming as she moved away and called out hello to William.

William answered back, but he looked unreachable.

She'd lost him for good. She didn't have to be a rocket scientist to know that. She'd crossed the line in their friendship; he'd crossed that line for some unknown reason, and now they were left with goodbyes to say. She hated goodbyes.

He paced toward her, giving her the hint of a smile, instead of the full one. Even then, the impact of his half smile made her want to dream. It took all her strength to fight the wish for those dreams and impact of his nearness. But could she stop the love in her heart for him?

No. Even when there was no hope for the kind of relationship she wanted with William, she still loved him. She couldn't even keep control of her feelings. How sad was that? Since she couldn't stop her feelings, she had to at least cover them up. Keep things light and on the surface. Friendly. Maybe then this goodbye between them wouldn't hurt so much. Because she'd already decided. This had to be goodbye.

She would not settle for friendship and secretly hope for him to change his mind. This was a good theory, but in practice, she couldn't pretend. It was one thing when she hoped he might feel this way, too. But another when kissing her had filled him with regret. He saw it as something to apologize for.

It had been her first kiss. A disastrous first kiss.

Remember, keep it friendly, Aubrey. No matter how tough that is to do.

The sun was in her eyes when they met in the middle of the lush green lawn fronting the hospital. William towered above her, silhouetted against the sky in all his broad-shouldered glory like a legend of old. She stood in his shadow and felt plain and very sensible. "You didn't have to stay, William."

"I had to. I feel terrible. Your friendship is the best blessing—the only blessing—I've had in a long while. And I just messed it up. I have to know if you can forgive me. If we can go back to things being the way they were."

Oh, if only it were possible. She knew it wasn't because right here and now, standing in his presence, there was only turmoil and an unsettled feeling of hurt inside that she could not still or quiet by force or willpower. There was no longer the peaceful, safe harbor they'd found together.

No, this raw-edged ache in her heart came from being with him. This had gone well beyond simple friendship for her, and she could not turn back the clock or change the truth in her heart. It hurt too much. She knew it always would.

She steadied her voice before she answered him. "Now it's my turn to be sorry. No, I don't think we can go back to the way things were between us."

"Maybe if we give it a little time?"

"I wish it were that simple."

"Me, too." William hung his head. He knew she was right, but he'd been hoping there was a way to salvage things. Neither of them had moved a hairbreadth closer, but he was intensely aware of her. How could he not notice the cute slope of her perfect nose? Or the porcelain-fine cut of her dear face? How she moved his spirit without saying a word?

He didn't want to be moved by her. He wanted to be Mount Everest, remote and cold and unreachable.

But despair moved through him, pulling at him like a lead weight, taking him down, keeping him under. Like a drowning man, he gulped for air, but there was none. The brightness faded from the day, the light from the sky.

This was over, just like that? He squeezed his eyes shut so he wouldn't have to look at her. So she would stop having this overwhelming, unstoppable effect on him.

Be strong, William. Whatever happened, he had to keep distance between them. He had to stop his heart from this terrible thaw. He could walk away now and save himself more pain. So, why did his feet refuse to move?

"If you ever change your mind, or think you can forgive me," he found himself saying. "If you miss the company of having a riding companion—"

"I know what you're saying, and I won't change my mind. This is goodbye, William."

Don't go, he wanted to say. He needed her friendship. He needed—he didn't know what he needed or why he felt the way he did. And to tell her all of this would be too honest. Make him too vulnerable. He wanted to be glacier cold, but instead he was as warm as the sun-baked earth.

Good going, William. If he kept going like this, he was going to lose all control completely. Every last shield would be down, and then where would he be?

"I'm sure Danielle and Jonas will be in touch," she said as she moved away. "Don't forget the auction next Saturday."

"Will you be there?"

"No." She'd be helping with the paperwork before

and after, but the gallery owner would handle the actual bidding. But explaining all that was more than she wanted to say to William. More than she could say.

What she had to do was to keep her dignity, to hold it all inside. She steeled her spine and tried to make her face as placid as possible, so that William had no hint of how she really felt. No hint at what was truly inside.

Tucking away her hopes, she gathered enough courage to do the right thing—walk away. After all, she'd known from the start that he wasn't looking for love. He probably never would be.

Walking away was the hardest thing she'd ever done. She was leaving forever the only man she'd ever loved. With every step across the grass she felt it more. The crash of those new, shining wishes for true love. The shatter of those dreams of loving William through a lifetime. Forever gone.

She could feel his gaze on her back as surely as the relentless beat of the sun, but the connection she'd felt with him, or maybe the tie she imagined, was no longer there. The sidewalk blurred ahead of her. She walked faster. The sooner she left William behind, the better. She didn't want him to ever guess how far she'd fallen for him. She never wanted him to know about the tears running down her cheeks, the first wave of the heartbreak to come.

She broke into an all-out run the instant she was in the parking garage, hoping to be in the privacy of Dorrie's car before the first sobs broke.

By the time William made it home, the sun was low in the sky, shining down on the proud profile of the

Rockies, painting them luminescent rose and purple. The color streaked like tracer missiles across the sky. He escaped the echoing emptiness of his house, but the painful lonesomeness of it followed him out onto the back step and also, regretfully, Aubrey's words. Aubrey's pain. *No, I don't think we can go back to the way things were between us. I wish it were that simple.*

He scrubbed his face with his hands, unable to escape the image of her looking so forlorn, her face schooled to hide her emotions, unaware that it did no good. To him, she was as transparent as glass. He'd learned to read the subtle changes in her eyes and face, revealing her heart.

It hurt too much. All he could see was her hesitating before she ran away. Waiting for him to call her back. To say what she wanted to hear. To be what she needed him to be. To say the words he could not allow into his mind, his heart or his soul.

I cannot love her. Even as he willed the words to be true, he knew that they weren't. He'd done everything he could, raised every shield and used his every defense so this wouldn't happen. So he wouldn't be here right now feeling as if he'd had his chest ripped open, bleeding from the inside out. But what good did it do?

He could hold on to that truth as hard as he wanted to, but it would make no difference. It would not make the pain inside him go away. It would not make the raw, open spaces in his heart close up and heal.

Because it was no longer the truth. The one thing he'd held on to so tightly with all his white-knuckled strength had become a falsehood and, even knowing that, he could not let go of it. Could not face what the truth had become.

He did love her. What could he do about that? He could sit here and try to hold back and change the tides of his heart.

Or he could simply wait and over time, these strong feelings for her would fade into nothing at all.

I will not love her.

He held on to that wish with all his inner strength and steely willpower. Although he feared it would do no good. He suspected that it was too late.

It had been a tough afternoon to get through, but she'd done it. She had her car back, her calm back and if her heart was still in a million pieces, nobody had to know. Aubrey pulled her sensible beige Toyota into the bridal shop's parking lot and recognized most of the parked cars—most of the family had beaten her here. Ava was just climbing out of her SUV.

"Hey, Aub? Are you okay?"

Aubrey startled. Her brain was foggy, but apparently she wasn't hiding her heartbreak well enough. Some things were too private to share. At least, right now. She shut her car door and studied her twin, who had strawberry icing streaked across the front of her bright yellow T-shirt. "Yeah, I'll survive."

"You don't look like it."

"It's been a long day." It was her story and she was sticking to it. She followed her twin toward the shop's front door. Everything felt like a mess—mind, body and soul. She gulped in a breath of hot, dry July air.

Pull it together, Aubrey. Somehow, she had to act

as if nothing had happened, and how impossible was that? She *wasn't* all right. With so much of her heart missing, how could she ever be okay again?

But finally, there was so much to celebrate—and without worry or tragedy. This was Katherine's final fitting for her wedding. There was so much to look forward to. Their grandmother's upcoming visit. Ava's engagement. Jonas's improvement. So much to be grateful for. She would concentrate on that.

Sounded like a good plan, right? Aubrey felt a crack of pain in her soul and she sealed up her feelings. Somehow, she had to put on a smile for her family. For herself. For her dignity.

Katherine must have seen them coming because she opened the door. She looked radiant; how could she not be? She'd found the love of her life. No one deserved a good man the way Katherine did.

"Ava, you're hardly late. This is like a major miracle. A once-in-a-lifetime occurrence." Katherine held the door wider.

"A total shocker," Aubrey found herself saying, as if the day hadn't happened. As if she had a whole heart beating within her chest.

Ava sparkled as she marched to the front door of the wedding boutique. "Hey, it's not as if I'm never on time."

"Just *almost* never on time," Katherine teased. She looked beautiful, as always, in a navy knit summer top and tasteful navy shorts. Her matching flats didn't seem to actually touch the ground. She looked so happy she seemed to float.

"Ooh, look at that dress!" Ava was immediately distracted by a shop crammed full of wedding gowns. "How am I ever going to decide for my wedding? This is torture. Who knew getting married was so agonizing? Which dress? Which bridesmaids' dresses? Where, when, how, and then trying to fit everything on my poor credit card."

Aubrey hung back, letting the door close behind her, trying to put her plan in place. She swallowed hard. Just because she was surrounded by beautiful, exquisite wedding dresses simply waiting to be worn, she didn't have to be reminded that she'd dared to secretly pick out her own gown long ago.

It was still there, a princess-style satin with hand-sewn pearls. She'd never dared to let herself think of wearing it before. She'd fallen in love with it long before she'd ever met William. But now, she realized it was one of those secret dreams she'd never let herself actually picture. But it was there, still, in the pieces of her heart.

Don't think about what you lost, Aubrey.

She turned her back on the dress. On the dream. On the wish. If only she could turn her back and deny how much she'd loved him. Still hopelessly loved him.

"This way, girls!" Dorrie squeezed between rows of white satin and tulle and popped into sight. "The dresses are laid out and ready. My, they're so beautiful. Aubrey, dear, are you all right?"

She suspected her stepmom had figured things out. She swallowed hard as Dorrie headed straight for her with that penetrating, motherly radar. There was no way she could hold it together if everyone knew. No, these feelings had to stay hidden for now, even if she felt so alone, without her sisters' comfort.

Aubrey forced what she hoped was a smile on her face. "I can't wait to try on my bridesmaid's dress."

"Aubrey's just had another date with William," Ava volunteered, looking even happier. "So you know she's got to be happy. William likes her."

Those words were like a knife twisting in her heart. Aubrey gasped from the pain. "N-no. You have that wrong. We're not a couple."

"Yet." Ava piped in. "You're just in the denial stage. I know. I was there a long time."

"I'm not in denial."

"Ha! That sounds like denial to me." Ava grinned. "What do you think, Katherine?"

"I think it's official."

How did she make them understand? "Oh no, you have it all wrong."

"Oh, sure we do." Ava wasn't believing a word of it.

"He's such a nice man." Katherine smiled her approval. "See? What did I tell you? Good things happen to good people."

She couldn't take it anymore. Aubrey opened her mouth to tell them the truth, but all her pain stuck in the middle of her throat. Only a squeak came out. How did she get them to change the subject? It was killing her to hear his name and to stand in this shop with happiness and the promise of wishes coming true all around her. Her heart cracked all the way down to her soul.

"You girls, look what you've done." Dorrie's scolding was loving and sympathetic as she took Aubrey by the shoulder. "Poor Aubrey is speechless. Come along and let's get these dresses on. Where is Rebecca? Is that her, driving up?"

Aubrey didn't think she'd ever been so grateful for her stepmom. Somehow, she managed to head toward the back where the dressing rooms were. She heard Ava call out, "No, that's not Becca. It's the teenager."

"How's she working out at the bakery?" Dorrie asked Ava as Aubrey ducked behind a long rack of exquisite silk dresses.

"Great," Ava said.

Aubrey spotted a chair and plopped into it. She smiled at the store worker who was prepping the changing rooms with bridesmaids' dresses in varying tones of soft pinks.

She'd never felt so alone.

Chapter Fourteen

Aubrey couldn't remember such a bleak night. Of course, her mood might have something to do with it. She'd successfully got through the dress fitting intact. Now, she had one more errand and then she could call her day done. The first thing she was going to do was head home to her apartment, draw a bath and try to soothe away all this horrible grief. Somehow she had to figure out a way to put herself back together. Who knew love—and losing it—could hurt so much?

She pulled her car to a stop in Danielle's driveway and turned off the ignition. The headlights died, leaving such a thick darkness that it felt as if she'd been turned inside out and she were looking at the contents of her heart.

She carefully gathered the plastic-encased bridesmaid dress from the seat beside her and stepped out into the darkness. The humid puff of wind was oppressive and smelled like steam. A storm was on the way. Already the sky was endless and moonless. Clouds had blotted out the stars on her drive over, and now it was hard to make out the steps to the front door, even with the ambient light from the street and the other neighbors' houses. Danielle's windows were dark. The kitchen window, the closest window to the door, was curtained and dark, too.

Not wanting to wake the kids, Aubrey found the key on her ring and unlocked the door. Danielle knew she was coming over with the dress, but she called out softly in the entryway, not wanting to startle her. "Dani?"

"In here," came a thin reply.

Aubrey followed the sound of her sister's voice through the dark to the living room, where a small reading lamp illuminated Danielle seated in an over-stuffed chair. The rest of the living room was dark and quiet, which was definitely not normal. Had something else happened when they'd been at the dress fitting, and then out to dinner? Worry ratcheted through her. "Are you all right? Jonas? He is all right?"

"Yes. I'm just tired."

Whew. Aubrey set her keys and the dress down on the couch and came farther into the room. "You look a lot more than tired."

"I think it's the letdown. I've been running on fear and adrenaline and willpower for so long, now that the crisis is over, I can't move."

"Then you don't have to. I can stay and help, if you want."

"You have done too much already, although there is one more thing. I could use a hug." Danielle stood and held out her arms. Her clothes hung on her. She'd lost so much weight. Exhaustion marked her lovely face.

Aubrey held her tight. Maybe she needed a hug, too. When she stepped back, she resolved to stay a little longer and make sure Danielle didn't need anything else. "The good news is that you can sleep all night in your own bed."

"Now that Jonas is sleeping peacefully, yes." Danielle took a step back, letting the dark take her. "It was all I could do to leave him, even when the doctors said he would be fine tonight."

"It's been a long road for you."

"Yes, but I haven't been on that road alone. How can I ever thank everybody? And you, too."

Just what I needed, Aubrey thought. A reminder of how full her life was and how blessed. "Thanks aren't necessary. Taking care of you is. Did you manage to get any supper?"

"Oh, I fed the kids some mac and cheese and nibbled on that. It was nice to be able to make their meal and give them their baths and put them to bed. Everything is going to go back to normal. And get better from here on out."

"That's what we're all praying for."

You know what? She was who she was—sensible, practical—and she was glad for that. Perhaps she would never be adorable like her twin or classy like Katherine or truly lovely like Danielle, but Aubrey didn't mind so much about that anymore. She made a difference being who she was. After all, *someone* had to be sensible.

She took Danielle by the hand. "Let me make your favorite sandwich. We'll get food in your stomach and put you to bed. A good night's sleep will make tomorrow easier to deal with. Do you want me to stay in the guest room? I can keep an ear out for the kids."

"No, the sandwich would be enough. If you don't mind."

"Are you kidding? It's my pleasure. Oh, and before I forget the reason I came over here in the first place, here's your bridesmaid's dress." Aubrey clicked on another lamp so they could both admire the exquisite gown.

Danielle sighed in admiration. "Katherine has such good taste. This is lovely."

"If you need any alterations, just give the dress lady a call. I'll put her card by the phone in the kitchen just in case." Aubrey snapped on lights and seated Danielle down at the table in the eating nook. "Here are some chips to munch on while I grill the sandwich."

"You didn't notice." Danielle sounded surprised as she tore open the new bag of Ruffles.

Aubrey knelt to drag the frying pan out of the lower cabinet. She slid it onto the stove's burner with a slight clatter. "Notice what?"

"Where I hung William's picture."

William. Like another blow to her heart, she almost lost her balance. She quickly grabbed onto the counter as her head began to spin. Her heart shattered all over again. The feelings she'd tucked away to deal with later rushing through her fortifications like a wall of water through a dam's concrete wall. She could feel every piece breaking. Every crack and fissure and fracture.

Why had he kissed her if he didn't love her? If he'd never loved her?

She gulped in air, refusing to cry. Knowing that it

was too late. Her eyes burned, and her vision blurred. And there was Danielle at her side, reaching to pull her into a sisterly hug and wipe her tears.

It was Danielle who was taking care of her now, leading her to the table, sitting down to comfort her. "What happened with William?"

"Nothing." It was the simple, painful truth. "Nothing at all."

Danielle's voice broke with sympathy. "Oh, honey, I'm so sorry. We all had such high hopes for the two of you."

"Me, too." It hurt even worse to admit. The tears came for a second time, blurring the picture hung on the wall, where light still found it, even in the shadowed recesses of the room. An image of faith, despite the tragedy of winter's numbing cold.

She laid her head in her hands and let go of the last of her hope. The last of her hope for William's love.

It was another perfect Montana summer's day, William thought as he guided Jet through the trailhead. The air smelled sweet. Birdsong filled the vastness of his mountain paradise. There was nothing but beauty in every direction, beauty which he'd managed to capture with his camera's lens. He was back among the living. He should be happy, right?

Not. There was the truth like a big dark hole stuck in the middle of his heart, sucking at the brightness of the day and draining any chance he had for peace. It was that truth he kept doing his best to avoid, to ignore, to go on as if it didn't exist.

He was not in love with Aubrey. He didn't want to be in love with anyone.

After nearly two weeks of telling himself that, he still didn't believe it. After two weeks of pretending his life would go back to what it was before Aubrey, that hadn't happened, either. Because he wasn't the same man he'd been before. He hadn't been happy back then. He hadn't been whole. He'd been too afraid to try to live again, and it had happened anyway, the same way summer had come to the mountains, coaxing flowers to bloom and the grass to ripen and the glacier caps to melt.

What did he do now, when staying tough and ice-cold had been his only defense?

I'm not in love with her. How many times did he have to say that to himself to convince his heart? A hundred? A thousand? A million? There was only one love ever in his lifetime that had been something he couldn't get over. And it felt just like this.

The realization shook him. He was all out of excuses.

This couldn't be love he was feeling. He didn't want it to be, and that hadn't been able to change it. He'd denied it, ignored it, called it by a different name, tried to let it fade away. It was still here, a tenacious light that he could not defeat.

"Whoa, boy." They'd reached the mailbox and he eased Jet to a stop. A package was already protruding out of the box. He gave it a tug, thinking it was probably his latest online book order.

But no, the return address was from Danielle and Jonas Lowell. How about that? Curiosity got the best of him. He'd been keeping their family in his nightly prayers for a while now.

He'd heard the auction was a huge success; it had been reported in the local paper. He hadn't had the heart to attend, although he'd been wondering how Jonas was doing. He kept hope that the state trooper would be restored to full health and be able to take his son to the upcoming county fair for his birthday. It was hard to forget the first time he'd met the little boy, for it had been the memorable evening when he'd met Aubrey.

Aubrey. Knowing her had forever changed him.

Wasn't admitting it the first step?

He tore through the tape holding the cardboard box, peeled back the top flaps and stared in disbelief. It was the ceramic bowls, in descending sizes, that he'd seen on Aubrey's worktable. Not, bowls, he corrected, her rain chimes that looked like hammered pewter. Like the lake where he'd taken her riding.

I do love her. The truth was there in his heart. But that wasn't enough. Not by a long shot. For with loving came too much risk. He didn't know if he could ever imagine risking so much again.

There was a letter, too, on Danielle's stationary. It was just a short note.

William,
All is well here, which is a welcome change. I picked something up at the auction for you. An original. One of a kind. Aubrey designed it, but didn't have the heart to make more than this single design. I suspect it hurts her too much.
Proverbs 13:12

It hurt *him* too much. Danielle's words hit a familiar note. So did her chosen passage. He knew it.

Hope deferred makes the heart sick, but a longing fulfilled is a tree of life. Remembering those words made hope move through with a powerful force.

Aubrey. There she was in his mind's eye. He could see, in memory, the image of her when they'd been riding to the lake. Her slim shadow had trailed at an angle beside him, staying directly within his line of sight through part of the ride. He could remember how the sun had beat against his back and shoulder, and how the feel of being with her was like the exact peace he always found in the mountains.

He closed his eyes, and he was seeing her with his heart, riding her dainty Arabian with a born horse-woman's grace. Sitting easily and straight backed in her saddle, her smile gentle and her quiet presence infinitely precious to him. She had become his innermost dream.

How was that possible? He was a man who'd lost so many dreams that he had none left. None.

Until now.

Loving again made him too vulnerable. It was too much to risk. After surviving what he'd been through, could he put everything he was on the line and open his heart to love? To Aubrey?

He did not know if he had enough hope for that.

Chapter Fifteen

It was another lovely Friday evening. Aubrey pulled into Danielle's driveway, leaving room for her to back her minivan out of the garage, and grabbed the big take-out bags she'd picked up on the way in. The wonderful spicy fragrance of Mr. Paco's Tacos made her stomach rumble.

At least she was starting to get her appetite back. It seemed that recovering from heartbreak was more complicated than she'd ever expected, but she was starting to feel more like herself. And surely copious amounts of nachos and Mexi-Fries would help.

Before she made it halfway to the front door, it swung open and there was Tyler in his fireman hat. He was sopping wet, as if he'd stood in a sprinkler for a full hour, and was dripping onto the entryway floor.

"Aunt Aubrey! I put out five whole fires."

"You did good today, kid."

"I know! An' we went grocery shoppin' an' a fire truck zoomed by an' Mom had to pull over and everything!"

"It's a good thing I brought extra tacos. I hear firemen get pretty hungry fighting fires."

"Yep. Did you bring Mexi-Fries?" Tyler tried to peer into one of the bags.

So she gave him the lightest one, with the enormous tub of Mexi-Fries. "How could I forget Mexi-Fries? Go put those on the table for me, okay, tiger?"

"Okay." He marched off, leaving wet sandal prints across the kitchen floor.

Danielle came around the corner of the kitchen with Madison on her hip, saw the water marks and sighed. "It's been a busy day. I'll get that mopped up."

"No, I'll take care of it." After all, she had a flair for taking care of things. "Go have dinner at the hospital with your husband."

"Since we can't have dinner out, I'm taking dinner to him." Madison was wiggling and leaning hard against Danielle's hold on her. "No way, kiddo. I'm going to belt you into your high chair."

Madison squealed a loud protest.

"Aubrey, I've been chasing her around all day. She's discovered if she runs at full speed when I'm not paying perfect attention, I might not be able to catch up to her for a while. Oh, and she's unlocking the door, too."

"Aw, freedom. I understand." Aubrey set the restaurant bag on the table next to Tyler's bag of Mexi-Fries. "I'll keep an eagle eye on her so she doesn't take off down the street."

"I have complete faith in you." Danielle stopped to kiss her kids' cheeks. "Okay, you know the drill. I rented a movie for Tyler to watch tonight—it's on the coffee table. I shouldn't be out too late."

"Take your time. I'm starting a new book tonight."

"One of those old thick ones?" Danielle smiled as she grabbed her purse and swung open the inside garage door. "I won't even tease you about that. Good night."

The door closed, and she was gone. It felt good having life back to normal. Well, almost normal, she thought, noticing William's picture on the wall.

Some things time didn't heal. She suspected the love she had for him was one of them. Neither rejection nor lost hope nor heartbreak had made a dent in that shining love.

The knock at the door had Tyler leaping up from the table before she could start the evening blessing.

"Who is it?" Tyler was all energy as he raced through the kitchen, dripping more water as he went.

"It's probably Rebecca. Maybe she forgot her key." Aubrey had half expected Rebecca to stop by at some point. They'd spent a good deal of time on the phone earlier. Things weren't going well with her boyfriend and Rebecca didn't want to spend a Friday evening alone.

"You're not Rebecca." Tyler declared once he'd yanked open the door.

"No, I'm not. Sorry, kid." That warm, cozy baritone sounded familiar.

William. She had to be hearing things. Missing him so sorely that she'd dreamed him up.

She wasn't aware of crossing the kitchen until her sneaker squeaked in a water puddle. She didn't remember reaching the door or even consider that maybe it would be best not to see William. Suddenly she was there, in front of him, gazing at him, wonderful him. So big and strong, he was all she could see. Her entire spirit brightened with joy.

Oh, Aubrey. You love this man too much. It was probably on her face. Lord knows it was a powerful light in her heart that would not fade. She tried to tuck down her feelings and manage what she hoped was a cordial—and not an adoring—smile.

She would always love him. It would hurt that he'd rejected her. But she was a sensible girl, and she could handle this. "You're looking for Danielle, right?"

"Uh, no. I came for you."

"Me?" Renewed pain cracked through her, soul deep. She thought she knew, but she had to ask. She had to hear it from his lips. "Why are you here?"

"Because I want to discuss this friendship thing. We didn't finish it that day at the hospital, and I have something to say."

She squeezed her eyes closed, trying against hope to keep the pain hidden. She feared she was failing at that, too. "No, I meant what I said. I can't go back to being friends."

"Exactly. That's what I want to talk to you about. Will you let me in?"

"You don't know how much this is hurting me. You don't know—"

"Yes, I do." He held out his hand, palm up, as if offering his heart to her like a knight of old in one of those aged, thick books she loved so well.

She'd never wanted anything more than to place her hand in his. But she could not accept what he was offering. Friendship was no longer enough. Madison chose that moment to start yelling and banging on her high-chair tray. The air conditioner kicked on, as warm air sailed into the house. Inviting him in was the practical thing to do.

She stepped back with a nod and headed straight to Madison. "Be careful of the water on the floor," she said over her shoulder and above Madison's ten-decibel-level shout for "taters."

"You look pretty busy," he said uncertainly. "I should come back at another time."

"No, say what you've come to say and then you can go." She didn't say the words unkindly.

"I need your forgiveness." William took a deep breath. This wasn't easy. He didn't know if he'd destroyed the only chance he had with her. Because he knew—soul deep—that she was his one hope for a real life. A real love. Real happiness.

"Hey, mister." Tyler skidded to a stop next to him and held up all five fingers on his left hand. "I'm gonna be this much tomorrow. We're havin' cake. Aunt Ava's making me a firehouse cake! With a truck an' a dog an' everything!"

"Happy birthday, little man." His throat ached as he watched the kid rush the rest of the way to the table and climb into his booster seat. That must mean Jonas was well enough, maybe not to leave the hospital, but to have guests visit with cake.

Now he had to face Aubrey. He waited while she oversaw Tyler's blessing and handed out the tacos and Mexi-Fries. The little girl in the high chair dug into her Tater Tots and a hot dog with gusto. They looked like happy kids. Just the way things should be. They had a happy ending. Now he was praying that there would be one for him, too.

Aubrey stopped before him, unaware that she was standing exactly where she'd been that first evening, holding a crying Madison, when he'd fallen, unknowingly, in love with her. Because he realized it now. Could see it for what it was. He didn't need the brush of evening's gentle rose light falling over her to know she was his future and his heart's reason for beating.

"You were right, Aubrey. We can't go back to being friends. I don't want to be friends."

Her eyes widened. She stood before him, so vulnerable and dear. "You don't?"

Was she really so surprised? "No. I'm in love with you. One hundred percent. Down to the soul. Forever and ever. I should have realized it. I should have—"

"You love me? That's why you're here?"

It was the hardest thing he'd ever done to see the pain in her eyes. To know his fears had done this. That's what made him take the final risk, and lay all of his heart on the line. "It's why I'm here. To ask you to forgive me. To ask if you love me like this, too."

"Forever and ever?" she asked, as if she were weighing and measuring what remained in her heart. "Down to the soul?"

He couldn't breathe or even blink. He'd never been so vulnerable.

Then she smiled. "Yes. That is exactly how I love you."

Relief left him dizzy. Until this moment he hadn't been sure. "I'm glad we have this deep love in common, too."

"This feels like a dream."

"I think it is. I found my dream, my heart, my purpose, and it's you, Aubrey."

She felt blinded by the overwhelming strength of her love for him. It grew stronger with each passing second. Each breath. Each heartbeat. Hope filled her until she couldn't speak, only feel.

She finally had her own happily-ever-after.

Epilogue

"It's time to throw the bouquet!"

Aubrey looked up at the sound of her twin's voice. Sure enough, there was Ava on the gazebo in her grandmother's backyard. She'd seized control of one of the microphones for the string quartet to make the announcement.

"All you single ladies, line up. C'mon. Don't be shy!"

William's hand tightened around hers. "I guess that means you, technically."

"You haven't official proposed, you know."

"I was waiting for the right moment. It's hard getting you alone. You have a lot of family." He smiled wide enough that his dimples showed. "First there was Katherine's wedding shower. Then your grandmother's homecoming. And now the wedding. There hasn't been a lot of time."

"I know. It's the hazard of having a large enmeshed family."

"That happens to be the kind I like." He pressed a

kiss to her cheek. "Go on. If you don't, your sister is never going to stop talking into the mike."

"It's true." She left him chuckling, but in truth, she was so happy she didn't think her slippers touched the ground as she floated toward the gazebo where Katherine had taken her flower-launching position.

He trailed after her and took a spot on the sidelines. Oh, he looked like a dream in his black tux. She stood there, oblivious to all the festive cheers and speeches, simply drinking in the sight of him. He was her own love, her true romantic hero. Each day spent with him was happier than the last. She had her best blessings in him.

"Okay!" Katherine's joyful voice vaguely pierced Aubrey's thoughts. "Is everyone ready? Catching stances, girls. Here it comes!"

Aubrey loved how the evening's sunlight seemed to find William. It caressed the strong line of his wide shoulders and highlighted him. He was a man of such strong character and kindness, this man she would love for the rest of her life.

Something smacked her against the side of her head.

"Aubrey!" It was Ava, scolding her. "You were supposed to catch it."

"What?" Okay, she was a little preoccupied. Being in love could do that to a girl. Sure enough, Katherine's lovely bouquet was at her feet. And something was glinting there. Something tied on to the lovely pink satin ribbon.

William knelt to pick up the bouquet. The glint became princess-cut diamonds on a platinum band. "I have a question to ask you."

"How handy that you're on one knee."

"Exactly." His smile was her heaven. "Aubrey Mc-Kaslin, will you marry me?"

The cheers from her family started and so she didn't bother saying it loud enough for everyone to hear. She leaned close to whisper, so that he could know first. "It would be an honor."

William's hand was shaking as he slipped the ring on her finger. The diamonds sparkled like all the promises he intended to make to her—and to keep.

He swung her into his arms for a romantic kiss— much to the delight of the wedding guests.

He'd found his happily-ever-after, too. He was, after all, a deeply hopeful man.

* * * * *

Dear Reader,

Thank you so much for choosing *Everyday Blessings*. I hope you enjoyed reading Aubrey and William's story as much as I did writing it. William has given up on living and on love—until Aubrey comes into his life. If you're going through a tough time, please take heart. There are so many wonderful, everyday blessings God has in store for all of us.

Wishing you the best of blessings,

Jillian Hart

We hope you enjoyed reading
this special collection.

If you liked reading these stories,
then you will love **Love Inspired®** books!

You believe hearts can heal. **Love Inspired**
stories show that faith, forgiveness and hope
have the power to lift spirits and change
lives—always.

Enjoy six new stories from
Love Inspired every month!

Available wherever books and
ebooks are sold.

**Uplifting romances of faith,
forgiveness and hope.**

SPECIAL EXCERPT FROM

Love Inspired®

A young Amish woman yearns for true love.
Read on for a preview of A WIFE FOR JACOB
by Rebecca Kertz, the next book in her
***LANCASTER COUNTY WEDDINGS** series.*

Annie stood by the dessert table when she saw Jedidiah Lapp chatting with his wife, Sarah. She'd been heartbroken when Jed had broken up with her, and then married Sarah Mast.

Seeing the two of them together was a reminder of what she didn't have. Annie wanted a husband—and a family. But how could she marry when no one showed an interest in her? She blinked back tears. She'd work hard to be a wife a husband would appreciate. She wanted children, to hold a baby in her arms, a child to nurture and love.

She sniffled, looked down and straightened the dessert table. And the pitchers and jugs of iced tea and lemonade.

"May I have some lemonade?" a deep, familiar voice said.

Annie looked up. "Jacob." His expression was serious as he studied her. She glanced down and noticed the fine dusting of corn residue on his dark jacket. "Lemonade?" she echoed self-consciously.

"*Ja.* Lemonade," he said with amusement.

She quickly reached for the pitcher. She poured his lemonade into a plastic cup, only chancing a glance at him when she handed him his drink.

"How is the work going?" she asked conversationally.

"We are nearly finished with the corn. We'll be cutting hay next." He lifted the glass to his lips and took a swallow.

Warmth pooled in her stomach as she watched the movement of his throat. "How's *Dat?*" she asked. She had seen him chatting with her father earlier.

Jacob glanced toward her *dat* with a small smile. "He says he's not tired. He claims he's enjoying the view too much." His smile dissipated. "No doubt he'll be exhausted later."

Annie agreed. "I'll check on him in a while." She hesitated. "Are you hungry? I can fix you a plate—"

He gazed at her for several heartbeats with his striking golden eyes. "*Ne,* I'll fix one myself." He finished his drink and held out his glass to her. "May I?"

She hurried to refill his glass. With a crooked smile and a nod of thanks, Jacob accepted the refill and left. The warm flutter in her stomach grew stronger as she watched him walk away, stopping briefly to chat with Noah and Rachel, his brother and sister-in-law.

Annie glanced over where several men were being dished up plates of food. She then caught sight of Jacob walking along with his brother Eli. The contrast of Jacob's dark hair and Eli's light locks struck her as they disappeared into the barn. They came out a few minutes later, Eli carrying tools, Jacob leading one of her father's workhorses.

As if he sensed her regard, Jacob looked over and locked gazes with her.

Will Annie ever find the husband of her heart?
Pick up A WIFE FOR JACOB to find out.
Available March 2015,
wherever Love Inspired® books and ebooks are sold.

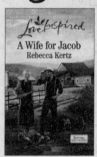

Use this coupon to save

$1.00

on the purchase of any Love Inspired® book.

Available wherever books are sold, including most bookstores, supermarkets, drugstores and discount stores.

Save $1.00

on the purchase of any Love Inspired® book.

Coupon valid until July 20, 2015. Redeemable at participating retail outlets in the U.S. and Canada only. Limit one coupon per customer.

52612262

Canadian Retailers: Harlequin Enterprises Limited will pay the face value of this coupon plus 10.25¢ if submitted by customer for this product only. Any other use constitutes fraud. Coupon is nonassignable. Void if taxed, prohibited or restricted by law. Consumer must pay any government taxes. Void if copied. Millennium1 Promotional Services ("M1P") customers submit coupons and proof of sales to Harlequin Enterprises Limited, P.O. Box 3000, Saint John, NB E2L 4L3, Canada. Non-M1P retailer—for reimbursement submit coupons and proof of sales directly to Harlequin Enterprises Limited, Retail Marketing Department, 225 Duncan Mill Rd., Don Mills, Ontario M3B 3K9, Canada.

5 65373 00076 2   (8100)0 12011

U.S. Retailers: Harlequin Enterprises Limited will pay the face value of this coupon plus 8¢ if submitted by customer for this product only. Any other use constitutes fraud. Coupon is nonassignable. Void if taxed, prohibited or restricted by law. Consumer must pay any government taxes. Void if copied. For reimbursement submit coupons and proof of sales directly to Harlequin Enterprises Limited, P.O. Box 880478, El Paso, TX 88588-0478, U.S.A. Cash value 1/100 cents.

LICOUP0215